THE FAR-OUT FUTURE

—An interstellar conspiracy to gain control of a brand new continent on earth.

—The Old Wild West transported intact into the Brave New World of the distant galactic colonies.

—a primitive race in a far-off solar system gaining control of supertechnology and using it for their own weird purposes.

—A strange civilization that takes very seriously the idea "You are what you eat."

—Super-mod fashions in the status-mad society of outer space.

These are but some of the bizarre and mind-boggling adventures that await you in

THE CONTINENT MAKERS

created by one of the truly great masters of modern science fiction, the one and only incredible

L. SPRAGUE de CAMP

Other SIGNET Science Fiction Titles
You Will Enjoy

The Continent Makers

and
Other Tales of the Viagens

by
L. Sprague de Camp

A SIGNET BOOK from
NEW AMERICAN LIBRARY
TIMES MIRROR

Acknowledgments:
"The Inspector's Teeth" was first published in *Astounding Science Fiction* for April, 1950; copyright 1950 by Street and Smith Publications, Inc.; reprinted in *The Continent Makers and Other Tales of the Viagens* (Twayne Publishers, Inc.), 1953.
"Summer Wear" was first published in *Startling Stories* for May, 1950; copyright 1950 by Better Publications, Inc.; reprinted in *The Best Science-Fiction Stories: 1951* (Frederick Fell), 1951, and in *TCM&OTOTV.*
"Finished" was first published in *Astounding Science Fiction* for November, 1949; copyright 1949 by Street & Smith Publications, Inc.; reprinted in *TCM&OTOTV.*
"The Galton Whistle" was first published as "Ultrasonic God" in *Future Fiction* for July, 1951; copyright 1951 by Columbia Publications, Inc.; reprinted under its present title in *TCM&OTOTV*, and as "Ultrasonic God" in *Novelets of Science Fiction* (Belmont Books), 1963.
"The Animal-Cracker Plot" was first published in *Astounding Science Fiction* for July, 1949; copyright 1949 by Street & Smith Publications, Inc.; reprinted in *TCM&OTOTV.*
"Git Along!" was first published in *Astounding Science Fiction* for August, 1950; copyright 1950 by Street & Smith Publications, Inc.; reprinted in *The Outer Reaches* (Pellegrini & Cudahy), 1951, and in *TCM&OTOTV.*
"Perpetual Motion" was first published as "Wide-Open Planet" in *Future Fiction* for September & October, 1950; copyright 1950 by Columbia Publications, Inc.; reprinted under its present title in *TCM&OTOTV.*
"The Continent Makers" was first published in *Thrilling Wonder Stories* for April, 1951; copyright 1951 by Standard Magazines, Inc.; reprinted in *TCM&OTOTV.*

Published by arrangement with L. Sprague de Camp

SIGNET, SIGNET CLASSICS, SIGNETTE, MENTOR AND PLUME BOOKS
are published by The New American Library, Inc.,
1301 Avenue of the Americas, New York, New York 10019

FIRST PRINTING, NOVEMBER, 1971

PRINTED IN THE UNITED STATES OF AMERICA

TO:

EVELYN P. and JOHN B. HATCHER

CONTENTS

IN RE SPRAGUE

On June 6, 1939, I dropped in at the office of Mr. John W. Campbell, editor of *Astounding Science Fiction*, to ask whether he had come to a decision about a story of mine which I had submitted a week earlier. He had, and handed back the manuscript to prove it. For once, however, a rejection threw me into something less than the usual delirium of despair, because he simultaneously introduced me to a tall, thinnish chap who was in the office with him.

He said, "This is L. Sprague de Camp."

I fell into an awestruck silence that persisted until Sprague left, surrounded, in my eyes, by that gold-dust aura an established writer has for the unsuccessful novice. Make no mistake, Sprague is an impressive fellow for anyone to meet suddenly. Tall and, at that time, thinnish; a thin, square-jawed face; dark hair and eyes; a snappy military mustache; and dark, luxurious eyebrows that can only be described as formidable, he looked like the younger son of a British peer. At the time, he frightened me silly.

(By a queer coincidence, Catherine de Camp, his wife, looked like the younger daughter of a British peer. For a long time I considered her the most beautiful blonde in science fiction.)

Thirty-two years have passed and Sprague has aged perhaps ten of them. He is not quite so thin as he used to be and he has a neat grayish chin beard. Now he looks like the English peer himself. My early awe and fright have long since given way to feelings of liveliest affection for a nice guy who happens to struggle under the disadvantage of an aristocratic cast of countenance.

Sprague, despite his cool, self-confident appearance, is essentially shy. People meet him once, combine his eyebrows, mustache, and shy silence in their own minds, and walk away with the impression of having met a cold personality. Not so! Underneath the cool exterior there is a friendly and affectionate nature; even, on occasion, a demonstratively affectionate nature. I have seen Sprague run madly across a large and crowded hotel room to hug a friend he had not seen in some months.

Perhaps the most amazing thing about Sprague de Camp is the amount of quaint and miscellaneous lore he has crammed within his head.

He is a historian of almost anything you can think of. It can be the Atlantis myth or magic and witchcraft; the abortive industrial age of Hellenistic times or Ostrogothic Italy; naval armament or hoaxes—he can write entertainingly and authoritatively on any of them, in the form of good history or excellently researched historical novels. I'm not just saying that. I can prove it. He *has* written entertainingly and authoritatively on all of them.

And this knowledge is not dry bones. He can give it out clothed with verve and life in speech as well as in writing. The enthusiasm with which he will hold forth on odd subjects conquers even his shyness.

I was once part of an admiring audience who heard Sprague give the details of a battle between Ptolemaic Egypt and Seleucid Syria; the only battle, he explained, in which one side used Indian elephants and the other, African. In colorful detail, he described the causes of the war, the events leading to the battle, the battle itself. He was by turns an Egyptian spearman and a Syrian mahout. Sometimes he was an elephant. He leaped about vigorously, wielding an imaginary spear (a large, heavy, imaginary spear) as he spoke. When he finished, he was breathless and so were we; he from exertion, we from laughter.

He is a world traveler who has been chased by hippopotami in Africa, seared by the sun in India, impressed by archaeological ruins everywhere—and everything gets into a book. Nor does age wither nor custom stale his infinite variety. He is currently planning to revisit Istanbul and is learning Turkish for the purpose. And where he goes, Catherine goes, too, often and anon.

Sprague has written serious books on naval armaments, dinosaurs, archaeology, history, patent law, and myths and legends. He is a linguist and a phonetician and has contributed serious articles on phonetics to weighty journals in the field. And he has written enough verse, both serious and comic, to make up a volume, which is about to appear.

Let's sum it up this way. Sprague can talk all evening, on any subject you can name, without boring you.

It is too easy to get the idea, listening to Sprague, that he was born, somehow, knowing all these things or, at the most, had picked them up by walking rapidly through the reference section of the New York Public Library, flipping the pages of books as he went by.

No, sir! I was disillusioned on that score a score of years ago when I spent a few days at his house. I was bedded down in his study, and the morning after the first night (being an early riser), I poked through such of his papers as he had not wisely put under lock and key.

I found a stack of books on "Daily Life in Ancient Athens," "Walks on the Acropolis," "I Fought at Marathon," "Why Persia Must Be Destroyed," and so on. (Those are not the exact titles.) I found maps of ancient Greece, large and small. I found a graph of lifetimes of famous Athenians and whether they were children, adults, or old people at the time.

I tackled him when he woke up. I pointed to the paraphernalia. I demanded an explanation. It turned out that he was writing "The Glory That Was." The setting was to be in ancient Athens, and, by Zeus, it was going to be accurate.

There is no doubt that Sprague is the greatest stickler for minutiae in science fiction and invests the most time and energy per story. And there's a return on the investment in that air of reality he gets into his stories, that extra grip upon your imagination.

I recall the time when his novel *Lest Darkness Fall* first appeared in *Unknown*. It was a Connecticut Yankee type of story in which a modern American found himself in the Italy of Cassiodorus and Belisarius (early sixth century, A.D.). I bought the magazine the day before I was due to take a final examination in physical chemistry. For reasons we need not go into here, I had to pass physical chemistry with a B or better to keep my academic career alive. For additional reasons we need not go into, I had grave doubts as to my ability to do this.

I sat down, in no very happy frame of mind, to study. To cheer myself up, since I reasoned that no man can study efficiently when in a state of depression, I decided to read just the tiniest little bit of *Lest Darkness Fall* before I opened my text. You guess the results? It was inevitable. You don't read a "little bit" of a de Camp novel. I finished the yarn at a sitting and I never did get around to studying.

Nor was I sorry. The story was tabbed "fantasy" but it was the best historical novel I had ever read. It still is. Furthermore, its excellence so cheered me up that I took the finals next day in stride and got an A in the course. I would love to recommend Sprague as a mental stimulant for all readers shaky in their college courses, but maybe I had better not. All I can say is that it seems to work for me.

My only complaint is that Sprague sometimes limits himself by his own damned conscientiousness. Take the *Viagens Interplanetarias* stories which compose this book. (*Viagens Interplanetarias,* by the way, means "interplanetary tours" in Portuguese. At the time interstellar travel is developed, Sprague supposes Brazil to be the dominant power on Earth, as it well may be some day. In that case, of course, Portuguese would be the dominant language of the spaceways.) In this series, Sprague's interstellar travel takes place in Earth's backyard, so to speak; among stars, that is, within a reasonable number of light-years from the sun. Further, his concept of interstellar travel has queer effects on the subjective passage of time. This makes the stories harder to write.

I once asked him why he did this, and he explained that since travel faster than the speed of light was impossible, it would take far too long to reach the really distant stars. I pointed out that if he used "hyperspace" as most writers did, that wouldn't matter. (Hyperspace is a mythical term among s-f writers and can be used in a vague and foggy way to excuse any speeds up to infinity.) Sprague said he didn't believe in hyperspace. I said neither did I, but I used it.

He just put his pipe in his mouth and shook his head. "If I don't believe a thing is possible," he said, "I try not to use it."

Sprague doesn't remain pure always. He has written time-travel stories, though he considers time travel impossible. But he is inhibited about such things. God knows how many stories he could write, but won't—on principle. That's Sprague.

But Sprague needs no one to teach him better habits. He has been among the top few in his profession for over a generation now. He sells regularly and will continue to do so, I am sure, while he lives and while editors are sane.

He has been repeatedly anthologized. In fact, three of the stories included here, "Summer Wear," "The Galton Whistle," and "Git Along!" have previously been anthologized, but here they are at last where they belong—with the other tales of the Viagens. They make fine rereading for themselves, but you will find them even richer in the context of the other tales.

But if what I am saying here has any meaning at all, you should be impatient to be off with me and on with Sprague. Perhaps you've already passed on to the book itself. If you have, I certainly can't blame you. If you haven't, what are you waiting for? Go ahead, turn the page——

                                        Isaac Asimov

AUTHOR'S NOTE

When men attained interstellar travel in the early twenty-first century, they named the planets of other stars after gods of various Terran pantheons, following the analogy of their own system. Tau Ceti, a K-type star like Sol but dimmer and yellower, had its planets named for Hindu gods, the three inhabited planets of the group (reading from the star outward) becoming Vishnu, Krishna, and Ganesha respectively. Krishna has a climate much like that of Earth; it is larger, but less dense, so that its surface-gravity is a little less though atmospheric pressure is a little greater. It is drier and smoother than Earth, having no true oceans but a lot of small seas; hence its land area is several times Earth's.

The planet Vishnu, closer to Tau Ceti than Krishna, is hotter than Krishna, though not too hot for unprotected human beings. Osiris, Isis, and Thoth are inhabited planets of the star Procyon (Osiris having the most Earth-like surface conditions) while Thor is a planet of Epsilon Eridani.

As a result of the Third World War the United States was reduced to a second-class power and the U. S. S. R. ceased to be a power at all. World leadership was taken over by fast-growing Brazil. Hence most early spatial exploration was done by Brazilians, and the government-owned space-transport system, the Viagens Interplanetarias, was largely Brazilian in control and personnel. The word *Viagens* rhymes roughly with "Leah paints", with *g* as in "rouge": *vee-uh-zhainhs*.

Don't worry about pronunciation of Krishnan names, because such is the multitude of languages and dialects that almost any guess will be right in one or another. The symbols, *q*, and *gh* stand for (a) a glottal stop or plosive (a cough), (b) a guttural variety of *k* and (c) a uvular roll like French *r*. If you're no linguist, ignore the first and pronounce the second and third as ordinary *k* and *g*. The letter *á* stands for "ah", and final *é* for "eh" or "ay." Samples: "Qarao" rhymes with "allow", "Laiján" with "by John", "Zerdai" with "hair-dye", "dour" with "slower", and "Balhib" with "Al Grebe". "Castanhoso" is about "cas-*tahn*-yo-soo"; "Katai-Jhogorai", "cat-eye jug-o'-rye".

L. Sprague de Camp

A.D. 2054-2088

The Inspector's Teeth

World-Manager Chagas sat waiting for the Osirian ambassador, mentally practicing the brisk handshake and the glassy smile. Across the conference-table the First Assistant to the Manager, Wu, chain-smoked, while the Minister of External Affairs, Evans, filed his nails. Although the faint rasp annoyed Chagas, he gave no sign, imperturbability being one of the qualities for which he was paid. The indirect lighting threw soft highlights from the silver skullcaps covering the shaven crania of the three.

Chagas said: "I shall be glad when I can let my hair grow again like a civilized man."

"My dear Chagas," said Wu, "with the hair you have, I don't see what difference it makes."

Evans put away his nail-file and said: "Gentlemen, when I was a kid a century ago, I wondered what it would be like to be on the inside of a great historical moment. Now I'm in on one, I find it queer I'm the same old Jefferson Evans, and not Napoleon or Caesar." He looked at his nails. "Wish we knew more Osirian psychology . . ."

Wu said: "Don't start that Neo-Paretan nonsense again about Osirians being guided by sentiments, so we need only know which one to play on, like pressing a button. Osirians are rational people; would have to be to invent space-travel independently of us. Therefore will be guided by their economic interests alone . . ."

"Neo-Marxist tapioca!" snapped Evans. "Sure they're rational, but also sentimental and capricious like us. There's no contradiction—"

"But there is!" said Wu excitedly. "Environment makes the man, and not the contrary . . ."

"Do not start that, I beg," said Chagas. "This is too important to get your systems full of adrenalin over theo-

17

ry. Thank God I am a plain man who tries to do his duty and does not worry about sociological theories. If he takes our terms, the Althing will ratify the treaty and we shall have an Interplanetary Council to keep peace. If he insists on the terms we privately think he is entitled to, the Althing will not ratify. Then we shall have separate sovereignties, and it will be the history of our poor Earth all over again."

"You borrow trouble, chief," said Wu. "There are no serious disputes between our system and the Procyonic. Even if there were, there is no economic advantage to a war at such distance, even though Osirians have capitalistic economy like Evans's country . . ."

"Who said wars are always fought for economic advantage?" said Evans. "Ever hear of the Crusades? Or the war that was fought over one pig?"

Wu said: "You mean the war some sentimental historian without grasp of social and economic factors *thought* was fought for pig—"

"Stop it!" said Chagas.

"Okay," said Evans. "But I'll bet you a drink, Wu, that the Osirian takes our offer as it stands."

"You are on," said Wu.

A bell chimed, bringing the men to their feet.

As the Osirian came in, they advanced with outstretched hands, uttering polite platitudes. The Osirian set down his bulging briefcase and shook their hands. He looked like a small dinosaur, a head taller than a man—one of the little ones that ran about on its hind legs with its tail stuck out behind to balance. A complex pattern of red-and-gold paint decorated his scales.

The Osirian took the backless chair that had been provided for him. "A kreat pleashure, chentlemen," he said slowly in an accent they could barely understand. This was natural, considering the difference between his vocal organs and theirs. "I haff stuttiet the offer of the Worlt Fetteration and reached my tecishion."

Chagas gave him a meaningless diplomatic smile. "Well, sir?"

The ambassador, whose face was not built for smiles, flicked his forked tongue out and back. With irritating deliberation he began ticking off points on his claws:

"On one hant, I know political conditions in the Solar System and on Earth in particular. Hence I know why you hat to ask me the things you dit. On the other, my people will not like some of these things. They will consitter many of your demants unchust. I could go ofer the grounts of opchection one py one. Howeffer, since you alretty know these opchections, I can make my point better py tellink you a little story."

Wu and Evans exchanged a quick glance of impatience.

The forked tongue flicked out again. "This is a true story, of the old tays when the mesonic drive had first enapled you to fly to other stars and put your system in touch with ours. Pefore there was talk apout galactic government, and pefore you learnt to guart akainst our little hypnotic powers with those pretty silfer hats. When a younk Sha'-akhfa, or as you say an Osirian, hat come to your Earth to seek wistom . . ."

When Herbert Lengyel, a junior, proposed that they bid Hithafea, the Osirian freshman, the Iota Gamma Omicron's council was thrown into turmoil. Herb persisted, glasses flashing:

"He's got everything! He's got money, and he's smart and good-natured, and good company, and full of college spirit. Look how he got elected yell-leader when he'd been here only a few weeks! Of course it would be easier if he looked less like a fugitive from the reptile house in the zoo, but we're civilized people and should judge by the personality inside . . ."

"Just a minute!" John Fitzgerald, being a three-letter man and a senior, threw much weight in the council. "We got too many queer types in this fraternity already."

He looked hard at Lengyel, though Herb, who would like to have punched his handsome face, was merely a sober and serious student instead of a rah-rah boy. Fitzgerald went on:

"Who wants the Iotas to be a haven for all the campus freaks? Next thing you'll find a thing like a bug, a praying-mantis a couple of meters high, sitting in your chair, and you'll be told that's the new pledge from Mars . . ."

"Ridiculous!" interrupted Lengyel. "Martians can't stand Earthly gravity and humidity for long—"

"That's not the point. I was speaking generally, and for my money a young dinosaur's not much improvement on a Martian . . ."

"Another thing," said Lengyel. "We have an anti-discrimination clause in our charter. So we can't bar this man—this student, I should say—"

"O yes we can," said Fitzgerald, stifling a yawn. "That refers only to the races of mankind; it don't apply to non-human beings. We're still a club of gentlemen—get that, gentle-men—and Hithafea sure ain't no man."

"Principle's the same," said Lengyel. "Why d'you think Atlantic's one of the few universities left with fraternities? Because the frats here have upheld the democratic tradition and avoided snobbery and discrimination. Now—"

"Nuts!" said Fitzgerald. "It isn't discriminatory to pick folks you think will be congenial. It wouldn't be so bad if Herb had merely proposed some guy from Krishna, where they look more or less human—"

"There aren't any Krishnans at Atlantic this year," muttered Lengyel.

"—but no, he has to foist a shuddery scaly reptile—"

"John's got a phobia against snakes," said Lengyel.

"So does every normal person—"

"Nuts to you, Brother Fitzgerald. It's merely a neurosis, implanted by—"

"You're both getting away from the subject," said Brother Brown, president of the chapter.

They went on like that for some time until a vote was called for. Since Fitzgerald blackballed Hithafea, Lengyel blackballed Fitzgerald's young brother.

"Hey!" cried Fitzgerald. "You can't do that!"

"Says who?" said Lengyel. "I just don't like the young lout."

After further wrangling, each withdrew his veto against the other's protegé.

On his way out, Fitzgerald punched Lengyel in the solar plexus with a thumb the size of a broomstick-end and said: "You're taking Alice to the game tomorrow for me, see? And be sure you give her back in the same condition as you got her!"

"Okay, Stinker," said Lengyel, and went to his room to study. Although they did not like each other, they managed to get along. Lengyel secretly admired Fitzgerald for being the perfect movie idea of Joe College, while Fitzgerald secretly envied Lengyel's brains. It amused Fitzgerald to turn over his coed to Lengyel because he regarded Herb as a harmless gloop who wouldn't dare try to make time with her himself.

Next day, the last Saturday of the 2054 football season, Atlantic played Yale on the home field. Herb Lengyel led Alice Holm into the stands. As usual, when he got near her his tongue got glued to the roof of his mouth. So he studied the pink card he found thumb-tacked to the back of the bleacher-seat in front of him. On this were listed, by number, the things he was supposed to do with a big square of cardboard, orange on one side and black on the other, when the cheerleader gave the command, in order to present a letter, number, or picture to the opposite side of the stadium.

He finally said: "D'I tell you we decided to bid Hithafea? Speak it not in Gath, though; it's confidential."

"I won't," said Alice, looking very blonde and lovely. "Does that mean that when John takes me to your dances Hithafea will ask to dance with me?"

"Not if you don't want him to. I don't know if he dances."

"I'll try not to shudder. Are you sure he didn't use his mysterious hypnotic powers to make you propose him?"

"Fooey! Professor Kantor in psych says all this talk about the hypnotic powers of the Osirians is bunk. If a man's a naturally good hypnotic subject he'll be hypnotizable, otherwise not. There aren't any mysterious rays the Osirians shoot from their eyes."

"Well," said Alice, "Professor Peterson doesn't agree. He thinks there's something to it, even though nobody has been able to figure out how it works—oh, here they come. Hithafea makes a divine yell-leader, doesn't he?"

Although the adjective was perhaps not well-chosen, the sight of Hithafea, flanked by three pretty coeds on each side, and prancing and waving his megaphone, was certainly unforgettable. It was made even more so by the fact that he was wearing an orange sweater with a big black A on the chest, and a freshman beanie on his head. His locomotive-whistle voice rose above the general uproar:

"Atlantic! A-T-L-A-N . . ."

At the end of each yell Hithafea flung out his arms with talons spread and leaped three meters into the air on his bird-like legs. He got much more kick out of the rooters' reaction to his yell-leading than the players did, since they were busy playing football. Hithafea himself had had hopes of going out for intercollegiate athletics, preferably track, until the coach had broken it to him as gently as possible that nobody would compete against a being who could broad-jump twelve meters without drawing a deep breath.

As both teams were strong that year, the score at the end of the first quarter still stood 0-0. Yale completed a pass and it looked as if the receiver were in the clear until

John Fitzgerald, the biggest of the fourteen right tackles of the Atlantic varsity, nailed him. Hithafea screamed:

"Fitzcheralt! Rah, rah, rah, Fitzcheralt!"

A drunken Yale senior, returning to his seat after visiting the gentlemen's room under the stands, got turned around and showed up on the grass strip in front of the Atlantic side of the stadium. There he tramped up and down and bumped into people and fell over the chairs of the Atlantic band and made a general nuisance of himself.

At last Hithafea, observing that everybody else was too much interested in the game to abate this nuisance, caught the man by the shoulder and turned him round. The man looked up at Hithafea and shrieked: "I got 'em! I got 'em!" and tried to break away.

He might as well have saved his trouble. The Sha'akhfi freshman held him firmly by both shoulders and hissed something at him. Then he let him go.

Instead of running away, the man threw off his hat with its little blue feather, his furry overcoat, his coat and vest and shirt and pants. Despite the cold he ran out on to the field in his underwear, hugging his bottle under one arm and pretending it was a football.

Before he was finally taken away, the man had caused Yale to be penalized for having twelve men on the field during a play. Luckily the Yale rooters were too far away on the other side of the stadium to understand what was happening, or there might have been a riot. As it was, they were pretty indignant when they found out later, feeling that somebody had pulled a fast one on them. Especially as the game ended 21-20 favor of Atlantic.

After the game Hithafea went to his mail-box in the Administration Building. All the other frosh were eagerly pushing around the pigeonholes to get theirs, for this was the day when fraternity bids were distributed. When Hithafea softly hissed: "Excuse me, please," they made plenty of room for him.

He took three little white envelopes from his box and scooted for his room in the freshman dorm. He burst in to find his roommate, Frank Hodiak, studying his one bid. Hithafea sat down on his bed with his tail curling up against the wall and opened his envelopes, slitting them neatly along the edge with his claws.

"Frank!" he cried. "They want me!"

"Hey," said Hodiak, "what's the matter with you? You're drooling on the rug! Are you sick?"

"No, I am cryink."

"What?"

"Sure. That is the way we Sha'akhfi cry."

"And why are you crying?"

"Pecause I am so happy! I am ofercome with emotion!"

"Well for goodness' sake," said Hodiak unfeelingly, "go cry in the sink, then. I see you got three. Which you gonna take?"

"I think the Iota Gamma Omicrons."

"Why? Some of the others got more prestige."

"I do not care. I am takink them anyway, for sentimental reasons."

"Don't tell me a cold-blooded reptile like you is sentimental!"

"Sure. All we Sha'akhfi are. You think we are not pecause we do not show our feelinks in our faces."

"Well," persisted Hodiak, "what are these sentimental reasons, huh?"

"First," (Hithafea counted on his claws) "pecause Herp Lengyel iss one. He was the first man on the campus to treat me like a fellow-beink. Second, pecause the kreat de Câmara was an Iota when he attendet Atlantic many years ako."

"Who's this guy de Câmara?"

"Dit you neffer know? My, some of you echucated Earthmen are iknorant of your own history! He was one of the great space-pioneers, the founter of the Viagens Interplanetarias, and the first Earthman to set foot on Osiris."

"Oh. Another Brazzy, eh?"

"Yes. It wass de Câmara, who prought the false teeth of our Chief Inspector Ficèsaqha back to Earth from Osiris, and gafe them to Atlantic when they presented him with an honorary degree. Pefore I leat yells at a game, I go up to the museum and gaze upon those teeth. Their sentimental associations inspire me. I am fery sentimental apout Senhor de Câmara, although some of our people claim he stole those teeth and other thinks as well when he left our planet."

At the first pledge-meeting, Hithafea squatted down humbly among his fellow-pledges, who looked at him with traces of distaste or apprehension. When the prospective members' duties had been explained to them, Fitzgerald and a couple of the other brothers undertook to have a little fun of the sadistic sort associated with initiations.

They brought out a couple of wooden paddles, like ping-pong racquets but heavier, and fired nonsensical questions at the freshmen. Those who failed to answer glibly were paddled for ignorance, whereas those who answered glibly were paddled for being fresh.

By and by Hithafea said: "Will nopody pattle me?"

"Why, Monster?" said Fitzgerald. "D'you wanna be?"

"Of course! It is part of peink a pletch. It would preak my heart if I were not pattled the same as the others."

The brothers looked at each other with expressions of bafflement. Brother Brown, indicating Hithafea's streamlined stern, asked:

"How the hell can we? I mean, where's his—uh—I mean, where shall we hit him?"

"Oh, anywhere!" said Hithafea.

Brother Brown, looking a bit unhappy about the whole thing, hauled off with his paddle and whacked Hithafea's scaly haunch. He hit again and again, until Hithafea said:

"I do not efen feel it. Are you sure you are not goink easy on me on purpose? It would wound my feelinks if you dit."

Brown shook his head. "Might as well shoot an elephant with a pea-shooter. You try, John."

Fitzgerald swung his massive arm and dealt Hithafea a swat that broke the paddle. He wrung his hand, looked at the other brothers, and said:

"Guess we'll have to consider you constructively paddled, Hithafea. Let's get on to business."

The other pledges grinned, evidently glad to escape any further beating. As the brothers had been made to feel a little foolish, the fun seemed to have gone out of paddling for the time being. The brothers sternly commanded the pledges to show up at the house the following night for the Thanksgiving dance, to do the serving and mess-work. Moreover they were told to bring three cats each to the next pledge-meeting, the following week.

Hithafea as ususal showed up an hour early for his duties at the dance, wearing a black bow tie around his scaly neck in deference to the formality of the occasion. John Fitzgerald, of course, brought Alice Holm, while Herbert Lengyel came stag and hovered uneasily, trying by an air of bored superiority to mask the fact that he would have liked to bring her himself.

When Hithafea stalked in bearing a tray of refreshments, some of the girls, who were not Atlantic coeds and so had never seen him before, shrieked. Alice, mastering her initial revulsion, said:

"Are you dancing, Hithafea?"

Hithafea said: "Alas, Miss Holm, I could not!"

"Oh, I bet you dance divinely!"

"It is not that. At home on Osiris I perform the fertility-tance with the pest of them. Put look at my tail! I should neet the whole floor to myself, I fear. You have no idea how much trouple a tail is in a worlt where peinks do not normally have them. Every time I try to go through a swingink door—"

"Let's dance, Alice," said Fitzgerald abruptly. "And you, Monster, get to work!"

Alice said: "Why John, I think you're jealous of poor Hithafea! I found him sweet!"

"Me jealous of a slithery reptile? Ha!" sneered Fitzgerald as they spun away in the gymnastic measures of the Zulu.

At the next pledge-meeting a great yowling arose when the pledges showed up with three cats apiece, for which they had raided alleys and their friends' houses and the city pound. Brother Brown said: "Where's Hithafea? The Monster's not usually late—"

The doorbell rang. When one of the pledges opened it he looked out, then leaped back with the alacrity if not the grace of a startled fawn, meanwhile making a froglike noise in his throat. There on the doorstep stood Hithafea with a full-grown lioness on a leash. The cats frantically raced off to other parts of the fraternity-house or climbed curtains and mantel-pieces. The brothers looked as if they would have done likewise if they had not been afraid of losing face before the pledges.

"Goot evenink," said Hithafea. "This is Tootsie. I rented her. I thought if I prought one cat bik enough it would do for the three I was tolt to pring. You like her, I trust?"

"A character," said Fitzgerald. "Not only a monster, but a character."

"Do I get pattled?" said Hithafea hopefully.

"Paddling you," said Fitzgerald, "is like beating a rhinoceros with a fly-swatter." And he set to work with a little extra vim on the fundaments of the other pledges.

When the pledge-meeting was over, the brothers went into conference. Brother Broderick said: "I think we'll have to give 'em something more original to do for next time. Specially Hithafea here. S'pose we tell him to bring—ah—how about that set of false teeth belonging to that guy—that emperor or whatever he was of Osiris, in the museum?"

Hithafea said: "You mean the teeth of our great Chief Inspector, Ficèsaqha?"

"Yeah, Inspector Fish—well, you pronounce it, but that's what I mean."

"That will be a kreat honor," said Hithafea. "Pefore we go, Mr. Fitzcherald, may I speak to you alone for a moment?"

Fitzgerald frowned and said: "Okay, Monster, but hurry it up. I got a date." He followed the Sha'akhfa out, and the other brothers heard Hithafea hissing something to him in the corridor.

Then Hithafea stuck his head in the doorway and said: "Mr. Lengyel, may I speak to you too, now?" And the same thing happened to Lengyel.

The other brothers did not listen to the conversation between Lengyel and Hithafea because they were more interested in what was happening in the parlor. John Fitzgerald came through, all slicked up in his best clothes, and the lioness tackled him and tried to wrestle with him. The more he tried to get away the more vigorously she wrestled. He finally gave up and lay on his back while Tootsie sat on his chest and licked his face. As having your face licked by a lion is something like having it gone over with coarse sandpaper, Fitzgerald was somewhat the worse for wear by the time Hithafea came back into the room and pulled his pet off.

"I am fery sorry," he told them. "She is playful."

The night before the next pledge-meeting, shadows moved in the shrubbery around the museum. The front door opened and a shadow came out—unmistakably that of a big, broad-shouldered man. The shadow looked about, then back into the darkness whence it had come. Sounds came from the darkness. The shadow trotted swiftly down the front steps and whispered: "Here!"

Another shadow rose from among the shrubs; not that of a man, but of something out of the Mesozoic. The human shadow tossed a package to the reptilian shadow just as the museum's watchman appeared in the doorway and shouted:

"Hey, you!"

The human shadow ran like the wind, while the reptilian shadow faded into the bushes. The watchman yelled again, blew on a police-whistle, and ran after the human shadow, but gave up, puffing, after a while. The quarry had disappeared.

"Be goddamned," muttered the watchman. "Gotta get the cops on this one. Let's see, who came in late this afternoon, just before closing? There was that little Italian-looking girl, and that red-haired professor, and that big football-type guy . . ."

Frank Hodiak found his roommate packing his few simple belongings, and asked:

"Where you going?"

"I am gettink retty to leave for the Christmas vacation," said Hithafea. "I got permission to leafe a few tays aheat of the rest." He shut his small suitcase with a snap and said: "Goot-pye, Frank. It is nice to have known you."

"Good-bye? Are you going right now?"

"Yes."

"You sound as if you weren't coming back!"

"Perhaps. Some tay. *Sahacikhthasèf,* as we say on Osiris."

Hodiak said: "Say, what's that funny-looking package you put in your—"

But before he finished, Hithafea was gone.

When the next pledge-meeting was called, Hithafea, hitherto the outstanding eager-beaver among the pledges, was absent. They called the dormitory and got in touch with Frank Hodiak, who said that Hithafea had shoved off hours previously.

The other curious fact was that John Fitzgerald had his right wrist bandaged. When the brothers asked him why, he said:

"Damn'f I know. I just found myself in my room with a cut on my wrist, and no idea how it got there."

The meeting was well under way and the paddles were descending when the doorbell rang. Two men came in: one of the campus cops and a regular municipal policeman.

The former said: "Is John Fitzgerald here?"

"Yeah," said Fitzgerald. "I'm him."

"Get your hat and coat and come with us."

"Whaffor?"

"We wanna ask you a few questions about the disappearance of an exhibit from the museum."

"I don't know anything about it. Run along and peddle your papers."

That was the wrong line to take, because the city cop brought out a piece of paper with a lot of fancy printing on it and said: "Okay, here's a warrant. You're pinched. Come—" and he took Fitzgerald by the arm.

Fitzgerald cut loose with a swing that ended, splash, on the cop's face, so that the policeman fell down on his back and lay there, moving a little and moaning. The other brothers got excited and seized both cops and threw them out the front door and bumpety-bump down the stone steps of the fraternity-house. Then they went back to their pledge-meeting.

In five minutes four radio patrol-cars stopped in front of the frat-house and a dozen cops rushed in.

The brothers, so belligerent a few minutes before, got out of the way at the sight of the clubs and blackjacks. Hands reached out of blue-clad sleeves towards Fitzgerald. He hit another cop and knocked him down, and then the hands fastened onto all his limbs and held him fast. When he persisted in struggling, a cop hit him on the head with a blackjack and he stopped.

When he came to and calmed down, on the way to the police-station, he asked: "What the hell is this all about? I tell you, I never stole nothing from a museum in my whole life!"

"Oh yes you did," said a cop. "It was the false teeth of one of them things from another planet. O'Riley, I think they call it. You was seen going into the museum around closing-time, and you left your fingerprints all over the glass case when you busted it. Boy, this time we'll sure throw the book at you! Damn college kids, think they're better than other folks ..."

Next day Herbert Lengyel got a letter:

Dear Herb:

When you read this I shall be enroute to Osiris with the teeth of Chief Inspector Ficèsaqha, one of our greatest heroes. I managed to get a berth on a ship leaving for Pluto, whence I shall proceed to my own system on an Osirian interstellar liner.

When Fitzgerald suggested I steal the teeth, the

temptation to recover this relic, originally stolen by de Câmara, was irresistible. Not being an experienced burglar, I hypnotized Fitzgerald into doing the deed for me. Thus I killed three birds with one stone, as you Earthmen say. I got the teeth; I got even with Fitzgerald for his insults; and I got him in Dutch to give you a clear field with Miss Holm.

I tell you this so you can save him from being expelled, as I do not think he deserves so harsh a penalty. I also gave you the Osirian hypnosis to remove some of your inhibitions, so you shall be able to handle your end of the project.

I regret not having finished my course at Atlantic and not being finally initiated into Iota Gamma Omicron. However, my people will honor me for this deed, as we admire the refined sentiments.

> Fraternally,
> Hithafea.

Lengyel put the letter away and looked at himself in the mirror. He now understood why he had felt so light, daring, and self-confident the last few hours. Not like his old self at all. He grinned, brushed back his hair, and started for the house 'phone to call Alice.

"So, chentlemen," said Hithafea, "now you unterstant why I have decidet to sign your agreement as it stants. I shall perhaps be criticized for giffink in to you too easily. But you see, I am soft-heartet apout your planet. I have been on many planets, and nowhere have I peen taken in and mate to feel at home as I was py the Iota Gamma Omicron fraternity, many years ago."

The ambassador began to gather up his papers. "Have you a memorantum of this meetink for me to initial? Goot." Hithafea signed, using his claw for a pen. "Then we can have a formal signink next week, eh? With cameras and speeches? Some tay if you feel like erecting a monument to the founders of the Interplanetary Council, you might erect it to Mr. Herbert Lengyel."

Evans said: "Sir, I'm told you Osirians like our Earthly alcoholic drinks. Would you care to step down to the Federation bar ..."

"I am so sorry, not this time. Next time, yes. Now I must catch an airplane to Baltimore, U.S.A."

"What are you doing there?" said Chagas.

"Why, Atlantic University is giving me an honorary degree. How I shall balance one of those funny hats with the tassel on my crest I do not yet know. But that was another reason I agreet to your terms. You see, we are a sentimental race. What is the matter with Mr. Wu? He looks sick."

Chagas said: "He has been watching his lifelong philosophy crumble to bits, that is all. Come, we will see you to your aircraft."

As Wu pulled himself together and rose with the rest, Evans grinned wryly at him, saying:

"After we're dropped the ambassador, I think I'll make it a champagne cocktail!"

A.D. 2104-2128

Summer Wear

Cato Chapman and Celia Zorn, the model, were waiting for the Moon ship to take off from Mohave Spaceport. Chapman, a brisk young man who sometimes reminded people of a chipmunk, said to his young cousin Mahoney: "If you can take enough time off from your precious paint, Ed, keep an eye on Miss Nettie. Don't want to come back in twenty-two years and find she's forgotten us."

"Sure," said Mahoney. "I like the old dame. She buys our paint. Tough customer, though, isn't she?"

Celia Zorn said: "I think 'formidable' is the word. But see to it she doesn't get some perfectly bizarre idea and go broke."

"Like selling summer clothes to critters that don't wear none and don't need 'em?" said Mahoney. "If she gets any crazier ones than that . . ."

Chapman punched his cousin's arm with friendly violence. "Not so nuts, Ed. Osirians go in for fads and fashions, and they're the only civilized extra-terrestrials with a real capitalistic system; less socialized even than that of the U.S."

Mahoney said: "What do I do if she does go loco?"

"I don't know," said Chapman, "but I'd hate to come back and find there wasn't any Greenfarb's of Hollywood . . ."

"All passengers! *Todos passageiros!*" bellowed the loudspeaker.

Chapman and Miss Zorn shook hands with Mahoney and walked up the ramp. Mahoney yelled after them: "Behave yourselves! Or if you can't . . ."

Chapman thought that if he had misbehavior in mind, he wouldn't pick a girl two inches taller than he. He forebore to say so, though, since he wanted to keep on friendly terms with Celia even if she did not appeal to the romantic side of his nature.

Seven hours later they alighted at Tycho station for the usual wrestle with red-tape before boarding the *Camões* for Osiris, otherwise Procyon XIV. The passenger *fiscal* said:

"You have a berth reserved for your *trunk*, senhor?"

"That's right," said Chapman.

"I do not understand. Contains this trunk a live creature?"

"Not at all. It is my sample trunk."

"Samples of what?"

"Clothes. I am the sales agent for Greenfarb's of Hollywood, summer wear, and Miss Greenfarb insists I sleep with that damned trunk until I've done my business."

The *fiscal* shrugged. "It is no business of mine, if your employer wishes to pay a couple of thousand dollars extra. There is another passenger on the *Camões* with a sample trunk like yours; he is in clothing too. Excuse me please . . .

Seeing that the next man in line was fidgeting, Chapman walked away, checking his tickets and passport.

"Yours okay?" he asked Celia.

"Yes. Wasn't that ticket-agent simply divine, Cato? I love these tall dark Latin types."

"Keep your mind on business," growled Chapman. As he was small and sandy, her remarks stung his *amour-propre*. Moreover he knew enough of her weaknesses to become apprehensive when she began to talk in that vein. He added:

"Seems we've got a rival aboard."

"What? How perfectly horrid! Who is he?"

"Dunno yet, but the *fiscal* said some guy has another sample trunk full of clothes."

"Oh." Celia's face took on that lugubrious expression. "One of the big Parisian cout—"

"Sh! We'll know soon enough. It's not *him*, anyhow," Chapman jerked his head towards an Osirian who stalked past on birdlike legs, carrying a suitcase. The Osirian (or Sha'akhfa, to give him his proper name) looked like a dinosaur seven feet tall: one of the little ones that ran around on their hind legs with a tail sticking out behind to balance. The creature's scaly hide was decorated with an elaborate painted pattern in many colors.

"Excuse me, pleass," said this being in a barely intelligible accent, "put what iss the correct moon time?"

Chapman told the Osirian (a male from his wattle) who set his wrist-watch and asked: "Are you too koink py the *Camões*?"

"Yes," said Chapman.

"So am I. Let uss introtuce ourselfs. I am Businessman-second-rank Fiasakhe."

Chapman introduced himself and the model and asked: "I wonder you don't wait for an Osirian ship, Mr. Fiasakhe?"

"I would, sir, but an urchent message from home . . . I came in with that cultural mission, you know, that iss to prepare the way for the export of the designs of Osirian arts and crafts . . ."

Celia said: "I should think you'd find one of our ships frightfully uncomfortable."

"I do! Always I am bumping my head on tor-frames or catching my tail in tors! Put then . . ." The creature managed a shrug with his negligible shoulders.

The steward showed Chapman his cabin and said: "Where shall we put this trunk you have a passenger-ticket for, senhor?"

"Middle bunk," said Chapman, picking up the printed passenger-list from the tiny dresser. He read:

> Barros, M. C., Rio de Janeiro.
> Bergerat, J.-J. M., Paris.
> Chapman, C. H., Hollywood.
> Chisholm, W. J., Minneapolis.
> Fiasakhe, 3*, Cefef Aqh, Osiris.
> Kamimura, A., Kobe.
> Kichik*, Dzidzigä, Thoth.
> Mpande, S., Molopololi, Bechuanaland.
> Popovich, I. I., Sofia.
> Savinkov, A. P., Paris.
> Sz, T.-E., Tientsin.
> Varga, M., Szolnok, Hungary.
> Zorn, C. E., Hollywood.

A footnote told him that the names with asterisks were those of extra-terrestrials . . .

"Cato!" said Celia's voice outside.

"Come in, Cee."

The tall dark girl did so. "I'm in with Senhora Barros

and Anya Savinkov. Anya is a model for Tomaselli's of Paris!"

"Ah," said Chapman. "Say who her boss was?"

"No, I've only just met her. She's the redhead."

"Hm. Our rival must be this Bergerat. I seem to remember that guy: the agent for Tomaselli's at the New York fair three years ago. A tall dark type, the kind you slobber over—"

"I do *not*! The nerve of you—"

"Okay, consider it unsaid. A slick operator, as I remember; pulled some fast ones on the New York department stores."

She looked at the list. "Fiasakhe we know. This Kichik must be an e. t. from Thoth. What are they like?"

"Monkey-rats, they sometimes call them; about a meter high, with seven fingers on each hand."

"How perfectly horrid!"

"They're harmless."

The door opened again and the steward ushered in a black man who turned out to be S. Mpande. After introductions Chapman said: "How about giving me the top bunk, Mr. Mpande? I'm better fitted for climbing into it."

Mpande patted his paunch and chuckled. "Right-o, old chap."

"See you later, Cee," said Chapman.

After the first few high-g hours following takeoff, Chapman got up from his bunk and went out to explore. On the opposite side of the narrow curving corridor, a little way around the circumference of the nose of the ship, was a door behind which, according to the legend in the Brazilo-Portuguese of the spaceways, lay the passengers' heavy baggage. The door was closed by a simple cylinder-lock—locked.

Following the corridor back in the other direction, Chapman came to the tiny saloon with its two little tables. Around one a game of sunburst was already under way among three human passengers and the Thothian, whose many fingers flipped the cards with ominous dexterity.

A tall dark young man unfolded himself and came over to extend a hand ornamented with a large and gaudy ring: " 'Ello, Meester Shapman! Remembair me from the New York Fair?"

"Hello, Jean-Jacques," said Chapman. "On your way to Osiris to drum up business?"

"Well, yes, maybe. I suspect that you and I, we are after the same thing."

"Got a line of summer wear?"

"Pour le sport, that is it. This is droll, no? What is this about keeping your sample trunk in your cabin?"

Chapman grinned. "Thought some sharp operator like you might be along, so . . ."

"I see, ha-ha. Me, I think Captain Almeida's locks will keep unwanted ones away. And I can imagine more amusing things to keep in my cabin than a trunk."

"No doubt," said Chapman. "But as there are only three females aboard . . ."

"Exactement. When the number does not come out even, the results are sometimes of the most amusing. Unless you count Kichik, who is neither one thing nor the other."

"Both," squeaked the Thothian. "Don't you envy me? Three spades."

It was hard to get Celia aside for private conversation because of the lack of space. He met the other passengers, including Bergerat's luscious redhead, who seemed a nice straightforward girl. At least she didn't tower over him as Celia did.

Since Mpande turned out to be a sunburst enthusiast, Chapman finally got a moment with his model in his cabin. He said: "I'm going to get a look at that trunk of Bergerat's."

"How, if it's locked up?"

"Didn't you know I once worked for a locksmith?"

"Now, look, Cato, don't start something like *that* again. You remember what happened to you in the case of that Argentine polo-player . . ."

"You leave this to me! I didn't say I was going to do anything to his trunk, did I?"

"No, but I know you—"

"And I know Jean-Jacques; the only way to treat that no goodnik is to beat him to the punch."

"I think he's perfectly nice!"

"Ha ha. You'll see."

Chapman went back down the corridor and studied the baggage-room door. Then he took life easy until chance introduced him to Zuloaga, the chief engineer of the *Camões.*

"Could I have a look around?" he asked after the amenities.

"I much regret, but it is a strict rule of the Viagens Interplanetarias that no passengers are allowed in the power-compartments."

"Then how about the machine-shop? I couldn't do any harm there."

Zuloaga wagged a forefinger. "Oh, you *Americanos do Norte* all want to get your hands greasy as soon as you come aboard. It must give you a feeling of virility, *pois não?* But come, you shall see our little shop."

In the shop Chapman cultivated the acquaintance of Chief Machinist Gustafson. Zuloaga left them puttering among the tools. When Chapman departed a quarter-hour later, he took with him a lump of beeswax and a length of wire which he had slipped into his pockets unseen.

When he was sure nobody was coming along the corridor, Chapman made an impression of the cross-section of the slot of the lock on the baggage-room door, and poked his wire into the slot until he knew how deep it was.

As the hours passed, some passengers took short-trance pills while others continued to play sunburst. Fiasakhe, whose claws were ill-shaped for holding playing-cards, sat folded in a corner of the saloon with his tail curled up against the wall, reading through a pile of slushy sentimental Earthly novels he had brought with him.

Chapman, after letting a decent interval elapse, found an excuse to get back into the machine-shop. Here he wheedled a couple of pieces of titanium brass out of Gustafson and began hammering and filing them into the shape he wanted. Gustafson appeared to believe the unlikely story that they were for Chapman's portable radio.

The two pieces of metal finally took the form of a couple of very slender cylinder-lock keys, one without any of the usual saw-toothed projections and the other with a single such projection. The two keys had handles offset in opposite directions. "For adjusting my germanium crystals," said Chapman.

"You must show me how to fix mine some time," said Gustafson.

"Sure. *Obrigado.*"

Chapman's next step was to walk off from the dinner-table with the pepper-shaker in his pocket. When Mpande was absent from the cabin, Chapman emptied the pepper into an ordinary envelope and put the envelope in his pocket.

Then he waited until nearly all the passengers were asleep, and Mpande was playing sunburst in the saloon. (On a space-ship there were always some individualists who preferred not to keep to the arbitrary waking-and-sleeping schedule of the majority.) He slipped out of his cabin with the brass gadgets in his pockets and went to the baggage-room. After looking nervously over his shoulders he slipped the plain brass finger into the lock and twisted hard. Then he slid the one with the projection into the remaining space in the slot and worked it in and out until all the little split pins inside caught at their opening levels. Click! Chapman opened the door.

First making sure that he would not be locking himself in, he closed the door behind him. He was in complete darkness except for the beam of his little pocket flashlight. The compartment was so jammed with baggage that there was little room to move. However, Chapman grinned when his light picked out Bergerat's big sample trunk in plain sight, with the legend: *J.-J. M. B.—Tomaselli of Paris.* He had to move only one suitcase to get at it.

He grinned wickedly at the thought that Monsieur Tomaselli, a notorious pinchfranc, had been unwilling to lay out a couple of grand more to assure a private berth for his samples; how nice! But what now? The trunk had a combination lock: a Kleinwasser, the peculiarity of which was that it had to be locked as well as unlocked by twirling the knob in a certain combination. The idea had been to discourage people from locking the combination into the trunk.

That knowledge, however, did him no good without the combination. Of course there were the tried and true methods of prying, drilling, or blasting. But even the unbrilliant Gustafson would get suspicious if he tried to borrow a jimmy or a drill, and blasting was quite out of the question. What then? Too bad he didn't have a hypnoscope to pry the combination out of Bergerat.

What other possibilities? The luscious redhead, Anya Savinkov, might prove pliable. In fact he wouldn't mind cultivating her on general principles. Although he knew many beauties in Hollywood, they'd all be middle-aged matrons by the time he returned. That was why only people like Celia and himself, without close family ties, went off on jaunts of this sort. In the five months' subjective time of their voyage, eleven years would be passing on the planets ...

He whirled at a sound, snapping off his light. Somebody moved and breathed in the corridor outside. Then the door opened and an arm came through the opening, to grope about the inside of the bulkhead for the light-switch.

Chapman saw enough of a shoulder and part of a head, silhouetted against the lighted corridor, to recognize Jean-Jacques Bergerat. In another second the lights would go on, and the trunks were too closely packed for him to hide among them on such short notice.

With one hand Chapman reached into his blouse pocket and brought out a small fistful of pepper. With the other, having stowed his flashlight, he seized the wrist groping for the switch. He threw the pepper in Bergerat's face and pulled hard on the wrist, jerking the man forward into the baggage-room. Chapman let go his victim and slipped past him out the door, which he closed behind him just as the air was rent by the first of a series of crashing sneezes.

Half an hour later a fist knocked on Chapman's door. "Let me in, Cato! A thing of the most strange has 'appened to me!"

Chapman looked around the room and took the water-carafe out of its bracket on the wall. In a pinch it would do.

Bergerat, however, seemed entirely friendly, though afflicted with a red face and bloodshot eyes. "My friend! It is something of incredible! I am walking along the corridor when I hear a noise coming from the baggage-room. Aha, I say, what is it that is there? Is somebody after my beautiful samples? I push the door. *Achoo!* It opens, though it should at all times be locked except when the steward or one of the officers is there. I reach inside to put on the lights. What happens? I am seized and drawn in, and pepper is thrown in my face. The intruder, he rushes past me and out. Fortunately the door cannot be locked from the inside or I should be there yet. *Achoo!*"

"Who was it?" said Chapman.

"I don't know, so quickly did the *fripon* move. For a moment I suspected even you. But that would be absurd; one agent of a great couturière to play such a trick on another? Then I thought maybe our friend Fiasakhe might have some fanatical idea that the custom of wearing clothes was indecent, and wished to prevent us from introducing it to his planet. But no, I am sure the hand that grasped my arm was that of a man, not an Osirian. Have you any ideas?"

Chapman asked innocently: "Is your model, Mademoiselle Savinkov, trustworthy?"

"That little one? I think that yes. Here, let us repair the ravages of time and misfortune." Bergerat brought out a silver flask with two small cups screwed over the outlet. "Good cognac."

Chapman sniffed suspiciously at his thimbleful of brandy and held it in his hand until Bergerat drank his. Then Chapman drank too.

"Let us go over the passenger-list," said Bergerat. "This Madame Barros, now, she is enroute to join her husband, so I think she is kosher. Mr. William Chisholm: do you know anything of him?"

"Only what he's told us. He's some kind of professor ..."

Chapman, sitting on the edge of Mpande's bunk, swayed. Then, before he even realized what was happening, he lost consciousness.

Cato Chapman awakened with a headache and a foul taste in his mouth. He moved a little experimentally, groaned, and sat up to hold his head.

"I say, are you all right, old thing?" said Mpande, sticking his head out from the bottom bunk. "I came in some hours ago, and found you stretched out on your bunk with your togs on."

"Guess I'll live, thanks," muttered Chapman. His watch told him it was nearly breakfast-time.

He got up and shaved. Then, as soon as Mpande left, Chapman leaped to his trunk. Finding it still locked, he hoped for a moment it had not been tampered with. When he got it open, however, the gorgeous raiment within was a slimy mess. Some of the garments were full of holes; others were partly dissolved into a kind of slush; others were whole but violently discolored.

He pulled himself together and pressed the intercom button in the bulkhead. "Miss Zorn, please ... Celia, this is Cato. Will you step over to my cabin, quick?"

When she saw the mess she clutched her head and moaned: "Cato! How perfectly ghastly! How did that happen?"

Chapman poked among the ruins and came up with a couple of slivers of thin glass. "See this cut on the outside?" He pointed to a semicircular gash that had been cut or burned in the metal of the trunk, and the resulting flap lifted up and pushed down again.

"It's Bergerat, of course. I thought that ring of his looked too big to be just an ornament. It's an energy-cutter. He knocked me out with that drink—God knows how—cut the trunk open, and stuck in an acid-bomb.

They're cute little things, used in strikes in the cleaning-business. There's a plastic covering about the size of an egg, and inside that a thin glass container with the acid and a sliding weight. You tap them hard on something and the weight breaks the glass and the acid dissolves the plastic."

While they examined the ruined samples he told her of his earlier encounter with Bergerat in the baggage-room.

She said: "He knew it was you, and decided to get even."

"For what? I hadn't hurt his damned trunk . . ."

"You mean not yet. You did fill his face with pepper, though. Why didn't you have the sense to leave him be, instead of going in for this perfectly ridiculous amateur burglary?"

"What do you mean, sense? Damn it, woman, I'm in charge and I won't be yelled at . . ."

"*Who's yelling at whom?*"

"*You are!*" he shouted.

"I AM NOT YELLING!"

"*YOU ARE TOO!*" Chapman took a firm grip on himself and laughed. "So'm I. Let's not fight; at least, not each other."

"But what'll we do? There's nothing usable except this one pair of swim-trunks, and we can't give a showing with that."

"We could give a sensational showing," he said, "but the Osirians wouldn't appreciate it."

"There's no way of turning back, say by being transferred to another ship, is there?"

"Certainly not. We've got enough energy stored in us, just from the speed we're going, to—to—"

They both held their heads. Ceilia Zorn finally said: "I knew nothing would come of letting you and Miss Nettie talk me into this crazy expedition. Even if we live to get back, the old hell-cat will fire us."

Chapman looked up. "There's one chance left." He took out his wallet and stuffed it up his sleeve.

"Cato! Are you planning something reckless?"

"You'll see. Anyway, what have we got to lose?"

In the saloon the first shift had just finished breakfast and were making way for the second. Chapman pushed towards Bergerat, said: "All right, you. . . ." adding several fruity epithets, and punched Bergerat's nose.

Instantly the saloon was filled with yells, silverware, and confusion. Bergerat got back one good right to Chapman's mouth before they clinched and fell, threshing about in the little space between the two tables.

"Stop this at once!" shouted an authoritative voice in Brazilo-Portuguese, and Chapman felt himself plucked from his antagonist. Captain Almeida was roaring at him: "Are you mad, man? What is the meaning of this outrage?"

"This twerp," said Chapman, blood trickling down his chin, "dopes me with a knockout drop, picks my pocket, and puts an acid-bomb in my sample trunk to ruin my stock, and you call it an outrage when I poke him one?"

"Liar!" said Bergerat. "I gave him a swallow of cognac and he passed out. Can I help it if he has no head for good liquor? I know nothing about his trunk and I never picked his pocket. Let me at the cheap chiseler . . ."

"Look in his pockets," said Chapman.

Zuloaga ran his hands over Bergerat's body and found Chapman's wallet.

"You see?" said Chapman.

"But—but I have no idea how that got there," said Bergerat. "He must have planted it while we were fighting . . ."

By now, however, Chapman had obviously captured the sympathy of the officers. "Let me show you my trunk," he said.

He showed them the remains of the samples, Bergerat denying his guilt all the while. Chapman thought with an inward chuckle that he could never have proved that Bergerat had done the crime he *had* committed if he hadn't first convinced the authorities that Bergerat had done another one he *hadn't*.

Bergerat said: "I came to see Mr. Chapman because I had just had another encounter with him in the baggage-room." He went on with an account of his peppery experience.

"He's making that up," said Chapman. "He has to have something to say, I suppose. Let's look at that trunk of his; maybe it's full of stolen goods."

They went down the hall, where the captain opened the baggage-room door. Chapman had a moment of panic lest somebody think to ask Gustafson what Mr. Chapman had been doing all that time in the machine-shop. But nobody did, and Bergerat's trunk proved undisturbed.

"Open it," said the captain.

Bergerat complied. Inside was a mass of neatly hung summer wear, mostly female: sun-suits, bathing-suits, tennis-clothes, and the like. None of the other passengers claimed any of these items as stolen property.

"You see," said Chapman. "Nobody's tried to break into his trunk."

"I see," said Captain Almeida. He slammed the trunk closed, spun the knob, and turned on Bergerat. "You, *amigo,* are under arrest for assault, burglary, theft, and any others I think up later. You will remain in Compartment K until we arrive, when formal charges will be preferred. Take him away."

Anya Savinkov protested: "But—but that is wrong—you should at least put them both in the cell. What will become of me? I am desolated—"

Chapman patted her arm. "That's all right, little one. I'll take care of you."

"Huh?" said Celia Zorn. "Watch out for him, Anya, when he starts talking that way . . ."

Chapman laughed at them and went back to his cabin, where he swabbed out the inside of his trunk. At the next sleeping-period he made sure Mpande was engrossed in a game in the saloon, dug his lock-pickers out of their hiding-place, and entered the baggage-compartment again. Captain Almeida, not knowing the peculiarity of the Kleinwasser lock, had simply given the knob a twirl, so that Bergerat's trunk was not really locked at all.

Half an hour later all Miss Greenfarb's ruined summer wear had been transferred to Bergerat's trunk, while Monsieur Tomaselli's assortment of similar garments reposed snugly in Chapman's trunk in Chapman's cabin.

Then he relaxed in the saloon by dragging Fiasakhe away from his sentimental novels for a bout of checkers.

After the *Camões* had landed and all the passengers had been through passport, health, and customs inspection, Chapman said: "Come along, girls. I think those birds in the waiting-room are our Osirian capitalists."

"What good will it do?" wailed Celia. "We haven't got any stock and we can't make any . . ."

"Leave it to me," said Chapman. "Oh, Fiasakhe!"

"Yess?"

"Will you act as interpreter for me for a few minutes? I don't know much of your language yet."

"Klatly."

They went up to the little herd of dinosaurs and Chapman told Fiasakhe: "Ask them if one of them is Thafahiya the curtain-maker."

After some hissing in the Sha'akhfi tongue, Fiasakhe reported: "That bik one is he." He indicated a tall Osirian whose scales were decorated with a peculiarly gorgeous pattern of blue-and-gold paint. "Say he get Miss Greenfarb's letter. Think it is a fine idea. You sell them the designs, they make the clothes. Naturally their answer will not haff reached Earth for many yearss yet. Will you come with them to their office to arranche the showink?"

"Come, girls," said Chapman, starting to follow his new associates. Through the glass doors he could see an Osirian automobile—a wheeled platform with handrails but no seats. With those tails a sedan body wouldn't be practical . . .

"Senhor Chapman!" It was one of the Viagens officials. "Just a minute, *por favor!*"

"What is it?" said Chapman in some annoyance.

"You must sign the complaint against the Senhor Bergerat. Otherwise we cannot try him."

"Don't want to press that complaint," said Chapman, feeling magnanimous. "Four months in Compartment K was enough punishment."

"But then we must let him go!"

"Okay, let him go."

The assembled Osirians hissed like a leaky boiler as Celia and Anya paraded in front of them in one outfit after another. Chapman, whose command of Sha'akhfi was yet meager, read his patter from a script in phonetic symbols: ". . . here, ladies and gentlemen, is an outfit for window-shopping on the boulevard. Notice the flare of the skirt . . ." He knew his accent was terrible, since some Sha'akhfi sounds simply could not be made by human vocal organs and vice versa. Naturally he did not tell them they were looking at the line of Tomaselli of Paris.

The female Osirians, he was gratified to see, were putting pressure on their males to buy them everything in sight. When it was over the males lined up and signed checks, using their claws as pens, as fast as Chapman could quote them prices. Although these prices were fantastically high they did not, of course, cover the cost of bringing the sample-trunk to Osiris, but there was no point either in giving the things away or in blowing a few grand more hauling them back to Earth.

After all the samples had been sold, the female Osirians wanted to buy the girls' personal clothes—all of them. It took all Chapman's persuasion to get rid of them.

"Whew!" he said as the last Osirian belle stalked out, a beret perched on her cockscomb and a halter around her breastless torso. "That—uh—that show you, eh, Thafahiya?"

"Magnificent!" said the Osirian. "We shall sign the contract forthwith. What a pity that with our bodily temperature-control, we have never felt the need of this charming custom of wearing clothes? Come, I shall give you your contract and your first payment. When may we expect our first portfolio of designs?"

"They—they on way," said Chapman in his stumbling Sha'akhfi. "Are being sent here by ship, for deposit with Viagens, and released to you if contract has been closed. Let us hurry, for we not want to miss *Camões's* return trip."

"No great matter; one of our own ships leaves for your star a few days later . . ."

Chapman hurried nevertheless. Osirians slept on the floor, did not use chairs, and subsisted on the meat of other reptiles which they domesticated. While he'd heard their space-ships made special provisions for human passengers, as those of the Viagens did for e. t.'s, he did not care to test their sleeping-accommodations and cuisine himself.

When he had stowed his copy of the contract between Greenfarb's and Thafahiya's syndicate safely in Captain Almeida's safe, Cato Chapman said: "Well, girls, guess our fortunes are made." Then he yelped as he saw Bergerat's name on the passenger-list.

"Well," said Celia, "what did you expect the poor man to do?"

Chapman said: "This may be embarrassing."

It did not, however, prove so. Bergerat grinned at him and said: "Where can we talk, my old? I have a proposition to make."

Later he said: "Look, I cannot go back to Tomaselli. He will not only fire me but will try to get me blacklisted in Paris. A very vengeful man, my little Tomaselli.

"Now you and I, we have fought with what you call the bare knuckles—or it is brass knuckles?—and you have won. *Bien.* I congratulate you. But why can I not go back to Hollywood with you? It is the world's other great style center. Perhaps you could put in a good word for me with your Miss Greenfarb."

"Hm," said Chapman. "An idea. Can't promise anything. Nettie'll probably think Tomaselli is trying to plant you in her shop as a spy. Are you sure he isn't?" Chapman looked hard at his friendly enemy.

"No, no! That is easily proved. True, there is another motive in the case."

"Huh?"

"A sentimental motive. Your Miss Zorn—ahum—ah . . ."

"Oh. Well, I'll do what I can. By the way, how'd you work that Mickey Finn trick on me? I carefully watched you drink the same stuff."

"That was simple," said Bergerat. "I used a barbiturate that is counteracted by caffein, and I filled myself with coffee before I visited your cabin. But we are all done with these games now, no?"

Five months later, subjective time, the shuttle-rocket from Pluto landed at Mohave Spaceport. Chapman, with Anya clinging to his arm, walked down the ramp. There would be changes in twenty-two years. Fortunately, because of the great lengthening of the human lifespan in the last century, most of his old acquaintances would still be around. Including Miss Nettie.

He puffed furiously on his pipe, the first smoke he'd been allowed since boarding the *Camões*. Behind him came Bergerat and Celia. As they passed through the inspection-rooms and into the waiting-room, Chapman stopped short. His pipe bounced from the floor unheeded.

Except for those who had come in on the ship, the people swarming in the waiting-room were all quite naked except for sandals. Moreover their hides were decorated with the fantastically interwoven designs in iridescent colors that the Osirians used for personal adornment.

As the four stood gawking, a man came up. "Cato Chapman?"

"Y-yes. Who are you?"

"Don't you know me?"

"By all the gods, you're my cousin Ed Mahoney! This is my wife Anya, and these are Mr. and Mrs. Bergerat. Remember Celia? She always wanted a tall dark type. The captain hitched us on the way back from Osiris."

Mahoney nodded. "I thought something like that might happen."

"But—but—where the hell are your clothes? And why is everybody going around looking like the tattooed woman in the circus?"

"Oh, that. That's the new Osirian style; it came in a couple of years ago. We don't wear clothes in hot weather any more."

"Yuk," said Chapman. "How come?"

"It seems some smart Osirians who came here on that so-called cultural mission started a syndicate to exploit the Osirian body-paint designs on Earth. That reminds me, you haven't got a job any more."

"What?"

"That's right. Nettie Greenfarb and all the other summer wear specialty-shops went broke. Last I heard of Nettie she had some government job. But maybe you'd like to try the paint business. It's doing swell, as you can imagine, and maybe I can find openings for you and your friend. Like me to fly you in to L.A.?"

Dumbly they followed him.

Finished

"It won't work forever," said Abreu gloomily. "Keep up a technological blockade, and at the same time allow communication between Krishnans and beings from other planets? Bah! Why doesn't the damned Interplanetary Council ask us something easy, like lighting the Sadabao Sea with a match?"

Comandante Silva, who had come over from his planet for the conference, looked amused. "We have no trouble on Vishnu, and moreover we run the station without red tape. Your forms, Senhor Cristôvão, are getting notorious—"

Abreu turned pink and began to bounce in his chair. "Easy for you to criticize, Senhor Augusto. You know Bembom's a little station compared to Novorecife, and that your Vishnuvans are simple-minded children compared to Krishnans."

"I only said your red tape was getting notorious, which—"

"But I tell you—"

"Which it is—"

"*Queira, senhores,*" interrupted Kennedy. As the Comandante of Novorecife was the S. O. P., the others subsided. "Let's not get personal. We all do the best we can with what we have."

"Well, it still won't work," grumped Abreu. "Some day they'll get something big through, and then we'll learn whether the I. C. is right in fearing that the backward Krishnans might start an interplanetary war once they have their scientific revolution."

Silva said: "I sympathize with you, at that. The I. C. is just a board, and a board may be defined as a long, narrow, and wooden thing. I've been writing them for a Vishnuvan year now to get—"

"Yes?" said Abreu. Gorchakov, the head customs inspector, had come in.

"You'd better be in on this, *chefe*," said Gorchakov. "You know that Earthman we cleared for travel a few ten-nights back—Akelawi? Ahmad Akelawi?"

"The tall Algerian engineer? *Sim*. What about him?"

"He's trying to take a mummy through customs."

"Excuse me, *senhores*," said Abreu. "I certainly do want to be in on this." The head security officer. of Novorecife heaved his bulk out of his chair and waddled after Gorchakov.

"What sort of mummy?" he asked.

"Some native king. He claims it's perfectly legal, and has a bill of sale to show for it."

Abreu prepared to bristle at the sight of Akelawi. Being short and fat, he suspected all tall men of evil designs, and the Algerian was perhaps the tallest man ever to set foot on this outpost of the Viagens Interplanetarias. Akelawi still wore his Krishnan makeup: antennae, green hair, and artificial points to his ears. He gazed down at Abreu from large dark eyes with an expression of melancholy reserve.

Abreu brusquely asked: "What's this all about, Senhor Ahmad?"

Akelawi sighed. "First I explain to the customs inspector, then to the head customs inspector, now to you, and I suppose after you to Comandante Kennedy—"

"Never mind that, my good sir. Just answer the question."

"Very well. As I've already said twice, I bought this mummy from Prince Ferrian of Sotaspé. Here's my bill of sale, with the prince's own signature."

"Why did you buy it?"

"To take to Earth as a museum piece. Even with the present freight-rates it'll pay the cost of my trip."

"Whose mummy is it? asked Abreu, bending over the object. *"Mãe do Deus*, it's ugly!"

Akelawi said: "It's supposed to be the remains of Manzariyé, the first and only king of Sotaspé."

"How so? Have they a republic, or what?"

"Not exactly. They have a legal fiction whereby King Manzariyé is still the legal ruler, and the reigning prince has only the status of a regent. The reasons are very complicated and legalistic—"

"Never mind them, then. Have you X-rayed it, *amigo*?"

"Not yet," said Gorchakov. "I thought you'd want to be present ..."

Half an hour later Abreu completed his examination. "I don't see why we shouldn't let you take it through," he told Akelawi. "But tell me: Why should Prince Ferrian sell the sacred relic of his ancestor?"

Akelawi shrugged his bony shoulders. "He didn't say. Perhaps he plans to make himself king in name as well as in fact."

"I see. What's the medal you're wearing?"

"The open glider-championship of Mikardand. If you'll let me start signing that mountain of papers, maybe I'll be through in time to catch the ship."

He signed out and departed with his mummy.

Three days later, after Akelawi had taken off on the *Lorêto*, a slim, burning-eyed young Krishnan stormed into Novorecife. His clothing was that of a rich islander from the Sadabao Sea, and his Brazilo-Portuguese was, if not broken, at least badly bent.

"I am Prince Ferrian of Sotaspé!" he shouted at the amazed Abreu. "What have you filthy animals done with our sublime king?"

"You mean that mummy Akelawi took with him?" asked Abreu.

"To you mummy, perhaps, but to us, sacred symbol of our eternal kingdom! Where is?"

Abreu explained.

"You mean," cried the prince, "that symbol of glory of our ancestors has gone millions miles away? That this thief, may Dupulán rot his intestines, has—"

"Wait a minute, my good sir," said Abreu. "Are you claiming that Akelawi stole this mummy, and didn't buy it from you as he said?"

"Of course he stole! Think you we are such poor things as sell our very king?"

Abreu told his secretary: "Get the photostat of Akelawi's bill of sale out of the files. If there's been a mistake, Dom Ferrian, we'll set it right ... Here you are. Isn't that your signature?"

"Looks like, but I never signed no such paper. He must have got it by trick. When does next space-ship leave for Earth?"

"In nine or ten days. But, my friend, you know there are difficulties to getting permission for Krishnans to travel on Viagens vehicles—"

"As if we were not oldest and proudest line in universe!" said Ferrian hotly. "Let me tell you, senhor, some day will be end to this discrimination—"

"Now, now, it's not a matter of thinking ourselves superior to the Krishnans. It's a question of your cultural fitness to absorb scientific knowledge. When you've adopted modern ideas on government and legal codes—"

Ferrian told Abreu, in guttural Gozashtandou, what to do with his legal codes.

Abreu, keeping a tight grip on his none-too-amiable temper, replied: "Why not let us handle it? The Viagens security organization can send a dispatch to Earth by the next ship. As soon as the message is received, the great Earthly police-forces will go into action and have your king back here in no time."

"What is no time?"

"Oh—Krishnan time, about twenty-five years. It takes that long for the message to reach Earth and the king to return."

"No! Can't wait. Must go myself. You think I let my poor ancestor be jerked all over universe without escort, lonesome, unprotected? You Terrans don't know nothing about respect due divine rulers."

"Very well. File your application in due form."

Thus it happened that the next space-ship for the planets of Sol's system bore Ferrian bad-Arjanaq, Prince Regent of Sotaspé. Since the space-traveller was, on one hand, a person of importance, while on the other he was still a native of a backward planet whose warlike people were not allowed access to technical information, Abreu sent his assistant security officer, the small and modest Herculeu Castanhoso, along as guardian.

When Abreu saw them off, they were arguing hotly about the Fitzgerald effect. Ferrian refused to believe that if it took a hundred and sixty-some days, subjective time, to get to Earth, something like three thousand days, objective time, would have meanwhile elapsed on Krishna.

"We have fairy-tale," he said scornfully, "about the miner Ghalaju who go to Fairyland and spend three days, and when he come back all his friends have grow old. But you don't expect me, adult and educated man, to take that sort of thing serious!"

Years passed.

There was a scandal about the introduction of the custom of kissing into Krishna. In the resulting shakeup

Abreu was transferred to Ganesha, though it hadn't been his fault at all. Then a similar shakeup, when the tobacco-habit spread to Krishna in the administration of his successor, brought him back again, thanks to Earthly geriatrics not visibly older.

Then one day the fast new *Maranhão* settled down on the Novorecife landing-area, and down the ramp trudged Castanhoso and Prince Ferrian.

"Well!" said Abreu, shaking hands vigorously. "I thought you two should be showing up soon. Did you get your mummy?"

"Yes," said Ferrian, in much improved Portuguese; "it was a most interesting journey, even though this watch-eshun of yours kept me confined like an aqebat in a cage. He'd let me read nothing, even, save a moldy old law-book he picked up somewhere."

"Those were his orders," said Abreu. "When Krishna achieves the interplanetary standards of law, ethics, and government, then maybe we'll let you have access—"

Ferrian made an impatient motion. "Save your lectures, my friend. Right now I'm more interested in arranging transportation to Majbur for myself and my king. While the trip didn't seem so long to me, the wait will have been interminable for my poor wives. I must see them again."

Abreu, a henpecked man, envied the prince his ability to manage not merely one wife but a whole platoon of them. However, like a wise bureaucrat, he kept his reflections to himself. When Ferrian was out of earshot he asked Castanhoso:

"How did you make out, Herculeu?"

"Not badly. He obeyed orders all right; the only trouble is he's too intelligent."

"How so?"

"He draws correct inferences from the least things. And he can turn on charm enough to lure a fish out of a pond when he wants to! I finally gave him that law-book to keep him quiet, thinking that Krishna could use some modern law."

"You did right. Did you know you'd been promoted?"

"Why—uh—thanks, but isn't there a mistake? I've just *been* promoted—"

"You forget, my boy, that was by subjective time, while for pay and seniority purposes, service is figured by objective time . . ."

Abreu saw to it that the prince and his mummy departed in a twenty-oar barge down the Pichidé River, then returned to his paperwork and put the kinglet out of his mind.

Until he got a letter from Gorbovast, the resident commissioner of King Eqrar of Gozashtand in the free city of Majbur. Gorbovast, in addition to representing King Eqrar, picked up a little change on the side by spying for Abreu. The missive read:

From the writer to the distinguished addressee, greeting:

O worthy one, a matter of interest to you has come to my notice. As you know, the Prince of Sotaspé has resided here for a ten-night or more, having with him the mummy of King Manzariyé. Today there docked here a vessel flying the banner of Sotaspé, carrying the Sotaspeo prime minister, Sir Qarao bad-Avé. 'Tis said a tame bijar flew a message to Sotaspé for this ship to come fetch the prince.

The matter of most interest, however, is the ship *Kerukchi* herself. For the means of propulsion on which she relies, besides sails, are not oars but a mechanical device. To either beam is affixed a great wheel having paddles of wood set about its rim so as to dip into the water as the wheel turns. The wheels are revolved by a machine within the hull, whose details I cannot give you because the Sotaspeva let none aboard their craft. 'Tis said, however, that the machine works by boiling water, and that smoke issues from a tall pipe amidships.

As the *Kerukchi* will probably sail soon, when the machine has been readied for the voyage, you must hasten if you'd view this craft. My respectful regards to you and yours.

Abreu, after reading the letter through again, buzzed furiously for Castanhoso.

"Herculeu!" he shouted. "Make an appointment with the barber for both of us! We're going out! Green hair and all the rest!"

Meanwhile in Majbur Prince Ferrian was giving his prime minister a proper dressing-down.

"You utter, unmitigated idiot!" he cried. "Has Sotaspé no ships of the conventional kind, that you must even bring the *Kerukchi* hither, where rumors of its being will surely reach the Earthmen at Novorecife? Take that, fool!" He slashed at the minister's head with an aya-whip.

Sir Qarao ducked, prostrated himself, and beat his head on the floor. "Have mercy, Your Sublimity!" he wailed. "You know I could never manage your harem!"

"What about my harem?"

"Why, this ill-starred venture was undertaken upon the insistence of your wife the Lady Tánzi, who said she sought to do you proper honor by sending the pride of our navy to fetch you!"

"Pride! Honor! *Ghuvoi* such talk! My wife the Lady Tánzi wished to score one over my wife the Lady Kurahi, did she not? Why sought you not the counsel of my wife the Lady Ja'li?"

"I did, but she's ill, and referred me to your wife the Lady Rovrai, who took the part of the Lady Tánzi . . ."

"I see," snarled Ferrian. "A proper muddle. Well, at least this error shall not be repeated, for when I return to Sotaspé there shall be a new law in the land. A law-book I read while among the Earthmen convinced me of its desirability."

"What's that?" said Qarao, raising his head from the floor.

"Compulsory monogamy, as among the Gozashtanduma."

"Oh, but Your Sublimity! What will you do with all your faithful wives?"

"Faithful, ha! I can imagine, after all these years . . . But to answer your question, I'll divorce all but one and pension them off. If they'd find other husbands, let 'em. They'll have little trouble, since they'll have wealth and prestige and we have a surplus of men."

"Which will you keep, godlike sir?"

"That I hadn't decided. The Lady Ja'li's the most sensible, but she's old; the Lady Dunbeni's the most beautiful, but she's cold; while the Lady Tánzi's the most loving, but lacks the wit the gods gave an unha . . ."

Two days later Abreu and his assistant stood before Gorbovast in Majbur. Gone were the trim Viagens security-force uniforms. To all appearances the Earthmen were a pair of raffish-looking Krishnans in divided kilts, stocking-caps, and cutlery.

"Right sorry am I, sirs," said King Eqrar's commissioner. "The *Kerukchi* departed at dawn, as I warned you she might, taking Prince Ferrian and his moldering mummy with her."

"That can't be helped," said Abreu in his fluent, accentless Gozashtandou. "What I need is a fast ship to catch them."

"There be some large merchantmen in harbor—"

"Scows! Too slow for a stern chase."

"Are you planning—"

"Never mind what I'm planning! Whatever happens, it'll be on the high seas where it's every man for himself. The only law that can touch me will be Sotaspeo law, and I don't intend to come under that jurisdiction. Where can I get a galley?"

Gorbovast raised his antennae. "Majbur Town will hardly rent out the ships of their navy."

"How about the King of Zamba?"

"No. He has no wish to become embroiled with Sotaspé."

"And anyway it would take too long to arrange," said Abreu. "Think, man, think!"

"I think," said Gorbovast. *"Ohé!* How about Captain Zardeku and his *Alashtir?*"

"What's that?"

"A tern bireme which Zardeku bought from Arisang last year and converted to a fast merchantman. He has eighty stout rowers pulling forty oars, and a good spread of sail, and can outrun aught hereabouts save Majbur's great quinquireme *Junsar.*"

"How on Krishna can he make a profit with eighty rowers to feed? They eat like bishtars. And there can't be much cargo-space."

"Ah, but 'tis for a special purpose! With the *Alashtir* he trades in the Va'andao Sea, in defiance of the monopoly claimed by Dur. Should any normal merchantman venture into those waters, the Duruma would catch him ere he'd gone ten hoda and throw his folk to the fish. Zardeku, however, dashes in and out and wiggles his tongue at 'em, for they can catch him no more than King Gedik could catch the rain-god in his net. Methinks some of the goods he brings to Majbur were obtained by plain piracy, though there's no proof of that. At all events, he was still here yester-eve; why seek you not him?"

Captain Zardeku turned out to be a tall heavy Krishnan lolling on a bench in a waterfront dive with an air of sleepy good-nature. Somebody had once flattened his flat

Krishnan nose still further with a blunt instrument. He said:

"For the terms ye mention, gentlemen, I'd take the *Alashtir* over the waterfall that legend used to place at the other end of the Sadabao Sea, where the water poured over the edge of the world. When would ye set forth?"

"This afternoon?" said Abreu.

"Nay, not quite so fast as that! 'Twill take me till the morrow to drag my sturdy boys from those entertainments that sailors seek ashore, and to get supplies aboard. If ye would, though, I'll cast off an hour ere dawn."

"Agreed," said Abreu. "I hope your men are willing to spend nights at sea."

"Aye, they'll do it if I so tell 'em. They've had to sleep on their benches ere this, when the Duro galleys were crawling on our track like the bugs from under a flat stone. And for a chase of this kind I'd better embark some supplementary rowers."

Captain Zardeku, almost as good as his word, cast off half a Krishnan hour before sunrise. The forty oars, two men to an oar, thumped in their locks as the prevailing westerlies carried them down the estuary and out into the Sadabao Sea. To the west, to landward, great piles of clouds swept in stately ranks across the greenish sky, but as they reached the shoreline they dissolved into nothing, so that the seaward half of the dome of heaven was clear.

The wind filled the three triangular lateen sails. " 'Tis a new rig in these parts," said Zardeku. "For fast maneuver a tern has it all over a two-sticker, and can sail closer to the wind, for ye can control the ends of your ship with the small sails. Howsomever, it looks as if our chase would be all running free, if this breeze holds. Would ye put in to Zamba?"

Abreu made the negative head-motion. "He's not likely to have stopped there, after such a short run from Majbur, unless the machinery broke down. We might sail a reach past the Reshr harbor, just to make sure he's not lying there, and go on to Jerud."

"One point to port!" said Zardeku, and went on to talk of piracy and nautical lore and ship-design; how the ship-wrights, before they found the trick of putting two or more men on the same oar, used to range the oars in several tiers, with all sorts of elaborate arrangements to keep the rowers out of each others' hair . . .

Although there was no sign of the *Kerukchi* in the harbor of Reshr, the harbor-master at Jerud told them:

"Yes, we saw this craft go past with a long stream of smoke blowing ahead of her. Thinking she was afire, we sent a galley out to help, and sore foolish they felt when the fire-ship signalled that all was well."

Captain Zardeku topped off his supplies of food and water for the gigantic hunger and thirst of his rowers, and set out again over the emerald waters. They stopped at Zá, where the folk have tails like those of the Koloft Swamp; at Ulvanagh, where Dezful the gold-plated pirate reigned before his singular demise; and at Varzeni-Ganderan, the isle of women, who allow the men of passing ships to company with them but let no grown males settle.

The dames of Varzeni-Ganderan had indeed seen the fire-ship go by on the horizon, but it had not stopped. This in itself was unusual.

"Small crew, or else he's in a hell of a hurry," mused Abreu. He told Zardeku: "We should find him soon. I think he'll have to stop for firewood for his machine."

They lost most of a night in Varzeni-Ganderan because the crew of the *Alashtir* scattered to enjoy the pleasures the place afforded, and rounding them up took hours. On the fourth day the *Alashtir* came in sight of Darya, where the folk wear coats of grease in lieu of clothes. They recognized the island by its two rocky peaks long before the rest of it came in sight.

The lookout called down: "Smoke in the harbor, but I see not what it means."

"Captain," said Abreu, "I think our man stopped here for wood and is just about to pull out. Hadn't you better rig your catapult and give the rowers a rest?"

"Aye-aye. You there!" Zardeku began giving orders in his usual mild tone, but little above the conversational. Abreu, however, noted that the crew hopped to it nevertheless.

While the rowers loafed and the ship eased towards the harbor under sail, the sailors brought up a mass of timbers and rope from below, which they assembled on the foredeck into a catapult. They piled beside it the missiles, which could be called either feathered javelins or oversized arrows.

"What now?" asked Zardeku.

"Heave to; we can't go into the harbor to take him."

Zardeku brought his ship's bow up-wind and let go his main sheet so that the big mainsail flapped, while the small fore and mizzen sails, as close-hauled as they could be braced, kept just enough way on the *Alashtir* to prevent her from drifting shorewards. The swells smacked obliquely against her bow, giving her an uneasy rotary motion.

Through a telescope Abreu could see the paddle-wheel steamer, her stack puffing angrily. They must be stoking her up, he thought. As the *Alashtir* worked slowly past the harbor, a quarter-hoda away, he got a view of his quarry from several angles. Another conversion job, evidently; he could see the places where the outriggers for the oarlocks had been attached when she had been a galley.

"Aren't we getting too far north?" he asked Zardeku. "If she heads south when she comes out we might have trouble catching her."

"Right ye be," said Zardeku. "Haul the main sheet! Let her fall off a point!"

As the ship gathered speed, Abreu asked: "Captain, why are we sailing directly away from the harbor?"

"To get sea-room to wear ship."

"But why can't you simply turn to the left?"

"Port helm and back sails? Think ye I'm mad? Y'only do that when 'tis a matter of dodging rocks!"

Abreu, realizing that he was no sailor, left the technical end of the art to Zardeku.

"The fire-ship's coming out!" called the lookout.

"Better hurry, Captain," said Abreu.

Zardeku gave more orders. The rowers ran out their oars. The helmsman swung the ship hard to starboard until the bow pointed toward shore, while the sailors let out the sheets until all three sails were flapping. The rowers backed, holding the ship immobile, the swells smashing against the stern.

"Have to see which way he turns," said Zardeku. Then, after a minute: "He's bearing south. Let go the luff braces; haul the leech braces; haul the sheets; starboard the helm!"

The high ends of the yards came down as the low ends rose. After much running about and hauling on ropes the ship shook herself out on the other reach and headed towards the *Kerukchi*, which had come out of harbor against the wind on her paddles alone and was now shaking out her sails. The *Alashtir's* rowers grunted as they dug in their oars.

The two ships sailed on converging courses until Castanhoso said: "They seem to be running up flags. What are they saying?"

Zardeku put eye to telescope. "Interrogatory. In other words, have we any business with them? Qorvé, run up 'heave to.' Hain, load the catapult."

The *Kerukchi*, instead of stopping, continued on her way, running up more flags. Abreu supposed that the proud prince was telling them what he thought of them.

Zardeku said: "They have a catapult too. On the poop."

The wind hissed through the rigging. Presently a thump came from the *Kerukchi*, and a shower of specks rose from her poop and arced towards the *Alashtir*. They plunked into the water before they reached the other ship.

"Bullets," said Zardeku. "I like that not; my rowers'll suffer." He put his megaphone to his mouth and roared: "Heave to, miserable *baghana*! We wish to parley!"

"What would you?" came back the answer.

"Tell him his ship," said Abreu.

"Your ship!"

"Go to Hishkak!" came the thin voice across the water, and there was another thump. This time a shower of lead balls over a kilo in weight bounced against the *Alashtir's* woodwork. There were yells from the benches, and Abreu saw one rower sprawled on the deck with his head mashed. A couple of relief rowers dragged him out of the way, and one took his place. Other men were laying weapons alongside the benches.

The *Alashtir's* own catapult whanged, sending a javelin over the *Kerukchi's* stern. The catapult-crew of the steamship ducked and scattered, to be bullied back to their weapon by the officer commanding the squad.

Abreu said: "Captain, if you can get further forward, they won't be able to reach us with that catapult because their rigging will be in the way."

"But then they could reach us with their ram," said Zardeku. "We have no ram; I took it off when I converted the ship." After a few seconds he added: "Besides, they seem to be gaining on us."

Although Zardeku called encouragement to his rowers, who responded with mighty grunts and visibly bent their oars, the stack of the *Kerukchi* was now smoking furiously. The spray kicked up by the wheels hid most of the stern of the ship, which began to inch ahead of the *Alashtir*. Thump! The lead balls flew high, making several holes in the sails. Whang! A javelin stuck in the *Kerukchi's* planking.

"If you can hit one of those wheels," said Abreu, "as I told you . . ."

Zizz! Abreu ducked as a couple of crossbow-bolts flew over his head. Up forward one of their sailors was down, and others were shooting back.

Zardeku went forward to oversee the catapult himself, trotting along the catwalk over the rowers' heads. The *Kerukchi* continued to forge ahead.

Whang! The javelin flew between the spokes of the *Kerukchi's* nigh paddle-wheel and buried its head in the planking behind. The wheel stopped with a groan, wedged fast, the shaft of the missile sticking out at an angle. The *Alashtir* seemed to jump ahead as the *Kerukchi* slowed, since her sails could not do much against the drag of the stationary paddles.

"Surrender!" came the voice of Zardeku through the megaphone.

A voice from the *Kerukchi* told him what to do to himself.

Zardeku persisted: "We'll board ye! Come, we would not murder ye all!"

More obscenities.

"Lay aboard," said Zardeku. "Grapnells out! Boarders muster!"

"Come, Herculeu," said Abreu, hefting a cutlass. "Take one. We must lead the charge, you know."

"Uk," said little Castanhoso, looking anything but Herculean. Nevertheless he put on his helmet with shaky fingers and joined the gang in the bows. The inboard man of each pair of rowers had armed himself and gone forward, leaving his mate to manage the oar. The boarders crouched behind the protection of the wales as more arrows and quarrels whizzed overhead. Meter by meter the hulls of the ships approached each other.

"Gangplanks out!" said Zardeku.

The sailors threw out several gangplanks with spikes on the far ends to hold them fast in the foe's woodwork.

"Boarders away!" said Zardeku.

Abreu, although he considered himself a little old for such lethal athletics, felt he must set an example for his subordinate. With astonishing agility he jumped up and ran across the nearest gangplank. The thunder of feet on the planks behind him told him that the rest of the boarders were with him.

At the far end of the gangplank a man was trying to pry the spikes out of the planking. Abreu cut at him, hit something, and kept on without waiting to see what damage he'd done. Yells and tramplings; clang of steel.

Abreu found himself facing a slim elegant figure in a skimpy suit of light armor, oxidized black and inlaid with gold, who handled a straight sword like a professional duellist. Behind the nasal of the helmet Abreu recognized Prince Ferrian.

"Give up?" he said.

"Never!" The prince danced at him in one of those fancy fencing lunges.

Abreu caught the prince's point on his buckler and whacked at his opponent. No fencer he, and anyway there was no time for fancy stuff. Others pressed by on either side of him. The prince, blood on his face, thrust wickedly at each of them, his blade flickering out like lightning, but there were too many. Suddenly he was holding the stump of a broken rapier. As he dropped it and stepped back to the rail, feeling at his belt for another weapon, a pike took him in the chest, and shoved him over the side. Splash!

"All over," said Zardeku, sheathing his sword. The outnumbered Sotaspeva had already fallen to their knees before they had either inflicted or suffered much damage. Castanhoso was obviously torn between pride in the drop of blood on his blade and concern for the well-being of the surrendered sailor whose arm he'd nicked.

"Who's the head man?" demanded Abreu. "You?"

"If it please Your P-pirateship," said Qarao. "What *is* all this?"

"Where's the mummy?"

"In the cabin, sir. May I show you . . . ?"

"Lead on." Abreu followed the minister to the cabin below the poop. "Ah!"

The mortal remains of King Manzariyé were no prettier than they had been on the previous occasion.

"What do you?" cried Qarao in sudden anguish. "Sacrilege!"

"Bunk!" snorted Abreu, slitting open the mummy with his dagger along the carefully sewn seam in the king's flank. "Look here!"

"Who be ye?" cried Qarao. "Men of Dur, or disguised Earthmen, or what?"

Ignoring the question, the security officer pried open the mummy and fished out a fistful of small books. "Look, Herculeu," he said. "Chemistry, structures, heat-engineering, electronics, calculus, strength of materials, aeronautics . . . He did a good job. Now, *you*!" He glared at the cringing Qarao. "Would you like to answer questions, or join your lamented master in the sea?"

"I—I'll answer, good my lord."

"Good. Who built this ship? I mean, who converted it to a steamship?"

"Ahmad Akelawi, sir."

"And Ferrian and he fixed up a scheme to take the mummy to Earth, stuff it full of technical literature, and bring it back to Krishna, yes?"

"Yes, sir."

"What did Akelawi get out of it?"

"Oh, His Sublimity had figured out a complicated scheme for converting some of his ancestral treasure into Earthly dollars. Also he was going to make Akelawi his Minister of Science, if Akelawi ever got back to Sotaspé."

"I see," said Abreu. "He's an original, this prince of yours; I'm sorry he's drowned."

"Do we arrest this one?" said Castanhoso in Portuguese. "We could take the mummy along for evidence."

"Hm," said Abreu. "It occurs to me that we made a serious mistake in letting the mummy back into Krishna without examining it more thoroughly, didn't we?"

"Pois sim."

Abreu mused: "And if we arrest this man, and so forth, that fact will come out. The results might be bad for the service, not to mention us."

"Yessir."

"If we drag Qarao back to Novorecife on charges of conspiracy to violate I. C. Regulation 368, Section 4, subsection 26, the native Krishnan states will make a terrible howl about illegal arrest, and we'll be called murderers and imperialists and all sorts of hard names. Whereas if we let this one and his men go with a warning, and burn the ship, the matter will be ended to the satisfaction of all. Since the unfortunate prince is now fish-food, and we'll be on the watch for Akelawi, there'll be no more violation of the technological blockade from this source."

"True," said Castanhoso, "but I hate to burn this handsome ship. It seems wicked to destroy knowledge."

"I know," snapped Abreu, "but we have a policy to carry out. The peace of the universe is more important . . ." He turned to Qarao and spoke in Gozashtandou: "We've decided that this conspiracy was not your fault, since you merely carried out your master's orders. Therefore, as soon as we've cleaned up and burned the ship—"

"*Iyá!* Generous masters, pray do not burn the pride of the Sotaspeo navy . . ." and Qarao began to shed big tears.

"Sorry, my good sir, but it must be. Zardeku, collect your men . . ."

Meanwhile Ferrian bad-Arjanaq, Prince of Sotaspé, clung to the lowest paddle of the port wheel with only his head out of water. He could not be seen from the deck of the *Kerukchi* because the other paddles and the wheel structure were in the way. He had thrown off his helmet and was worming his way between duckings out of his mail-coat. After much straining exertion he got the thing off. It sank silently. Now at least he could swim.

Although he could hear voices on deck, he could not make out the words over the sounds of wind and water, especially since the larger waves ducked him from time to time. A couple of loud splashes told him that the fatal casualties of the fight were being disposed of. More tramping and voices, and sounds of things being broken up and moved about.

Then a crackling that he could not at first identify. It took him some minutes to realize that the smell of wood-smoke which normally clung to the *Kerukchi* was much stronger than could be accounted for by stoking up the engine. When he realized that his prize ship was actually burning, he cursed by all the gods of his pantheon and added a salt tear or two to the Sadabao Sea.

Well, he couldn't hold this paddle all day. Presumably the other ship would push off from the *Kerukchi's* side and stand off a safe distance to windward to make sure that her prey was fully consumed. Nor would the *Keruk-chi* simply burn down to the water and then lie sloshing, a waterlogged hulk, as would most ships. The weight of the machinery would take her to the bottom.

Prince Ferrian wormed out of his remaining clothes and struck out for shore, keeping the blazing *Kerukchi* between him and the *Alashtir*. The fresh afternoon breeze blew a long streamer of smoke down over him, making him cough and swallow water but also helping to hide him. The customs of Darya being what they were, he could go ashore as he was without fearing arrest for impropriety.

A ten-night later the merchantman *Star of Jazmurian* docked at Sotaspé, and Prince Ferrian, followed by two men carrying a large box, came ashore. Those who saw him almost fell over with astonishment.

"Your Serenity!" babbled a man. "We all thought you dead! Your cousin Prince Savarun is about to declare your eldest son Prince Regent . . ."

"We'll soon fix that, my good fellow," said Ferrian. "Get me an aya! I'm for the palace."

After the excitement had died down, Prince Ferrian made a speech.

"First," he said, "my thanks to my dutiful subjects who have kept the kingdom running so faithfully in my absence. How many rulers could go away for years and return to find their thrones still their own?

"Second, you know that we've suffered a grievous loss. Our sacred relic, our king, is no more. However, I had a replica made of wood in Darya, which will be used in place of the true king. I got the idea from a law-book I read while among the Terrans.

"Third, polygamy is hereby abolished. While I appreciate the devotion my wives have given me these many years, there are sound reasons against the institution. I might mention that petty jealousy among my wives caused my great design to fail. (No, no, Tánzi, stop your weeping. You'll be taken care of.)

"Fourth, since my plan for industrializing Sotaspé has failed, I've been forced to find a substitute. Why, thought I, should we strain every nerve to steal the secrets of Terran science? Why not develop our own? While reading that book on the history of Earthly law I learned of a system whereby the Earthmen have long promoted knowledge and invention on their own planet. 'Tis called a patent system, and as soon as the Privy Council can work out the details, Sotaspé shall have one too . . ."

Abreu, wearing the slightly smug air which success always conferred upon him, reported to Comandante Kennedy on the outcome of his foray into the Sadabao Sea. He ended:

"Far be it from me to brag, Senhor William, but thanks to the efforts of the good Herculeu and myself, the most dangerous threat in years against the technological blockade is now over, smashed, finished!"

And a few ten-nights later Prince Ferrian, who loved speech-making and public appearances, stood at the head of the great flight of marble steps in front of Coronation

Hall. Before him knelt a shabby little Sotaspeu with his arm in a sling. Ferrian, in stentorian tones, read a proclamation:

". . . our subject, Laiján the carriage-maker has combined the glider wherewith the mainland sportsmen amuse themselves by soaring through the air with the fireworks wherewith we celebrate astrological conjunctions, to create a new and useful device, to wit: a rocket-powered flying-machine with which one can fly like an aqebat whither one wishes. Although the range of the device be yet short, and its control be yet imperfect (as you see from Master Laiján's broken arm) these difficulties shall be overcome in time.

"Therefore I, Ferrian bad-Arjanaq, Prince of the Realm, do confer up you, Laiján bad-Zagh, Patent Number 37 of the Sotaspeo patent system, together with the rank of knight in recognition of the outstanding quality of the invention."

He touched the kneeling man with his sceptre. "Rise, Sir Laiján." He hung a medal around the little man's neck. "And now," he finished, "let a full holiday be declared, with feasting and fireworks. Henceforth this day shall be known as Liberation Day, for this day the walls of ignorance in which the tyrannical Terrans have long sought to imprison us are overthrown, blasted, *finished!*"

The Galton Whistle

Adrian Frome regained consciousness to the sound of harsh Dzlieri consonants. When he tried to move, he found he was tied to a tree by creepers, and that the Vishnuvan centaurs were cavorting around him, fingering weapons and gloating.

"I think," said one, "that if we skinned him carefully and rolled him in salt . . ."

Another said: "Let us rather open his belly and draw forth his guts little by little. Flaying is too uncertain; Earthmen often die before one is half done."

Frome saw that his fellow-surveyors had indeed gone, leaving nothing but two dead zebras (out of the six they had started out with) and some smashed apparatus. His head ached abominably. Quinlan must have conked him from behind while Hayataka was unconscious, and then packed up and shoved off, taking his wounded chief but leaving Frome.

The Dzlieri yelled at one another until one said: "A pox on your fancy slow deaths! Let us stand off and shoot him, thus ridding ourselves of him and bettering our aim at once. Archers first. What say you?"

The last proposal carried. They spread out as far as the dense vegetation allowed.

The Dzlieri were not literally centaurs in the sense of looking like handsome Greek statues. If you imagine the front half of a gorilla mounted on the body of a tapir you will have a rough idea of their looks. They had large mobile ears, a caricature of a human face covered with red fur, four-fingered hands, and a tufted tail. Still, the fact that they were equipped with two arms and four legs apiece made people who found the native name hard call them centaurs, though the sight of them would have scared Pheidias or Praxiteles out of his wits.

"Ready?" said the archery enthusiast. "Aim low, for his head will make a fine addition to our collection if you spoil it not."

"Wait," said another. "I have a better thought. One of their missionaries told me a Terran legend of a man compelled by his chief to shoot a fruit from the head of his son. Let us therefore . . ."

"No! For then you will surely spoil his head!" And the whole mob was yelling again.

Lord, thought Frome, how they talk! He tested his bonds, finding that someone had done a good job of tying him up. Although badly frightened, he pulled himself together and put on a firm front: "I say, what are you chaps up to?"

They paid him no heed until the William Tell party carried the day and one of them, with a trader's stolen rifle slung over his shoulder, approached with a fruit the size of a small pumpkin.

Frome asked: "Does that gun of yours shoot?"

"Yes," said the Dzlieri. "I have bullets that fit, too!"

Frome doubted this, but said: "Why not make a real sporting event of it? Each of us put a fruit on our heads and the other try to shoot it off?"

The Dzlieri gave the gargling sound that passed for laughter. "So you can shoot us, eh? How stupid think you we are?"

Frome, thinking it more tactful not to say, persisted with the earnestness of desperation: "Really, you know, it'll only make trouble if you kill me, whereas if you let me go . . ."

"Trouble we fear not," roared the fruit-bearer, balancing the fruit on Frome's head. "Think you we should let go such a fine head? Never have we seen an Earthman with yellow hair on head and face."

Frome cursed the coloration that he had always been rather proud of hitherto, and tried to compose more arguments. It was hard to think in the midst of this deafening racket.

The pseudo-pumpkin fell off with a thump. The Dzlieri howled, and he who had placed it came back and belted Frome with a full-armed slap across the face. "That will teach you to move your head!" Then he tied it fast with a creeper that went over the fruit and under Frome's chin.

Three Dzlieri had been told off to loose the first flight.

"Now look here, friends," said Frome, "you know what the Earthmen can do if they—"

T-twunk! The bowstrings snapped; the arrows came on with a sharp whistle. Frome heard a couple hit. The pumpkin jerked, and he became aware of a sharp pain in his left ear. Something sticky dripped onto his bare shoulder.

The Dzlieri shouted. "Etsnoten wins the first round!"

"Was that not clever, to nail his ear to the tree?"

"Line up for the next flight!"

"Hoy!" Hooves drummed and more Dzlieri burst into view. "What is this?" asked one in a crested brass helmet.

They explained, all jabbering at once.

"So," said the helmeted one, whom the others addressed as Mishinatven. (Frome realized that this must be the insurgent chief who had seceded from old Kamatobden's rule. There had been rumors of war . . .) "The other Earthman knocked him witless, bound him, and left him for us, eh? After slaying our fellows there in the brush?" He pointed to the bodies of the two Dzlieri that had fallen to the machine-gun in the earlier skirmish.

Mishinatven then addressed Frome in the Brazilo-Portuguese of the spaceways, but very brokenly: "Who—you? What—name?"

"I speak Dzlieri," said Frome. "I'm Frome, one of the survey-party from Bembom. Your folk attacked us without provocation this morning as we were breaking camp, and wounded our chief."

"Ah. One of those who bounds and measures our country to take it from us?"

"No such thing at all. We only wish . . ."

"No arguments. I think I will take you to God. Perhaps you can add to our store of the magical knowledge of the Earthmen. For instance, what are these?" Mishinatven indicated the rubbish left by Quinlan.

"That is a thing for talking over distances. I fear it's broken beyond repair. And that's a device for telling direction, also broken. That—" (Mishinatven had pointed to the radar-target, an aluminum structure something like a kite and something like a street-sign) "is—uh—a kind of totem-pole we were bringing to set up on Mount Ertma."

"Why? That is my territory."

"So that by looking at it from Bembom with our radar— you know what radar is?"

"Certainly; a magic eye for seeing through fog. Go on."

"So you see, old fellow, by looking at this object with

the radar from Bembom we could tell just how far and in what direction Mount Ertma was, and use this information in our maps."

Mishinatven was silent, then said: "This is too complicated for me. We must consider the deaths of my two subjects against the fact that they were head-hunting, which God has forbidden. Only God can settle this question." He turned to the others. "Gather up these things and bring them to Amnairad for salvage." He wrenched out the arrow that had pierced Frome's ear and cut the Earthman's bonds with a short hooked sword like an oversized linoleum-knife. "Clamber to my back and hold on."

Although Frome had ridden zebras over rough country (the Viagens Interplanetarias having found a special strain of Grévy's zebra, the big one with narrow stripes on the rump, best for travel on Vishnu where mechanical transport was impractical) he had never experienced anything like this wild bareback ride. At least he was still alive, and hoped to learn who "God" was. Although Mishinatven had used the term *gimoa-brtsqun,* "supreme spirit," the religion of the Dzlieri was demonology and magic of a low order, without even a centaur-shaped creator-god to head its pantheon. Or, he thought uneasily, by "taking him to God" did they simply mean putting him to death in some formal and complicated manner?

Well, even if the survey was washed up for the time being, perhaps he could learn something about the missing missionary and the trader. He had come out with Hayataka, the chief surveyor, and Pete Quinlan, a new man with little background and less manners. He and Quinlan had gotten on each other's nerves, though Frome had tried to keep things smooth. Hayataka, despite his technical skill and experience, was too mild and patient a little man to keep such an unruly subordinate as Quinlan in line.

First the Dzlieri guide had run off, and Quinlan had begun making homesick noises. Hayataka and Frome, however, had agreed to try for Mount Ertma by travelling on a magnetic bearing, though cross-country travel on this steaming soup kettle of a planet with its dense jungle and almost constant rain was far from pleasant.

They had heard of the vanished Earthfolk yesterday when Quinlan had raised Comandante Silva himself on the radio: ". . . and when you get into the Dzlieri country, look for traces of Sirat Mongkut and Elena Millán. Sirat Mongkut is an entrepreneur dealing mainly in scrap-metals with the Dzlieri, and has not been heard of for a

Vishnuvan year. Elena Millán is a Cosmotheist missionary who has not been heard of in six weeks. If they're in trouble, try to help them and get word to us . . ."

After signing off, Quinlan had said: "Ain't that a hell of a thing, now? As if the climate and bugs and natives wasn't enough, it's hunting a couple of fools we are. What was that first name? It don't sound like any Earthly name I ever heard."

Hayataka answered: "Sirat Mongkut. He's a Thai—what you would call a Siamese."

Quinlan laughed loudly. "You mean a pair of twins joined together?"

Then this morning a party of Dzlieri, following the forbidden old custom of hunting heads, had rushed the camp. They had sent a javelin through both Hayataka's calves and mortally wounded the two zebras before Frome had knocked over two and scattered the rest with the light machine-gun.

Quinlan, however, had panicked and run. Frome, trying to be fair-minded, couldn't blame the lad too much; he'd panicked on his first trail-trip himself. But when Quinlan had slunk back, Frome, furious, had promised him a damning entry in his fitness report. Then they had bound Hayataka's wounds and let the chief surveyor put himself out with a trance-pill while they got ready to retreat to Bembom.

Quinlan must have brooded over his blighted career, slugged Frome, and left him for the Dzlieri, while he hauled his unconscious supervisor back to Bembom.

After a couple of hours of cross-country gallop, the party taking Frome to Amnairad began to use roads. Presently they passed patches of clearings where the Dzlieri raised the pushball-sized lettuce-like plants they ate. Then they entered a "town," which to human eyes looked more like a series of corrals with stables attached. This was Amnairad. Beyond loomed Mount Ertma, its top hidden in the clouds. Frome was surprised to see a half-dozen zebras in one of the enclosures; that meant men.

At the center of this area they approached a group of "buildings"—inclosed structures made of poles with sheets of matting stretched between them. Up to the biggest structure the cavalcade cantered. At the entrance a pair of Dzlieri, imposing in helmets, spears, and shields, blocked the way.

"Tell God we have something for him," said Mish-inatven.

One of the guards went into the structure and presently came out again. "Go on in," he said. "Only you and your two officers, Mishinatven. And the Earthman."

As they trotted through the maze of passages, Frome heard the rain on the matting overhead. He noted that the appointments of this odd place seemed more civilized than one would expect of Dzlieri, who, though clever in some ways, seemed too impulsive and quarrelsome to benefit from civilizing influences. They arrived in a room hung with drapes, of native textiles and decorated with groups of crossed Dzlieri weapons: bows, spears and the like.

"Get off," said Mishinatven. "God, this is an Earthman named Frome we found in the woods. Frome, this is God."

Frome watched Mishinatven to see whether to prostrate himself on the pounded-clay floor or what. But as the Dzlieri took the sight of his deity quite casually, Frome turned to the short, burly man with the flat Mongoloid face, wearing a pistol and sitting in an old leather armchair of plainly human make.

Frome nodded, saying: "Delighted to meet you, God old thing. Did your name used to be—uh—Sirat Mongkut before your deification?"

The man smiled faintly, nodded, and turned his attention to the three Dzlieri, who were all trying to tell the story of finding Frome and shouting each other down.

Sirat Mongkut straightened up and drew from his pocket a small object hung round his neck by a cord: a brass tube about the size and shape of a cigarette. He placed one end of this in his mouth and blew into it, his yellow face turning pink with effort. Although Frome heard no sound, the Dzlieri instantly fell silent. Sirat put the thing back in his pocket, the cord still showing, and said in Portuguese:

"Tell us how you got into that peculiar predicament, Senhor Frome."

Unable to think of any lie that would serve better than simple truth, Frome told Sirat of his quarrel with Quinlan and its sequel.

"Dear, dear," said Sirat. "One would almost think you two were a pair of my Dzlieri. I am aware, however, that such antipathies arise among Earthmen, especially when a few of them are confined to enforced propinquity for a considerable period. What would your procedure be if I released you?"

"Try to beat my way back to Bembom, I suppose. If you could lend me a Grévy and some rations. . . ."

Sirat shook his head, still smiling like a Cheshire-cat. "I fear that is not within the bourne of practicability. But why are you in such a hurry to get back? After the disagreement of which you apprised me, your welcome will hardly be fraternal; your colleague will have reported his narrative in a manner to place you in the worst possible light."

"Well, what then?" said Frome, thinking that the entrepreneur must have swallowed a dictionary in his youth. He guessed that Sirat was determined not to let him go, but on the contrary might want to use him. While Frome had no intention of becoming a renegade, it wouldn't hurt to string him along until he learned what was up.

Sirat asked: "Are you a college-trained engineer?"

Frome nodded. "University of London; Civil Engineering."

"Can you run a machine-shop?"

"I'm not an expert machinist, but I know the elements. Are you hiring me?"

Sirat smiled. "I perceive you usually anticipate me by a couple of steps. That is, roughly, the idea I had in mind. My Dzlieri are sufficiently clever metal-workers but lack the faculty of application; moreover I find it difficult to elucidate the more complicated operations to organisms from the pre-machine era. And finally, Senhor, you arrive at an inopportune time, when I have projects under way news of which I do not desire to have broadcast. Do you comprehend?"

Frome at once guessed Sirat was violating Interplanetary Council Regulation No. 368, Section 4, Sub-section 26, Paragraph 15, which forbade imparting technical information to intelligent but backward and warlike beings like the Dzlieri without special permission. This was something Silva should know about. All he said, though, was:

"I'll see what I can do."

"Good." Sirat rose. "I will patch up your ear and then show you the shop myself. Accompany us, Mishinatven."

The Siamese led the way through the maze of mat-lined passages and out. The "palace" was connected by a breezeway with a smaller group of structures in which somebody was banging on an anvil; somebody was using a file; somebody was pumping the bellows of a simple forge.

In a big room several Dzlieri were working on metal parts with homemade tools, including a crank-operated lathe and boring-mill. In one corner rose a pile of damaged native weapons and tools. As his gaze roamed the room, Frome saw a rack holding dozens of double-barrelled guns.

Sirat handed one to Frome. "Two-centimeter smooth-bores, of the simplest design. My Dzlieri are not yet up to complicated automatic actions, to say nothing of shock-guns and paralyzers and such complex weapons. That is why the guns they expropriate from traders seldom remain long in use. They will not clean guns, nor believe that each gun requires appropriate ammunition. Therefore the guns soon get out of order and they are unable to effect repairs. But considering that we are not yet up to rifling the barrels, and that vision is limited in the jungle, one of these with eight-millimeter buckshot is quite as effective as an advanced gun.

"Now," he continued, "I contemplate making you my shop foreman. You will first undergo a training-course by working in each department in turn for a few days. As for your loyalty—I trust to your excellent judgment not to attempt to depart from these purlieus. You shall start in the scrap-sorting department today, and when you have completed your stint, Mishinatven will escort you to your quarters. As my Dzlieri have not yet evolved a monetary economy, you will be recompensed in copper ingots. Lastly, I trust I shall have the gratification of your companionship for the evening repast tonight?"

The scrap-sorting room was full of piles of junk, both of human and of native origin. Idznamen, the sorter, harangued Frome on such elementary matters as how to tell brass from iron. When Frome impatiently said: "Yes, yes, I know that," Idznamen glowered and went right on. Meanwhile Frome was working up a state of indignation. An easy-going person most of the time, he was particular about his rights, and now was in a fine fury over the detention of him, a civil servant of the mighty Viagens, by some scheming renegade.

During the lecture Frome prowled, turning over pieces of junk. He thought he recognized a motor-armature that had vanished from Bembom recently. Then there was a huge copper kettle with a hole in its bottom. Finally he found the remains of the survey-party's equipment, including the radar-target.

Hours later, tired and dirty, he was dismissed and taken by Mishinatven to a small room in this same building. Here he found a few simple facilities for washing up. He thought he should mow the incipient yellow beard in honor of dining with God, but Mishinatven did not know what a razor was. The Dzlieri hung around, keeping Frome in sight. Evidently Sirat was taking no chances with his new associate.

At the appointed time, Mishinatven led him to the palace and into Sirat's dining-room, which was fixed up with considerable elegance. Besides a couple of Dzlieri guards, two people were there already: Sirat Mongkut and a small dark girl, exquisitely formed but clad in a severely plain Earthly costume—much more clothes than human beings normally wore on this steaming planet.

Sirat said: "My dear, allow me to present Senhor Adrian Frome; Senhor, I have the ineffable pleasure of introducing Senhorita Elena Millán. Will you partake of a drink?" he added, offering a glass of *moikhada*.

"Righto," said Frome, noticing that Sirat already held one but that Miss Millán did not.

"It is contrary to her convictions," said Sirat. "I hope to cure her of such unwarranted extremism, but it consumes time. Now narrate your recent adventures to us again."

Frome obliged.

"What a story!" said Elena Millán. "So that handsome North European coloring of yours was almost your death! You Northerners ought to stick to the cold planets like Ganesha. Not that I believe Junqueiros's silly theory of the superiority of the Mediterranean race."

"He might have a point as far as Vishnu is concerned," said Frome. "I do notice that the climate seems harder on people like Van der Gracht and me than on natives of tropical countries like Mehtalal. But perhaps I'd better dye my hair black to discourage these chaps from trying to collect my head as a souvenir."

"Truly I regret the incident," said Sirat. "But perhaps it is a fortunate misfortune. Is there not an English proverb about ill winds? Now, as you observe, I possess a skilled mechanic and another human being with whom to converse. You have no conception of the *ennui* of seeing nobody but extraterrestrials."

Frome watched them closely. So this was the missing missionary! At least she had a friendly smile and a low sweet voice. Taking the bull by the horns he asked:

"How did Miss Millán get here?"

Elena Millán spoke: "I was travelling with some Dzlieri into Mishinatven's territory, when a monster attacked my party and ate one of them. I should have been eaten, too, had not Mr. Sirat come along and shot the beast. And now . . ."

She looked at Sirat, who said with his usual smile: "And now she finds it difficult to accustom herself to the concept of becoming the foundress of a dynasty."

"What?" said Frome.

"Oh, have I not enlightened you? I am imbued with considerable ambitions—exalted, I think, is the word I want. Nothing that need involve me with Bembom, I trust, but I hope before many years have elapsed to bring a sizable area under my sovereignty. I already rule Mishinatven's people for all practical purposes, and within a few weeks I propose to have annexed old Kamatobden's as well. Then for the tribe of Romeli living beyond Bembom . . ." He referred to the other intelligent species of the planet, six-limbed ape-like beings who quarreled constantly with the Dzlieri.

"You see yourself as a planetary emperor?" said Frome. This should certainly be reported back to his superiors at Bembom without delay!

Sirat made a deprecating motion. "I should not employ so extravagant a term—at least not yet. It is a planet of large land area. But—you comprehend the general idea. Under unified rule I could instill real culture into the Dzlieri and Romeli, which they will never attain on a basis of feuding tribes." He chuckled. "A psychologist once asserted that I had a power-complex because of my short stature. Perhaps he was correct; but is that any pretext for neglecting to put this characteristic to good use?"

"And where does Miss Millán come in?" asked Frome.

"My dear Frome! These primitives can comprehend the dynastic principle, but are much too backward for your recondite democratic ideals, as the failure of attempts to teach the representative government has amply demonstrated. Therefore we must have a dynasty, and I have elected Miss Millán to assist me in founding it."

Elena's manner changed abruptly and visibly. "I never shall," she said coldly. "If I ever marry, it will be because the Cosmos has infused my spiritual self with a Ray of its Divine Love."

Frome choked on his drink, wondering how such a nice girl could talk such tosh.

Sirat smiled. "She will alter her mind. She does not know what is beneficial for her, poor infant."

Elena said: "He walks in the darkness of many lives' accumulated karma, Mr. Frome, and so cannot understand spiritual truths."

Sirat grinned broadly. "Just a benighted old ignoramus. I suppose, my love, you would find our guest more amenable to your spiritual suasion?"

"Judging by the color of his aura, yes." (Frome glanced nervously about.) "If his heart were filled with Cosmic Love, I could set his feet on the Seven-Fold Path to Union with the Infinite."

Frome almost declared he wouldn't stand by and see an Earthwoman put under duress—not while he had his health—but thought better of it. Such an outburst would do more harm than good. Still, Adrian Frome had committed himself mentally to helping Elena, for while he affected a hardboiled attitude towards women, he was secretly a sentimental softhead towards anything remotely like a damsel in distress.

Sirat said: "Let us discuss less rarefied matters. How are affairs proceeding at Bembom, Mr. Frome? The information brought hither by my Dzlieri is often garbled in transit."

After that the meal went agreeably enough. Frome found Sirat Mongkut, despite his extraordinarily pedantic speech, a shrewd fellow with a good deal of charm, though obviously one who let nothing stand in his way. The girl, too, fascinated him. She seemed to be two different people—one, a nice normal girl whom he found altogether attractive; the other, a priestess of the occult who rather frightened him.

When Sirat dismissed his guests, a Dzlieri escorted each of them out of the room. Mishinatven saw to it that Frome was safely in bed (Frome had to move the bed a couple of times to avoid the drip of rain-water through the mat ceiling) before leaving him. As for Adrian Frome, he was too tired to care whether they mounted guard over him or not.

During the ensuing days Frome learned more of the workings of the shop and revived his familiarity with the skills that make a metal-worker. He also got used to being tailed by Mishinatven or some other Dzlieri. He supposed he should be plotting escape, and felt guilty because he had not been able to devise any clever scheme for doing so. Sirat kept his own person guarded, and Frome under constant surveillance.

And assuming Frome could give his guards the slip, what then? Even if the Dzlieri failed to catch him in his flight (as they probably would) or if he were not devoured by one of the carnivores of the jungle, without a compass, he would get hopelessly lost before he had gone one kilometer and presently die of the deficiency-diseases that always struck down Earthmen who tried to live on an exclusively Vishnuvan diet.

Meanwhile he liked the feeling of craftsmanship that came from exercising his hands on the tough metals, and found the other human beings agreeable to know.

One evening Sirat said: "Adrian, I should like you to take tomorrow off to witness some exercises I am planning."

"Glad to," said Frome. "You coming, Elena?"

She said: "I prefer not to watch preparations for the crime of violence."

Sirat laughed. "She still thinks she can convert the Dzlieri to pacifism. You might as well instruct a horse to perform on the violin. She tried it on Chief Kamatobden and he thought her simply deranged."

"I shall yet bring enlightenment to these strayed souls," she said firmly.

The exercises took place in a large clearing near Amnairad. Sirat sat on a saddled zebra watching squadrons of Dzlieri maneuver at breakneck speed with high precision: some with native weapons, some with the new shotguns. A troop of lancers would thunder across the field in line abreast; then a square of musketeers would run onto the field, throw themselves down behind stumps and pretend to fire, and then leap up and scatter into the surrounding jungle, to reassemble elsewhere. There was some target practice like trapshooting, but no indiscriminate firing; Sirat kept the ammunition for his new guns locked up and doled it out only for specific actions.

Frome did not think Sirat was in a position to attack Bembom—yet. But he could certainly make a sweep of the nearby Vishnuvan tribes, whose armies were mere yelling mobs by comparison with his. And then ... Silva *must* be told about this.

Sirat seemed to be controlling the movements in the field, though he neither gestured nor spoke. Frome worked his way close enough to the *renegado* to see that he had the little brass tube in his mouth and was going through the motions of blowing into it. Frome remembered: a Galton whistle, of course! It gave out an ultrasonic blast above the limits of human hearing, and sometimes people back on Earth called their dogs with them. The Dzlieri must have a range of hearing beyond 20,000 cycles per second.

At dinner that night he asked Sirat about this method of signalling.

Sirat answered: "I thought you would so conjecture. I have worked out a system of signals, something like Morse. There is no great advantage in employing the whistle against hostile Dzlieri, since they can perceive it also; but with human beings or Romeli ... For instance, assume some ill-intentioned Earthman were to assault me in my quarters when my guards were absent? A blast would bring them running without the miscreant's knowing I had called.

"That reminds me," continued the adventurer, "tomorrow I desire you to commence twenty more of these, for my subordinate officers. I have decided to train them in the use of the device as well. And I must request haste, since I apprehend major movements in the near future."

"Moving against Kamatobden, eh?" said Frome.

"You may think so if you wish. Do not look so fearful, Elena; I will take good care of myself. Your warrior shall return."

Maybe, thought Frome, that's what she's scared of.

Frome looked over the Galton whistle Sirat had left with him. He now ran the whole shop and knew where he could lay hands on a length of copper tubing (probably once the fuel-line of a helicopter) that should do for the duplication of the whistle.

With the help of one of the natives he completed the order by nightfall, plus one whistle the Dzlieri had spoiled. Sirat came over from the palace and said: "Excellent, my dear Adrian. We shall go far together. You must pardon my not inviting you to dine with me tonight, but I am compelled to confer with my officers. Will you and Miss Millán carry on in the regular dining-room in my absence?"

"Surely, Dom Sirat," said Frome. "Glad to."

Sirat wagged a forefinger. "However, let me caution you against exercising your charm too strongly on my protégée. An inexperienced girl like that might find a tall young Englishman glamorous, and the results would indubitably be *most* deplorable for all concerned."

When the time came, he took his place opposite Elena Millán at the table. She said: "Let us speak English, since some of our friends here" (she referred to the ubiquitous Dzlieri guards) "know a little Portuguese, too. Oh, Adrian, I'm so afraid!"

"Of what; Sirat? What's new?"

"He has been hinting that if I didn't fall in with his dynastic plans, he would compel me. You know what that means."

"Yes. And you want me to rescue you?"

"I—I should be most grateful if you could. While we are taught to resign ourselves to such misfortunes, as things earned in earlier incarnations, I don't think I could bear it. I should kill myself."

Frome pondered. "D'you know when he's planning this attack?"

"He leaves the day after tomorrow. Tomorrow night the Dzlieri will celebrate."

That meant a wild orgy, and Sirat might well take the occasion to copy his subjects. On the other hand, the confusion afforded a chance to escape.

"I'll try to cook up a scheme," he told her.

Next day Frome found his assistants even more restless and insubordinate than usual. About noon they walked out for good. "Got to get ready for the party!" they shouted. "To hell with work!"

Mishinatven had vanished, too. Frome sat alone, thinking. After a while he wandered around the shop, handling pieces of material. He noticed the spoilt Galton whistle lying where he had thrown it the day before; the remaining length of copper tubing from which he had made the whistles; the big copper kettle he had never gotten around either to scrapping or to fixing. Slowly an idea took shape.

He went to the forge-room and started the furnace up again. When he had a hot fire, he brazed a big thick patch over the hole in the kettle, on the inside where it would take pressure. He tested the kettle for leakage and found none. Then he sawed a length off the copper tube and made another Galton whistle, using the spoilt one as a model.

In the scrap-sorting room he found a length of plastic which he made into a sealing-ring or gasket to go between the kettle and its lid. He took off the regular handle of the kettle, twisted a length of heavy wire into a shorter bail, and installed it so that it pressed the lid tightly down against the gasket. Finally he made a little conical adapter of sheet-copper and brazed it to the spout of the kettle, and brazed the whistle to the adapter. He then had an air-tight kettle whose spout ended in the whistle.

Then it was time for dinner.

Sirat seemed in a rollicking good humor and drank more moikhada than usual.

"Tomorrow," he said, "tomorrow we cast the die. What was that ancient European general who remarked about casting the die when crossing a river? Napoleon? Anyway, let us drink to tomorrow!" He raised his goblet theatrically. "Will you not weaken, Elena? Regrettable; you do not know what you miss. Come, let us fall upon the provender, lest my cook decamp to the revellers before we finish."

From outside came Dzlieri voices in drunken song, and sounds of a fight. The high shriek of a female Dzlieri tore past the palace, followed by the laughter and hoofbeats of a male in pursuit.

These alarming sounds kept the talk from reaching its usual brilliance. When the meal was over, Sirat said:

"Adrian, you must excuse me; I have a portentous task to accomplish. Please return to your quarters. Not you, Elena; kindly remain where you are."

Frome looked at the two of them, then at the guards, and went. In passing through the breezeway he saw a mob of Dzlieri dancing around a bonfire. The palace proper seemed nearly deserted.

Instead of going to his room he went into the machine-shop. He lit a cresset to see by, took the big copper kettle out to the pump, and half filled it with several liters of water. Then he staggered back into the shop and heaved the kettle up on top of the forge. He clamped the lid on, stirred the coals, and pumped the bellows until he had a roaring fire.

He hunted around the part of the shop devoted to the repair of tools and weapons until he chose a big spear with a three-meter shaft and a broad keen-edged half-meter head. Then he went back to the forge with it.

After a long wait, a faint curl of water-vapor appeared in the air near the spout of the kettle. It grew to a long plume, showing that steam was shooting out fast. Although Frome could hear nothing, he could tell by touching a piece of metal to the spout that the whistle was vibrating at a tremendous frequency.

Remembering that ultrasonics have directional qualities, Frome slashed through the matting with the broad blade of the spear until the forge-room lay open to view in several directions. Then he went back into the palace.

By now he knew the structure well. Towards the center of the maze Sirat had his private suite: a sitting-room, bedroom, and bath. The only way into this suite was through an always-guarded door into the sitting-room.

Frome walked along the hallway that ran beside the suite and around the corner to the door into the sitting-room. He listened, ear to the matting. Although it was hard to hear anything over the racket outside, he thought he caught sounds of struggle within. And from up ahead came Dzlieri voices.

He stole to the bend in the corridor and heard: ". . . surely some demon must have sent this sound to plague us. In truth it makes my head ache to the splitting-point!"

"It is like God's whistle," said the other voice, "save that it comes not from God's chambers, and blows continually. Try stuffing a bit of this into your ears."

The first voice (evidently that of one of the two regular guards) said: "It helps a little; remain you here on guard while I seek the medicine-man."

"That I will, but send another to take your place, for God will take it amiss if he finds but one of us here. And hasten, for the scream drives me to madness!"

Dzlieri hooves departed. Frome grinned in his whiskers. He might take a chance of attacking the remaining guard, but if the fellow's ears were plugged there was a better way. Sirat would have closed off his bedroom from the sitting-room by one of those curtains of slats that did duty for doors.

Frome retraced his steps until he was sure he was opposite the bedroom. Then he thrust his spear into the matting, slashed downward, and pushed through the slit into a bedroom big enough for basketball.

Sirat Mongkut looked up from what he was doing. He had tied Elena's wrists to the posts at the head of the bed, so that she lay supine, and now, despite her struggles, was tying one of her ankles to one of the posts at the foot. Here was a conqueror who liked to find his dynasties in comfort.

"Adrian!" cried Elena.

Sirat's hand flashed to his hip—and came away empty. Frome's biggest gamble had paid off: he assumed that just this once Sirat might have discarded his pistol. Frome had planned, if he found Sirat armed, to throw the spear at him; now he could take the surer way.

He gripped the big spear in both hands, like a bayon-etted rifle, and ran towards Sirat. The stocky figure leaped onto the bed and then to the floor on the far side, fumbling for his whistle. Frome sprang onto the bed in pursuit, but tripped on Elena's bound ankle and almost sprawled headlong. By the time he recovered he had staggered nearly the width of the room. Meanwhile Sirat, having avoided Frome's rush, put his whistle to his mouth, and his broad cheeks bulged with blowing.

Frome gathered himself for another charge. Sirat blew and blew, his expression changing from confidence to alarm as nobody came. Frome knew that no Dzlieri in the neighborhood could hear the whistle over the continuous blast of the one attached to the kettle. But Sirat, unable to hear ultrasonics, did not know his signals were jammed.

As Frome started towards him again, Sirat threw a chair. It flew with deadly force; part of it gave Frome's knuckles a nasty rap while another part smote him on the forehead, sending him reeling back. Sirat darted across the room again on his short legs and tore from the wall one of those groups of native weapons he ornamented his palace with.

Down with a clatter came the mass of cutlery: a pair of crossed battle-axes, a gisarme, and a brass buckler. By the time Frome, having recovered from the impact of the chair, came up, Sirat had possessed himself of the buckler and one of the axes. He whirled and brought up the buckler just in time to ward off a lunge of the spear. Then he struck out with his ax and spun himself half around as he met only empty air. Frome, seeing the blow coming, had leaped back.

Sirat followed, striking out again and again. Frome gave ground, afraid to parry for fear of having his spear ruined, then drove Sirat back again by jabs at his head, legs, and exposed arm. They began to circle, the spear-point now and then clattering against the shield. Frome found that he could hold Sirat off by his longer reach, but could not easily get past the buckler. Round they went, *clank! clank!*

Sirat was slow for a second and Frome drove the spear-point into his right thigh, just above the knee . . . But the thrust, not centered, inflicted only a flesh-wound and a great rip in Sirat's pants. Sirat leaped forward, whirling his ax, and drove Frome back almost to the wall before the latter stopped him with his thrusts.

They circled again. Then came a moment when Sirat was between Frome and the door to the sitting-room. Quick as a flash Sirat threw his ax at Frome, dropped his shield, turned, and ran for the curtained door, calling "Help!"

Frome dodged the ax, which nevertheless hit him a jarring blow in the shoulder. As he recovered, he saw Sirat halfway to safety, hands out to wrench the curtain aside. He could not possibly catch the Siamese before the latter reached the sitting-room and summoned his delinquent guards to help him.

Frome threw his spear like a javelin. The shaft arced through the air and the point entered Sirat's broad back. In it went. And in, until half its length was out of sight.

Sirat fell forward, face down, clutching at the carpet and gasping. Blood ran from his mouth.

Frome strode over to where the would-be emperor lay and wrenched out the spear. He held it poised, ready to drive home again, until Sirat ceased to move. He was almost sorry ... But there was no time for Hamlet-like attitudes; he wiped the blade on Sirat's clothes, carried it over to the bed, and sawed through Elena's bonds with the edge. Without waiting for explanations he said:

"If we're quick, we may get away before they find out. That is, if the guards haven't heard the noise in here."

"They will think it was he and I," she replied. "Before he dragged me in here he told them not to come in, no matter what they heard, unless he whistled for them."

"Serves him right. I'm going down-street to get some of his zebras. Where's that bloody gun of his?"

"In that chest," she said, pointing. "He locked it in there, I suppose because he was afraid I'd snatch it and shoot him—as though I could kill any sentient being."

"How do we get into—" Frome began, and stopped as he saw that the chest had a combination lock. "I fear we don't. How about his ammunition-chest in the store-room?"

"That has a combination lock, too."

"*Tamates!*" growled Frome. "It looks as though we'd have to start out without a gun. While I'm gone, try to collect a sack of tucker from the kitchen, and whatever else looks useful." And out he went through the slit.

Outside the palace, he took care to saunter as if on legitimate business. The Dzlieri, having cast off what few inhibitions they normally possessed, were too far gone in their own amusements to pay him much heed, though one or two roared greetings at him.

Catching the zebras, though, was something else. The animals dodged around the corral, evading with ease his efforts to seize their bridles. Finally he called to a Dzlieri he knew:

"Mzumelitsen, lend a hand, will you? God wants a ride."

"Wait till I finish what I am doing," said the Dzlieri.

Frome waited until Mzumelitsen finished what he was doing and came over to help collect three zebras. Once caught, the animals followed Frome back to the palace tamely enough. He hitched them to the rail in the rear and went into the machine-shop, where he rummaged until he found a machete and a hatchet. He also gathered up the radar-target, which looked still serviceable if slightly battered.

When he got back he found that Elena had acquired a bag of food, a supply of matches, and a few other items. These they loaded on one of the zebras, and the other two they saddled.

When they rode out of Amnairad, the Dzlieri celebration was still in its full raucous swing.

Next day they were beginning to raise the lower slopes of the foothills of Mount Ertma when Frome held up a hand and said: "Listen!"

Through the muffling mass of the Vishnuvan jungle they heard loud Dzlieri voices. Then the sound of bodies moving along the trail came to their ears.

Frome exchanged one look with Elena and they broke into a gallop.

The pursuers must have been coming fast also, for the sounds behind became louder and louder. Frome caught a glimpse of the gleam of metal behind them. Whoops told them the Dzlieri had seen them, too.

Frome said: "You go on; I'll lead them off the trail and lose them."

"I won't! I won't desert you—"

"Do as I say!"

"But—"

"Go on!" he yelled so fiercely that she went. Then he sat waiting until they came into sight, fighting down his own fears, for he had no illusions about being able to "lose" the Dzlieri in their native jungle.

They poured up the trail towards him with triumphant screams. If he only had a gun ... At least they did not seem to have any, either. They had only a few guns that would shoot (not counting the shotguns, whose shells were still locked up) and would have divided into many small parties to scour the trails leading out from their center.

Frome turned the zebra's head off into the jungle. Thank the gods the growth was thinner here than lower down, where the jungle was practically impassable off the trails.

He kicked his mount into an irregular run and vainly tried to protect his face from the lashing branches. Thorns ripped his skin and a trunk gave his right leg a brutal blow. As the Dzlieri bounded off the trail after him, he guided his beast in a wide semicircle around them to intersect the trail again behind his pursuers.

When he reached the trail, and could keep his eyes open again, he saw that the whole mob was crowding after him and gaining, led by Mishinatven. As the trail bent, Sirat's lieutenant cut across the corner and hurled himself back on the path beside the Earthman. Frome felt for his machete, which had been slapping against his left leg. The Dzlieri thundered at him from the right, holding a javelin up for a stab.

"Trickster! Deicide!" screamed Mishinatven, and thrust. Frome slashed through the shaft. As they galloped side by side, the point grazed Frome's arm and fell to the ground.

Mishinatven swung the rest of the shaft and whacked Frome's shoulders. Frome slashed back; heard the clang of brass as the Dzlieri brought up his buckler. Mishinatven dropped the javelin and snatched out his short sword. Frome parried the first cut and, as Mishinatven recovered, struck at the Dzlieri's sword-hand and felt the blade bite bone. The sword spun away.

Frome caught the edge of the buckler with his left hand, pulled it down, and hacked again and again until the brass was torn from his grip by the fall of his foe.

The others were still coming. Looking back, Frome saw that they halted when they came to their fallen leader.

Frome pulled on his reins. The best defense is a bloody strong attack. If he charged them now ... He wheeled the zebra and went for them at a run, screeching and whirling his bloody blade.

Before he could reach them, they scattered into the woods with cries of despair. He kept right on through the midst of them and up the long slope until they were far behind and the exhaustion of his mount forced him to slow down.

When he finally caught up with Elena Millán, she looked at him with horror. He wondered why until he realized that with blood all over he must be quite a sight.

They made the last few kilometers on foot, leading their zebras zigzag among the immense boulders that crested the peak and beating the beasts to make them buck-jump up the steep slopes. When they arrived at the top, they tied the beasts to bushes and threw themselves down to rest.

Elena said: "Thank the Cosmos that's over! I could not have gone on much further."

"We're not done yet," said Frome. "When we get our breath we'll have to set up the target."

"Are we safe here?"

"By no means. Those Dzlieri will go back to Amnairad and fetch the whole tribe, then they'll throw a cordon around the mountain to make sure we shan't escape. We can only hope the target brings a rescue in time."

Presently he forced himself to get up and go to work again. In half an hour, with Elena's help, the radar target was up on its pole, safely guyed against the gusts.

Then Adrian Frome flopped down again. Elena said: "You poor creature! You're all over bruises."

"Don't I know it! But it might have been a sight worse."

"Let me at least wash those scratches, lest you get infected."

"That's all right; Vishnuvan germs don't bother Earth-folk. Oh, well, if you insist . . ." His voice trailed off sleepily.

He woke up some hours later to find that Elena had gotten a fire going despite the drizzle and had a meal laid out.

"Blind me, what have we here?" he exclaimed. "I say, you're the sort of trail-mate to have!"

"That is nothing. It's you who are wonderful. And to think I've always been prejudiced against blond men, because in Spanish novels the villain is always pictured as a blond!"

Frome's heart, never so hard as he made it out to be, was full to overflowing. "Perhaps this isn't the time to say this but—uh—I'm not a very spiritual sort of bloke, but I rather love you, you know."

"I love you too. The Cosmos has sent a love-ray . . ."

"Oi!" It was a jarring reminder of that other Elena. "That's enough of that, my girl. Come here."

She came.

When Peter Quinlan got back to Bembom with the convalescing Hayataka, Comandante Silva listened eagerly to Quinlan's story until he came to his flight from Mishinatven's territory.

". . . after we started," said Quinlan, "while Hayataka was still out, they attacked again. I got three, but not before they had killed Frome with javelins. After we beat them off I buried—"

"Wait! You say Frome was killed?"

"Pois sim."

"And you came right back here, without going to Ertma?"

"Naturally. What else could I do?"

"Then who set up the radar target on the mountain?"

"What?"

"Why yes. We sent up our radars on the ends of the base-line yesterday, and the target showed clearly on the scopes."

"I don't understand," said Quinlan.

"Neither do I, but we'll soon find out. *Amigo,*" he said to the sergeant Martins, "tell the aviation group to get the helicopter ready to fly to Mount Ertma, at once."

When the pilot homed on the radar target, he came out of the clouds to see a kite-like polygonal structure gleaming with a dull gray aluminum finish on top of a pole on the highest peak of Mount Ertma. Beside the pole were two human beings sitting on a rock and three tethered zebras munching the herbage.

The human beings leaped to their feet and waved wildly. The pilot brought his aircraft around, tensely guiding it through gusts that threatened to dash it against the rocks, and let the rope-ladder uncoil through the trapdoor. The man leaped this way and that, like a fish jumping for a fly, as the ladder whipped about him. Finally he caught it.

Just then a group of Dzlieri came out of the trees. They pointed and jabbered and ran towards the people whipping out javelins.

The smaller of the two figures was several rungs up the ladder when the larger one, who had just begun his ascent, screamed up over the whirr of the rotor-blades and the roar of the wind:

"Straight up! Quick!"

More Dzlieri appeared—scores of them—and somewhere a rifle barked. The pilot (just as glad it was not he dangling from an aircraft bucking through a turbulent overcast) canted his blades and rose until the clouds closed in below.

The human beings presently popped into the cabin, gasping from their climb. They were a small dark young woman and a tall man with a centimeter of butter-colored beard matted with dried blood. Both were nearly naked save for tattered canvas boots and a rag or two elsewhere, and were splashed with half-dried mud. The pilot recognized Adrian Frome, the surveyor.

"Home, Jayme," said Frome.

Frome, cleaned, shaved and looking his normal self once more except for a notch in his left ear, sat down across the desk from Silva, who said: "I cannot understand why you ask for a transfer to Ganesha now of all times. You're the hero of Bembom. I can get you a permanent P-5 appointment; perhaps even a P-6. Quinlan will be taken to Krishna for trial; Hayataka is retiring on his pension; and I shall be hard up for surveyors. So why must you leave?"

Frome smiled a wry, embarrassed smile. "You'll manage, *chefe*. You still have Van der Gracht and Mehtalal, both good men. But I'm quite determined, and I'll tell you why. When Elena and I got to the top of that mountain we were in a pretty emotional state, and what with one thing and another, and not having seen another human female for weeks, I asked her to marry me and she accepted."

Silva's eyebrows rose. "Indeed! My heartiest congratulations! But what has that to do with—"

"Wait till you hear the rest! At first everything was right as rain. She claimed it was the first time she'd been kissed, and speaking as a man of some experience I suppose it was. However, she soon began telling me *her* ideas. In the first place this was to be a purely spiritual marriage, the purpose of which was to put my feet on the sevenfold path of enlightenment so I could be something better than a mere civil engineer in my next incarnation— a Cosmotheist missionary, for example. Now I ask you!

"Well, at first I thought that was just a crochet I'd get her over in time; after all we don't let our women walk over us the way the Americans do. But then she started preaching Cosmotheism to me. And during the two and a half days we were up there, I'll swear she didn't stop talking five minutes except when she was asleep. The damndest rot you ever heard—rays and cosmic love and vibrations and astral planes and so on. I was never so bored in my life."

"I know," said Silva. He too had suffered.

"So," concluded Frome, "about that time I began wishing I could give her back to Sirat Mongkut. I was even sorry I'd killed the blighter. Although he'd have caused no end of trouble if he'd lived, he was a likeable sort of scoundrel at that. So here I am with one unwanted fiancée, and I just *can't* explain the facts of life to her. She once said as a joke that I'd be better off on Ganesha, and damned if I don't think she was right. Now if you'll just indorse that application ... Ah, *muito obrigado,* Senhor Augusto! If I hurry I can just catch the ship to Krishna. Cheerio!"

A.D. 2120

The Animal-Cracker Plot

The chief pilot of the ship that had just landed at Bembom on Vishnu handed Luther Beck his cargo manifest, fuel check, flight permit, passenger list, radio transcript, and log. He said: "Only one passenger this time, Luther."

"Who?" said Beck, fumbling through the papers with pudgy fingers.

"Darius Koshay."

"What!"

"Yeah. You know the guy, don't—hey, where you going?"

Beck, not stopping to reply, ran down the corridor and burst into the *Comandante's* office without knocking. *"Chefe!"* he yelled, "Koshay's back!"

"Realmenté?" said Silva, raising frosty eyebrows. *"Tamates,* that'll complicate life, though I wouldn't shout so that Senhor Darius can hear us from here. What's he brought this time?"

"I haven't examined—"

"Then you'd better do so. We shall then know better what he's up to."

Beck shrugged. "Of course. I just thought you'd want to know *imediatamente."*

"Obrigado; I do. Be sure you give him the works. With a microscope."

The plump little customs agent of the Viagens Interplanetarias found Darius Koshay awaiting him in the customs shed, slim, dark, and looking like Hollywood's gift to the frustrated female. The entrepreneur had already stripped down to the costume of Earthmen on Vishnu and was sweating like a team of percherons.

"Alô, Senhor Luther," said Koshay. "As you see, I

couldn't have anything up my sleeve. And if you'll turn on your tube I'll prove I haven't swallowed anything either."

Beck, rushing Koshay through the X-ray examination, said: "What's all that junk?"

"*Por favor,* my good man, don't call my factory junk!"

"A factory to make what? Looks like a bunch of old stoves and things to me."

"Crackers."

"Crackers?"

"Crackers."

"Are you nuts?"

"Not at all. I learned last time that both the Romeli and the Dzlieri are crazy mad about sweet crackers. Since it wouldn't pay to import them over a distance of several light-years, I propose to make my own."

"Where?" said Beck, rummaging through the cooking equipment.

"On that little plot I leased from old Kamatobden. My lease should still be good, even though I left last time— ah—a little more suddenly than I expected."

"Where will you get the stuff to make them?"

"Easy. I'll use Vishnuvan wheat for flour, buy my salt, sugar, and spices from the natives, and import my shortening, syrup, and powdered milk from Novorecife."

There must be a catch, thought Beck. Either that or Darius Koshay must have reformed—a less likely supposition. These ovens and pots looked harmless enough; no secret compartments for contraband weapons or drugs.

After some mental calculations he asked: "Did you bring all this stuff from Earth? The freight must have been something astronomical."

"No, most of it's surplus I picked up at Novorecife and repaired myself."

"Still, you'll have to sell your crackers for their weight in natural diamonds to get your money back."

Koshay lit up. "Naturally I expect to be paid well, or I wouldn't let myself in for a year of tea and salt-tablets. My kidneys must be so tanned now you could use 'em for shoe-leather. When you finish snooping, here are the permits and visas and things."

Luther Beck did not want to finish snooping, being still unconvinced that all was kosher. However, the equipment was nothing but a lot of metal sheets fastened together in simple forms. He even held a couple of the pots in front of the fluroscope, finding nothing suspicious.

He gave up finally and went through Koshay's personal

luggage. The trader, who seemed to be getting a quiet boot out of all this, said: "Really, Inspector, you'll find everything in order. I'm shoving off as soon as I visit Gwen."

"How are you going to get this stuff through the jungle?"

"I'll hire a couple of the tame Dzlieri as pack-horses. Are there any in Bembom now?"

"They'll be drifting in now that the rutting-season's over."

"Still angling for that scholarship, my learned friend?"

"Uh-huh."

"You know," said Koshay, blowing a ring, "I could have one of those long-haired jobs without any stupid courses. I know more about extra-terrestrial life than most professional xenologists. But I could never stand the red tape you civil-service guys have to put up with."

Beck grunted. "I know. You're the strong, adventurous type, impatient of the restraints of civilization." He finished his examination and checked Koshay's papers. Try as he might he could find no discrepancies and was forced to sign the man out.

With his usual luck, Koshay hired a pair of Dzlieri the same day; they wandered in out of the wilds with pleas for packing jobs. When the man even persuaded them to fetch a mare of their kind to carry him personally, Beck thought, the rascal's a wizard with them; the most exasperating thing about his bragging is that it's mostly true. Beck saw him disappear into the steaming drizzle perched impudently on the back of the female, while the two stallions, waving their hands and gabbling, swayed behind under their loads.

After the ship took off for Novorecife on Krishna, life at Bembom settled into its usual round. Beck was busy for some days checking the cargo that had come in. An entrepreneur came out of the jungle, deposited his goods, drew supplies, and vanished into the woods again. A member of the *Viagens* ground-crew took sick and died of some mysterious disease, and all held their breaths waiting to see if an epidemic would develop. Sparks quarreled with Slops over the doxy and both had to be psyched by Sawbones to straighten them out . . .

Then one day a battered Romeli crawled into the station and croaked a request for first aid. Stamps saw him first and called Sawbones, who patched the native's slaty skin and assured him that his middle eye was not seriously hurt. Meanwhile Stamps told the *Comandante*, who fetched the sergeant and Beck for the interview. Sergeant Martins was wanted as the person most concerned in case of shooting-trouble with the Vishnuvans, while Beck was interested as ranking peace officer.

The interview was halting, since the Romeli knew only a few words of Portuguese, and of the three men only the sergeant was fluent in Romeli. The aborigine lay on his back twiddling his twenty-four fingers and toes while the *sargento* translated.

The commandant asked: "What was the fight about?"

The Romeli replied via interpreter: "I would not agree with the new war-plan, so they drove me out."

"What war-plan?"

"The plan of Mogzaurma against the Dzlieri." (Beck knew Mogzaurma as the high-priest of the neighboring tribe of the Romeli species, and a slippery customer.)

"What plan is that?" continued Silva.

"The plan of Mogzaurma—"

"*Não*, I mean what are the details?"

"Magic."

"What magic?"

"The great Senhor Augusto knows what magic is."

Silva earned his salary by keeping calm and courteous no matter how irritating his Vishnuvan visitors proved themselves. He said quietly: "There are times when I miss the good old Earth, and this is one. Ask him about this spell or whatever it is."

"The spell," said the Romeli, "calls for the destruction of the Dzlieri."

"Yes, but *how?*"

The Romeli scratched his bandage with his right middle limb. "I know little of magic. That is for the priests."

"What do you know of this particular spell?"

"I—I think it has something to do with destroying effigies of the Dzlieri."

"What sort of effigies?"

"That's all I know."

Silva said: "If the Romeli and Dzlieri want to make a lot of silly spells against each other, it's none of our business. They've always fought, and I suppose they always will. That's what comes of having two species of intelligent life on the same planet. I don't think another planet has that condition. Tell him—"

"Wait, *chefe*," said Beck. "I still have a feeling Koshay's mixed up in this. Let me question him a while. Maybe I can find something. Mteli, how are these effigies to be destroyed?"

"I told you I don't know," grumbled Mteli.

"Were they to be—eaten?"

"You seem to know all about it, so why ask me?"

"Were they?"

"It's none of your business how we deal with our enemies."

"Oh yes it is, since you asked us for help. How'd you like us to rip those bandages off and drive you out of Bembom? Huh?"

"You wouldn't do that. You're supposed to be kind to us. I know about the Viagens policy too."

"That's all right; we didn't have to admit you in the first place and we'd be just back where we started. Now, will you answer my questions like a good fellow? Were they to be eaten?"

"Unh, yes."

"That's better. Were they to be little biscuits?"

"Yes."

"And what led you to disagree with this plan?"

"I thought these little biscuits would be too dangerous to spread around among the tribe. We might start using them on each other. Daatskhuna has always been afraid of an outbreak of witchcraft among us."

"Were you to buy them from Darius Koshay?"

"I shouldn't tell you that—"

"We'll find out anyway. You know our mysterious ways."

"I suppose so. All right, we were."

"There you are," said Beck. "I told you he was up to something. Koshay makes sweet crackers all right—animal crackers in the form of Dzlieri, so the Romeli can eat them to kill their enemies by sympathetic magic. How were you going to pay him, Mteli?"

The Romeli answered: "He says his people back on Earth have a magical rite they call dancing, which they do to music. He says they are mad about dancing to our tribal songs, so they will pay him mountains of money for them. According to the contract, therefore, he gives us the crackers and we let him copy down the songs, with little marks to show the notes."

"Now," said Silva, "I've seen everything. I've heard of ingenious ways of getting around the freight charges to Earth, but this one takes the *bolo*. It's true the people home in Rio were absolutely crazy about some of these Romeli tunes which a xenologist had brought back, the last time I was there. However, I still don't know whether we ought to try to interfere."

The sergeant said: "*Comandante,* we can't allow a major outbreak among these damned Vishnuvans just when we've gotten the trade-routes stabilized. Also, they'll murder our entrepreneurs in the general excitement."

"Would there be an outbreak?" said Silva. "Or would they just stay home and eat their crackers?"

"I'll ask," said the sergeant. "Mteli, were your people going to atttack the Dzlieri physically after they had whittled 'em down with their magic?"

"Naturally. How could we seize their property otherwise?"

"Still," said Silva cautiously, "I don't see what law Koshay has broken."

"He's sold arms to the Vishnuvans," said Beck.

"How can you call animal-crackers arms? Come, Senhor Inspector, you're not superstitious; you don't believe Koshay's little crackers work that way, whatever these poor deluded ones think about them!"

"They do so work!" cried the Romeli, who seemed to have caught the gist of the statement. "And we're not poor deluded anything. I've seen it done. Mogzaurma brought in a captive Dzlieri and worked the rite on him, and he died at once."

"Maybe he was already sick or wounded," said Silva.

"No! No!"

"Maybe he was scared to death," said the sergeant. "You know how natives are."

"Don't you call me a native!" said Mteli, struggling up.

"Well, aren't you?" said the sergeant.

"Please, *calma,*" said Silva. "Sergeant Martins meant no insult, my dear friend. I *have* heard of primitives on Earth who died when they heard the local witch-doctor had put a hex on them. But that's not the law; I can't help it if beings get frightened over nothing."

Beck shook his head. "If I scare you to death on purpose I've killed you just as if I'd conked you with a blunt instrument. And as the sergeant says, we can't let them knock off our entrepreneurs, who are human beings even if they are free-lancers. I'd stretch a point."

"How?"

"Go to Koshay's plot and pinch him."

"You're mad, my young friend," said Silva.

"Listen to the eager beaver," said the sergeant. "Sonny, don't you know how easy it is to disappear in that muck?"

"I know all about it," said Beck. "I've travelled all over that country and never had any trouble. If I can yank Koshay out quickly, the source of all this disturbance will be gone."

Silva explained: "Senhor Luther wants a scholarship to study to be a xenologist, and figures that a few coups like this will get it for him."

"Why not?" said Beck. "If I show I can deal with extraterrestrials—"

"There's one sure way to do *that*," said the sergeant, slapping his holster. "What we need is a reconnaisance in force to put the fear of God into them. No schoolboys—"

"Who you calling a schoolboy?" yelped Beck. "You'd just start a general war of Vishnuvans against Bembom, and first thing you know—"

"*Faça o favor* to be quiet, my dear friends!" cried Silva. "Are we civilized men? We get ourselves excited for nothing. Now, my idea is to try to bring in Kamatobden and Daatskhuna for a quiet discussion—"

"You tried that!" said Beck. "They wanted to kill each other the minute they set eyes—"

The argument raged for another half-hour, at the end of which Luther Beck won by sheer lung-power and loquacity. It was decided that he should try his plan first; if it didn't work, then it would be time enough to attempt another. Anyway, if Beck's plan failed, he would probably not be around to argue against any that the others might want to try.

The pilot said: "These damn maps are practically useless, on account of the stuff grows so fast . . . Here, I think we got it."

He pointed to a spot on the radar scope that corresponded to Koshay's house on the top-map. The craft sank slowly until the cleared ground around the house appeared out of the fog a few meters below. When they were less than a man's height from the ground, Beck climbed out and lowered himself down the rope ladder to the ground.

He told the pilot: "Watch and see what happens." Then he walked boldly up to Koshay's door and pushed the buzzer. The fog swirled about him as the rotor of the helicopter sucked it down from above and blew it out in all directions from where the craft hovered.

When there was no answer after several minutes, Beck

took out a key and opened the door. Gun in hand he slipped in. The last time there had been Koshay trouble he had made a duplicate of Koshay's door-key without telling the owner: not strictly legal, perhaps, but one of those dodges officers of the peace have to resort to sometimes.

A search of the premises discovered no Senhor Darius. The general neatness implied that Koshay had gone away at his own convenience. Beck inspected the kitchen where the animal-crackers were made, finding a pair of little molds for stamping them out, one cut in the form of a Dzlieri and one in that of a Romeli.

"Both ends against the middle," thought Beck. There were a couple of canisters half full of the things: one of Romeli and the other of Dzlieri crackers. He ate a few, found them good, and then was oppressed by the ever-present need of water in this Turkish-bath atmosphere. He washed down a couple of salt-tablets, wondering if being a Turk had anything to do with Koshay's liking for Vishnu.

Beck went outside again and looked around. The mud was full of footprints, some new, some leading to the house and others away. Most were plainly the three-toed prints of the Dzlieri. After a diligent search, Beck found also a trail of human footprints leading away from the house. After a few steps, however, they stopped. There were indications the person who had made them had turned at right angles and then hopped on one foot. Evidently Koshay had mounted one of his centaurine visitors and ridden off on it.

Beck called up to the pilot: "Throw me down my stuff, will you? I'm going to trail this guy, and I'll probably have to stay down overnight."

"You crazy?" replied the pilot, but nevertheless he tossed down the pack, the canteen, and the stick. Beck caught them, slung the first two over his shoulders and gripped the third. He called: "Come back for me here each day at this time, will you? *Até logo!*" and set out along the trail. The pilot, unable to follow him into the jungle, flew away.

Beck's high canvas boots, supposed to keep out borers, sank into the black slime with each step and came out with squilching sounds. Where the path was flooded he poked with the steel-shod end of his staff to make sure the footing was sound. Perspiration ran off him in rivers; Luther Beck sometimes wondered himself how he kept both stout and active in a climate that wrung most men to lean washed-out rags.

A sudden shower made him no wetter than he was

already. A reptilian swamp-dweller gaped a pair of great jaws at him from beside the trail, but a whack on the nose sent it slithering off. Beck was glad he had not had to shoot, for he feared alerting his quarry.

He considered himself lucky when signs indicated that he was approaching a main corral well before dark. Here the vegetation had been thinned out and the ground was higher and drier.

The plop-plop of hooflike feet sent Beck bolting into the brush. There he crouched, hoping that he did not share his hiding-place with anything poisonous, while half a dozen Dzlieri trotted past. Four were stallions with crested brass helmets on their heads, shields on their arms, and great quivers of javelins strapped to the upright part of their bodies. A war-party making up, he thought.

Beck resumed his approach, very cautiously this time. By flitting from bush to bush he got within sight of the corral, and by scouting around he found a place with a good view. Glasses were almost useless in this pea-soup atmosphere, with the fog billowing a few metres overhead.

The clearing swarmed with Dzlieri all talking at the tops of their naturally loud voices. Beck could make out no individual words above the general uproar. Sure enough, there was Koshay sitting on old Kamatobden's back.

A couple of the creatures had rifles slung over their backs as well as their more usual weapons. Stolen from entrepreneurs in times past, thought Beck; probably without ammunition and rusted to uselessness. Still, the Dzlieri were pretty smart at metalwork and would some day perhaps start making their own, the way some primitives on Earth had done. In fact there were rumors ... What would then happen to Bembom? Silva was a skilled diplomat and an awfully nice man personally, but Beck doubted that he had the spine for a shooting war. Silva was always one to gloss over and postpone in an effort to put the best face on things. Then command would devolve in fact upon the bluff and sometimes brutal sergeant, who lacked the imagination needed. As for himself, Luther Beck, it was no doubt true that he was too impulsive ...

Some of the Dzlieri were throwing big leaves and other vegetable matter into a wooden bowl six metres in diameter. One of them poured liquid from a leather bottle over the mixture; another threw in handfulls of powders; a couple more vigorously stirred the mess with spears.

Meanwhile others were mixing the Dzlieri cocktail in another bowl, a mere metre in diameter.

Somebody blew a whistle and the noise died. An old Dzlieri whom Beck recognized as Dastankhmden, the medicine-man, appeared with what looked like (and probably was) an Earthly beer-bottle. He shrilled something of which Beck caught only; "May the gods ..." and emptied the bottle into the smaller bowl. A faint but pungent smell stole out to where Beck crouched behind his bush. This must be the secret bitters of the Dzlieri, for which such fabulous prices could be obtained on Earth after the stuff had been cut to one-thousandth of its original strength so that human throats could tolerate it. Could it be—it must be—that Koshay would take his pay from these indigenes in bitters?

The Dzlieri lined up with mugs and one by one scooped their drinks out of the bowl. They held some sort of drinking ceremony in which they paired off and drank with locked arms, Koshay pairing with Kamatobden. (Something with a lot of legs was crawling on Beck's arm.)

Then the chief banged for silence on the edge of the large bowl and began a harangue: "You all know our dear friend Darius, thanks to whose generosity we are at last to wipe our immemorial enemies, the vile Romeli, off the face of the planet. In time I see a great alliance among all the tribes of Dzlieri to exterminate all the tribes of Romeli, even those that live across the great seas.

"Fetch forth the charms! Here they are, created by the invincible magic of the Earthmen on their far world, and smuggled from there over millions of miles, through the terrible emptiness of space, by our faithful friend at terrible risk and staggering cost." (What a lot of fertilizer, thought Beck.) "Now the Reverend Dastankhmden will explain their use."

The priest spoke: "First I will repeat the charm so you can become familiar with it. Then each of you will take one cracker, hold it up, and repeat each line of the charm after me. While you do that, try to keep a picture of a Romeli clearly in your minds. As you finish each line, you will bite off, chew, and swallow a small piece from your cracker. Just a small piece, mind you, since one cracker has to last through the entire charm. Are you ready? Here it is:

" 'As this cracker is consumed so may your life-force—' Hey, Dzalgoniten! I said this was just a rehearsal! You're not supposed to be eating your cracker yet! Get another one and listen quietly.

"'As this cracker is consumed, so may your life-force be eaten away.

"'As this cracker is chewed, so may your hopes be ground to bits.

"'As this cracker goes down—'"

"Wow!" A piercing yell just behind Beck made him jump to his feet and whirl. He reached for his pistol just as a Dzlieri, who had stolen up behind him, let fly a lasso he had been whirling. Before Beck could draw, the rope settled over his head. It tautened with a jerk, pinning his arms, and pulled him off his feet.

"Yeow!" screamed his captor, hauling him bumpety-bump over roots and through bushes out into the clearing. "Look what we have!"

Strong arms jerked Beck, who was still a little dazed, to his feet. They relieved him of his gear. "Anybody know this Earthman?" bellowed Kamatobden. "He looks familiar, but they all look alike."

Koshay said: "He's the customs inspector at Bembom."

"Now I know him," said the chief. "What's he doing here?"

"How should I know?"

"Which shall we do to him?"

Koshay shrugged. "That's up to you."

"All right." Kamatobden raised his powerful voice: "There are only two things to do: either kill him quickly now, or wait until after the salad and give him a proper execution, with refinements. All in favor of the first . . ."

The later and more lingering death carried by a large majority. Beck was hustled over to the far side of the corral and thrust into a well-made cage of wooden bars the thickness of his arm and not much farther apart than they were thick. The door shut with a clank and a Dzlieri locked it with an iron key a foot long.

At least the smell of the herd was less overpowering here than in the middle of the corral. The Dzlieri who had locked the door was evidently the official guard, for he hung Beck's belt over one shoulder and tapped the holster affectionately. "I know how to shoot one of these things," he said with a leer. "So no tricks."

Beck doubted that he did know how to shoot a pistol, since under the strict Viagens control a Vishnuvan was lucky if he got a chance to fire a real gun once in a lifetime. However, this was something to remember; no use taking unnecessary chances.

The other Dzlieri went back to their party, and the medicine-man resumed his instructions. After he finished, the Dzlieri in charge of the mixing-bowl was kept busy by the continuous line of customers waiting their turn for a refill. The party got noisier, some of the creatures singing hoarsely and others demonstrating that the breeding-season was not after all quite over.

Koshay came up to the bars with a mug in his hand and looking a little upset. He said: "You damn fool, why didn't you mind your own business? Now that you've come snooping around here I can't help you."

"You didn't try very hard just now," said Beck, wondering how the entrepreneur could drink the Dzlieri cocktail straight.

"Why should I? I know them. They'd kill you no matter what I said, and if I interfered it would only make trouble for me."

"You might try to steal that key and slip it to me."

"While the sentry's standing a couple of metres away watching us? And then have you get out and try to spoil my deal? How silly do I look, anyway?"

"But—"

"Serves you right for not keeping your nose where it belongs, though I personally wouldn't have punished you so drastically. *Adeus!*"

Koshay strolled off, leaving Beck to mutter curses after him. A couple of the Dzlieri had gotten into a fist-fight, and pounded each other mightily until others separated them.

Beck, trying to fight off despair, got the sentry's attention and said in halting Dzlieri: "You—you make big mistake. That Koshay, he sell magic crackers to your enemies too, so you—uh—all get killed while he get rich . . ."

"Stow it," growled the guard. Another Dzlieri brought him a drink, and when he had drunk that one he yelled until somebody brought him another.

A Dzlieri stumbled up to the cage with an armful of canes and shoved them through, saying: "Here—hic—Earthman, we can't decide on a death horrible enough, so this'll keep you alive for a few hours."

As he lurched off, Beck remembered that these organisms had fast digestive systems. No doubt they thought that his was equally active and required nourishment soon if he were not to die of starvation. A Dzlieri spent about two-thirds of his waking time just eating. Beck chewed on the end of one of the canes and found it sweet. Well, he might as well die on a full stomach.

The pearly fog overhead was darkening when the party ended in general stupor. The corral was full of Dzlieri lying about in odd attitudes as if they had been machine-gunned, feet in the air, tongues lolling, and fragments of the salad scattered about. The place snored like a sawmill. Koshay had passed out early and even Beck's sentry was laid out like the rest.

Beck wondered if he couldn't take advantage of the situation. The key to his cage was hanging in plain sight from his jailer's harness, and Beck's belt with its holster and pouches lay around his neck. However, the sentry had prudently passed out beyond Beck's reach.

Beck looked around the cage. The only loose objects that might possibly be used for reaching were the canes he had been chewing. He handled a few of them and chose one that seemed stiffer than the rest.

It would not reach.

That was a hell of a thing, thought Beck. Surely there must be some way. Wouldn't he look stupid if he thought of the answer to this little puzzle after the Dzlieri had come to and were flaying him alive? Then he remembered that when he was boning up on biology for his scholarship (which now, alas, seemed more remote than ever) he had read a book on the Earthly great apes. It seemed that a genius of a chimpanzee named Sultan had once reached a fruit outside his cage by taking two sticks and fitting one into a socket in the other to make one long stick.

Well, Beck thought, at least I should be as smart as a chimpanzee. The canes were not ideal for the purpose, being soft, but at length he succeeded in telescoping two of them one into the end of the other. With this extended arm he found he could reach the key easily enough.

The only trouble was that the key was looped by a stout cord to a snap-ring on the Dzlieri's harness, and try as he might he could not work it loose from that distance, nor yet undo the knot in the cord. He thought some more. If he could get his belt . . .

He eased the belt off the sentry's head—a tough job, for the belt was heavy with gear and the canes bent. Finally the belt came adrift, and Beck scraped it slowly toward the cage. At least he now had his gun.

What next? While he knew a little about picking locks

as a result of his customs work, he had no tools suitable for the purpose. He made a resolve never to set forth on an expedition like this without a length of heavy iron wire for lock-picking.

Of course he had the gun, but so what? Could he hold up the herd and force them to let him go? They didn't look as if they would be aroused even by gunshots. And if he did arouse them, would they obey him, or would they rush the cage and spear him despite his fire, or would they scatter into the woods and leave him there to starve? Unless he could be sure they would follow the first of these courses there was no point in killing a few, which would merely enrage the rest.

Could he open fire now and massacre the lot before they awoke? He had 42 shots—fourteen in the gun and two spare magazines—but there were over a hundred Dzlieri present. And anyway he did not know how sound asleep they were. So that was out, especially since he was not sure he could make every shot count in this fading light. Could he blast the lock with his pistol? Maybe, but the ironwork looked solid if crude, and perhaps he would merely jam the works so the door could not be opened without a cutting-torch, and even if he succeeded they might wake up . . .

No, altogether shooting did not seem to be the answer except as a last-ditch measure. He went through the pockets and attachments that hung from his belt. The most promising item seemed to be the sheath-knife. If he had a stout cord to fasten the knife to the end of his pole with, perhaps he could saw the cord that held the key. Unfortunately he had not brought any string along either, and the nearest cord was that which held the key in question.

Well, perhaps he could improvise some string. The canes had twigs with long slim leaves, and by twisting a lot of these together he managed to achieve a fairly secure lashing. Then with the knife on the end of the pole, he reached out and began to saw the cord. He dreaded pricking the Dzlieri with the knife-point and bringing the extraterrestrial up with a roar of rage, but he had to take that chance. And he couldn't exert any really powerful force on the knife for fear of breaking his slender canes or his precarious lashing.

His arms ached from muscular tension. At this rate it would be black by the time he finished . . . And then the cord parted. Beck scraped the key towards himself, losing it in the semi-darkness several times and having to feel for it. But at last it was his.

He stowed the knife and the string from the key, released the safety of his pistol, and unlocked the door. The screech of the lock he expected to bring all the Dzlieri up standing, but it failed to arouse them. He picked his way through the gloom among the sprawled Vishnuvans until he found Koshay, whose shoulder he shook.

"Que quer você?" mumbled the entrepreneur, rubbing his eyes. These eyes widened suddenly when they took in Beck. Koshay tensed himself for action, but subsided when Beck shoved the pistol into his face.

"Shut up," whispered Beck. "One yell and it'll be your last. Roll over on your face and put your hands behind your back."

When Koshay had obeyed, Beck sat on him and tied his wrists together with the key-string. When he felt what was happening, Koshay started to struggle. However, the pressure of the muzzle on the back of his head quieted him.

"Now come along," said Beck. He marched Koshay over to the edge of the corral, looking about him as he did so. He could not find his walking-stick, and for negotiating the swampy parts of the trail a pole or staff of some sort was a practical necessity. Therefore he finally pulled a javelin from one of the Dzlieri's quivers.

As they plunged into the woods, the darkness compelled Beck to use his flashlight. This confronted him with a problem: he needed three hands for light, javelin, and pistol. Not daring to entrust any of these articles to his prisoner, Beck compromised by leaving the pistol in its holster and following Koshay at a distance of three paces with the light in his left hand and the javelin in his right. Now, if Koshay tried to run, he could throw the spear at him and still draw and fire before the man could get out of range. Nobody, he thought, could be very agile with his hands tied behind him.

"Hey," said Koshay, "if I'm going ahead, untie my hands and give me the javelin to feel my way."

"And have you stick me with it? No sir!"

"Then at least give me the light so I can see where I'm walking."

"So you can put it out and bolt?"

"Oh my God, what a suspicious character! Then you go ahead and let me follow."

"And trust you behind me? How silly do *I* look, anyway?"

"But say, I'm liable to walk into a hole and go in over my head! Or step on some monster. I knew a man once who stepped into the mouth of a mud-worm on a trail like this, and it swallowed him down, gulp, before he could even yell."

"That would be a small loss in your case."

"Don't you care what happens to me? After all we are fellow-human beings . . ."

"I care about as much as you did what happened to me a couple of hours ago. Go on."

They plowed through the slime. The occasional stir of an animal in the vegetation halted them. The hair on Beck's neck prickled.

Koshay grumbled: "You're not so damn smart as you think. Anybody could figure out a way to get away from those dumb Dzlieri."

And again: "You think you're brave as all hell, don't you? Well, you're not. You're just one of those optimistic dopes who thinks everything will always come out right for him. You'll see. When the Dzlieri wake up they'll come after us."

"Not at night," said Beck, "and tomorrow'll be too late. Pipe down and keep going."

Because of the darkness, and the fact that Koshay in his bound condition had to go slowly, the hike back to Koshay's house took nearly all night. They arrived in the pre-dawn twilight. Koshay was covered with mud and filth from having stepped into holes and fallen down; Beck heartlessly had forced him to scramble up again as best he could.

Then there was nothing to do but wait for the helicopter.

On the ship for Krishna, Koshay made a nuisance of himself. He remembered, for instance, that he was supposed to be a pious Muslim, and pestered Beck five times a day to ask the navigator to calculate the direction of the Solar System so he could pray towards Mecca, though sometimes he almost had to stand on his head to do so. Beck was glad to deliver him into the custody of the regular *policía* at Novorecife.

Preliminary hearings were being held that session by Judge Keshavachandra, whose brows soared up his bald brown forehead like a bird taking off when he heard the case against the prisoner.

"You mean," he said, "that you intend to prosecute this man for arms-traffic because he sold animal-crackers to these warring tribes?"

"That's right, your honor," said Beck.

"But how in the Galaxy can animal-crackers be considered arms?"

Beck explained.

Koshay protested: "That's ridiculous, your honor. Suppose I sold golf-clubs to the human beings here at Novorecife—you do have a course, don't you?—well, if I did, and then a golfer killed another with a club in a fit of rage, that wouldn't make me guilty of arms-running."

"It's a matter of intent, your honor," said Beck. "If Senhor Darius sold golf-clubs with the intent that they should be used as golf-clubs, well and good; but if he sold them as weapons, then it's a violation of the statute. See the case of—*People versus Terszczansky*, I think it was; the regular prosecutor can tell you. And if you don't think this magic is effective against beings who believe in it, I urge that you bind the prisoner over while I go back to Vishnu and fetch a Dzlieri and a Romeli. It'll only take a couple of weeks, since the planets are almost in conjunction."

"And what then?"

"We'll stage a duel to demonstrate."

"You mean to have that centaur and that six-legged ape stand up on opposite sides of my courtroom and eat animal-crackers at each other?"

"Yes sir."

The judge sighed, then said with a twinkle: "We'd be famous for all time, no doubt, but it wouldn't be law. If the stunt didn't work we'd make ourselves ridiculous and accomplish nothing, while if it did we'd all be accessories to a murder. No, I'm afraid I shall have to discharge your man with a warning. Don't take it too hard, Inspector Beck. Morally you're right, and I'm going to see what I can do about revoking his entrepreneur's license. However, you'd never make your charge stand up at a regular trial, I can assure you."

Beck left the court with chin up but spirits drooping, not looking back lest he meet Koshay's triumphant grin. He had begun to feel like that fellow in the myth who was condemned to roll a boulder up hill again and again. Good-bye to his scholarship!

When the next ship for Vishnu took off some days later,

Beck was exasperated to learn that Koshay was a fellow-passenger.

"What are you up to now, Senhor Koshay?" he said.

Koshay grinned unregenerately. "I've got a load of golf-clubs and balls. You remember that crack of mine at the hearing? Well, it gave me an idea. I bought up all the surplus equipment at Novorecife and made arrangements with the shop to make me some more. I'm betting the Romeli will make great golfing enthusiasts."

"Where'd you get the money?"

"Oh, I salvaged enough of those Romeli songs, so my credit's good. This time I'll really hit the jackpot."

"Is your license still valid?"

"Nobody had said otherwise up to the time I left. I've got friends, you know. And if old Keshavachandra did get it revoked, that wouldn't affect me until somebody caught up with me and delivered the news. Which might not be easy."

There's a catch somewhere, thought Beck gloomily, and kept away from Koshay the rest of the trip.

When Beck resumed his post as customs inspector at Bembom, his first customer was naturally Darius Koshay. Again, however, the baggage proved to have nothing objectionable in it. Koshay, whistling cheerfully, rented the light tractor and trailer to haul his gear out to his house, and vanished into the jungle.

A couple of hours later he was back, panting, with an arrow sticking in his gluteus maximus. While Sawbones extracted it he told his story to Comandante Silva, Inspector Beck, and Sergeant Martins:

"I never saw anything like it; a party of mixed Romeli and Dzlieri, and instead of fighting each other they took after me! I just managed to get turned around in time, and I had to cut loose the trailer with all my stuff on it. You should have seen me bouncing along that lousy little road with the things whooping after me! If they hadn't stopped to pull my baggage apart they'd have had me."

"I told you they weren't fighting any more," said Silva.

"Yes, I know you did, but why aren't they?"

"I arranged a treaty between them."

"You did? I don't think it can be done!"

"Yes; that's the mixed border patrol you saw. They police the boundary zone between the tribes to see that none of either species crosses it and starts more trouble. I warned you not to go in there."

"You might have made it more specific," growled the

sufferer. "Hell, this is no place for a real man any more. I can see it's going to be all fouled up with red tape like the rest of the universe. I'm clearing out. When does the *Cabot* leave? Tomorrow? Swell."

When Koshay had limped off to gather his remaining belongings, Beck asked: *"Chefe,* what's this treaty really? How did you work it?"

"Simple enough. I persuaded Kamatobden to visit Koshay's house with me, and showed him that Koshay was supplying both sides. It took the evidence of the stored crackers to do it, because those types are stubborn. Then I did the same with Daatskhuna, and in that way I got them together for a friendly talk for the first time in known history."

Beck said: "That's fine. I wish I'd had a hand in it, though. I nearly got killed, and all I got to show for it was the merry ha-ha after that hearing on Krishna."

"Oh, you'll be all right, Luther. If you hadn't taken Koshay out of circulation so he wasn't there to foul things up, I could never have worked on the chiefs. As a reward I've recommended you for that scholarship, and I'm sure you'll get it—hey, doctor! I think he's going to faint!"

A.D. 2135-2148

Git Along!

Darius Mehmed Koshay looked at the fat slob across the table, and then at the prettier though hardly rounder wall clock. In three hours the ship from Earth would arrive at the Uranus spaceport, bearing, nine chances out of ten, a warrant for the arrest of Darius Koshay.

Three hours in which somehow to convert the fat slob into a means of escape from the Solar System. Escape to where his talents would be appreciated instead of thwarted. More to the point, escape to where Earthly writs did not run—at least not for such minor errors as an over-enthusiastic prospectus for a new company to raise Gaeneshan doodle-birds on Mars.

It was a gruesome choice between the clock and Moritz Gloppenheimer, who was not only fat but also a loud-mouthed vulgar bounder. Gloppenheimer, in fact, must have been the man for whom the English word "slob" had been invented. He had dirt under his nails—Koshay stole a look at his own fastidiously-manicured digits—and an unpleasant breath.

And most unkindest cut of all, the slob had hit upon a scheme that Koshay wished he had thought of. In fact Koshay was sure he *would* have thought of it if given a little time. Therefore the scheme by rights belonged to him—

"Go on, pal," said Koshay with an ingratiating smile, like the smile that caused a certain legendary heroine to remark: "What big teeth you have, Grandma!"

The encouragement was hardly necessary, for Gloppenheimer was a nonstop talker. The problem was to turn him off once he got started—like a Scotch faucet in reverse:

"... *und so,* when I saw this adwertisement for a chenu-

108

ine American dude ranch in the Bawarian Alps, I said to myself: why cannot you use the idea use, my boy? You have the cinema dealing with the American wild West many times seen. You can a month at this ranch to pick up the tricks of the trade shpend, and away you go!"

"Where to?" said Koshay, with just the right mixture of interest and nonchalance to encourage his acquaintance without rousing his suspicions.

"To a not-too-distant, humanoid-inhabitants-possessing, to Earthly-private-enterprises-hospitable planet. So, I inwestigate. What find I? Mars and Wenus are for this purpose useless; Mars had not enough air and its people are too insectlike, while Wenus is too hot and has no intelligent inhabitants at all. The most promising planet from my point of wiew is Osiris in the Procyonic System. The people are reptilian but highly ciwilized, friendly, with an extreme capitalistic economy, and to Earthly fads and fashions giwen. To Osiris then shall I, as soon as I can my materials collect, go."

"What materials?" asked Koshay, lighting a cigarette.

"Ah. A cowboy suit of the old American type. I know all this costumery a choke is; not for centuries have the Americans by such picturesque methods their cattle reared. I have once a ranch in Texas seen—like a laboratory, with the cowboys walking about in white coats, carrying test tubes and taking their animals' temperatures. But there is in this dude-ranch business still money to be gained. It even gives a *dzudzu ranchi* in Japan, I am told.

"But to get back to my materials: A rope or lasso. An ancient single-action rewolwer-type pistol, such as one sees in museums. Textbooks and romantic nowels dealing with the wild West. A guitar, bancho, or similar song-accompanying instrument in the evening by the campfire to play. I wisit the ranch; I buy the materials—"

"How's the monetary exchange between the Procyonic System and ours?" said Koshay.

Gloppenheimer belched loudly. "Wide open! One can Osirian money to World Federation dollars limitlessly convert. Of course one must first a partner or shponsor find. It is a rule for strange planets, a native partner to get, and one's own operations in the background to keep. Otherwise some day arises a character crying: 'The Earthman exploits us; tear the monster to pieces!' "

"Have you got all this stuff with you?"

"Yes, yes. Oh, waiter!" barked Gloppenheimer. "Bring another round. At once, you undershtand?"

Koshay smiled. "Put it on my bill," he added softly. A plan was beginning to form which, if successful, would well repay him for treating the oaf from his dwindling cash.

Three rounds later Gloppenheimer showed a tendency to drop his head on his forearms and go to sleep. Koshay said:

"Let me help you back to your room, Herr Gloppenheimer."

"Wery goot," mumbled Gloppenheimer. "A true friend. Remind me to set my alarm; my ship goes soon. *Ja,* I should not so much drinken. My third wife always said—" And the slob began to blubber, presumably over the memory of his third wife.

They zigzagged through the passageways, ricocheting from one bare bulkhead to the other like animated billiard balls until they reached Gloppenheimer's compartment. This lay two doors from Koshay's own room in the transient section of this underground rabbit warren. (Neptune and Pluto had similar spaceports; Uranus was at this time the transfer-point to the Procyonic and Sirian systems because it alone happened to be on the right side of the Solar System.)

Gloppenheimer flopped onto his bunk and began to snore like a sawmill almost before his head hit the pillow.

When he had satisfied himself that Gloppenheimer could not be roused even by severe shaking, Koshay went through the man's papers and effects. He took Gloppenheimer's keys from his pocket and opened the trunk standing upright by the door. There hung the cowboy outfit and its accessories. Gloppenheimer's ordinary clothes lay in his suitcase. This suitcase, about the size of Koshay's own, was covered by an almost identical fabric. A piece of luck! Allah was evidently going to see to it that Koshay got his just due.

Koshay examined Gloppenheimer's passport for some minutes.

Finally he tiptoed back to his own compartment, picked up his own suitcase, and looked cautiously out of his door. The room between his and Gloppenheimer's was occupied by an eight-legged native of Isis who looked like the result of an incredible miscegenation between an elephant and a dachshund. As the Isidian normally kept his door closed to enjoy a raised air pressure like that of his own planet, he was unlikely to burst out suddenly. Still, you couldn't be too careful.

He listened. From the Isidian's room, muffled by the door, came the faint *tonk-tonk* of the occupant's phonograph; Isidian music, Koshay knew, was made by a lot of Isidians holding little hammers in their trunks and hitting pieces of wood of various sizes and shapes with them. The effect was ultra-Cuban, and not much improved by the background of Gloppenheimer's snores.

Koshay carried his suitcase swiftly to Gloppenheimer's room and, after making sure that Gloppenheimer was still somnolent, opened it. Out of a false bottom came an assortment of pens, ink bottles, stamps, engraving tools, and other equipment not usually carried by honest travelers. Out also came several passports with Koshay's fingerprints and photograph, but without the passport-holder's name.

He stamped the name "Moritz Wolfgang Gloppenheimer" in the appropriate places so that it looked like typescript. Then he practiced Gloppenheimer's signature a few times on a sheet of stationery and signed the document.

He looked again at Gloppenheimer's passport. If he could only furnish Gloppenheimer with a similar passport made out to Darius Mehmed Koshay— But he lacked equipment for such a comprehensive job of forgery. He did the next best thing, which was to forge for Gloppenheimer, with his own name, a little identity-card bearing the legend, in the Brazilo-Portuguese of the spaceways:

TEMPORARY CARD
ISSUED ON LOSS OF PASSPORT
PENDING RECEIPT OF NEW PASSPORT

He then took a small strip of fabric like that which covered his suitcase and ran it through a gadget that stamped "M. W. G." on it in gold letters. He picked with his nails at the initials on his own suitcase until a corner of a similar strip came up, and then tore it off altogether and glued the new strip on in place of the old. Then he glued a strip bearing the initials "D. M. K." over the initials on Gloppenheimer's suitcase, so that unless you looked closely you would have thought that this suitcase bore Koshay's initials.

Then he checked through Gloppenheimer's clothes to make sure none of them had any initials or other marks of identity. When he finished the job he exchanged wallets with Gloppenheimer, checking all the papers, cards, tickets, and other things in both. He kept his regular passport and enough papers to identify him as Darius Koshay if necessary, packing these in the false bottom of his bag. The ticket to Osiris was especially welcome, as he did not have enough money to buy one of his own.

Koshay's pride troubled him a little during this transfer of identities, for he usually considered himself above vulgar thievery. To salve his sense of fitness he made a vague resolution to repay Gloppenheimer some day, when he could do so without personal sacrifice or inconvenience. Although he had made these resolutions before when circumstances had forced him to bend even his very pliable moral code, nothing had ever come of them.

And anyway, a man had to stand up for his rights, didn't he?

The passenger agent of the Viagens Interplanetarias looked up to see a man, one of that last lot that came in from Earth on the *Antigonos,* standing before him.

"Que quer você, senhor?" asked the *fiscal.*

"Excuse me," said the man in excellent Portuguese, "but I'm Moritz Gloppenheimer, en route from Earth to Osiris, and I have Compartment 9 in the Transient Section."

(The official wondered a little at this. He seemed to remember Gloppenheimer as fat, blond, boorish, and voluble, with a strong German accent, while this fellow was slim, dark, elegant, quiet, and younger-looking. No doubt he had confused the names.)

"One of my fellow-travelers," continued Koshay, "has passed out in the corridor in front of my door. Will you take care of the poor chap?"

"Do you know who he is?" said the agent, rising.

"I know who he said he was: Darius Koshay. We were drinking in the bar when he said he felt sick and excused himself. Later in going to my room I found him."

Just then a little door behind the *fiscal* opened and the head security officer of the port came in and whispered to the agent. Both men turned eyes on Koshay. The *fiscal* said:

"A thousand thanks to you, *senhor*; it transpires that the man is wanted on Earth. A warrant just came in on the *Kepler.* Had you not told us, he might have slipped away on the outgoing *Cachoeira* before we could get the alarm out."

"*Tamates*, that reminds me!" said Koshay. "I have about fifteen minutes to get aboard the *Cachoeira* myself. *Até à vista!*"

A few minutes later two processions passed each other in the corridors. One consisted of a porter trundling Gloppenheimer's trunk and Koshay's suitcase on an electric truck, and behind him Koshay ambling along with hands in pockets. The other comprised three Viagens policemen and a staggering, half-asleep Gloppenheimer, blubbering through his tears:

"*Aber, ich bin doch nicht dieser Koshay!*" (Belch.) "*Ich habe von dem Kerl niemals gehört!*"

The Viagens men, who probably did not understand German, paid no attention. Meanwhile Koshay blessed the prudence that had inhibited him from telling Gloppenheimer his name. What people didn't know—

Six months later—subjective time—Darius Koshay, still posing as Moritz W. Gloppenheimer, sat—or rather squatted—in conference with the three mayors of Cefef Aqh, Osiris. (The Osirians had explained to him that they used committees of three for all executive positions because they feared that one Osirian by himself might commit impulsive or sentimental acts.) They looked like small bipedal dinosaurs, a head taller than a man.

"No," he said firmly in the Sha'akhfi tongue, in which he was becoming as fluent as one lacking Sha'akhfi vocal organs could. "I will not form a partnership with you all. I will form a stock corporation with one of you, whichever gives me the best deal. Which shall it be?"

The three Sha'akhfi, like three Shakespearean witches, looked uneasily at Koshay and then at each other. Their forked tongues flicked out nervously. The one called Shishirhe, with scales covered with solid silver paint, said: "You mean whichever of us offers you the largest share of the stock?"

"Precisely," said Koshay. The Sha'akhfi knew all about corporation finance. In fact their economy reminded visitors of the wildest days of unregulated capitalism on Earth in the late nineteenth century.

Yathasia, the one with the red-and-black pattern painted on his hide, jumped up and began pacing back and forth on his birdlike feet. "That is not how I understood it at all when I introduced you to this honorable committee.

I thought we should each take a fourth, as is the custom."

Koshay said: "I am sorry if you got the wrong idea, but those are my terms. If you don't like them, I shall go hunting another trio of mayors."

"Most unfair!" cried Yathasia. "The monster is trying to set us one against the other. Let us refuse to deal with him!"

"Well?" said Koshay, looking at the other two.

Shishirhe, after some hesitation, said: "I will offer thirty percent."

"What?" cried Yathasia. "You surprise me, honorable colleague. I had thought you a person of more refined sentiments. However I will not let you have the corporation for the asking. Forty percent!"

Koshay looked towards the third of the trio, Fessahen, the one with the blue-green-and-orange pattern.

The latter waved his claws in the gesture of negation. "I am not in on this, having too many interests already. You, Shishirhe?"

"Forty-five," said Shishirhe.

"Forty-nine," hissed Yathasia.

"Fifty," said Shishirhe.

"Fifty-two," said Yathasia, his shrillness suggesting rage.

Fessahen observed: "Are you mad, Yathasia? That will give the Earthman control of the corporation!"

"I know," said Yathasia, "but our laws will protect my interest, and he knows how to run the business better than I in any case."

"Fifty-five," said Shishirhe.

(Koshay all the while was desperately translating the numbers, which they gave in their own octonary number-system, into his own decimal system. Their "percents" were actually sixty-fourths, and instead of "fifty percent" Shishirhe had said "forty" and meant "thirty-two.")

Yathasia hesitated, then picked up his brief case and threw it through the window. *Crash!*

"I have been grossly betrayed and insulted!" he shrieked in a voice like a calliope on the down-grade, hopping about in his fury. "I could never do business with a cold, calculating schemer like you, Mr. Glopphenheimer! Not only are you without a spark of sentiment, but worse, you do not even appear ashamed of the fact! And I am ashamed of you other two for not backing me up! You are as bad as the monster! Good day, honorable sirs!"

Fessahen said: "I apologize for my colleague, Mr.

Gloppenheimer. He is excitable. Not but that you gave him some cause to feel provoked. If you will excuse me, I will leave you two to work out the details of your deal. I have an engagement to inspect our new sewage-disposal plant."

"Will you step this way?" said Shishirhe. He thrust aside the heavy leather curtain in one of the doorways that led out of the conference room. Osirians did not build doors, no doubt for fear of catching the long tails that stuck out behind them to balance their bodies.

Koshay, tired of squatting, was glad to find a sort of hassock in Shishirhe's office on which he could sit.

"First," he said, "I shall need a sizable tract of land."

"That can be furnished," said Shishirhe. "I control a large piece a few *sfisfi* beyond the limits of Cefef Aqh. What else?"

"I need an introduction to makers of textiles who can duplicate the ranch clothes I brought from Earth—with such modifications as are necessary to fit the Sha'akhfi shape."

"I think that can be done, despite the fact that we never wrap ourselves in pieces of curtain as you Earthmen do. However, we have skilled workers."

"And finally, does your law provide any sort of monopoly for the inventor or introducer of new ideas? The kind of thing we Earthmen call a patent."

"I know what you mean. We do have such an exclusive license for all new types of business, good for one year."

Koshay was a little disappointed by the shortness of the period until he remembered that an Osirian year equaled half a dozen years on Earth.

A year later, Earth time, Darius Koshay sat in his ranch house waiting for his dudes to return from their three-day camping trip to the Fyasen'iç Waterfall. He was a little concerned; it had been the first such trip on which he had not gone with them, and he hoped Haqhisae the head wrangler could handle them. He'd have gone except that he'd been a little lame from the scratch he'd got the day before in the swimming pool. A friend of one of the dudes had come out with a half-grown son, and had urged Koshay to give the creature a swimming lesson, something never before heard of on this comparatively dry planet. And the infant had got panicky and kicked out with its hind claws.

All too well he remembered that horrible time when

that no-good cowboy Sifirhash seduced the daughter of that astronomy professor—or rather of that family group of which the astronomy professor was one of the husbands. (In the multiple Sha'akhfi families nobody ever knew which of the adults were the actual biological parents of which offspring.) However, the Sha'akhfi, at least in this province, were fussier in some respects about such matters than Earthmen. There was one consolation: He, personally, couldn't get into any trouble of that sort with these amiable if impulsive reptiles.

Or could he? There was Afasiè, the niece of one of the Inspectors of the Province, to whom Shishirhe had introduced him. Since she had such important relatives it behooved him to be nice to her, with the result that she had practically taken up a permanent residence at the ranch. He had been glad of an excuse to stay home from this camping trip in order to get away from her for once.

The sound of an Osirian automobile caused him to look up from his highball. The bare little wheeled platform with its hand-rails and levers drew up in front of the door of the ranch house. The tame lhaehe chained in the yard in front of the house gave a whistle of recognition, and Koshay's partner Shishirhe came in.

"Hello, partner," said the latter, doffing a ten-gallon hat and scaling it across the room, where it settled over one of the horns of the skull of the sassihih nailed to the wall. Shishirhe also wore a colored handkerchief around his neck, but had drawn the line at crowding his clawed feet into a pair of embroidered Western high-heeled boots with jingly spurs such as Koshay and most of his dudes wore.

"Hello, yourself," said Koshay. "Have a highball. How are the accounts?"

"Thank you," said Shishirhe, mixing a highball in one of the native drinking-vessels resembling a long-spouted oil can. "The accounts are doing well. We shall be out of debt in another score of days."

Koshay beamed at the thought of lovely money at last rolling in. "Any more trouble with the professor?"

"Not a bit. After that cowboy of ours was wedded to his daughter, the professor used influence to have the fellow made an assistant in the Physical Education Department. She has acquired two more husbands and a co-wife since then, and if the first clutch of eggs arrives ahead of schedule, nobody will be so discourteous as to mention the fact. How are you making out with little Afasiè?"

"Too well, if anything," said Koshay, and told of his troubles with that adhesive young female.

Shishirhe wagged his tongue in the Osirian equivalent of a grin. "If the idea were not too revolting to contemplate, one would almost think that she had— Well, anyway, you should get a wife of your own species, Gloppenheimer. That is, if you Earthmen recognize the sacred sentiment of matrimony."

"Some do," said Koshay. "And I manage. I have friends among the human colony in Cefef Aqh."

"By the way, it looks as though we should soon have competition of a sort."

Koshay sat up suddenly. "What sort?"

"Another Earthman arrived recently and went into business with my fellow-mayor, Yathasia. His name is"— the Sha'akhfa struggled with unfamiliar sounds—"Sarius Khoshay."

"What?" Koshay almost leaped up to protest that a vile imposter was taking his name in vain, when it occurred to him that he was doing the same thing. "Is this Koshay a fat fellow with yellow hair?"

"That is right."

"What sort of business is he starting?"

"Something called the Cefef Aqh Hunt Club. I do not know the details, though apparently it does not infringe our patent."

Koshay thought: Must keep track of this guy, who'll be after my blood. He must have beaten the rap I cooked up for him and set out after me, taking my name.

Shishirhe said: "If you will excuse me, I will take a dip in the pool."

"Are you going to try to swim at last?" asked Koshay.

"You mean go in over my head? Horrors, no! Such an outlandish sport is all very well for the young. By the way, there are those in Cefef Aqh who do not like your introduction of this strange sport to our land. They say the water washes off our body paint, and that it is not decent for us to mix unpainted with those outside our families. However, it is nothing serious—" and he squirted the rest of his drink into his open mouth and went out.

Koshay refilled his glass and brooded over it until his meditations were interrupted by the sound of galloping, as the dudes poured up to the ranch house on their 'aheahei. These were beasts somewhere between large long-legged lizards and small brontosauri which the Sha'akhfi had ridden back in their premechanical age.

Koshay had collected a herd of 'aheahei for his "horses," while for "cattle" he used the efaefan, a great horned reptile something like an Earthly triceratops, which the Sha'akhfi reared for food. Little by little he had introduced the methods of an Earthly dude ranch. The Sha'akhfi, however, had balked at branding—said it was cruel, and efaefin should continue to be marked as before, by stenciling.

The dudes crowded into the ranch house, hissing the story of their wonderful trip. The shortest of the females bustled up to Koshay, her chaps of efaefan-hide flapping. It was Afasiè, who gushed:

"Oh, dear Mr. Gloppenheimer—she said "Lhaffenhaimen"—"we had such a marvelous time, but we missed you so!" She pulled off her big hat, which had been held in place on her crest by an elastic chin strap. "Had I but known, I should have planned to stay here at the ranch house with you! And this evening may we have another square dance? The last was delightful, except that we got mixed up and went bumping into one another. This time why do you not let Haqhisae call the numbers while you dance with us? You never have, and I am sure you are very good at it. Would you consider me bold and unmaidenly if I asked you to be my partner? It will make the other girls simply slobber with jealousy! After all I am the only one of them who does not tower over you. You poor dear Earthman, it must give you a dreadful feeling of inferiority, between your short stature and your horrible soft pink skin. But there, I should not remind you of your shortcomings, should I? And then afterwards you can get out your guitar and sing us that wonderful song about 'Git along, little dogies.' By the way, if the singer is supposed to be driving cattle, as you told us, why does he speak of 'dogies,' which I always thought to be small domestic animals on your planet used for pets instead of food?"

For several days life at the ranch ran smoothly, save that a dude was gored by a bull efaefan whom he had, in the manner of dudes, foolishly and wantonly provoked. Koshay was planning a roundup for the amusement of the dudes—an easy day's ride out to watch his cowboys work and back. (He wondered whether he ought not to try to introduce an element into the proceedings corresponding to rustlers or hostile Indians, but gave it up, as too complicated. Still, Haquisae would look remarkable in a feathered war bonnet.)

Afasiè hung around bothering him. When he tried to send her on rides she said:

"Oh, but you are so much more fascinating, dear Mr. Gloppenheimer! Tell me more about the Earth. Ah, that my uncle would send me on a tour of the Solar System, like that which my fourth cousin Ahhas took last year! But being an honest politician he cannot afford it—"

The gruesome thought that the creature was in love with him oppressed Koshay more and more. If such were the case, he'd better sell out and beat it!

But where to? That warrant was still out for him in the Solar System, and he couldn't get to the Centaurine group, where he had good contacts, without stopping at at least one of the Solar planets. For the Osirian space-line did not run ships beyond Sol in that direction, and even the Viagens Interplanetarias did not run direct service from the Procyon-Sirius group to the Centaurine group. Furthermore these trips were so costly that he'd land as bare as an Osirian's hide, without a decent stake.

Then how about the other galactic directions? Sirius IX had a race about as humanoid as the Sha'akhfi, but an antlike culture with a rigid communistic economy; no place for an enterpriser like himself.

He asked Afasiè: "Are you coming to the roundup tomorrow?"

"You are going, are you not?"

"Yes," he said.

"Then I will most certainly go. I would not miss the sight of your roping and shooting. Where did you learn those arts?"

"Oh, I learned to rope on Vishnu, among the Dzlieri, and I learned to shoot when I was a kid on my native Earth. But this old gun is worn more for atmosphere than looks; compared to a modern gun it's so inaccurate that you might as well hit your victim over the head with it."

"May I see how it works?"

"Sure. You pull back this thing with your thumb, and sight through this little notch. Watch out, she's—"

Bang! The Colt leaped like a bucking 'aheahea in the Sha'akhfa's hand and shot out a tongue of yellow flame. Koshay could have sworn he felt the wind of the bullet. He snatched the pistol back.

"Now look at that hole in the roof!" he said. "Young lady, don't monkey with machinery you don't understand. You might have killed one of us."

"I am so sorry, Mr. Gloppenheimer, but I did not know

its battery was charged. What can I do? I will reshingle your roof myself. Give me your lovely boots that I may shine them."

Koshay refrained with effort from grinding his teeth. "The most useful thing you can do is to run along and let me alone. I am working up the next order for supplies."

Sulkily she went.

The party rode out to the scene of the roundup, brave in pseudo-Western finery. Most of the dudes dismounted while Koshay, still astride his 'aheahea, directed operations. Afasiè insisted upon riding beside him, the wind whipping the brim of her ten-gallon hat. As he bossed his reptilian wranglers, Koshay privately reflected that this was no way to rear efaefin for commercial purposes—chivvying them about this way must work hundreds of kilos off them.

The herd was finally bullied into a solid mass. The bulls took station around it in a circle, horns pointing outwards. Now if they could only get them moving in the right direction—

A strange sound came over the hills—the silvery notes of a horn. The scaly cowpokes looked this way and that.

Then a reptile scuttled over the brow of the nearest rise and raced through the scattered dudes, who leaped up with a shrill hiss. It was a theyasfa, the small wild relative of the lhaehe, over a meter long and looking like a lizard with big pointed ears.

Koshay, twisting in his saddle to see, heard Afasiè's voice: "Rope him, Mr. Gloppenheimer!"

Good idea, thought Koshay, provided his roping was good enough. He adjusted the loop in his lasso and turned his mount. The big rowels of his spurs dug into the leathery flanks of the 'aheahea, which broke into a gallop on a course converging with that of the theyasfa. Koshay leaned forward, whirling his lariat.

The loop shot out, whirling into a circle that settled around the forebody of the quarry. Koshay steered his mount to the other side to tighten the noose, and began to reel his rope in.

The theyasfa scrambled to its feet and began lunging wildly; one lunge carried it under the 'aheahea. As Koshay shortened his rope, the theyasfa, feeling its hindlegs pulled off the ground, snapped its jaws shut on the nearest leg of the 'aheahea.

The 'aheahea grunted and reared. Koshay, caught by surprise, fell backwards—right on top of the theyasfa.

"*Yeow!*" yelled Koshay, leaping up. He had come down in a sitting position, and the theyasfa had bitten him. The beast started to run again, dragging Koshay, who had retained his grip on the rope. He dug in his high heels and stopped the lunge.

Then he became aware of a growing clamor—the hiss of a pack of lhaehi, the cries of many mounted Sha'akhfi, and a human shout of: "Wiew hallo! Tally-ho! Yoicks! Yoicks!"

They poured towards him—first the lhaehi, a dozen or more. Then a 'aheahea bearing the fat form of Moritz Wolfgang Gloppenheimer, carrying a hunting horn and clad in black riding boots, white breeches, a red tailcoat, and a black silk top hat. Behind Gloppenheimer rode a score of Sha'akhfi similarly clad, except that they did without the white riding pants. (Considering their long tails it was not surprising.)

At this point Koshay's "cattle" stampeded away from the ranch, despite the yells of the cowboys. The theyasfa, terrified, began to run round and round Koshay, so that the rope wrapped itself around his legs and he lost his balance and sat down. The lhaehi raced towards the theyasfa and its captor, whistling like leaky radiators.

Koshay snatched out the old revolver and yelled in English: "Get 'em back! Call 'em off or I'll shoot!"

"Let go our fox, *Schweinhund!*" bawled Gloppenheimer. "Cut your rope! Let go!"

Koshay had no time to comply, for a couple of lhaehi threw themselves upon him with fangs bared. They were scarcely a meter away when he let fly: *bang, bang!* A third shot dropped another, and the rest laid their ears back and raced away in all directions, up gullies and over hills. The theyasfa bit through Koshay's rope and scampered away likewise.

As Koshay stood up and untangled himself, Gloppenheimer rode up yelling: "You will my hunt shpoil, will you? You will my hounds shlaughter, will you? You will my passport and baggage shteal, will you? Take that!"

The whip in his hand whistled and came down with a stinging crack on Koshay's shoulder. Koshay, smarting from the blow, jumped back, but a second slash stung the side of his face and carried away his cowboy hat. The whip snaked back and up for a third blow.

Bang! Without consciously meaning to, Koshay fired at

his assailant. Between the quick movement of the target, the fact that he shot from the hip without sighting, and the inaccuracy of the old Colt .45, he missed Gloppenheimer and buried the slug in the haunch of the man's mount. The 'aheahea bellowed and bucked, catapulting Gloppenheimer into the air.

Before the Master of the Hunt struck the ground there was a sharp *crack!* and Koshay's muscles jerked violently. An Osirian electrostatic gun had appeared in the hand of one of the red-coated huntsmen. A faint beam of violet light and the buzz of the ionizer, and then the piercing crack and blue flash of the discharge. The pistol flew from Koshay's hand and the world spun in front of him.

He came to sitting with his back against a tree. The young Afasiè was supporting him. The air was filled with the whistling Sha'akhfi tongue; the reptiles, in cowboy hats and silk toppers, were standing in groups and garruling. The real Gloppenheimer had fallen into a hellhiash bush which had punched him unmercifully with its knobs until he had rolled free. He got up and looked disgustedly at his smashed top hat.

"What happened?" Koshay asked Afasiè.

"Did you not recognize the other two mayors in the hunting party? Yathasia's bodyguard winged you to stop you from shooting Mr. Koshay. You will be all right."

"I hope so," muttered Koshay, trying to move his right arm.

A Sha'akhfi came forward. In the gap in the front of his red coat Koshay recognized the paint-pattern of Fessahen, the senior mayor of Cefef Aqh. The latter said:

"Have you recovered? Good. We mayors have decided to constitute a tribunal to try you on the spot."

"For what?" asked Koshay.

"For slaying your fellow-Earthman."

"But he is not dead!" cried Koshay. "Look at him!"

"That makes no difference; in Osirian law the intent is all, the degree of success nothing. Our judicial system, in case you are unfamiliar with it, gives us much latitude in trying beings from other planets. To be fair, we modify our own system as far as we can to conform to the legal concepts of the being's home world. In your case they would be those of the western United States—"

"They would not!" interrupted Koshay. "I'm a native of Istanbul, Turkey!"

"No, since your cultural pattern is that of a Western American, you will be deemed to be such. We all know the legal system prevailing there from having read Earthly novels and seen Earthly cinemas. A quick summary trial, no lawyers, and when convicted the accused is hanged to the nearest tree—"

"Hey!" said Koshay. "That's how it was centuries ago, maybe, but not now! The western United States is as civilized as any place! I know because I have been there! They have plumbing, libraries—"

"An unlikely story," said Fessahen. "We have read and seen many accounts, and all agree on this point. Surely if the West were as civilized as you say, there would be some indication of the fact in your Earthly literature."

"Shishirhe!" said Koshay. "Do something!"

Shishirhe, who had ridden out with the dudes, spread his claws. "I have already opposed this proceeding, but I am outvoted."

"If you are ready," said Fessahen, "we—"

"I am not ready," yelled Koshay, struggling to his feet. "I shall appeal to the Earthly ambassador! And why aren't you trying the other man, too? He started it!"

"One thing at a time. When we have disposed of you we shall take up the case of Mr. Koshay. Of course if you have been destroyed by then it is unlikely he will be convicted. Will you act with decorum, or must we bind and gag you? This honorable court is now in session and all spectators are warned to keep order. Spread out, you people. Mr. Koshay"—he indicated Gloppenheimer—"as the prosecution's main witness, you shall squat there."

Koshay looked around. His pistol had been taken away, he was surrounded, and even the friendly Afasiè had disappeared. The other Sha'akhfi seemed neither friendly nor hostile; just curious. You couldn't tell from the expressionless scaly faces what was going on in those mercurial minds.

The trial took a couple of Earthly hours, in the course of which the whole story of Koshay's theft of Gloppenheimer's name and effects came out.

Fessahen said: "The trial is over. Honorable Shishirhe, how do you vote?"

"Not guilty," said Koshay's partner.

"Honorable Yathasia, how say you?"

"Guilty!" said Gloppenheimer's partner.

"I, too, vote guilty," said Fessahen. "We must teach these creatures that wild West barbarism is not tolerated on our planet.

"Therefore, Gloppenheimer . . . I mean Koshay . . . I

sentence you to be hanged forthwith by the neck to a suitable branch of this qhaffaseh tree until you are dead. I believe that in the wild West it is customary to seat the culprit on his mount with the rope about his neck, and stimulate the animal, causing the beast to move away leaving the felon dangling. It will be sentimentally appropriate to do it that way, and will furthermore remind the prisoner of his native planet during his last minutes. As an even more delicate touch of sentiment, let us use his own rope."

All the Sha'akhfi cheered. Koshay made as if to break for freedom, but they grabbed him and tied his hands.

"Ha, ha!" said Gloppenheimer. "I laugh! I knew you were born to be hung the moment I saw you, you shcoundrel! And because you have so kindly in my name the title to the majority shtock of your ranch made out, I may be able to eshtablish ownership to it. Ha."

Koshay said: "Turn me loose long enough to sock that *sfasha'*, won't you?"

"No," said Fessahen, though several Sha'akhfi murmured approval of the idea. They boosted Koshay astride an 'aheahea, tied his rope around his neck, and tossed the other end over a branch. One of them belayed the loose end.

Shishirhe said: "Farewell, partner; I grieve that your sojourn ended thus. Would I could help you."

"You're not half so sorry as I am," said Koshay.

Fessahen said: "When I say 'go!', strike his mount. Go!"

The whip cracked, the beast jumped, and the rope pulled Koshay off its back. Since he had no long drop and since the Sha'akhfi were not experts at nooses, he was doomed to die by slow strangulation instead of by a quick breaking of the neck. He spun, kicking frantically.

So intent was the crowd that they did not even notice that an aircraft had dropped to the ground nearby, rotors whistling, and a couple of Sha'akhfi with badges around their necks and shock-guns around their middles got out. These rushed up to the tree and cut the rope, letting the nearly unconscious Koshay fall to the ground. As the roaring in his ears lessened he felt the cord being unwound from his wrists.

Fessahen said: "Why have the Provincial Inspectors sent men to interfere with the decision of a duly constituted municipal court?"

One of the new arrivals answered: "Your court was not

duly constituted, because Judge Yathasia is the plaintiff's partner and hence has an interest in the outcome. I am also told that other features of this trial constitute reversible errors as well. In any case, the case will be transferred to the Provincial Court of Appeals."

The crowd cheered this outcome even more loudly than they had the original sentence.

Koshay, feeling his neck, croaked: "How did you two get here in the nick of time?"

The provincial policeman said: "One of your dudes, Afasiè, rode back to your ranch house and called her uncle, Inspector Eyaèsha, on the communicator. He ordered us out to stop this proceeding, on the grounds I mentioned. Can you stand now, Earthman?"

"I think so," said Koshay.

"Stop them!" cried Fessahen, and the police leaped to do so. For Gloppenheimer had picked up a large stone and was rushing at Koshay, and Koshay had picked up a stout piece of dead branch and stood awaiting his assault, and both had manslaughter in their eyes.

Afasiè and Shishirhe visited Koshay in his cell in Cefef Aqh. The former said: "They have decided to deport both of you, dear, dear Mr. Glopp . . . I mean Mr. Koshay. My liver will be broken."

Koshay said: "There are worse fates, I suppose. Anyway, thanks for saving my worthless life."

"It was nothing. Ah, were your spirit in the body of a Sha'akhfa instead of in that of a hideous monster—but I speak folly. It can never be." She leaned forward, flicked out her forked tongue, and touched his cheek in the Osirian kiss. "Farewell! I go before emotion strips me of my last maidenly reticence!"

Koshay watched her go with some relief. Shishirhe said: "Poor girl! Such sweet sentiment; just like that Earthly fairytale of Beauty and the Beast. Now as for you, partner, you will be shipped out tomorrow on Number 36 for Neptune."

"How about the money from the ranch? Do I get any?"

"I am sorry, but your share will be confiscated as a fine by the Province."

"Oh, well," said Koshay. "As long as I never see that slob Gloppenheimer again— I suppose he feels the same about me. In fact the worst punishment you could give us would be to put us in the same room—"

"Oh-oh," said Shishirhe. "I regret that is just what will

happen. Number 36 has but one compartment for non-Osirian passengers, and you two will be confined to it for the duration of your trip. But do not look so upset. It will be over in but half one of your Earthly years, subjective time. May you have a pleasant voyage!"

A.D. 2137

Perpetual Motion

"My good senhor," said Abreu, "where the devil did you get those? Raid half the Earth's pawnshops?" He bent closer to look at the decorations on Felix Borel's chest. "Teutonic Order, French Legion of Honor, Third World War, Public Service Award of North America, Fourth Degree of the Knights of St. Stephen, Danish Order of the Elephant, something-or-other from Japan, Intercollegiate Basketball Championship, Pistol Championship of the Polícia do Rio de Janeiro . . . *Tamates*, what a collection!"

Borel smiled sardonically down on the fat little security-officer. "You never can tell. I might be a basketball champion."

"What are you going to do, sell these things to the poor ignorant Krishnans?"

"I might, if I ran short. Or maybe I'll just dazzle them so they'll give me whatever I ask for."

"Humph. I admit that in that private uniform, with all those medals and orders, you're an awe-inspiring spectacle."

Borel, amusedly watching Abreu fume, knew that the latter was sore because he had not been able to find any excuse to hold Borel at Novorecife. Thank God, thought Borel, the universe is not yet so carefully organized that personal influence can't perform a trick or two. He would have liked to do Abreu a bad turn if for no better reason than that he harbored an irrational prejudice against Brazzies, as though it were Abreu's fault that his native country was the Earth's leading power.

Borel grinned at the bureaucrat. "You'd be surprised how helpful this—uh—costume of mine has been. Flunkeys at spaceports assume I'm at least Chief of Staff of the

World Federation. 'Step this way, Senhor! Come to the head of the line, Senhor!' More fun than a circus."

Abreu sighed. "Well, I can't stop you. I still think you'd have a better chance of survival disguised as a Krishnan, though."

"And wear a green wig, and false feelers on my forehead? No thanks."

"That's your funeral. However, remember Regulation 368 of the Interplanetary Council rules. You know it?"

"Sure. 'It is forbidden to communicate to any native resident of the planet Krishna any device, appliance, machine, tool, weapon, or invention representing an improvement upon the science and technics already in existence upon this planet . . .' Want me to go on?"

"Não, you know it. Remember that while the Viagens Interplanetarias will ordinarily let you alone once you leave Novorecife, we'll go to any length to prevent and punish any violation of that rule, even to withholding your longevity-doses."

Borel yawned. "I understand. If the type has finished X-raying my baggage, I'll be pushing off. What's the best route to Mishé at present?"

"You could go straight through the Koloft Swamps, but the wilder tribes of the Koloftuma sometimes kill travellers for their goods. You'd better take a raft down the Pichidé to Qou, and follow the road southwest from here to Mishé."

. . . *"Obrigado.* The Republic of Mikardand is on a gold standard, isn't it?"

"Pois sim."

"And what's gold at Novorecife worth in terms of World Federation dollars on Earth?"

"Oh, *Deus meu!* That's takes a higher mathematician to calculate, what with freight and interest and the balance of trade."

"Just approximately," persisted Borel.

"As I remember, a little less than two dollars a gram."

Borel stood up and shook back his red hair with a characteristic gesture. He gathered up his papers. *"Adeus,* Senhor Cristôvão; you've been most helpful."

He smiled broadly as he said this, for Abreu had obviously wanted to be anything but helpful and was still gently simmering over his failure to halt Borel's invasion of Krishna.

The next day found Felix Borel drifting down the

Pichidé on a timber-raft under the tall clouds that paraded across the greenish sky of Krishna. Next to him crouched the Koloftu servant he had hired at Novorecife, tailed and monstrously ugly.

A brisk shower had just ended. Borel stood up and shook drops off his cloak as the big yellow sun struck them. Yerevats did likewise, grumbling in broken Gozashtandou: "If master do like I say, put on poor man clothes, could take tow-boat and stay close to shore. Then when rain came, could put up tarpaulin. No get wet, no be afraid robbers."

"That's my responsibility," replied Borel, moving about to get his circulation going again. He gazed off to starboard, where the low shore of the Pichidé broke up into a swarm of reedy islets. "What's that?" he asked, pointing.

"Koloft Swamps," said Yerevats.

"Your people live there?"

"No, not by river. Further back. By river is all *ujerö*." (He gave the Koloftou name for the quasi-human people of the planet, whom most Earthmen thought of simply as Krishnans because they were the dominant species.) "Robbers," he added.

Borel, looking at the dark horizontal stripe of reeds between sky and water, wondered if he'd been wise to reject Yerevats's advice to buy the full panoply of a *garm* or knight. Yerevats, he suspected, had been hoping for a fancy suit of armor for himself. Borel had turned down the idea on grounds of expense and weight; suppose one fell into the Pichidé in all that stove-piping? Also, he now admitted to himself, he had succumbed to Terran prejudice against medieval Krishnan weapons, since one Earthly bomb could easily wipe out a whole Krishnan city and one gun mow down a whole army. Perhaps he hadn't given enough weight to the fact that where he was going, no Earthly bombs or guns would be available.

Too late now for might-have-beens. Borel checked over the armament he had finally bought: a sword for himself, as much a badge of status as a protection. A cheap mace with a wooden handle and a star-shaped iron head for Yerevats. Sheath-knives of general utility for both. Finally, a crossbow. Privately Borel, no swashbuckler, hoped that any fighting they did would be at as long a range as possible. He had tried drawing a longbow in the Outfitting Shop at Novorecife, but in his unskilled grip it bobbled about too much, and would have required more practice than he had time for.

Borel folded his cloak, laid it on his barracks bag, and sat down to go over his plans again. The only flaw he could see lay in the matter of getting an entrée to the Order of Qarar after he arrived at Mishé. Once he'd made friends with members of the Brotherhood, the rest should be easy. By all accounts the Mikardanduma were natural-born suckers. But how to take that first step? He'd probably have to improvise after he got there.

Once he'd gotten over that first hurdle, his careful preparation and experience in rackets like this would see him through. And the best part would be that he'd have the laugh on old Abreu, who could do absolutely nothing about it. Since Borel considered honesty a sign of stupidity, and since Abreu was not stupid for all his pompous ways, Borel assumed that Abreu must be out for what he could get like other wise joes, and that his moral attitudes and talk of principles were mere hypocritical pretense.

"Ao!" The shout of one of the raftmen broke into Borel's reverie. The Krishnan was pointing off towards the right bank, where a boat was emerging from among the islets.

Yerevats jumped up, shading his eyes with his hairy hand. "Robbers!" he said.

"How can you tell from here?" asked Borel, a horrid fear making his heart pound.

"Just know. You see," said the Koloftu, his tail twitching nervously. He looked appealingly at Borel. "Brave master kill robbers? No let them hurt us?"

"Sh-sure," said Borel. He pulled out his sword halfway, looked at the blade, and shoved it back into its scabbard, more as a nervous gesture than anything else.

"Ohé!" said one of the raftmen. "Think you to fight the robbers?"

"I suppose so," said Borel.

"No, you shall not! If we make no fight, they will slay only you, for we are but poor men."

"Is that so?" said Borel. The adrenalin being poured into his system made him contrary, and his voice rose. "So you think I'll let my throat be cut quietly to save yours, huh? I'll show you *baghana!"* The sword whipped out of the scabbard, and the flat slapped the raftman on the side of the head, staggering him. "We'll fight whether you like it or not! I'll kill the first coward myself!" He was screaming at the three raftmen, now huddled together fearfully. "Make a barricade of the baggage! Move that stove forward!" He stood over them, shouting and swishing the air with his sword, until they had arranged the movables in a rough square.

"Now," said Borel more calmly, "bring your poles and crouch down inside there. You too, Yerevats. I'll try to hold them off with the bow. If they board us anyway, we'll jump out and rush them when I give the signal. Understand?"

The boat had been slanting out from the shore on a course converging toward that of the raft. Now Borel, peering over the edge of his barricade, could make out the individuals in it. There was one in the bow, another in the stern, and the rest rowing—perhaps twenty in all.

"Is time to cock bow," muttered Yerevats.

The others looked nervously over their shoulders as if wondering whether the river offered a better chance of safety than battle.

Borel said: "I wouldn't try to swim ashore. You know the monsters of the Pichidé." Which only made them look unhappier.

Borel put his foot into the stirrup at the muzzle end of the crossbow and cocked the device with both hands and a grunt. Then he opened the bandoleer he had bought with the bow and took out one of the bolts: an iron rod a span long, with a notch at one end, and at the other a flattened, diamond-shaped head with a twist to make the missile spin in its flight. He inserted the bolt into its groove.

The boat came closer and closer. The man in the front end called across the water: "Surrender!"

"Keep quiet," said Borel softly to his companions. By now he was so keyed up that he was almost enjoying the excitement.

Again the man in the boat hailed: "Surrender and we'll not hurt you! 'Tis only your goods we want!"

Still no reply from the raft.

"For the last time, give up, or we'll torture you all to death!"

Borel shifted the crossbow to cover the man in the front. Damn, why hadn't these gloops put sights on their gadgets? He'd taken a few practice shots at a piece of paper the day before and thought himself pretty good. Now, however, his target seemed to shrink to mosquito size every time he tried to draw a bead on it, and something must be shaking the raft to make the weapon waver so.

The man in the bow of the boat had produced an object

like a small anchor with extra flukes, tied to the end of a rope. He held this dangling while the grunting oarsmen brought the boat swiftly towards the raft, then whirled it around his head.

Borel shut his eyes and jerked the trigger. The string snapped loudly and the stick kicked back against his shoulder. One of the raftmen whooped.

When Borel opened his eyes, the man in the front of the boat was no longer whirling the grapnel. Instead he was looking back towards the stern, where the man who had sat at the tiller had slumped down. The rowers were resting on their oars and jabbering excitedly.

"Great master hit robber captain!" said Yerevats. "Better cock bow again."

Borel stood up to do so. Evidently he had missed the man he aimed at and instead hit the man in the stern. However, he said nothing to disillusion his servant about his marksmanship.

The boat had reorganized and was coming on again, another robber having taken the place of the one at the tiller. This time there were two Krishnans in front, one with the grapnel and the other with a longbow.

"Keep your heads down," said Borel, and shot at the archer; the bolt flew far over the man's head. Borel started to get up to reload, then realized that he'd be making a fine target. Could you cock these damned things sitting down? The archer let fly his shaft, which passed Borel's head with a frightening *whisht*. Borel hastily found that he could cock his crossbow in a sitting position, albeit a little awkwardly. Another arrow thudded into the baggage.

Borel shed his military-style cap as too tempting a target and sighted on the boat again. Another miss, and the boat came closer. The archer was letting off three arrows to every one of Borel's bolts, though Borel surmised that he was doing so to cover their approach rather than with hope of hitting anybody.

Borel shot again; this time the bolt banged into the planking of the boat. The man with the grapnel was whirling it once more, and another arrow screeched past.

"Hey," said Borel to one of the raftmen, "you with the hatchet! When the grapnel comes aboard, jump out and cut the rope. You other two, get ready to push the boat off with your poles."

"But the arrows—" bleated the first man spoken to.

"I'll take care of that," said Borel with more confidence than he felt.

The archer had drawn another arrow but was holding it steady instead of releasing it. As the boat came within range of the grapnel, the man whirling it let go. It landed on the raft with a thump. Then the man who had thrown it began to pull it in hand over hand until one of the flukes caught in a log.

Borel looked around frantically for some way of tempting the archer to shoot, since otherwise the first to stand up on the raft would be a sitting duck. He seized his cap and raised it above the edge of the barricade. Snap! and another arrow hissed by.

"Go to it!" shrieked Borel, and sighted on the archer. His crew hesitated. The archer reached back to his quiver for another arrow, and Borel, forcing himself to be calm, drew a bead on the man's body and squeezed.

The man gave a loud animal cry, between a grunt and a scream, and doubled over.

"Go on!" yelled Borel again, raising the crossbow as if to beat the raftmen over the head with it. They sprang into life; one severed the rope with a chop of his hatchet while the other two poked at the boat with their poles.

The remaining man in the front of the boat dropped his rope, shouted something to the rowers, and bent to pick up a boathook. Borel shot at him, but let himself get excited and missed, though it was practically spitting-distance. When the boathook caught in the logs, the man hauled the bow of the boat closer, while a few of the forward rowers stopped rowing to cluster around him with weapons ready.

In desperation Borel dropped his crossbow, grabbed the end of the boathook, wrenched it out of the wood, and jerked it towards himself. The man on the other end held on a second too long and toppled into the water, still gripping the shaft. Borel pulled on it with some idea of wrenching it away and reversing it to spear the man in the water. However, the latter held on and was hauled to the edge of the raft, where he made as though to climb aboard. Meanwhile the raftmen had again pushed the boat away with their poles, so that those who had been gathering themselves to jump across thought better of the idea.

Thump! Yerevats brought his mace down on the head of the man in the water, and the mop of green hair sank beneath the surface.

The raftmen were now yelling triumphantly in their

own dialect. A robber, however, had picked up the longbow from the bottom of the boat and was fumbling with
an arrow. Borel, recovering his crossbow, took pains with
his next shot and made a hit just as the new archer let fly.
The arrow went wild and the archer disappeared, to bob
up again a second later cursing and holding his shoulder.

Borel cocked his crossbow again and aimed at the man
in the boat. This time, however, instead of shooting, he
simply pointed it at one man after another. Each man in
turn tried to duck down behind the thwarts, so that
organized rowing became impossible.

"Had enough?" called Borel.

The robbers were arguing again, until finally one called
out: "All right, don't shoot; we'll let you go." The oars
resumed their regular rhythm, and the boat swung away
towards the swamp. When it was safely out of range some
of the robbers yelled back threats and insults, which Borel
could not understand at the distance.

The raftmen were slapping each other's backs, shouting:
"We're good! Said I not we could lick a hundred robbers?"
Yerevats babbled about his wonderful master.

Borel felt suddenly weak and shaky. If a mouse, or
whatever they had on Krishna that corresponded to a
mouse, were to climb aboard and squeak at him, he was
sure he'd leap into the muddy Pichidé in sheer terror.
However, it wouldn't do to show that. With trembling
hands he inserted a cigarette into his long jewelled holder
and lit it. Then he said:

"Yerevats, my damned boots seem to have gotten
scuffed. Give them a shine, will you?"

They tied up at Qou that evening to spend the night.
Felix Borel paid off the raftmen, whom he overheard
before he retired telling the innkeeper how they had (with
some help from the Earthman) beaten off a hundred
river-pirates and slain scores. Next morning he bade them
goodby as they pushed off down the river for Majbur at
the mouth of the Pichidé, where they meant to sell their
logs and catch a towboat back home.

Four long Krishnan days later Borel was pacing the
roof of his inn in Mishé. The capital of the Republic of
Mikardand had proved a bigger city than he had expected. In the middle rose a sharp-edged mesa-like hill sur-
mounted by the great citadel of the Order of Qarar. The
citadel frowned down upon Borel, who frowned right back
as he cast and rejected one plan after another for penetrat-

ing not only the citadel but also the ruling caste whose stronghold it was.

He called: "Yerevats!"

"Yes, master?"

"The *Garma Qararuma* toil not, neither do they spin, do they?"

"Guardians work? No sir! Run country, protect common people from enemies and from each other. That enough, not?"

"Maybe, but that's not what I'm after. How are these Guardians supported?"

"Collect taxes from common people."

"I thought so. Who collects these taxes?"

"Squires of Order. Work for treasurer of Order."

"Who's he?" asked Borel.

"Is most noble *garm* Kubanan."

"Where could I find the most noble Sir Kubanan?"

"If he in citadel, no can see. If in treasury office, can."

"Where's the treasury office?"

Yerevats waved vaguely. "That way. Master want go?"

"Right. Get out the buggy, will you?"

Yerevats disappeared, and presently they were rattling over the cobblestones towards the treasury office in the light one-aya four-wheeled carriage Borel had bought in Qou. It had occurred to him at the time that one pictured a gallant knight as pricking o'er the plain on his foaming steed rather than sitting comfortably behind the steed in a buggy. However, since the latter procedure promised to be pleasanter, and Yerevats knew how to drive, Borel had taken a chance on the Mikardanders' prejudices.

The treasury office was in one of the big graceless rough-stone buildings that the Qararuma used as their official architectural style. The doorway was flanked by a pair of rampant stone yekis: the dominant carnivores of this part of the planet, something like a six-legged mink blown up to tiger size. Borel had had the wits scared out of him by hearing the roar of one on his drive down from Qou.

Borel gathered up his sword, got down from the buggy, assumed his loftiest expression, and asked the doorman:

"Where do I find the receiver of taxes, my good man?"

In accordance with the doorman's directions he followed a hall in the building until he discovered a window in the side of the hall, behind which sat a man in the drab dress of the commoners of Mikardand.

Borel said: "I wish to see whether I owe the Republic

any taxes. I don't wish to discuss it with you, though; fetch your superior."

The clerk scuttled off with a look compounded of fright and resentment. Presently another face and torso appeared at the window. The torso was clad in the gay coat of a member of the Order of Qarar, but judging from the smallness of the dragonlike emblem on the chest, the man was only a squire or whatever you'd call the grade below the true *garma*.

"Oh, not you," said Borel. "The head of the department."

The squire frowned so that the antennae sprouting from between his brows crossed. "Who are you, anyhow?" he said. "The receiver of taxes am I. If you have anything to pay—"

"My dear fellow," said Borel, "I'm not criticising you, but as a past Grand Master of an Earthly Order and a member of several others, I'm not accustomed to dealing with underlings. You will kindly tell the head of your department that the *garm* Felix Borel is here."

The man went off shaking his head in a baffled manner. Presently another man with a knight's insignia stepped through a door into the corridor and advanced with hand outstretched.

"My dear sir!" he said. "Will you step into my chamber? 'Tis a pleasure extraordinary to meet a true knight from Earth. I knew not that such lived there; the Terrans who have come to Mikardand speak strange subversive doctrines of liberty and equality for the commonality— even those who claim the rank, like that Sir Erik Koskelainen. One can tell you're a man of true quality."

"Thank you," said Borel. "I knew that one of the *Garma Qararuma* would know me as spiritually one of themselves, even though I belong to another race."

The knight bowed. "And now what's this about your wishing to pay taxes? When I first heard it I believed it not; in all the history of the Republic no man has ever offered to pay taxes of his own will."

Borel smiled. "I didn't say I actually *wanted* to pay them. But I'm new here and wanted to know my rights and obligations. That's all. Better to get them straightened out at the start, don't you think?"

"Yes—but—are you he who came hither from Qou but now?"

"Yes."

"He who slew Usharian the river-pirate and his lieutenant in battle on the Pichidé?"

Borel waved a deprecating hand. "That was nothing. One can't let such rogues run loose, you know. I'd have wiped out the lot, but one can't chase malefactors with a timber-raft."

The Qararu jumped up. "Then the reward is due you!"

"Reward?"

"Why, knew you not? A reward of ten thousand *karda* was lain on the head of Usharian for years! I must see about the verification of your claim . . ."

Borel, thinking quickly, said: "Don't bother. I don't really want it."

"You don't *wish* it?" The man stared blankly.

"No. I only did a gentleman's duty, and I don't need it."

"But—the money's here—it's been appropriated—"

"Well, give it to some worthy cause. Don't you have charities in Mishé?"

The knight finally pulled himself together. "Extraordinary. You must meet the treasurer himself. As for taxes—let me see—there is a residence tax on metics, while on the other hand we have treaties with Gozashtand and some of the other states to exempt each other's gentlefolk. I know not how that would affect you—but concern yourself not, in view of your action in the matter of the reward. I'll put it up to the treasurer. Can you wait?"

"Sure. Mind if I smoke?"

"Not at all. Have one of these." The knight dug a bunch of Krishnan cigars out of a desk drawer.

After a few minutes, the official returned and asked Borel to come to the treasurer's office, where he introduced the Earthman to the treasurer of the Order. Sir Kubanan was that rarity among Krishnans, a stout man, looking a little like a beardless Santa Claus.

The previous conversation more or less repeated itself, except that the treasurer proved a garrulous old party with a tendency to ramble. He seemed fascinated by Borel's medals.

"This?" said Borel, indicating the basketball medal. "Oh, that's the second degree of the Secret Order of Spooks. Very secret and very powerful; only admits men who've been acquitted of a murder charge . . ."

"Wonderful, wonderful," said Kubanan at last. "My dear sir, we will find a way around this tax matter, fear not. Perish the thought that one so chivalrous as yourself should be taxed like a vulgar commoner, even though the Order be sore pressed for funds."

This was the opening Borel had been waiting for. He pounced. "The Order would like additional sources of revenue?"

"Why, yes. Of course we're all sworn to poverty and obedience" (he contemplated his glittering assortment of rings) "and hold all in common, even our women and children. Nevertheless, the defense of the Republic puts a heavy burden upon us."

"Have you thought of a state lottery?"

"What might that be?"

Borel explained, rattling through the details as fast as his fair command of the language allowed.

"Wonderful," said Kubanan. "I fear I could not follow your description at all times, though; you do speak with an accent. Could you put it in writing for us?"

"Sure. In fact I can do better than that."

"How mean you?"

"Well, to give you an example, it's much easier to tell how to ride an aya than to do it, isn't it?"

"Yes."

"Just so, it's easy to tell you how a lottery works—but it takes practical experience to run one."

"How can we surmount that difficulty?"

"I could organize and run your first lottery."

"Sir Felix, you quite take my breath away. Could you write down the amounts involved in this scheme?"

Borel wrote down a rough estimate of the sums he might expect to take in and pay out in a city of this size. Kubanan, frowning, said: "What's this ten percent for the Director?"

"That's the incentive. If you're going to run this thing in a businesslike manner after I've left, we'd better set it up right. And one must have an incentive. The first time I'd be the director, naturally."

"I see. That's not unreasonable. But since members of the Order aren't allowed private funds beyond mere pocket-money, how would the commission act as incentive?"

Borel shrugged. "You'd have to figure that one out. Maybe you'd better hire a commoner to run the show. I suppose there are merchants and bankers among them, aren't there?"

"True. Amazing. We must discuss this further. Won't you come to my chambers this evening to sup? I'll pass you in to the citadel."

Borel tried to hide his grin of triumph as he said: "It's my turn to be overwhelmed, your excellency!" The Borel luck!

At the appointed hour Borel, having presented his pass at the gate of the citadel, was taken in tow by a uniformed guide. Inside Mishé's Kremlin stood a lot of huge plain stone buildings wherein the Guardians led their antlike existence. Borel walked past playgrounds and exercise-grounds, and identified other buildings as apartment-houses, armories, office-buildings, and an auditorium. It was just as well to memorize such details in case a slip-up should require a hasty retreat. Borel had once spent six months as a guest of the French Republic in consequence of failing to observe this precaution. He passed hundreds of gorgeously arrayed *garma* of both sexes. Some looked at him sharply, but none offered interference.

For the quarters of one sworn to poverty, the treasurer's apartment was certainly sumptuous. Kubanan cordially introduced Borel to a young female Mikardandu who quite took his breath away. If one didn't mind green hair, feathery antennae, and a somewhat flat-featured Oriental look, she was easily the most beautiful thing he'd seen since Earth, especially since the Mikardandu evening-dress began at the midriff.

"Sir Felix, my confidential secretary, the Lady Zerdai." Kubanan lowered his voice in mock-confidence. "I *think* she's my own daughter, though naturally one can never know for sure."

"Then family feeling does exist among the Guardians?" said Borel.

"Yes, I fear me it does. A shameful weakness, but natheless a most pleasant one. Heigh-ho, at times, I envy the commoners. Why, Zerdai herself has somehow bribed the women in charge of the incubator to show her which is her own authentic egg."

Zerdai sparkled at them. "I was down there but today, and the maids tell me it's due to hatch in another fifteen days!"

"Ahem," said Borel. "Would it be good manners to ask who's papa? Excuse me if I pull a boner occasionally; I'm not entirely oriented yet."

Kubanan said: "No offense, sir. He was Sir Sardu, the predecessor of Sir Shurgez, was he not, Zerdai?"

"Yes," she agreed. "But our petty affairs must seem dull to a galaxy-traveller like you, Sir Felix. Tell us of the

Earth! I've long dreamed of going thither; I can fancy nought more glamorous than seeing the New York Stock Exchange, or the Moscow Art Theater, or the Shanghai night-clubs with my own eyes. It must be wonderful to ride in a power-vehicle! To talk to somebody.miles distant! And all those marvelous inventions and factories . . ."

Kubanan said dryly: "I sometimes think Lady Zerdai shows an unbecoming lack of pride in her Order, young though she be. Now about this lottery: will you see to have the certificates printed?"

"Certainly," said Borel. "So you do have a printing-press here?"

"Yes; from the Earthmen we got it. We'd have preferred a few Earthly weapons to smite our enemies; but no, all they'll let us have is this device, which bodes ill for our social order. Should the commoners learn reading, who knows what mad ideas this ill-starred machine may spread among them?"

Borel turned on the charm, thankful that supper consisted of some of the more palatable Krishnan dishes. On this planet you were liable to have something like a giant cockroach set before you as a treat. Afterwards all three lit cigars and talked while sipping a liqueur.

Kubanan continued: "Sir Felix, you're old enough in the ways of the world to know that a man's pretext is often other than his true reason. Your Earthmen tell me they hide their sciences from us because our culture is yet too immature—by which they mean our gladiatorial shows, our trials by combat, our warring national sovereignties, our social inequalities, and the like. Now, I say not that they're altogether wrong—I for one should be glad had they never introduced this accursed printing-press. But the question I'd ask you is: What's their real reason?"

Borel wrinkled his forehead in the effort of composing a suitable reply. Being an adventurer and no intellectual he'd never troubled his head much about such abstract questions. At last, he said:

"Perhaps they're afraid the Krishnans, with their war-like traditions, would learn to make space-ships and attack their neighboring planets."

"A fantastic idea," said Kubanan. " 'Tis not so long since there was a tremendous uproar over the question of whether the planets were inhabited. The churches had been assuring us that the planets were the very gods, and crucifying heretics who said otherwise. No wonder we hailed as gods the first beings from Earth and the other planets of your sun!"

Borel murmured a polite assent, privately thinking that the first expedition to this system ought, if they had any sense, to have been satisfied with being gods and not go disillusioning the Krishnans. That's what came of letting a bunch of sappy do-gooders . . .

Kubanan was going on: "Our problem is much more immediate. We're hemmed and beset by enemies. Across the Pichidé lies Gozashtand, whose ruler has been taking an unfriendly line of late; and Majbur City is a veritable hotbed of plots and stratagems. If a way could be found to get us—let's say—one gun, which our clever smiths could copy, there's nothing the Order would not do . . ."

So, thought Borel, that's why the old boy is so hospitable to a mere stranger. He said:

"I see your point, excellency. You know the risks, don't you?"

"The greater the risk, the greater the reward."

"True, but it would require most careful thought. I'll let you know when I've had time to think."

"I understand." Kubanan rose, and to Borel's surprise said: "I leave you now; Kuri will think I've forgotten her utterly. You'll stay the night, of course?"

"Why, I—thank you, your excellency. I'll have to send a note out to my man."

"Yes, yes, I'll send you a page. Meanwhile the Lady Zerdai shall keep you company, or if you've a mind to read there are ample books on the shelves. Take the second room on the left."

Borel murmured his thanks and the treasurer departed, his furred robe floating behind him. Then, having no interest whatever in Kubanan's library, he sat down near Zerdai.

Eyes aglow, Zerdai said: "Now that we need talk finance no more, tell me of the Earth. How live you? I mean, what's your system of personal relationships? Have you homes and families like the commoners, or all in common as we Guardians do?"

As Borel explained, the girl sighed. With a far-away look she said: "Could I but go thither! I can imagine nought more romantic than to be an Earthly housewife with a home and a man and children of my own! And a telephone!"

Borel reflected that some Earthly housewives sang a

different tune, but said gently: "Couldn't you resign from the Order?"

"In theory, yes—but 'tis hardly ever done. 'Twould be like stepping into another world, and what sort of welcome would the commoners give? Would they not resent what they'd call one's airs? And to have to face the scorn of all Guardians ... No, it would not do. Could one escape this world entire, as by journeying to Earth ..."

"Maybe that could be arranged too," said Borel cautiously. While he was willing to promise her anything to enlist her coöperation and then ditch her, he didn't want to get involved in more schemes at once than he could handle.

"Really?" she said, glowing at him. "There's nought I wouldn't do ..."

Borel thought, they all say there's nothing they wouldn't do if I'll only get them what they want. He said:

"I may need help on some of my projects here. Can I count on your assistance?"

"With all my heart!"

"Good. I'll see that you don't regret it. We'd make a wonderful team, don't you think? With your beauty and my experience there's nothing we couldn't get away with. Can't you see us cutting a swath through the galaxy?"

She leaned toward him, breathing hard. "You're wonderful!"

He smiled. "Not really. You are."

"No, you."

"No, you. You've got beauty, brains, nerve—Oh well, I'll have plenty of chance to tell you in the future. When I get this lottery organized."

"Oh." This seemed to bring her back to Krishna again. She glanced at the time-candle and put out her cigar, saying: "Great stars, I had no idea the hour was so late! I must go to bed, Sir Felix the Red. Will you escort me to my room?"

At breakfast Sir Kubanan said: "Thanks to the stars the Grand Council meets this forenoon. I'll bring up your lottery suggestion, and if they approve we can start work on it today. Why spend you not the morning laying your plans?"

"A splendid idea, excellency," said Borel, and went to work, after breakfast on the design of lottery tickets and advertising posters. Zerdai hung around, asking if she couldn't help, trying to cuddle up beside him and getting in the way of his pen arm, all the time looking at him with such open adoration that even he, normally as embarrassable as a rhinoceros, squirmed a little under her gaze.

However, he put up with it in a good cause, to wit: the cause of making a killing for Felix Étienne Borel.

By the middle of the day Kubanan was back jubilant. "They approved! At first Grand Master Juvain boggled a little, but I talked him round. He liked not letting one not of our Order so deep into our affairs, saying, how can there be a secret Order if all its secrets be known? But I bridled him. How goes the plan?"

Borel showed him the layouts. The treasurer said: "Wonderful! Wonderful! Carry on, my boy, and come to me for aught you need."

"I will. This afternoon I'll arrange for printing this stuff. Then we'll need a booth. How about setting it up at the lower end of that little street up to the gate of the citadel? And I'll have to train a couple of men as ticketsellers, and some more to guard the money."

"All shall be done. Harken, why move you not hither from your present lodgings? I have ample room, and 'twould save time as well as augment comfort, thus slaying two unhas with one bolt."

"Do come," sighed Zerdai.

"Okay. Where can I stable my aya and quarter my servant?"

Kubanan told him. The afternoon he spent making arrangements for printing. Since Mishé had but two printers, each with one little hand press, the job would not be finished for at least twenty days.

He reported this to Kubanan at supper, adding: "Will you give me a draft on the treasury of the Order for fifteen hundred karda to cover the initial costs?" (This was more than fifty percent over the prices the printers had quoted, but Kubanan assented without question.)

"And now," continued Borel, "let's take up the other matter. If Zerdai's your confidential secretary, I don't suppose you mind discussing it in front of her."

"Not at all. You've found a way to get around the technological blockade?"

"Well—yes and no. I can assure you it'll do no good for me to go to Novorecife and try to smuggle out a gun or plans for one. They have a machine that looks right through you, and they make you stand in front of it before letting you out."

"Have they no regard for privacy?"

"Not in this matter. Besides, even if one did succeed, they'd send an agent to bring one back dead or alive."

"Of those agents I've heard," said Kubanan with a slight shudder.

"Moreover I'm no engineer—a base-born trade—so I can't carry a set of plans in my head for your people to work from. Guns are too complicated for that."

"What then?"

"I think the only way is to have something they want so badly they'll ease up on the blockade in return for it."

"Yes, but what have we? There's little of ours that they covet. Even gold, they say, is much too heavy to haul billions of miles to Earth with profit, and almost everything we make, they can make more cheaply at home once they know how. I know; I've discussed it with the Viagens folk at Novorecife. Knight though I be, my office requires that I interest myself in such base commercial matters."

Borel drew on his cigar and remarked: "Earthmen are an inventive lot, and they'll continue thinking up new things for a long time to come."

Kubanan shuddered. "A horrid place must this Earth of yours be. No stability."

"So, if we had an invention far ahead of their latest stuff, they might want the secret badly enough to make a deal. See?"

"How can we? We're not inventive here. No gentleman would lower himself by tinkering with machines while the common people lack the wit."

Borel smiled. "Suppose *I* had such a secret?"

"That would be different. What is it?"

"It's an idea that was confided to me by a dying old man. Although the Earthmen had scorned him and said his device was against the laws of nature, it worked. I know because he showed me a model."

"But what *is* it?" cried Kubanan.

"It would not only be of vast value to the Earthmen, but also would make Mikardand preëminent among the nations of Krishna."

"Torture us not, Sir Felix!" pleaded Zerdai.

"It's a perpetual-motion machine."

Kubanan asked: "What's that?"

"A machine that runs forever, or at least until it wears out."

Kubanan frowned and twitched his antennae. "Not sure

am I that I understand you. We have water-wheels for operating grain-mills which run until they wear out."

"Not quite what I mean." Borel concentrated on putting a scientific concept into words, a hard thing to do because he neither knew nor cared much about such matters. "I mean, this machine will give out more power than is put into it."

"Wherein lies the advantage of that?"

"Why, Earthmen prize power above all things. Power runs their space-ships and motor-vehicles, their communications equipment and factories. Power lights their homes and milks their cows ... I forget, you don't know about cows. And where do they get their power? From coal, uranium, and things like that. Minerals. They get some from the sun and the tides, but not enough, and they worry about exhaustion of their minerals. Now, my device takes power from the force of gravity, which is the very fundamental quality of matter." He was striding up and down in his eagerness. "Sooner or later Krishna is bound to have a scientific revolution like that of Earth. Neither you nor the Viagens Interplanetarias can hold it off forever. And when—"

"I hope I live not to see it," said Kubanan.

"When it comes, don't you want Mikardand to lead the planet? Of course! No need to give up your social system. In fact, if we organize the thing right, it'll not only secure the rule of the Order in Mikardand, but extend the Order's influence over all Krishna!"

Kubanan was beginning to catch a little of Borel's fire. "How propose you to do that?"

"Ever heard of a corporation?"

"Let me think—is that not some vulgar scheme Earthmen use in trade and manufacture?"

"Yes, but there's more to it than that. There's no limit to what you can do with a corporation. The Viagens is a corporation, though all its stock is owned by governments ..." Borel plunged into corporation finance, not neglecting to say: "Of course, the promoter of a corporation gets fifty-one percent of the stock in consideration of his services."

"Who would the promoter be in our case?"

"I, naturally. We can form this corporation to finance the machine. The initial financing can come from the Order itself, and later the members can either hold—"

"Wait, wait. How can the members buy stock when they own no money of their own?"

"Unh. That's a tough one. I guess the treasury'll have to keep the stock; it can either draw profits from the lease of the machines, or sell the stock at an enormous profit—"

"Sir Felix," said Kubanan, "you make my head to spin. No more, lest my head split like a melon on the chopping-block. Enticing though your scheme be, there is one immovable obstacle."

"Yes?"

"The Grand Master and the other officers would never permit—you'll not take offense?—would never permit an outsider such as yourself to acquire such power over the Order. 'Twas all I could do to put over your lottery scheme, and this would be one thing too many, like a second nose on your face."

"All right, think it over," said Borel. "Now suppose you tell me about the Order of Qarar."

Kubanan obliged with an account of the heroic deeds of Qarar, the legendary founder of the Order who had slain assorted giants and monsters. As he talked, Borel reflected on his position. He doubted if the Qararuma would want to take in a being from another planet like himself, and even if they did, the club rules against private property would handicap his style.

He asked: "How do Mikardanders become members? By being—uh—hatched in the official incubator?"

"Not always. Each child from the incubator is tested at various times during its growth. If it fail any test, 'tis let out for adoption by some good commoner family. On the other hand, when membership falls low, we watch the children of commoners and any that show exceptional qualities are admitted to training as wards of the Order."

The treasurer went on to tell of the various grades of membership until he got sleepy and took his leave.

Later Borel asked Zerdai: "Love me?"

"You know I do, my lord!"

"Then I have a job for you."

"Aught you say, dearest master."

"I want one of those honorary memberships."

"But Felix, that's for notables like the King of Gozash-tand only! I know not what I could accomplish—"

"You make the suggestion to Kubanan, see? And keep needling him until he asks me. He trusts you."

"I will try, my dearest. And I hope Shurgez never returns."

While ordinarily Borel would have investigated this last

cryptic remark, at the moment his head was too full of schemes for self-aggrandizement. "Another thing. Who's the most skilled metal-worker in Mishé? I want somebody who can make a working model that really works."

"I'll find out for you, my knight."

Zerdai sent Borel to one Henjaré bad-Qavao the Brazer, a gnomish Mikardandu whom Borel first dazzled with his façade and then swore to secrecy with dreadful-sounding oaths of his own invention.

He then presented the craftsman with a rough plan for a wheel with a lot of rods with weights on their ends, pivoted to the circumference so that they had some freedom to swing in the plane of rotation of the wheel. There was also a trip arrangement so that as the wheel rotated, each rod as it approached the top was moved from a position leaning back against a stop on the rim to a straight-out radial position. Hence the thing looked as though at any time the weights on one side stood out farther from the center than those on the other, and therefore would over-balance the latter and cause the wheel to turn indefinitely.

Borel knew just enough about science to realize that the device would not work, though not enough to know why. On the other hand, since these gloops knew even less than he did, there should be no trouble in selling them the idea.

That night Kubanan said: "Sir Felix, a brilliant thought has struck me. Won't you accept an honorary membership in our proud Order? In truth, you'll find it a great advantage while you dwell in Mikardand, or even when you journey elsewhere."

Borel registered surprise. "Me? I'm most humbly grateful, excellency, but is an outsider like myself worthy of such an honor?" Meanwhile he thought: good old Zerdai! If I were the marrying kind ... For a moment he wavered in his determination to shake her when she'd served her turn.

"Nonsense, my lad, of course you're worthy. I'd have gone farther and proposed you for full membership, but the Council pointed out that the constitution allows that only to native-born Mikardanders of our own species. As 'tis, honorary membership will provide you with most of the privileges of membership and few of the obligations."

"I'm overcome with happiness."

"Of course there's the little matter of the initiation."

"What?" Borel controlled his face.

"Yes; waive it they would not, since no king are you. It

amounts to little; much ceremony and a night's vigil. I'll coach you in the ritual. And you must obtain ceremonial robes; I'll make you a list."

Borel wished he'd hiked the printing charges on the lottery material by another fifty percent.

The initiation proved not only expensive, but an inter-planetary bore as well. Brothers in fantastic robes and weird masks stood about muttering a mystic chant at intervals. Borel stood in front of the Grand Master of the Order, a tall Krishnan with a lined face that might have been carved from wood for all the expression it bore. Borel responded to interminable questions: since the language was an archaic dialect of Gozashtandou, he did not really know what he was saying half the time. He was lectured on the Order's glorious past, mighty present, and boundless future, and on his duties to protect and defend his interests. He called down all sorts of elaborate astrological misfortunes on his head should he violate his oaths.

"Now," said the grand master, "art thou ready for the vigil. Therefore I command thee: strip to thy underwear!"

Wondering what he was getting into now, Borel did so.

"Come with me," said Grand Master Sir Juvain.

They led him down stairs and through passages that got progressively narrower, darker, and less pleasant. A couple of the hooded brethren carried lanterns, which soon became necessary in order to see the way. We must be far below the ground-level of the citadel, thought Borel, stumbling along in his socks and feeling most clammy and uncomfortable.

When they seemed to have descended into the very bowels of the planet they halted. The grand master said:

"Here shalt thou remain the night, O aspirant. Danger will come upon thee, and beware how thou meetest it."

One of the brothers was measuring a long candle. He cut it off at a certain length and fixed it upright to a small shelf in the rough side of the tunnel. Another brother handed Borel a hunting-spear with a long, broad head.

Then they left him.

So far he had carried off his act by assuring himself that all this was a lot of bluff and hokum. Nothing serious could be intended. As the brothers' footfalls died away, however, he was no longer so sure. The damned candle seemed to illuminate for a distance of only about a metre in all directions. Fore and aft the tunnel receded into utter blackness.

His hair rose as something rustled. As he whipped the spear into position it scuttled away; some rat-like creature no doubt. Borel started pacing. If that damned dope Abreu had only let him bring his watch! Then he'd at least have a notion of the passage of time. It seemed he'd been pacing for hours, though that was probably an illusion.

Borel became aware of an odd irregularity in the floor beneath his stockinged feet, and he bent down and explored it with his fingers. Yes, a pair of parallel grooves, two or three centimeters deep, ran lengthwise along the tunnel. He followed them a few steps each way, but stopped when he could no longer see what he was doing. Why should there be two parallel grooves like a track along the floor?

He paced until his legs ached from weariness, then tried sitting on the floor with his back against the wall. When he soon found his eyelids drooping, he scrambled up lest his initiators return to find him asleep. The candle burned slowly down, its flame standing perfectly still for minutes at a stretch and then wavering slightly as some tiny air-current brushed it. Still silence and darkness.

The candle would soon be burned down to nothing. What then? Would they expect him to stand here in complete darkness?

A sound made him jump violently. He could not tell what sort of sound it was; merely a faint noise from down the tunnel. There it came again.

Then his hair really rose at a low throaty vocal noise, the kind one hears in the carnivore-cage of the zoo before feeding-time. A sort of grunt, such as a big cat makes in tuning up for a real roar. It came again, louder.

The dying candle-flame showed to Borel's horrified gaze something moving fast towards him in the tunnel. With a frightful roar a great yeki rushed into the dim light with gleaming eyes and bared fangs.

For perhaps a second (though it seemed an hour) Felix Borel stood helplessly holding his spear poised, his mouth hanging open. In that second, however, his mind suddenly worked with the speed of a tripped mousetrap. Something odd about the yeki's motion, together with the fact of the grooves in the floor, gave him the answer: the animal was a stuffed one pushed towards him on wheels.

Borel bent and laid his spear diagonally across the floor of the tunnel, and stepped back. When the contraption struck the spear it slewed sideways with a bang, rattle, and thump and stopped, its nose against the wall.

Borel recovered his spear and examined the derailed yeki at close range. It proved a pretty battered-looking piece of taxidermy, the head and neck criss-crossed with seams where the hide had been slashed open and sewn up again. Evidently it had been used for initiations for a long time, and some of the aspirants had speared it. Others had doubtless turned tail and run, thus flunking the test.

Footsteps sounded in the corridor and lanterns bobbed closer just as the candle on the shelf guttered out. The grand master and the masked brethren swarmed around Borel, including one with a horn on which he had made the yeki-noises. They slapped him on the back and told him how brave he was, then led him back up many flights to the main hall, where he was allowed to don his clothes again. The grand master hung a jewelled dragon insignia around his neck and welcomed him with a florid speech in archaic style:

"O Felix, be thou hereby accepted into this most noble, most ancient, most honorable, most secret, most puissant, most righteous, most chivalrous, and most fraternal Order, and upon thee be bestowed all the rights, privileges, rank, standing, immunities, duties, liabilities, obligations, and attributes of a knight of this most noble, most ancient, most honorable . . ."

The long Krishnan night was two-thirds gone when the hand-shaking and drinking were over. Borel and Kubanan, arms about each other's necks, wove their way drunkenly to the latter's apartment while Borel sang what he could remember of an Earthly song about a king of England and a queen of Spain, until Kubanan shushed him, saying:

"Know you not that poetry's forbidden in Mikardand?"

"I didn't know. Why?"

"The Order decided it was bad for our—*hic*—martial spirit. B'sides, poets tell too damned many lies. What's the nex' stanza?"

Next morning Sir Felix, as he tried to remember to think of himself, began to press for consideration of his perpetual-motion scheme. He obtained an interview with Grand Master Juvain in the afternoon and put his proposal. Sir Juvain seemed puzzled by the whole thing and Borel had to call in Kubanan to help him explain.

Juvain finally said: "Very well, Brother Felix, tell me when your preparations are ready and I'll call a general meeting of the members in residence to pass upon your proposal."

Then, since the working model was not yet ready, Borel had nothing to do for a couple of days except breathe down the neck of Henjaré the Brazer and superintend the building of the lottery ticket-booth. The printing-job was nowhere near done.

Therefore he whistled up Yerevats to help him pass the time by practicing driving the buggy. After a couple of hours he could fairly well manage the difficult art of backing and filling to turn around in a restricted space.

"Have the carriage ready right after lunch," he ordered.

"Master go ride?"

"Yes. I shan't need you though; I'm taking it myself."

"Unh. No good. Master get in trouble."

"That's my lookout."

"Bet master take girl out. Bad business."

"Mind your own business!" shouted Borel, and made a pass at Yerevats, who ducked and scuttled out. Now, thought Borel, Yerevats will sulk and I'll have to spend a day cajoling him back into a good humor or I'll get no decent service. Damn it, why didn't they have mechanical servants with no feelings that their masters had to take into account? Somebody had tried to make one on Earth, but the thing had run amok and mistaken its master for a cord of firewood . . .

The afternoon saw him trotting down the main avenue of Mishé with Zerdai by his side looking at him worshipfully. He could not get quite used to the curious sound made by the six hooves of the aya when it trotted.

He asked: "Who has the right of way if somebody comes in from the side?"

"Why, you do, Felix! You're a member of the Order, even if not a regular Guardian!"

"Oh." Borel, though he had about as little public spirit as a man can have, had been exposed to the democratic institutions of Earth long enough so as to find these class distinctions distasteful. "In other words, because I'm now an honorary knight, I can tear through the town at full gallop hollering '*byant-hao!*' and if anybody gets run over that's too bad?"

"Naturally. What think you? But I forget you're from another world. 'Tis one of your fascinations that beneath your hard adventuresome exterior you're more gentle and considerate than the men of this land."

Borel hid a smile. He'd been called a lot of things before, including thief, swindler, and slimy double-crossing heel, but never gentle and considerate. Maybe that was an example of the relativity the long-haired scientists talked about.

"Where would you like me to drive you?" he asked.

"To Earth!" she said, putting her head on his shoulder. For a moment he was almost tempted to renege on his plan to leave her behind. Then the resolute selfishness that was the adventurer's leading trait came to his rescue, and he reminded himself that on a fast getaway, the less baggage the better. Love 'em and leave 'em. Anyway, wouldn't she be happier if they parted before she learned he was no do-gooder after all?

"Let's to the tournament ground outside the North Gate. Today's the battle betwixt Sir Volhaj and Sir Shusp," she said.

"What's this? I hadn't heard of it."

"Sir Shusp forced a challenge on Sir Volhaj; some quarrel over the love of a lady. Shusp has already slain three knights in affrays of this kind."

Borel said: "If you Guardians are supposed to have everything in common like the Communists we used to have on Earth, I don't see what call a knight has to get jealous. Couldn't they both court her at once?"

"That's not the custom. A maid should dismiss the one before taking another; to do otherwise were in bad taste."

They reached the North Gate and ambled out into the country. Borel asked: "Where does this road go?"

"Know you not? To Koloft and Novorecife."

Beyond the last houses, where the farmed fields began, the tournament grounds lay to the right of the road. It reminded Borel of a North American high-school football field: same small wooden grandstands, and tents at the ends where the goal-posts should be. In the middle of one stand a section had been built out into a box in which sat the high officers of the Order. Hawkers circulated through the crowd, one crying:

"Flowers! Flowers! Buy a flower with the color of your favorite knight! Red for Volhaj, white for Shusp. Flowers!"

The stands were already full of people who, from the predominant color of the flowers in their hats, seemed to favor Shusp. Borel ignored Zerdai's suggestion that he pitch some commoner out of his seat and claim it for himself, and led her to where the late arrivals clustered standing at one end of the field. He was a little annoyed with himself for not having come in time to lay a few bets. This should be much more exciting than the ponies on Earth, and by shaving the odds and betting both ways he might put himself in the enviable position of making a profit on these saps no matter who won.

As they took their places a trumpet blew. Nearby, Borel saw a man in Moorish-looking armor, wearing a spiked helmet with a nose-guard and a little skirt of chain-mail; he was sitting on a big tough-looking aya, also wearing bits of armor here and there. This Qararu now left his tent to trot down to the middle of the field. From the red touches about his saddle and equipment Borel judged him to be Sir Volhaj. Volhaj as the challenged party had his sympathy, in line with his own distaste for violence. Why couldn't the other gloop be a good fellow about his girl friend? Borel had done that sort of thing and found nobody the worse for it.

From the other end of the field came another rider, similarly equipped but decorated in white. The two met at the center of the field, wheeled to face the grand master, and walked their mounts forward until they were as close as they could get to the booth. The grand master made a speech which Borel could not hear, and then the knights wheeled away and trotted back to their respective ends of the field. At the near end Sir Volhaj's squires, or seconds, or whatever they were, handed him up a lance and a smallish round shield.

The trumpet blew again and the antagonists galloped towards each other. Borel winced as they met with a crash in the middle of the field. When Borel opened his eyes again, he saw that the red knight had been knocked out of the saddle and was rolling over and over on the moss. His aya continued on without him, while the white knight slowed gradually as he approached Borel's end of the field, then turned and headed back.

Volhaj had meanwhile gotten up with a visible effort in his weight of iron and clanked over to where his lance lay. He picked it up, and as Shusp bore down on him he planted the butt-end in the ground and lowered the point to the level of the charging aya's chest, where the creature's light armor did not protect it. Borel could not see the spear go in, but he judged that it had when the beast reared, screamed, threw its rider, and collapsed kicking. Borel, who felt strongly about cruelty to animals, thought indignantly that there ought to be an interplanetary S. P. C. A. to stop this sort of thing.

At this point the crowd began to jostle and push with cries of excitement, so Borel had to take his eyes off the fight long enough to clear a space with his elbows for Zerdai. When he looked back again the knights were at it on foot, making a tremendous din, Shusp with a huge two-handed sword, Volhaj with his buckler and a sword of more normal size.

They circled around one another, slashing, thrusting, and parrying, and worked their way slowly down to Borel's end of the field, till he could see the dents in their armor and the trickle of blood running down the chin of Sir Volhaj. By now, both were so winded that the fight was going as slowly as an honest wrestling-match, with both making a few swipes and then stopping to pant and glare at each other for a while.

Then in the midst of an exchange of strokes, Sir Volhaj's sword flew up, turning over and over until it came down at Shusp's feet. Sir Shusp instantly put a foot on it and forced Sir Volhaj back with a swing of his crowbar-like blade. Then he picked up the dropped sword and threw it as far away as he could.

Borel asked: "Hey, is he allowed to do that?"

"I know not," said Zerdai. "Though there be few rules, mayhap that's against them."

Shusp now advanced rapidly on Volhaj, who was reduced to a shield battered all out of shape and a dagger. The latter gave ground, parrying the swipes as best he could.

"Why doesn't the fool cut and run?" asked Borel.

Zerdai stared at him. "Know you not that for a knight of the Order the penalty for cowardice is flaying alive?"

At the rate Volhaj was backing towards them he'd soon be treading on the toes of the spectators, who in fact began to spread out nervously. Volhaj was staggering, disheartening Borel, who hated to see his favorite nearing his rope's end.

On a sudden impulse, Borel drew his own sword and called: "Hey, Volhaj, don't look now but here's something for you!" With that he threw the sword as if it had been a javelin, so that the point stuck into the ground alongside of Volhaj. The latter dropped his dagger, snatched up the sword, and tore into Shusp with renewed vigor.

Then Shusp went down with a clang. Volhaj, standing over him, found a gap in his armor around the throat, put the point there, and pushed down on the hilt with both hands ... When Borel opened his eyes again, Shusp's legs were giving their last twitch. Cheers and the paying of bets.

Volhaj came back to where Borel stood and said: "Sir Felix the Red, I perceive you succored me but now."

"How d'you know that?"

"By your empty scabbard, friend. Here, take your sword with my thanks. I doubt the referee will hold your deed a foul, since the chief complainant will no longer be present to press his case. Call on me for help any time." He shook hands warmly and walked wearily off to his wigwam.

" 'Twas a brave deed, Felix," said Zerdai, squeezing his arm as they walked back to the buggy through the departing crowd.

"I don't see that it was anything special," said Borel truthfully.

"Why, had Sir Shusp won, he'd have challenged you!"

"Gluk!" said Borel. He hadn't thought of that.

"What is it, my dearest?"

"Something caught in my throat. Let's get back to dinner ahead of the crowd, huh? Giddap, Galahad!"

However, Zerdai retired after dinner, saying she would not be back for supper; the excitement had given her a headache.

Kubanan said: " 'Tis a rare thing, for she's been in better spirits since your arrival than was her wont since Sir Shurgez departed."

"You mean she was grieving for a boy-friend until I came along and cheered her up?" Borel thought, Kubanan's a nice old wump; too bad he'll have to be the fall guy for the project. But business is business.

"Yes. Ah, Felix, it's sad you're of another species, so that she'll never lay you an egg! For the Order can use offspring inheriting your qualities. Even I, sentimental old fool that I am, like to think of you as a son-in-law and Zerdai's eggs as my own grandchildren, as though I were some simple commoner with a family."

Borel asked: "What's this about Shurgez? What happened to him?"

"The grand master ordered him on a quest."

"What quest?"

"To fetch the beard of the King of Balhib."

"And what does the Order want with this king's beard? Are you going into the upholstery business?"

Kubanan laughed. "Of course not. The King of Balhib has treated the Order with scorn and contumely of late, and we thought to teach him a lesson."

"And why was Shurgez sent?"

"Because of his foul murder of Brother Sir Zamrán."

"Why did he murder Zamrán?"

"Surely you know the tale—but I forget, you're still new here. Sir Zamrán was he who slew Shurgez's lady."

"I thought Zerdai was Shurgez's girl."

"She was, but afterward. Let me begin at the beginning. Time was when Sir Zamrán and the Lady Fevzi were lovers, all right and decorous in accord with the customs of the Order. Then for some reason Lady Fevzi cast off Zamrán, as she had every right to do, and took Sir Shurgez in his stead. This made Sir Zamrán wroth, and instead of taking his defeat philosophically like a true knight, what does he do but come up behind Lady Fevzi at the ball celebrating the conjunction of the planets Vishnu and Ganesha, and smite off her head just as she was presenting a home-made pie to the grand master!"

"Wow!" said Borel with an honest shudder.

"True, 'twas no knightly deed, especially in front of the grand master, not to mention the difficulty of cleansing the carpet. If he had to slay her he should at least have taken her outside. The grand master, most annoyed, would have rebuked Zamrán severely for his discourtesy, but he's hardly past the preamble when Sir Shurgez comes in to ask after his sweetling, sees the scene, and leaps upon Zamrán with his dagger before any can stay him. So then we have two spots on the rug to clean and the grand master in a fair fury. The upshot was that he ordered Shurgez on this quest to teach him to issue his challenges in due form and not go thrusting knives among the ribs of any who incur his displeasure. No doubt he half hoped that Shurgez would be slain in the doing, for the King of Balhib is no effeminate."

Borel was sure now that nothing would ever induce him to settle permanently among such violent people. "When did Shurgez get time to—uh—be friends with Zerdai?"

"Why, he couldn't leave before the astrological indications were favorable, to wit for twenty-one days, and during that time he enjoyed my secretary's favor. Far places have ever attracted her, and I think she'd have gone with him if he'd have had her."

"What's the word about Shurgez now?"

"The simplest word of all, to wit: no word. Should he return, my spies will tell me of his approach before he arrives."

Borel became aware that the clicking sound that had puzzled him was the chatter of his own teeth. He resolved to ride herd on Henjaré the next day to rush the model through to completion.

"One more question," he said. "Whatever became of Lady Fevzi's pie?" Kubanan could not tell him that, however.

The model was in fact well enough along so that Borel asked the grand master for the perpetual-motion meeting the following day. Although he expected an evening meeting, with all the knights full of dinner and feeling friendly, it turned out that the only time available on the grand master's schedule was in the morning.

"Of course, Brother Felix," said Sir Juvain, "if you prefer to put it off a few days . . ."

"No, most mighty potentate," said Borel, thinking of the Shurgez menace. "The sooner the better for you, me, and the Order."

Thus it happened that the next morning, after breakfast, Felix Borel found himself on the platform on the main auditorium of the citadel, facing several thousand knights of the Order of Qarar. Beside him on a small table stood his gleaming new brass model of the perpetual-motion wheel. A feature of the wheel not obvious to the audience was a little pulley on the shaft, around which was wound a fine but strong thread made of hairs from the tails of shomals, which led from the wheel off into the wings where Zerdai stood hidden from view. It had taken all Borel's blandishments to get her to play this role.

He launched into his speech: " . . . what is the purpose and function of our noble Order? Power! And what is the basis of power? First, our own strong right arms; second, the wealth of the Order, which in turn is derived from the wealth of the commons. So anything that enriches the commons increases our power, does it not? Let me give you an example. There's a railroad, I hear, from Majbur to Jazmurian along the coast, worked by bishtars pulling little strings of cars. Now, mount one of my wheels on a car and connect it by belt or chain to the wheels. Start the wheel revolving, and what happens? The car with its wheel will pull far more cars than a bishtar, and likewise it never grows old and dies as an animal does, never runs amok and smashes property, and when not in use stands quietly in its shed without needing to be fed. We could build a railroad from Mishé to Majbur and another from Mishé to Jazmurian, and carry goods faster between the coastal cities than it is now carried by the direct route.

There's a source of infinite wealth, of which the Order would of course secure its due share.

"Then there is the matter of weapons. I cannot go into details because many of these are confidential, but I have positive assurance that there are those who would trade the mighty weapons of the Interplanetary Council for the secret of this little wheel. You know what that would mean. Think it over.

"Now I will show you how it actually works. This model you see is not a true working wheel, but a mere toy, an imitation to give you an idea of the finished wheel, which would be much larger. This little wheel will not give enough power to be very useful. Why? Friction. The mysterious sciences of my native planet found centuries ago that friction is proportionately larger in small machines than in large ones. Therefore the fact that this little wheel won't give useful power is proof that a larger one would. However, the little wheel still gives enough power to run itself without outside help.

"Are you watching, brothers? Observe: I release the brake that prevents the wheel from turning. Hold your breaths, sirs—ah, it moves! It turns! The secret of the ages comes to life before you!"

He had signalled Zerdai, who had begun to pull on the thread, reeling in one end of it while paying out the other. The wheel turned slowly, the little brass legs going click-click-click as they reached the trip at the top.

"Behold!" yelled Borel. "It works! The Order is all-rich and all-powerful!"

After letting the wheel spin for a minute or so, Borel resumed: "Brothers, what must we do to realize on this wonderful invention? One, we need funds to build a number of large wheels to try out various applications: to power ships and rail-cars, to run grist-mills, and to turn the shafts of machines in workshops. No machine is ever perfect when first completed; there are always details to be improved. Second, we need an organization to exploit the wheel; to make treaties with other states to lease wheels from us and to give us the exclusive right to exploit wheels within their borders; and to negotiate with the powers that be to exchange the secret of the wheel for—I need go no further!

"On Earth we have a type of organization called a corporation for such purposes . . ." And he launched into the account he had previously given Kubanan and Juvain.

"Now," he said, "what do we need for this corporation?

The officers of the Order and I have agreed that to start, the treasury shall advance the sum of 245,000 karda, for which the Order shall receive forty-nine percent of the stock of the company. The remaining fifty-one percent will naturally remain with the promoter and director of the company; that's the arrangement we've found most successful on Earth. However, before such a large sum can be invested in this great enterprise, we must in accordance with the constitution let you vote on the question. First I had better stop our little wheel here, lest the noise distract you."

The clicking stopped as Borel put his hand against the wheel. Zerdai broke the thread with a quick jerk, gathered it all in, and slipped away from her hiding-place.

Borel continued: "I therefore turn the meeting back to our friend, guide, counsellor, and leader, Grand Master Sir Juvain."

The grand master put the vote, and the appropriation passed by a large majority. As the knights cheered, Kubanan led a line of pages staggering under bags of coins to the stage, where the bags were ranged in a row on the boards.

Borel, when he could get silence again, said: "I thank you one and all. If any would care to examine my little wheel, they shall see for themselves that no trickery is involved."

The *Garma Qararuma* climbed up *en masse* to congratulate Borel. The adventurer, trying not to seem to gloat over the money, was telling himself that once he got away with this bit of swag he'd sell it for World Federation dollars, go back to Earth, invest his fortune conservatively, and never have to worry about money again. Of course he'd promised himself the same thing on several previous occasions, but somehow the money always seemed to dissipate before he got around to investing it.

Sir Volhaj was pushing through the crowd, saying: "Sir Felix, may I speak to you aside?"

"Sure. What is it?"

"How feel you?"

"Fine. Never better."

"That's good, for Shurgez has returned to Mishé with his mission accomplished."

"What's that?" said Kubanan. "Shurgez back, and my spies haven't told me?"

"Right, my lord."

"Oh-oh," said the treasurer. "If he challenges you, Sir

Felix, you will, as a knight, have to give him instant satisfaction. What arms own you besides that sword?"

"*Gluk,*" said Borel. "N-none. Doesn't the challenged party have a choice of weapons?" he asked with some vague idea of specifying boxing-gloves.

"According to the rules of the Order," said Volhaj, "each fighter may use what weapons he pleases. Shurgez will indubitably employ the full panoply: lance, sword, and a mace or ax in reserve, and will enter the lists in full armor. As for you—well, since you and I are much of a size, feel free to borrow aught that you need."

Before Borel could say anything more, a murmur and a head-turning apprised him of the approach of some interest. As the crowd parted, a squat, immensely muscular, and very Mongoloid-looking knight came forward.

"Are you he whom they call Sir Felix the Red?" asked the newcomer.

"Y-yes," said Borel, icicles of fear running through his viscera.

"I am Sir Shurgez. It has been revealed to me that in my absence you've taken the Lady Zerdai as your companion. Therefore I name you a vile traitor, scurvy knave, villainous rascal, base mechanic, and foul foreigner, and shall be at the tournament-grounds immediately after lunch to prove my assertions upon your diseased and ugly body. Here, you thing of no account!"

And Sir Shurgez, who had been peeling off his glove, threw it lightly in Borel's face.

"I'll fight you!" shouted Borel in a sudden surge of temper. "*Baghan! Zeft!*"

He added a few more Gozashtandou obscenities and threw the glove back at Shurgez, who caught it, laughed shortly, and turned his back.

"That's that," said Kubanan as Shurgez marched off. "Sure am I that so bold and experienced a knight as yourself will make mincemeat of yon braggart. Shall I have my pages convey the gold to your chamber while we lunch?"

Borel felt like saying: "I don't want any lunch," but judged it impolitic. His wits, after the first moment of terror-stricken paralysis, had begun to work again. First he felt sorry for himself. What had he done to deserve this? Why had he joined this crummy club, where instead of swindling each other like gentlemen the members settled differences by the cruel and barbarous methods of physical combat? All he'd done was to keep Zerdai happy while this blug was away . . .

Then he pulled himself together and tried to think his way out of the predicament. Should he simply refuse to fight? That meant skinning alive. Could he sprain an ankle? Maybe, but with all these people standing around . . . Why hadn't he told that well-meaning sap Volhaj that he was sick unto death?

And now how could he get away with the gold? It was probably too heavy for the buggy; he'd need a big two-aya carriage, which couldn't be obtained in a matter of minutes. How could he make his getaway at all before the fight? With his dear damned friends clustering round . . .

They were filling him with good advice: "I knew a man who'd begin a charge with lance level, then whirl it around his head as 'twere a club . . ." "When Sir Vardao slew that wight from Gozashtand, he dropped his lance altogether and snatched his mace . . ." "If you can get him around the neck with one arm, go for his crotch with your dagger . . ."

What he really wanted was advice on how to sneak out of the acropolis and make tracks for Novorecife with a third of the Order's treasury. When he had gulped the last tasteless morsel, he said:

"Good sirs, please excuse me. I have things to say to those near to me."

Zerdai was crying on her bed. He picked her up and kissed her. She responded avidly; this was an Earthly custom on which the Krishnans had eagerly seized.

"Come," he said, "it's not that bad."

She clung to him frantically. "But I love only you! I couldn't live without you! And I've been counting so on going with you to far planets . . ."

Borel's vestigial conscience stirred, and in a rare burst of frankness he said: "Look, Zerdai, it'll be small loss no matter how the fight comes out. I'm not the shining hero you think I am; in fact some people consider me an unmitigated heel."

"No! No! You're kind and good . . ."

" . . . and even if I get through this alive I may have to run for it without you."

"I'll die! I could never companion with that brute Shurgez again . . ."

Borel thought of giving her some of the gold, since he couldn't hope to get it all away himself. But then with the Guardians' communistic principles she couldn't keep it, and the Order would seize all he left in any case. Finally he unpinned several of his more glittery decorations and handed them to her, saying:

"At least you'll have these to remember me by." That seemed to break her down completely.

He found Yerevats in his own room and said: "If the fight doesn't go my way, take as much of this gold as you can carry, and the buggy, and get out of town fast."

"Oh, wonderful master must win fight!"

"That's as the stars decide. Hope for the best but expect the worse."

"But master, how shall pull buggy?"

"Keep the aya too. Volhaj is lending me his oversized one for the scrap. Tell you what: when we go out to the field, bring one of those bags inside your clothes."

An hour later Yerevats buckled the last strap of Borel's borrowed harness. The suit was a composite, chain-mail over the joints and plate-armor elsewhere. Borel found that it hampered him less than he expected, considering how heavy it had seemed when he hefted before putting it on.

He stepped out of the tent at his end of the field, where Volhaj was holding the big aya, which turned and looked at him suspiciously from under its horns. At the far end Shurgez already sat his mount. Borel, though outwardly calm, was reviling himself for not having thought of this and that: he should have hinted that *his* weapon would be a gun; he should have bought a bishtar and sat high up on its elephantine back, out of reach of Shurgez, while he potted his enemy with his crossbow . . .

Yerevats, bustling about the animal's saddle, secured the bag he had brought with him. Although he tried to do so secretly, the jingle of coin attracted the attention of Volhaj who asked:

"A bag of gold on your saddle? Why do you that, friend?"

"Luck," said Borel, feeling for the stirrup. His first effort to swing his leg over his mount failed because of the extra weight he was carrying, and they had to give him a boost. Yerevats handed him up his spiked helmet, which he carefully wiggled down on to his head. At once the outside noises acquired a muffled quality as the sound was filtered through the steel and the padding. Borel buckled his chin-strap.

A horn blew. As he had seen the other knights do the

day of the previous battle, Borel kicked the animal into motion and rode slowly down the field towards his opponent, who advanced to meet him. Thank the Lord he knew how to ride an Earthly horse! This was not much different save that the fact that the saddle was directly over the aya's intermediate pair of legs caused its rider to be jarred unpleasantly in the trot.

Borel could hardly recognize Shurgez behind the nasal of his helmet, and he supposed that his own features were equally hidden. Without a word they wheeled towards the side of the field where the grand master sat in his booth. They walked their animals over to the stand and listened side by side while Sir Juvain droned the rules of the contest at them. Borel thought it an awful lot of words to say that, for all practical purposes, anything went.

Beside the grand master sat Kubanan, stony-faced except at the last, when he tipped Borel a wink. Borel also caught a glimpse of Zerdai in the stands; catching his eye, she waved frantically.

The grand master finished and made motions with his baton. The fighters wheeled away from each other and trotted back to their respective tents, where Volhaj handed Borel his lance and buckler, saying: "Hold your shaft level; watch his . . ." Borel, preoccupied, heard none of it.

"Get you ready," said Volhaj. The trumpet blew.

Borel, almost bursting with excitement, said: "Goodbye, and thanks."

The hooves of Shurgez's mount were already drumming on the moss before Borel collected his wits enough to put his own beast into motion. For a long time, it seemed, he rode towards a little figure on aya-back that got no nearer. Then all at once the aya and its rider expanded to life-size and Borel's foe was upon him.

Since Shurgez had started sooner and ridden harder, they met short of the mid-point of the field. As his enemy bore down, Borel rose in his stirrups and threw his lance at Shurgez, then instantly hauled on the reins braided into the aya's mustache to guide it to the right.

Shurgez ducked as the lance hurtled toward him, so that the point of his own lance wavered and missed Borel by a meter. Borel heard the thrown spear hit sideways with a clank against Shurgez's armor. Then he was past and headed for Shurgez's tent at the far end. He leaned forward and spurred his aya mercilessly.

Just before he reached the end of the field he jerked a look back. Shurgez was still reining in to turn his mount.

Borel switched his attention back to where he was going and aimed for a gap on one side of Shurgez's tent. The people around the tent stood staring until the last minute, then frantically dove out of the way as the aya thundered through. Yells rose behind.

Borel guided his beast over to the main road towards Novorecife, secured the reins to the projection on the front of the saddle, and began shedding impedimenta. Off went the pretty damascened helmet, to fall with a clank to the roadway. Away went sword and battle-ax. After some fumbling he got rid of the brassets on his forearms and their attached gauntlets, and then the cuirass with its little chain sleeves. The iron pants would have to await a better opportunity.

The aya kept on at a dead run until Mishé dwindled in the distance. When the beast began to puff alarmingly, Borel let it slow to a walk for a while. However, when he looked back he thought he saw little dots on the road that might be pursuers, and spurred his mount to a gallop once more. When the dots disappeared he slowed again. Gallop—trot—walk—trot—gallop—that was how you covered long distances on a horse, so it should work on this six-legged equivalent. Oh, for a nice shiny Packard! After this he'd confine his efforts to Earth, where at least you knew the score.

He looked scornfully down at the bag of gold clinking faintly at the side of his saddle. One bag was all he had dared to take for fear of slowing his mount. It was not a bad haul for small-time stuff, and would let him live and travel long enough to case his next set of suckers. Still, it was nothing compared to what he'd have made if the damned Shurgez hadn't popped up so inopportunely. If, now, he'd been able to get away with the proceeds both of the stock sale and of the lottery . . .

Next morning found Borel still on the aya's back, plodding over the causeway through the Koloft Swamps. Flying things buzzed and bit; bubbles of stinking gas rose through the black water and burst. Now and then some sluggish swamp-dwelling creature roiled the surface or grunted a mating-call. A shower had soaked Borel during the night, and in this dank atmosphere his clothes seemed never to dry.

With yelping cries, the tailed men of Koloft broke from the bushes and ran towards him: Yerevats's wild brethren with stone-bladed knives and spears, hairy, naked, and fearful-looking. Borel spurred the aya into a shambling trot. The tailed men scrambled to the causeway just too late to seize him; a thrown spear went past his head with a swish.

Borel threw away his kindness-to-animals principle and dug spurs into the aya's flanks. The things raced after him; by squirming around he could see that they were actually gaining on him. Another spear came whistling along. Borel flinched, and the spearhead struck the cantle of his saddle and broke, leaving a sliver of obsidian sticking into the saddle as the shaft clattered to the causeway. The next one, he thought gloomily, would be a hit.

Then inspiration seized him. If he could get his money-bag open and throw a handful of gold to the roadway, these savages might stop to scramble for it. His fingers tore at Yerevats's lashings.

And then the twenty-kilo weight of the gold snatched the whole bag from his grasp. Clank! Gold pieces spilled out of the open mouth of the sack and rolled in little circles on the causeway. The tailed men whooped and pounced on them, abandoning their chase. While Borel was glad not to have to dodge any more spears, he did think the price a little steep. However, to go back to dispute possession of the money now would be merely a messy form of suicide, so he rode wearily on.

He reeled into Novorecife about noon, and was no sooner inside the wall than a man in the uniform of Abreu's security force said: "Is the senhor Felix Borel?"

"Huh?" He had been thinking in Gozashtandou so long that in his exhausted state the Brazilo-Portuguese of the spaceways at first was entirely meaningless to him.

"I said, is the senhor Felix Borel?"

"Yes. Sir Felix Borel to be exact. What—"

"I don't care what the senhor calls himself; he's under arrest."

"What for?"

"Violation of Regulation 368. *Vamos, por favor!*"

Borel demanded a lawyer at the preliminary hearing, and since he could not pay for one, Judge Keshavachandra appointed Manuel Sandak. Abreu presented his case.

Borel asked: "Senhor Abreu, how the devil did you find out about this little project of mine so quickly?"

The judge said: "Address your remarks to the court, please. The Security Office has its methods, naturally. Have you anything pertinent to say?"

Borel whispered to Sandak, who rose and said: "It is

the contention of the defense that the case presented by the Security Office is *prima facie* invalid, because the device in question, to wit: a wheel allegedly embodying the principle of perpetual motion, is inherently inoperative, being in violation of the well-known law of conservation of energy. Regulation 368 specifically states that it's forbidden to communicate a device 'representing an improvement upon the science and technics already existing upon this planet.' But since this gadget wouldn't work by any stretch of the imagination it's no improvement on anything."

"You mean," sputtered Abreu, "that it was all a fake, a swindle?"

"Sure," said Borel, laughing heartily at the security officer's expression.

Abreu said: "My latest information says that you actually demonstrated the device the day before yesterday in the auditorium of the Order of Qarar at Mishé. What have you to say to that?"

"That was a fake too," said Borel, and told of the thread pulled by Zerdai in the wings.

"Just how is this gadget supposed to work?" asked the judge. Borel explained. Keshavachandra exclaimed: "Good Lord, that form of perpetual-motion device goes back to the European Middle Ages! I remember a case involving it when I was a patent lawyer in India." He turned to Abreu, saying: "Does that description check with your information?"

"Yes, your Excellency." He turned on Borel. "I knew you were a crook, but I never expected you to brag of the

"No personalities," snapped Judge Keshavachandra. fact as part of your defense against a legal charge!"

"Bureaucrat!" sneered Borel.

"I'm afraid I can't bind him over, Senhor Cristôvão."

"How about a charge of swindling?" said Abreu hopefully.

Sandak jumped up. "You can't, your honor. The act was committed in Mikardand, so this court has no jurisdiction."

"How about holding him until we see if the Republic wants him back?" said Abreu.

Sandak said: "That won't work either. We have no extradition treaty with Mikardand because their legal code doesn't meet the minimum requirements of the Interplanetary Juridical Commission. Moreover the courts hold that a suspect may not be forcibly returned to a jurisdiction where he'd be liable to be killed on sight."

The judge said: "I'm afraid he's right again, senhor. However we still have some power over undesirables. Draw me a request for an expulsion order and I'll sign it quicker than you can say *'non vult.'* There are ships leaving in a few days, and we can give him his choice of them. I dislike inflicting him on other jurisdictions, but I don't know what else we can do." He added with a smile: "He'll probably turn up here again like a bad anna, with a cop three jumps behind him. Talk of perpetual motion, he's it!"

Borel slouched into the Nova Iorque Bar and ordered a double comet. He fished his remaining money out of his pants pocket: about four and a half karda. This might feed him until he took off. Or it might provide him with a first-class binge. He decided on the binge; if he got drunk enough he wouldn't care about food in the interim.

He caught a glimpse of himself in the mirror back of the bar, unshaven, with eyes as red as his hair and his gorgeous private uniform unpressed and weather-beaten. Most of the bravado had leaked out of him. If he'd avoided the Novorecife jail, he was still about to be shipped God knew where, without even a stake to get started again. The fact that he was getting his transportation free gave him no pleasure, for he knew space-travel for the ineffable bore it was.

Now that Zerdai was irrevocably lost to him, he kidded himself into thinking that he'd really intended to take her with him as he'd promised. He wallowed in self-pity. Maybe he should even go to work, repugnant though the idea appeared. (He always thought of reforming when he got into a jam like this.) But who'd employ him around Novorecife when he was in Abreu's black books? To go back to Mikardand would be silly. Why hadn't he done this, or that . . .

Borel became aware of a man drinking down the bar; a stout middle-aged person with a look of sleepy good-nature.

Borel said: "New here, senhor?"

"Yes," said the man. "I just came in two days ago from Earth."

"Good old Earth," said Borel.

"Good old Earth is right."

"Let me buy you a drink," said Borel.

"I will if you'll let me buy you one."

"Maybe that can be arranged. How long are you here for?"

"I don't know yet."

"What do you mean, you don't know yet?"

"I'll tell you. When I arrived, I wanted a good look at the planet. But now I've finished my official business and seen everything in Novorecife, and I can't go wandering around the native states because I don't speak the languages. I hoped to pick up a guide, but everybody seems too busy at some job of his own."

Borel, instantly alert, asked: "What sort of tour did you have in mind?"

"Oh, through the Gozashtando Empire, perhaps touching the Free City of Majbur, and maybe swinging around to Balhib on my way back."

"That would be a swell tour," said Borel. "Of course it would take you through some pretty wild country, and you'd have to ride an aya. No carriages. Also there'd be some risk."

"That's all right, I've ridden a horse ever since I was a boy. As for the risk, I've had a couple of centuries already, and I might as well have some fun before I get really old."

"Have another," said Borel. "You know, we might be able to make a deal on that. I just finished a job. My name's Felix Borel, by the way."

"I'm Semion Trofimov," said the man. "Would you be seriously interested in acting as a guide? I thought from your rig that you were some official . . ."

Borel barely heard the rest. Semion Trofimov! A big-shot if ever there was one; a director of Viagens Interplanetarias, member of various public boards and commissions, officer of capitalistic and coöperative enterprises back on Earth . . . At least there'd be no question of the man's ability to pay well, and to override these local bureaucrats who wanted to ship Borel anywhere so long as it was a few light-years away.

"Sure, Senhor Semion," he said. "I'll give you a tour such as no Earthman ever had. There's a famous waterfall in northern Ruz, for instance, that few Earthmen have seen. And then do you know how the Kingdom of Balhib is organized? A very interesting set-up. In fact I've often thought a couple of smart Earthmen with a little capital could start an enterprise there, all perfectly legal, and clean up. I'll explain it later. Meanwhile we'd better get our gear together. Got a sword? And a riding-outfit? I know an honest Koloftu we can get for a servant, if I can find him, and I've got one aya already. As for that Balhib scheme, an absolutely sure thing . . ."

A.D. 2153

The Continent Makers

I.

Gordon Graham looked up from his calculations as the telephone on his wrist tinkled. When he activated the receiver, the voice of his brother Ivor spoke from the little instrument:

"Gordon?"

"Yeah, what is it?" drawled Gordon Graham.

"Busy tonight?"

"We-ell, I'm doing some figuring on the Project . . ."

"Look, will you come down out of your scientific cloud long enough to take over one of my tourists this evening?"

"Huh? What sort of tourist?" said Gordon Graham in tones of alarm.

He had been through this before. Once he'd promised to show New York night-life to a member of Ivor's guided tour when Ivor was otherwise occupied. The tourist had turned out to be an ostrich-man from Thor with a voice like a foghorn in disrepair. All evening, far from enjoying the sight of the noted strippeuse, Ayesha van Leer, doing her famous fig-leaf song, the Thorian had honked into Gordon's ear his bitter complaints about the "partition" of his planet.

It seemed that nearly a hundred years previously, in the early days of interstellar exploration, a party of Earthmen had bought a thinly-inhabited Thorian continent from the chiefs of its primitive natives for some ridiculous price: a record-player with a stack of symphonic records and a case of Irish whiskey, or something like that. When the Irish was gone and the player broken, the Thorians had demanded their continent back. Wherefore there had been a little war in which the Thorians with their spears and boomerangs had come off second best.

By the time the civilized Thorians of the other continents

had roused themselves to take a serious view of the matter, a Terrestrial colony was flourishing and a whole new Earthly generation had grown up on the disputed continent. These circumstances led the Interplanetary Supreme Court to decide that the Thorians might not expel the Earthmen, who had come legally and had been allowed to live there undisturbed for many decades. On the other hand the Interplanetary Council had adopted rules to prevent advanced peoples from taking advantage of backward ones again . . .

All of which Gordon's Thorian had recounted in molecular detail in his honking accent until Gordon had nearly gone mad from boredom.

And then there had been the time he let Ivor talk him into taking one of the latter's tourists to the zoo. The tourist had proved to be an Osirian, a scaly creature like a small bipedal dinosaur a head taller than a man, with a complicated design painted on its bare hide. The animals had thrown such fits that the keepers ordered Gordon and his companion out, much to Gordon's embarrassment.

"It's a Krishnan this time," said Ivor. "A girl. Practically human, too; you'll like her."

"Yeah?" said Gordon Graham. "You said I'd like that ostrich-man from Thor . . ."

"No, no, this isn't like that at all. She's a member of the tour from the republic of Katai-Jhogorai, which is the most cultured state on the planet; all carefully selected people too. This being Sunday, the other gawkers are resting at the Cosmo, but I promised to take Jeru-Bhetiru— that's her name—out to Boonton to visit relatives in the extra-terrestrial colony. That was okay, but she met some Osirian out there who told her about some society that meets in the Bronx tonight and sold her the idea of going. Since her boy-friend who's studying Earthly law at N.Y.U.,—since he was busy, I said I'd take her, forgetting I already had a date of my own. So—uh—I thought,— especially since she's a beauty and an interesting personality—"

"Okay, I'll t-take her," said Gordon Graham. "Where do I meet you?"

"Just a minute while I look at the time-table . . . We'll be on the Boonton Branch train, Lackawanna Division, that gets into the K. S. T. at seventeen fifty-two."

"All right. See you."

Gordon Graham broke the connection, got up, and looked around vaguely for some clean clothes. Such was the warmth of the late June air that he wouldn't bother with a blouse; he cared nothing for other people's ideas of formality. He looked at his long-nosed face in the mirror to see if he needed a second shave, and decided against it. Then his mind wandered off among the differential equations describing magmatic vortices, on which he'd been working, and he stood lost in thought for ten minutes without moving a muscle.

Finally he pulled himself out of his trance, sat down, and wrote a few equations lest he forget them. Then he resumed his preparations. It was later than he had thought, so he hurried a bit, as much as he ever hurried. Not that it would do Ivor and his extra-terrestrial girl-friend any great harm to wait a few minutes for him . . .

At last he left the small four-apartment house in Englewood, New Jersey, where he and Ivor shared one of the apartments, to walk to the tube station. On the way to the station he passed the helicab lot and toyed for a moment with the idea of taking one of the cabs. It would set him down on the roof of the Columbus Circle Terminal (initials K. S. T. in the new spelling) in ten minutes. On the other hand the time he'd save would not be worth the extra cost.

On the tube train his mind wandered hazily between his beloved equations and the blind date he'd committed himself to. A Krishnan girl *might* be beautiful even from the Earthly standard, despite blue-green hair, pointed ears, and feathery smelling-antennae sprouting from between her eyebrows. And she could presumably talk instead of having to communicate by sign-language with writhing tentacles like an Ishtarian. Still she would not be a human being; her internal organs . . .

Well, maybe that was just as well. For Gordon Graham had sworn a great oath, by the founders of the science of geophysics, not—repeat not—to fall in love on first sight again, after all the misery it had caused him the last three or four times. It was all very well for the extroverted Ivor to tell him that what he needed was to get married; how could you when all the squids you asked laughed at you?

He got off the train at the K. S. T. In walking through the maze of passages in the terminal he let his mind wander off into some of the more abstruse problems of geophysics. When he came to he was on the escalator going down to the High Speed Line platforms at the lowest level of the station . . .

As the escalator was slowly crawling down two deep decks, Graham saved time by reaching up, seizing a crossbar with a directional sign on it, and swinging his long legs easily from the down escalator to the up one next to it. The feat brought startled stares from the other escalator passengers, especially as the sober-looking Graham did not seem like a young man to put on an impromptu public trapeze-act.

He finally found the gate through which passengers issued from trains of the Lackawanna Division of the North American Railroads. His watch showed him that he was just in time to meet the 1752 train of the Boonton division—or "Buunton" as the announcement-board said it in reformed spelling. (Graham was always forgetting to sign his checks "Goordon Greiam" and getting in trouble with his bank in consequence.)

The passengers presently streamed out, Ivor among them, almost as tall as Gordon but looking much shorter because he was broader. Ivor Graham, ex-football-hero and now local New York guide for the Tilghman Travel Agency (GUIDED TOURS TO ALL PLANETS) introduced his brother to the Krishnan girl.

Jeru-Bhetiru was almost as tall as Gordon Graham— not unnatural, as Krishnans averaged about the stature of the tallest human races. Something to do with lesser surface-gravity of that planet. She possessed external organs of smell, that looked something like a pair of blue-green feathers or perhaps like elongated supernumerary eyebrows, rising from above the bridge of her nose. Her hair was a glossy bluish-green and grew in a not-quite-human pattern on her head. Her features bore a slightly flattish Mongoloid look, so that while she would, with other coloration, have made a passably pretty American-Caucasoid girl, she would have been simply ravishing as a Chinese or Indonesian. Her skin bore a faintly greenish tinge too, and her large pointed ears stuck up like those of the Little People in children's picture-books. She wore the frontless Minoan-style dress of her native planet: an outfit to arrest attention even in that sophisticated city and age, rising primly to a high collar in back but in front bare to the midriff, so that it was patent that the wearer, though oviparous, was still definitely a mammal.

Gordon Graham gulped, reflecting that convergent evolution had certainly outdone itself in producing the Krishnans, so human-looking that it was possible for the two species to enjoy the pleasures of carnal love with each other. (Though of course without issue; the chromosome-mechanism of the Krishnans was entirely different from that of Terrans.) The mere thought made Gordon Graham tingle, blush, and clear his throat.

"G-g-glad to know you, Miss Bhetiru," he said at last.

Ivor corrected him: "If you must say 'Miss,' say 'Miss Jeru.' They put surnames first like the Chinese. I call her 'Betty.' "

"Glad to know you—uh—Betty," said Gordon solemnly.

She smiled warmly. "I am glad to know you too. Of course in my language if you wanted to use the familiar form, you would call me Jera-Bhetira, but I shall be happy with 'Betty.' "

Ivor explained: "Her old man is Jeré-Lagilé. You know, the Earthly representative of Katai-Jhogorai for all those years. After her tour finishes its New York stay, she's going to leave it and stay on for a few months to study our Earthly child psychology. Doesn't look like a snakepitter, does she?"

Gordon had to admit she didn't. Despite the oriental look of her Krishnan features, she was all that Ivor had promised and then some.

Ivor continued: "Gordon's a big-shot scientist on the Gamanovia Project, Betty, as well as an instructor of geophysics at Columbia. He's really a brilliant guy in spite of that sappy look."

"What is the Gamanovia Project?" asked Jeru-Bhetiru.

"Oh, don't you know? It's that scheme for increasing the land-area of the Earth by making some new continents."

"My ancestors! How do they do that?"

"You tell her, Gordon," said Ivor.

Gordon Graham cleared his throat. "The fact is, Miss—uh—Betty, that we've found how to control currents in the amorphous magmatic substratum—"

"Please!" she said, "I do not know all those big words! Can you not make it more simple?"

Gordon collected himself. "Well, you know that if you go down below the surface on a planet like this fifty or sixty miles, you'd find yourself in a mass of white-hot lava, which however can't flow freely like a true liquid because it's under such terrific pressure. But it will flow slowly, under long-continued stresses, like cold pitch, and these currents cause movements in the crystalline crust that lies on top of this substratum. That's how we get mountain ranges and oceanic deeps and things. Now, we find that by setting off atomic charges in the substratum at a controlled rate of disintegration, we can control these magmatic currents, as they're called, so as to cause parts of the ocean bed to rise to the surface, and other parts to sink deeper so as not to flood the existing land-surfaces."

"How do you get the charges down there?"

"By a 'maggot,' a kind of mechanical mole, remote-controlled from the surface ... Say, what's next on the program, Ivor? Have you folks eaten yet?"

Ivor Graham directed them to the K. S. T. restaurant, while Gordon, now warmed up to fine professorial fettle, went on with his explanation.

Jeru-Bhetiru asked: "Why do they call it 'Gamanovia?' "

"Because that will be the name of the first new experimental continent. It's to be raised in the South Atlantic around Ascension Island, and every nation in the World Federation had its own idea of what it should be named. Most of 'em had their pet national heroes in mind; the Indians wanted 'Nehruvia,' for instance. Somebody suggested 'Atlantis,' but it was objected that in the first place Plato's imaginary Atlantis was in the North Atlantic, and in the second, if this experiment worked, we'd probably want to raise another continent in the North Atlantic and we'd better save that name for it.

"Brazil wanted to name the new continent either after Vasco da Gama, the first European to navigate those waters, or João da Nova, who discovered Ascension Island a few years later. When the others said 'Gamia' and 'Novia' would be lousy names for continents, the Brazzies just grinned and said: 'All right, senhores, we'll run them both together and call it "Gamanovia." ' And being the world's leading power ..."

"Here we are," said Ivor. "Hey, Gordon, don't you want to wash your hands?"

Gordon Graham looked and saw that he did indeed want to wash his hands—and literally, not as a euphemism. For the steel bar by which he had swung from one escalator to the other had borne a thick coating of dust on its upper surface. He got lost a couple of times before he found a men's wash-room on the next lower story.

As this was Sunday, the room happened to be entirely empty at the moment. As Graham was soaping his hands a smallish dark man came in nervously puffing a cigarette, apparently on a similar errand. But then the man suddenly spoke:

"Ain't you Dr. Gordon Graham?"

"Uh?" said Graham vaguely, startled out of his day-dream of the beautiful Bhetiru. "Y-yes—that is, I haven't got my Ph.D. yet, but I am Gordon Graham."

"Good. I must spick to you soon. Are you goink places tonight?" The man seemed to have a slight Slavic accent.

"Yes, b-but who are you?"

"My name is Sklar. I will tell you more about myself later."

"And—uh—what do you want to see me about?"

"About your Gamanovia Project. You'll have to teck my word that it is important; I can't go into details now. What time do you get home from work tomorrow?"

"Let's see, that's Monday—oh, about fifteen hundred."

"Good, I will see you there—"

The man broke off and whirled as two other men, much larger than he, came in through the door and stalked swiftly towards the two who already occupied the washroom. One of them had his right hand in his blouse pocket, which bulged as if the man were pointing a gun, inside the pocket, towards the self-styled Sklar. The other faced Graham, placed a large hand on his chest, and gave a sharp push.

Graham sighed. It was always that way. People looking for trouble, deceived by his long soupy look and unaware that boxing had been his undergraduate sport in college, insisted on picking on him, and then he just had to take measures. He took them now: he put away his glasses and followed this act with a lead with his left to the ribs and a long straight right to the man's right eye.

The man tottered and fell backwards, supine, his head hitting the tiles with a distinct thud.

The other man turned at the sound, and Graham wondered in a flash if he had been so stupid as to provoke the man to shooting him. It really wasn't worth—

However, Sklar instantly did something that shot a stream of vapor from the ring he wore into the second man's face, so that the victim began at once to blink, sneeze, cough, and sputter. Then Sklar stepped close to the man. His hand came out of a pocket with a blackjack. *Thwuck!* went the sap against the man's skull, and this man, too, swayed and collapsed like a felled Douglas fir.

But now the man Graham had hit was getting up, his still-open left eye glaring furiously. Sklar took a whack at him, too, but the man saw him coming and knocked him aside with a sweep of an arm like the loom of a galley-oar. A fist came around and jolted Graham's jaw, staggering him. For a few seconds they mixed it. Graham, taking advantage of his orangutanian reach, landed a couple more good ones to the face. Then a repeated thud told Graham that Sklar was working on the man's cranium with his blackjack from behind. And although the man's skull seemed to be one of more than ordinary thickness, this man at last folded up on the tiles also.

"Now, ain't this somethink?" said Sklar, staring at the bodies. He quickly bent and searched the men, taking a pistol out of the pocket of one and stowing it in his own. "Help me get them out of here, quick," he said.

"Huh? What d'you mean?" said Graham. "Why don't you call a cop?"

"I *am* a cop!" said the small man impatiently, whipping out a wallet and flapping it in Graham's face. Graham got a glimpse of the identification card of Reinhold Sklar, World Federation Constable, Second Grade. (Some sort of Central European, Graham surmised.) Sklar continued: "So I don't want no city poliss buttink into my case."

Sklar looked swiftly around, still puffing on the same cigarette he had been smoking when the fight started. In the far corner of the washroom there was a small green door bearing the words KIIP AUT—the kind of door found all over large modern buildings. Everybody walks by them without even wondering whether they conceal broom-closets, back-stairs, or what. Sklar pushed it and it opened.

"Lucky for us some pipple is laxative about locking doors," he said. "Take that one's shoulders, now; they are too big for me to move all by myself. Quick before somebody comes in."

Graham, a bit bewildered by all this, did as he was told. Between them they lugged both unconscious forms through the small door and out onto an iron platform a little more than a meter square. This platform in turn gave access to a circular iron staircase that extended up and down from it. Upwards it disappeared into a tangle of dimly-lit girders, while downwards it ended on the extreme end of one of the loading-platforms of the High Speed Line, on the lowest level of the K. S. T. They were definitely backstage, now.

"Down," said Sklar softly, and they began hauling one of the bodies down the helical stair. When they had dropped the first on the concrete they went back for the second. The platform tapered at the end like the bow of a ship, and a couple of meters back of the stair was a huge square concrete pillar that cut off the view of the rest of the platform. They stood in shadow and in near-silence, except for the occasional distant rumble of a train on one of the higher levels.

Graham whispered: "What *is* all this about? Who are these gloops? And what's it got to do with me?"

"Tell you tomorrow," snapped Sklar, peering around the right side of the pillar. Below them gleamed the single ground-rail of the High Speed Line, twice the size of a normal railroad rail, while the overhead rail, which kept the cars upright, glimmered above. A few meters from where they stood, on the other side of the pillar, the smooth nose of a High Speed articulated car, tapering to a rounded point like that of an artillery-shell, reflected the lights of the station. Somewhere under the rounded body the air-compressor chugged faintly.

"That one only goes to Washington, and won't live for half an hour," said Sklar. "Should be one comink in on the other track soon."

As he spoke there came a click of relays from the other side of the platform, and a purr of motors, and another car crawled into view on the empty track. The nose came closer and closer and did not stop until it was even with the surface of the pillar behind which Sklar and Graham stood.

Sklar made a warning motion. "Wait till the yard motorman lives his cab," he said. "Then we put these characters in the mail-compartment."

After a few seconds' wait, Graham heard a door-latch click, and the sound of retreating footsteps. Sklar murmured:

"All right, now we got about two minutes. Help me!"

When they dragged the first body around the corner of the pillar, Graham fully expected to run into a flock of people: railroad employees and passengers. But the platform was empty. Sklar opened a door in the side of the car, and they lugged the man in. Then they repeated the operation with the other. As this one was showing signs of coming to, he had to be quieted by another tap of the blackjack.

"Graham," said Sklar, "stand by the door. If you see anybody comink alunk the platform, tell me."

And he fell to work with the expertness of long practice

to bind and gag the men with handkerchiefs, shoe-laces, and other items of clothing.

"Nobody there?" he whispered. "Good. Hold this guy up so as I can get this mail-bag over his head."

When both men had been stowed in mail-bags and shoved into a corner, Sklar dusted his hands and said:

"All right, now we go. Your brother will be missink you. Not a word about this, you understand. Will you be alone in your apartment tomorrow afternoon?"

"I—uh—guess so," said Graham. "Ivor never gets in before eighteen hundred and usually not till late in the evening."

"Good." Sklar took a last look at the car in which they had hidden their attackers. An electric truck piled with mail-bags was rumbling towards them down the platform, and beyond it Graham could see a few early passengers coming down the escalator to board the car. Sklar said:

"We just made it. I wrote 'Kansas City' on their tags, so unless some blip gets curious as to what's in them, they will be in Kansas City in another fourtin hours. I only wish the Line ran on to Los Angeles."

He led the way back up the circular staircase and into the washroom, where he coolly removed traces of the recent fracas. Graham, watching him with some slight awe, did likewise.

"Hurry, Graham," said Sklar. "I don't want your friends askink what you have been up to. Tomorrow at fiftin hundred, yes? Okusdokus. So lunk. See you." And he was gone.

II.

"And—er—what d'you think of Earth, Betty?" said Gordon Graham.

"Hey," said Ivor Graham, "how'd you get your knuckles skinned? Been in a scrap?"

Gordon shook his head and kept looking at Jeru-Bhetiru, who answered: "Fascinating, but so much water! It would give me a complex to know the land is nothing but an island surrounded by water."

"My Osirian tourists feel the same," said Ivor. "Not having any oceans, none of 'em knows how to swim; in fact the mere suggestion makes 'em shudder. On the other hand the monkey-rats of Thoth, having nothing but one big ocean with a lot of islands . . ."

"Can swim," Gordon broke in. "Go on, Betty."

"And there are so few young ones!"

"With the lengthening of human life the old ones have become relatively more numerous, and we have to control our increase or there'd soon be standing room only. How about our human culture?"

"I was trying to say—" said Ivor.

Jeru-Bhetiru paid him no more attention than did his brother. She said:

"It fascinates me too. To us poor backward Krishnans the Earth is a kind of glamorous fairyland. But most of all I am interested in human psychology. There is of course my—line, I think you call it? It is much like yours, but different in some ways. I should like to analyze you, for example."

"Wh-what?" said Gordon, pinkening. "You mean you'd want me to lie down on a couch and Tell All?"

"Don't waste your time on him," said Ivor. "You wouldn't get anything interesting. Gordon's heart is pure even if his strength isn't the strength of ten, but only two point seven. Now me—"

Gordon said: "Uh—don't let him fool you, Betty. Ivor wouldn't appreciate the purity of your motives. Couches make him think of things other than scientific research."

"Depends on what you call research," said Ivor. "If you two will stop gazing into each other's eyes, I've been trying to say it's time to go to your meeting. I'm going anyway; here's my half of the check."

Gordon Graham and Jeru-Bhetiru looked up in some confusion, but pulled themselves together to say good-bye to Ivor. After some further discussion of psychology Gordon Graham said:

"Guess he's right. We'd best be going."

She took his arm as they walked slowly out, almost wandering through the door before a whistle from the cashier reminded Graham that he had not paid for his dinner. He laughed a silly laugh, let the cashier short-change him without noticing, and continued on out. So busy were he and the Krishnan girl with each other that they bumped into two pillars and five pedestrians and got lost three times before they found the exit to the subway.

For Gordon Graham the world was beginning to take on that rosy glow it assumed when he had just met the latest girl of his dreams. His previous resolutions? Fooey. What if his friends would look askance on the idea of his marrying a being of another species? He cared nothing about that; let the morrow take care of itself. He'd found an ornamental companion, a soul-mate, and a listener. What else mattered?

They took a Concourse Express to Bedford Park Boulevard and walked east towards where Mosholu Parkway emerges from Bronx Park, with the late June sunset at their backs. Among the apartment houses stood a sprinkling of old one-family houses, some going back centuries.

"Should be somewhere along here," drawled Graham. "Sa-ay, Betty, what is this Churchillian Society?"

She replied: "The'erhiya told me it tries to prove that a twentieth-century playwright named George Bernard Shaw could not have composed the plays he is supposed to have written, but that, instead, they must have been conceived by a statesman of the time named Winston Churchill."

"Churchill? Wasn't he an early British labor-leader who wrote socially-conscious novels around 1900?"

"I should not know, Gorodon." (She always made three syllables of his name, a fault of enunciation he found wholly charming.)

"We can look it up later, but isn't it funny for an Osirian to be interested in such things? Who's The'erhiya?"

"My friends in Boonton told me he is a famous speculator. I met him at this party, with his partner, the Thorian Adzik. He carried Adzik around in the crook of his arm—"

"Hey! Are you sure you don't mean Adzik the Thothian?"

"Why?"

"Thorians are too big to be carried on anybody's arm. Ostrich-men, we call 'em."

"You must be right. Thorian, Thothian, I confuse your Earthly names for other planets. Why did they choose two so much alike?"

"Just happened. You see we called the planets of our own system after Roman gods back before space-travel, and when we found other planets we named 'em after other mythologies. Your star got Indian gods; Epsilon Eridani, Norse gods; and Procyon, Egyptian gods."

"Why must you give your own names to other stars and planets? It seems—a little arrogant."

"Because when we ask the natives of a strange planet what they call it, they give us answers in a hundred different languages, half of which we can't pronounce and all meaning something like 'home' or 'ground.' Some don't even speak, but talk by waving their tentacles. But go on about The'erhiya."

"Well, he carried the Thothian—is that right?—in the crook of his arm like—like—"

"Like a teddy-bear, I guess you'd say."

"Teddy-bear? Anyway, I do not much like Osirians, even this The'erhiya, who was polite enough. They frighten me with their big sharp teeth and that pseudo-hypnotic power they are said to have."

"Oh, I dunno," said Graham generously. "I've met some that weren't bad sorts, in spite of their scales and that weird hissing accent. They're kind of impulsive and sentimental, but otherwise not so different from Earthmen and Krishnans mentally. What more did The'erhiya tell you?"

"Not much, because he—how do you say it—passed out."

"Really?"

"Yes. You know they cannot drink out of our kind of cups and glasses, but use a thing like an oil-can. And the first thing we knew, there was The'erhiya the famous speculator sprawled in a corner, with these empty vessels with the long spouts all around him, and the little Thothian making clucking noises to show how unhappy he was about it all."

Graham tore his attention away from Jeru-Bhetiru long enough to look at a house-number. He exclaimed: "Oh, shucks, we walked past our number. Have to go back."

When they finally turned in at the right address, which proved to be one of the old private houses, a man standing in the shadow inside the doorway said: "Good evening."

Graham said: "Good evening. Is this where the Churchillian Society meets?"

"Yes indeed. Wait a minute—aren't you Gordon Graham the geophysicist?"

"Yeah, that's me. Why, how did you know?"

"Oh, you're a better-known man than you think, Mr. Graham. And we're *very* glad to see you. Won't you step in?"

Light chairs were arranged in rows in what had evidently once been a living-room. Some people occupied some of these chairs while others stood around talking. The room's main decoration was a large portrait photograph of Winston Churchill, wearing the necktie and stiff collar of his period.

As Graham led Jeru-Bhetiru to a pair of vacant seats,

another man—a stout bald fellow—said: "Good evening, Mr. Graham." Graham was sure he had never seen either this man or the man at the door before. Something was going on that he didn't understand. First the strange encounter with Sklar and the two men who had attacked them; now this. He was sure he had never been here before, either. He didn't even have that feeling of pseudo-memory the psychologists called *déjà vu* . . .

The stout bald man, whom somebody referred to as "Mr. Warschauer," called the meeting to order. There ensued the usual tedious round of discussion of membership, dues, and other topics of no interest to outsiders. (Graham kept whispering to Jeru-Bhetiru, earning disapproving frowns from his neighbors.) Then Mr. Warschauer introduced a Mr. Donaghy, a small white-haired man, as the speaker of the evening.

Mr. Donaghy got up in front and launched into an impassioned oration on his favorite subject:

" . . . and what do we know of this George Bernard Shaw, as he called himself? All we have to go on is a few biographies, mostly biased, and which don't agree with each other in many vital respects; and microfilm records of the notoriously corrupt and unreliable press of the twentieth century.

"Well, who was this so-called Shaw, anyway? From what little trustworthy evidence there is, he would not seem to have been a man of distinguished antecedents, which in those days of class distinction were necessary before a man could rise to intellectual eminence. So far from being a man of noble lineage, or a descendant of distinguished litterateurs, he was the son of a corn-merchant! It is known that Shaw, as he is called, never attended school after the age of fourteen. Furthermore, to judge from the eccentric spellings by which he anticipated the modern curse of the so-called reformed orthography, he never paid much attention to learning even when it was offered to him . . ."

Graham, having almost immediately caught the general drift of Donaghy's argument, paid it no more attention, devoting himself to gazing at Jeru-Bhetiru's profile.

" . . . five years working in a real-estate office, of all places! How could the author of 'Pygmalion' and 'Candida' have endured such a stultifying atmosphere? A man of such sensitivity of soul would have gone mad in a week! And when he did at last abandon the sordid career of rent-collector to try to earn a literary livelihood, he soon showed himself utterly incapable of doing so. In the first nine years of his new career he earned by his pen just six pounds, or about 28 modern World Federation dollars. The publishers rejected four novels, as they were called, one after the other. In one of these he showed his depraved tastes by setting his scene in the prize-fighting business. Try to imagine, if you can, the author of 'Saint Joan' writing about brutal and vulgar pugilists! And associating with them to pick up the necessary background and color . . ."

Graham shook his head vigorously to keep from falling asleep. Donaghy, seeing the motion, said sharply: "Do you have a question, young man?"

"N-no," said Graham, reddening. "I—ah—I went swimming and got water in my ear."

"Ahem. To resume: Finally obtaining a toe-hold on the fringe of the profession of letters, the *soi-disant* Shaw engaged in the lowest form of the craft: literary criticism. Even so, he showed not enough stability of character to hold any one job for long, but instead drifted from one publication to another . . ."

Graham let his hand steal out on a foraging-mission of its own until it found one of Jeru-Bhetiru's and clasped it. She not only did not try to draw away, but even returned his squeeze. The thumping of his heart all but drowned out what Mr. Donaghy was saying—not that Graham cared a damn what Donaghy said . . .

"Then who *did* write these plays, if not the so-called Shaw? Ah, who indeed?

"There was at that time one young man in Britain whose mind was in truth afire with the creative urge, but who could not have openly avowed his ambition in this direction because of the social and political tabus of the time. For such an aristocrat, son of a lord and grandson of a duke, playwriting was not an acceptable occupation in those distant days. Nor were theatrical people welcomed into exclusive circles like his. Moreover the plays he had stirring in his unconscious would gravely have compromised the political career for which he was destined both by his own transcendent ability and by the tradition of his family . . .

"Therefore, we are persuaded—nay, forced—to believe, this great man must have made a deal with the alleged Shaw, to let the plays he wrote but could not sign be published under the name of this seedy hanger-on. Shaw, for his part, was willing enough to have his name used in this fashion, though he himself lacked the talent . . ."

For final proof of his thesis, Mr. Donaghy drew on the blackboard an anagram consisting of the names of 23 of the plays of "the so-called Shaw," so arranged that one vertical row of letters read "WINSTON SPENCER CHURCHILL."

Everybody clapped loudly. Everybody, that is, except Graham and Jeru-Bhetiru, who could not do so without letting go each other's hands, and who were not enough impressed by Mr. Donaghy to do that.

It all seemed pretty thin to Graham, though he hardly knew enough about the literary history of the Century of Catastrophe to argue the matter. One thing he was sure of: He had evidently confused Winston Churchill with a couple of other fellows. He'd have to look him up in the Encyclopaedia.

Moreover he was surprised to see, on looking at his watch, that two hours had passed since they had sat down.

People were rising to leave. Some had gathered round Donaghy to argue or to praise him. Graham was leading out Jeru-Bhetiru when the fat Warschauer materialized in front of them, saying:

"I'm so glad you've come at last, Mr. Graham; we've been looking forward to meeting you."

"Really?" said Graham. How the devil could they have been looking forward to meeting him when he had never heard of them before this afternoon, was not at all interested in their screwball literary theories, and had nothing in common with them?

"Yes, really," said Warschauer. "Will you step back into our board room? The other officers of our little society are most eager to meet you too."

"We really must be getting along . . ." said Graham.

"No, really, my dear young people, you simply must step in for a minute. Only for a minute. We have a proposal I think you'll find interesting, and if you don't like it you can run right along."

"Let us see what this nice man wants, Gorodon," said Jeru-Bhetiru. "I am in no hurry."

Against his better judgment Graham gave in and preceded Warschauer to the rear of the house. Here he found himself in an ex-dining room facing a couple of other men. Warschauer said: "This is Mr. Lundquist" (indicating a jowly, red-faced, gray-haired man) "and Mr.

Edwards" (the small wiry red-haired man who had met Graham at the front door). "Go ahead, Chris."

"So glad to know you," said Lundquist. "How you doing?"

"All right," said Graham. "What's this proposition Mr. Warschauer was hinting about?"

Lundquist said: "This business conference will bore the young lady. Jim, why don't you take care of her in the next room?" When Edwards had taken Jeru-Bhetiru out, he continued: "You admit, Dr. Graham, that scientists ain't paid enough, don't you?"

"Oh, I don't know. I suppose you might argue that way. Why?"

"But you'd like to make more, now, wouldn't you?"

"Who wouldn't? But what's all this got to do with Shaw and Churchill?" Graham admitted to himself that these did not seem much like desperate characters; but then, never having known any desperate characters, how could he judge?

Lundquist smiled. "Nothing at all, my friend. We're thinking of a deal more in line with your scientific work. You know, on that Ganna—Gamanovia Project."

"Huh? How come?"

"We can't go into details because the chief is away tonight. All I can say is it has to do with geophysics, and it could be very profitable to you. What I want now is for you to tell us you'll come back here tomorrow at this time and talk it over with the boss."

"Who's the boss? I thought you were."

Lundquist smiled. "Not quite."

Still things did not seem quite right. Graham said: "How did you know about me? I haven't published anything on Gamanovia, and I've only been working part-time on it, as a consultant."

"Oh, we've had our eye on you for some time. By the way—" Lundquist turned to Warschauer "—what's happened to Smith and Magazzo? They called from the K. S. T. around eighteen, saying they had their eyes on our friend here, but they ain't come in and ain't reported since. They don't just disappear into thin air, now."

Graham's mind, however fuzzy at times, reacted instantly to this statement. Lundquist must have had him tailed by the pair whom he and Sklar had tangled with earlier. If Sklar was kosher, the group operating behind the front of the Churchillian Society weren't. He rose.

"Sorry," he said, "b-but Miss Jeru and I have to run

along. Right n-now. If you have a proposal to make, you can write me care of Columbia University. Oh, *Betty!*"

"Yes, Gorodon?" She opened the door from the next room. Behind her Graham could see a table with a chessboard set up on it, pieces in play, and two chairs, one occupied by Edwards. The latter, also, got up and moved towards this door. Graham deliberately took off his glasses, put them in their case, and put the case in his pocket.

"C-c-come on, Betty," said Gordon Graham, and started for the door.

But the stout Warschauer barred his way, saying: "Now, now, just a min, Dr. Graham. Let's not be hasty. Nothing will be asked of you that's against your principles ..."

That was as far as he got, because Graham's bony fist caught him in the nose, slamming his head back against the door with a resounding boom. Warschauer's legs went out from under him as he slid into a Billiken-like sitting posture, legs extended and back still against the door.

Graham, however, now found that he could not open the door so long as Warschauer sprawled against it. If he could lug the body to one side quickly enough, he might still be able to get them both out before the others grabbed them ... But even as he heaved at the heavy body, hands caught him from behind and dragged him back. As he turned he found himself grappling with Edwards, who, it transpired, was a strong little man.

Graham nevertheless got a couple of good short ones into Edwards's ribs, at the same time calling out: "Run, B-Betty! Get the cops! Yell for help!"

Instead of yelling, Jeru-Bhetiru grabbed a light chair by the back, as if intending to wallop Edwards with it. Before she could do so, however, Lundquist snatched the chair away from her and threw it across the room. Then he caught her arm with one hand and with the other brought out a thing like a paint-sprayer. Graham recognized it as an Osirian electrostatic gun.

"Better not," said Lundquist, pointing the shock-gun at the Krishnan girl. "You too, Graham; calm down or I'll burn her."

Graham cautiously disentangled himself from Edwards, who went over to help the fallen Warschauer to his feet. The latter was holding a bloody handkerchief in front of his face, muttering: "He busted by doze! What the hell busidess has a sciedtist got, pudchig people id the doze?"

"Now, my friends," said Lundquist, "we'll talk business.

I'm afraid we'll have to hold Miss What's-her-name here to make sure you coöperate with us. It would have been nicer if you'd done it of your own accord, but if that's the way it is, that's the way it is. During the lecture you acted like you think she's a pretty sweet little squid; is that right?"

Graham, feeling that he had probably talked too much for his own good already, stared silently.

Warschauer kept muttering through his nosebleed: "I got to get to a doctor to fix up by doze!"

"I guess we can take it you wudden want to see her killed, now would you?" Lundquist continued. "So you'll do this, my friend. You'll leave here quietly and go home without saying nothing to nobody about what happened here, or about the Churchillian Society, or any goddam thing at all, get me? Then you'll come back here tomorrow night like I asked you in the first place. Miss What's-her-name won't be here, but we'll be taking good care of her. And you can be sure if you try anything you won't never see her alive again. Do you understand what I'm saying, huh?"

"You mean you'll m-murder her?" said Graham.

"Not exactly. You can only muider human beans, and she's only some kind of animated vegetable from some goddam planet. But you get the idea. Well, my friend?"

"Okay," said Graham wearily.

He exchanged one last look with Jeru-Bhetiru. In his imagination, her appealing expression implied that she expected him to leap upon Lundquist, wrest the weapon from him, and massacre the miscreants. Graham, however, knew as well as the next man that as long as Lundquist remained alert, he could not possibly leap the gap between them before Lundquist's finger tightened on the trigger.

Then he went out, hearing at the last the plaintive voice of Warschauer behind him:

" . . . by poor doze!"

III.

Graham's ride home was the most miserable of his life. Not only did he feel the self-loathing of one who has let a loved one down, but also he was assailed by pettier fears.

For instance, what in God's name should he tell Ivor when the latter asked him what had become of his tourist? If he told him simply what had happened, the impulsive Ivor might do something leading to Jeru-Bhetiru's destruction. While he got along well enough with his brother, he didn't trust Ivor's judgment for a minute, at least not in enterprises of great pith and moment. Lundquist had impressed him, not as a preternaturally clever man, but one with the simple and direct brutality that in some circumstances makes a man even more formidable; and Graham thought he would do what he threatened to do. This idea of treating murderers as psychiatric cases had given all would-be killers a wonderfully secure feeling that they could get away with anything.

If he'd only had the sense to pretend to agree with them, until he and Betty were allowed to go free, and then . . .

As Ivor was not in when Gordon Graham got home, Gordon went to bed forthwith. When Ivor did come in a little later, Gordon pretended to be already asleep to forestall questions.

Next morning, as usual, he had to get up at the same time as Ivor. The latter, however, seemed to sense nothing unusual. He slapped Gordon on the back, saying:

"Boy, you sure hit it off with the little squid! Don't go falling for her the way you did with that last dame I introduced you to. She's not really human, you know. So there wouldn't be any—ah—issue to your union, if I may put it delicately. Not that you couldn't have fun trying . . ."

While Ivor rattled on, Gordon Graham smiled a sickly smile and went out to take the tube to work. He found himself counting the hours until Sklar had promised to call on him. If anybody would know what to do, Sklar would. But did he dare tell even Sklar? Wouldn't he consider it his duty to pounce on the gang, undeterred by such considerations as the life of an e. t. tourist? Or—was he even a real World Federation constable? In his present mood Gordon Graham felt suspicious of everybody from his brother down.

As the spring term was over, his main work at Columbia was correcting the last batch of papers. He rushed through this chore and took the subway back to Englewood without spending his usual hour in the library.

Back home, he tried to bury himself in a recent report by the South African Geological Survey on bathymagnetic fields in the substratum—all the time listening with one ear for the buzzer. At last it sounded.

He quickly admitted his caller, expecting Sklar, to whom he had finally decided to pour out his tale of woe. Instead it turned out to be a young-looking Krishnan in

Earthly costume, with antennae and green hair, as tall as Graham and wider in the shoulders. A fine figure of a man, in fact.

"Are you Gordon Graham?" said the visitor, in better English than Sklar used.

"Yes. What—"

"Then what have you done with Jeru-Bhetiru?" The young man pushed into the Graham apartment in a menacing manner.

"Nothing," said Gordon Graham. "Who are you and what are you after, anyway?"

The Krishnan put fists on hips. "I am Varnipaz bad-Savarun, chief lawyer—I think you would say Attorney-General—to Prince Ferrian bad-Arjanaq of Sotaspé, an island on the planet Krishna. Jeru-Bhetiru is my—ah—fiancée, I think you say."

"Gluk," said Graham as he digested this news. This must be the boy-friend Ivor had mentioned. If Ivor had come right out and said "fiancé" he might have been better prepared . . .

Varnipaz continued: "She was staying at the Cosmo Hotel in New York with the other members of the guided tour she is on, and last night she went out with you. Now, do not misunderstand me. I do not mind that she goes out with you; it is not as if she and I were in love or anything foolish like that. But when I called her hotel this morning she had not come back, and your brother, who takes these tourists around the sights of New York, did not know what had become of her. Now will you talk?"

"I'd be glad if I could," said Graham. "But I don't know where she is now either."

"What happened?" said the newcomer, his voice rising to a shout.

"I can't tell you that yet. If—uh—you'll wait a while—"

"You mean wait while you think up some plausible-sounding lie! Mr. Graham, either you tell me all you know right now, or . . ."

"Or what?" said Graham, taking off his glasses.

"You shall see. Will you tell?"

"N-no, I w-w-"

Graham ducked as Varnipaz's fist hurtled towards him. Graham got back a stiff left before Varnipaz could avoid it, rocking the extra-terrestrial back. Then Graham prepared to move in with a killing right. If he could just line Varnipaz up . . .

Instead of trying to avoid or block the blow, Varnipaz

stepped into it before it had gotten well started, and grappled.

Crash! They carried away a picture hanging on the wall, and fell to the ground, trying to use elbows and knees while keeping their grip on each other. Graham got a fist loose long enough to give Varnipaz a couple where his kidneys ought to be—if Krishnans had kidneys, and had them in the same place as human beings, which was unlikely.

Varnipaz retaliated by fastening his fingers around Graham's left thumb and twisting until Graham tore it loose. They broke for an instant and scrambled up. Graham knocked Varnipaz backwards with a quick one-two, bringing the floor-lamp down in ruin; then stepped forward for a knockout punch. As he did so, however, Varnipaz, staggering a little, threw himself into another clinch and skillfully tripped Graham. Down they went again, thrashing and kicking. Over went a chair. They got up, still struggling.

"Yeow!" yelped Graham as Varnipaz sank his teeth into his forearm. "I'll fix you!" and snapped a knee towards the Krishnan's crotch. Varnipaz, however, saw it coming and twisted his body so that the knee bounced off his hip. Graham realized that while he might be the better boxer, his antagonist had the edge in wrestling. Thinking the smelling-antennae might be sensitive, he groped towards them . . .

"Okay, break it up!" said a voice from the doorway.

Both fighters looked around to see Sklar standing there with his hat on the side of his head, a cigarette in the corner of his mouth, and one hand making a significant bulge in his blouse pocket.

"We might as well," said Graham. "He's got us covered."

They disengaged themselves, each watching the other carefully against a treacherous blow. Varnipaz had the makings of a fine black eye, while Graham had toothmarks on his arm and a cut on one hand from broken glass. He began picking up the debris.

"Looks like a tomato had been through here," said Sklar. "What's this all about?"

Both Graham and Varnipaz launched into an explanation at once. After a few minutes Sklar held up a hand.

"I get the idea so far," he said. "Mr. Graham, maybe you better tell us what *did* happen last night."

"With him here?" said Graham. "I think it has to do with—uh—you know—that trouble we had in the station."

"That's all right. I know about Varnipaz, and I think we can trust him."

"Perhaps you know me," said Varnipaz, "but I do not know you. Will you explain yourself, please?"

Sklar brought out his wallet and showed his credentials to the Krishnan, saying: "Go on pliz, Mr. Graham."

Graham had stepped into the kitchenette for a paper bag, and he was now squatting and picking up pieces of glass. As he worked he told the whole story of the visit to the meeting of the Churchillian Society—omitting only the fact that he had fallen in love with Jeru-Bhetiru, and that he suspected her of returning the sentiment. Despite Varnipaz's curious remark earlier about not being in love with his affianced, Graham thought it a little tactless to mention his own feelings in front of him.

Graham finished: " . . . and now maybe you can tell *me* what's happening. Here I am, the most p-p-peaceable sort of guy you could find, who hasn't been in a brawl since he was a kid. And now I've been in three fights in the last twenty-four hours; and I've been involved in kidnapping, assault, and goodness knows what else. What the hell goes on?"

Sklar put another cigarette in his mouth, drew quickly on it to light it, and said:

"This gank, as you call them, is up to somethink; just what, I am supposed to find out. It has some connection with the Gamanovia Project, as you know yourself, and there are rumors that it is really run by extra-terrestrial interests. What sort of e. t.'s I don't know either. Can you offer any suggestions, Prince?"

Varnipaz waved a deprecating hand. "I do not use the title here on Earth, where you are nearly all republicans. Besides it makes people confuse me with my cousin Ferrian, the Prince Regent. As for your question, I do not know either. Not counting the other Mr. Graham's tourists, there are only about twenty Krishnans on Earth, and I know most of them personally. You people screen us very carefully to make sure nobody tries to break your technological blockade. But I do not know why any should be especially interested in Gamanovia; we have no oceans to fish continents out of."

Graham said: "Wouldn't the fact that Lundquist used

an—uh—Osirian electric gun indicate that there was an Osirian in it?"

"Might," said Sklar. "Earthmen seldom use the shock-gun because it ain't practical in cities. When you shoot it you burn out the electric wiring for mitters around. But that still don't give a risen. Osirians haven't got oceans either, have they?"

"Not as I remember. It's a dry planet."

"Well then, who'd want to interfere with the Gamanovia Project?"

"Could it be somebody thinks this increased land area would increase our military potential so as to violate the arms limitation treaty?"

Sklar shook his head. "Fetched pretty far, if you don't mind me saying so. How about that island where you got all that control equipment, that will be in the middle of the continent? Who owns it?"

"Ascension? A Spaniard named Teófilo March who raises turtles."

"How'd this guy get the island? He must have folding money."

"When the World Federation took over the strategic islands and waterways like Gibraltar and the Panama Canal they got Ascension. Then a few years ago they sold some of these pieces of real estate at auction, and Señor March bought this one. Now we've got a contract to buy it back before the continent rises. Since he's doing all right on the deal I don't see why he should object."

"What Government has sovereignty of Ascension?"

"None," said Graham.

"You can't do that! If none of the national governments has it, it must come under W. F. jurisdiction."

"No, that's the funny thing. W. F. territory is limited by its constitution to certain kinds of land like the Kalahari Preserve and Antarctica. When the W. F. gave up Ascension it would normally have reverted to Great Britain, but the British refused it on grounds that it would cost more to administer this useless pile of volcanic clinkers than it was worth."

"So this March could call himself Emperor of Ascension if he wanted to?"

"I suppose he could. But look here, instead of theorizing, now that you know about the Churchillian Society, why don't you raid the place and run in the lot?"

"First," said Sklar, "because we'd only catch the small fries; they are smart enough not to let their right hands know what their lefts are doink. Second, because they would probably kill Miss Jeru if they were threatened. You wouldn't like that, would you?"

"No!" exclaimed the two younger men at once.

"So, we have to do what we can. You know, Graham, that was not so smart of you to rouse them up by defyink them while they still had you and the yonk lady in their power. You should have pretended to agree—"

"I know that now," said Graham. "It was the stupidest thing I've done since I was a frosh. But I'm new at bulldogging."

"I understand. But then they ain't supermen either, and they made mistakes too. Most battles is won by the side that mecks the fewest mistakes, you know. That gun, for instance. And tippink you off that two of their men was missink, so you connected them with the fight earlier."

"What about Smith and Magazzo?" asked Graham.

"I hope to have a receptions committee when they arrive in Kansas City," said Sklar. "We should be able to hold them on some charge for a few days at list. If they were arrested here in New York, the gank would find out about it."

Varnipaz said: "This talk is all very well, but what shall we do? I cannot sit making abstract remarks on crime and punishment while your vile Earthly gang kills my fiancée. At home I should buckle on my best sword, mount my noble aya, and gallop off to the rescue. But how does one do that on Earth where all is done by pushing electric buttons?"

Sklar thought a minute and said: "Do you two both want to help me?"

"Yes," they replied in chorus.

"Good. I nid your help too, and I know enough about you to think I can trust you. I can deputize you both right here and now. I can't have you taken up for pay without a civil-service examination and a training-course, but I can give you authority to carry arms and make arrests. Can you take the time off from your regular work?"

"Yes," they said again.

"Good. Raise your right hands and repit after me . . ."

" . . . and now you know what will happen to you if you break your oath to the Federation," said Sklar, "we will go on to your orders. Varnipaz, I am thinkink of sendink you to Rio, where is the headquarters of the Gamanovia Project. Do you spick Portuguese?"

"Enough to travel on the Viagens Interplanetarias by myself, but not well. It is funny: my fiancée and I have to speak to each other in English or in Portuguese, because she does not know Sotaspeou, which is a close relative of Gozashtandou, while I do not speak her *lala rakáta-rajhogora* either. When we are married something will have to be done, I suppose. But excuse me, I am wasting your time."

"So," said Reinhold Sklar. "The only eternity is to send you as an *Americano do Norte.* But try not to let people get you to spick English; you have trouble with your consonants and bowels. Graham, you still got to go back to that Churchillian house this ivnink, don't you? And since there may be Osirians in this case, we better take a little precaution. If your room is picked up, you will both come over to my place. We'll disgust your plans on the way."

An hour later the new deputy constables looked at one another and at their own images in Sklar's mirror. (Sklar had a room in a cheap hotel.) Gordon Graham looked no different, despite the fact that his head had been completely shaved, and he wore next to his naked scalp a cap of thin silver disguised by a wig that fairly well matched his original hair.

Varnipaz, on the other hand, was a complete Earthman, his antennae hidden by a flap of false skin that came down low on his forehead. His wig was brown instead of his natural green, and bushy enough to hide the points of his ears.

Sklar explained: "Nobody knows how works the pseudo-hypnosis of the Osirians; whether some kind of ray or what. But it works, that is the main point, and the only protection is this kind of cap. It also gives a *little* protection against blows on the head, but don't trust it too far in that direction. Now, you got all your orders straight? Remember, Graham, roll with the punch, as they say in fist-fightink. Don't think you can get word to me izzily, without being caught, at list until the boss thinks he has you under his pseudo-hypnotic control. And don't try no gallant rescues except as a last resort; live that kind of think to us. Understand? Good. So lunk!"

Having an hour to kill, Graham offered to accompany Varnipaz to the ticket-agency where the latter would make a reservation on an airplane for Rio de Janeiro. On the way he asked:

"What's this law-course you're taking?"

"Oh, Prince Ferrian has some advanced ideas about law-codes, and I am to make myself familiar with the International Basic Code and its origins—English common law, the Code Napoleon, the Japanese Constitution of 1998, and so on. You know the agreement under which Thoth was admitted to the Interplanetary Council?"

"No," said Graham.

"Since their legal system was below the minimum standards of the I. K., though they were in other respects a highly civilized people, they had to agree to follow the precedents of the International Basic Code in their courts, with such differences as are made necessary by the fact they are bisexual and so forth. Now, Ferrian thinks that some day we may get a world government on Krishna and apply for admission to the I. K. And when that happens he intends to have the most advanced legal code on Krishna, to give him control of the situation. I shall be amused to see how he fits the very democratic Japanese Constitution into his—I suppose you would say benevolent despotism."

Graham queried: "What strikes you most about our Earthly law?"

Varnipaz thought. "I suppose the care with which your constitutions safeguard the individual's rights against the state. Why is that?"

"We had experience with the other kind of state—with unlimited power over the individual—and it didn't work so well."

"What happens if an emergency arises that requires one of these states to exceed its powers?"

"Then you amend the constitution. That's hard to do, though."

"Why?" asked Varnipaz.

"Because the science of geriatrics has more than doubled our life-span, so that our average age is much greater than it was a couple of centuries ago."

"And that makes you conservative?"

"Exactly. What else have you noticed?"

"I notice how carefully the powers of the World Federation are limited. For instance I should think a world government would control migration from one continent to another; but no, that is reserved to the several nations."

"There's a reason for that. Several nations—Brazil, the United States, Australia—were afraid of being swamped with immigrants from countries where they'd let their population get out of hand. So the other nations had to agree to get any kind of Federation."

"And from what I understand, you had to have a Federation to keep you from blowing up your planet."

"Exactly. Besides, there was a reaction against centralization in government at that time, following the Third World War."

"I see. But law—*chá!* What are a lot of dusty lawbooks when one's betrothed is in peril? I wish I had those Churchillians on Krishna!" Varnipaz made thrust-and-parry motions.

Gordon Graham left Varnipaz and walked to the subway entrance. Although the Krishnan had apologized handsomely for starting the fight that afternoon, Graham still did not altogether trust him. Maybe he was a bit too knightly to be true. And was Sklar so smart, or had he let himself be glamorized? While Earthmen loved to boast of their democratic institutions, they were easily beguiled by extra-terrestrial titles.

As the train bore him away, Graham felt as if he had been shut up in one of the Gamanovia Project's maggots just as the device was about to burrow down into the white-hot substratum of the earth's crust, with an atomic charge aboard.

IV.

Gordon Graham's heart beat faster as he walked towards the old house where the Churchillian Society had met the previous evening. Though he hardly expected to find Jeru-Bhetiru still there, he would at least be definitely on her trail.

What on earth was this proposal they kept talking about? What could they possibly want with the Gamanovia Project, which was no secret military undertaking, but an open and above-board endeavor to provide more space for the inhabitants of the over-crowded Earth? He could make no sense of it.

The house, as he remembered, should be in the next block.

In a few minutes he'd know, or at least he'd be in a position to ask questions. Whether they'd answer was another matter. Anybody who deliberately put himself into the power of a group of determined and dangerous men like these, as he was doing, was several kinds of damn fool . . .

He felt a rising resentment against Sklar, the W. F. Constabulary, and all the other law-enforcement agencies. Why hadn't they stopped this mysterious conspiracy before it got that far? What were they good for, letting a bunch of nogoodniks meet openly to hatch some nefarious plot against the welfare of the world and the peace of ordinary citizens like himself? And then instead of dealing with the matter themselves, they roped in an inexperienced amateur like him to do their dirty work for them. They reminded him of these fictional detectives who buzz around busily detecting while the murderer kills off the entire cast of characters, one by one.

Some of his irritation even spread to include Jeru-Bhetiru. If he hadn't gotten silly over the girl; if he hadn't let Ivor talk him into getting involved in a situation that was none of his business . . .

But then his annoyance dissolved in a wave of sentimental tenderness. She hadn't known what she was getting into either, any more than he, so he shouldn't blame her. She was a stranger on a strange planet, while the villains were men of his own species. He was acting like Adam in *Genesis*: "The woman thou gavest me . . ." He should be ashamed of himself for even thinking such thoughts.

The old yellow clapboard two-storey house came into view.

Soon, now, he'd know. And maybe he'd have a chance to rescue her in the best romantic tradition. Or at least he'd get word to Sklar and so be the ultimate instrument of her rescue. That is, if they didn't shoot him full of holes first. Somehow he couldn't see Lundquist, if he had determined to kill somebody, doing anything so stupid as to waste time taunting his victim or telling him all his plans, while the victim contrived means to escape. Rather, Lundquist would calmly and sensibly blow the victim's head off, saving the talk till later.

Now he was walking up the front steps. The house had the dark eyeless look of an empty domicile. A few bats or owls under the eaves would have been in keeping with the general atmosphere.

He rang the bell, hearing the faint jangle from inside. Then he stood, weight on the balls of his feet, leaning a little forward with his head turned to catch the faintest sound, like a heron wading for minnows.

But no sound of approaching footsteps did he hear. And a while he rang again. Still silence.

What am I supposed to do now, he wondered, burgle

the joint? Unfortunately the training for the degrees of
Bachelor of Science and Master of Science in Geophysics
did not include instruction in housebreaking.

An automobile purred past on the street behind him; an
occasional pedestrian walked by. The darkness deepened.
Sounds of city traffic filtered softly into this quiet neighborhood. Kids were yelling somewhere in a nearby block.

A third ring still brought no response. Graham was
beginning to have the uneasy feeling that he had mistaken
the house—though a look at the number showed that he
had not. Or that he had dreamed the last night's episode.
No; the tender spots on his knuckles, face, and elsewhere
bore witness to the fights he'd been in.

Hands deep in pockets, he slouched gloomily down the
sagging front steps and strolled pensively towards the
street. It made you feel even sillier, when you've worked
up the pitch of courage required to put your head into the
lion's mouth, to learn that the lion has fled.

At the street he looked back towards the house, silhouetted darkly against the evening sky, in which stars had
begun to scintillate. What now? Report back to Sklar for
more orders, he supposed . . .

"Get in, Graham," said a low voice behind him in a
matter-of-fact tone.

Gordon Graham whirled. Behind him, by the curb,
stood an automobile: a long gray Ksenzov. Beside the car
stood a man. Graham couldn't be sure in the dim light,
but thought he recognized the small wiry Edwards of the
previous night.

"Okay," he sighed and bent his long form to enter the
car.

It was a roomy nine-passenger sedan with a couple of
men in the rear seat—no poor man's automobile. The
attachments for helicopter components showed it to be a
convertible.

Graham sat between the two men while Edwards occupied one of the jump-seats. Before Graham had a chance
to identify the driver, somebody pushed a button and an
opaque partition slid up to cut off that part of the car
from his vision. A limousine, no less. The windows seemed
likewise to be frosted so that he could not see out.

A feeling of acceleration told him that they were under
way, though there was no sound. The car, he thought,
must have good maintenance because most automobiles,
despite all the engineers could do, developed at least a
faint turbine-whine before they had gone many thousand

kilometers. The light from the streetlamps bloomed and faded against the frosted windows. The machine banked inwards a couple of times for turns and decelerated to a stop.

Edwards opened the door and slipped out; Graham caught a glimpse of a parking-lot before the door closed again. His two companions sat in pregnant silence on either side of him.

Mechanical sounds from outside suggested that Edwards, and no doubt the driver as well, were attaching a set of rotors and a tail-boom. There were sounds of speech, muffled by the windows; Graham caught the words: "Check that nut again . . ."

Then Edwards got back in. The vehicle shuddered slightly and the swish-swish of rotors became audible. A slight increase of seat-pressure told Graham that they were rising. The lights on the frosted windows died out, leaving the inside of the car in almost complete darkness. Edwards pushed another button that turned on a little red dome-light which shed just enough illumination to see a human shape by.

After that there was nothing, except the occasional irregular movement of the car as it met an air-current, for at least half an hour . . .

A slight bump told Graham that they had arrived. The rotor-swish ceased. Again Edwards got out, and sounds indicated that the rotors and the tail-boom were being taken off. Then Edwards got back in, and off they went.

After various turns and twists they stopped again. The door opened into the darkness. Somebody said: "Hurry up, Graham."

He was hustled out of the car and along a concrete walk to an old house of much the same type as that in the Bronx from which he had set out. There was one marked difference, though: instead of sounds of city traffic, from somewhere nearby came the booming of a surf and the smell of sea air. The house seemed to be one of a rather widely scattered row facing the street on which the Ksenzov stood. Little patches of sand on the concrete crunched under Graham's feet, while overhead he saw stars but no moon. The lot around the house looked like the unsuccessful result of an attempt to landscape a sand-dune area.

The time was a little after twenty-one hundred. That meant they must have brought him to some point on one of the nearby coasts—which coast, he couldn't yet tell.

The door opened and Graham went in, in the midst of the little group of men. For an instant they clustered in the hall, while somebody switched on a light.

Graham found himself leaning against a small table on which stood a table-lamp. The rays of the lamp shone on a brass tray on which lay a small pile of letters. This was an unexpected and unearned break! As the men crowded him past, Graham took a quick look at the topmost letter, the address on which read:

> Mr. Joseph Aurelio
> 1400 South Atlantic Ave.
> Bay Head, N. J.

The name "Aurelio" seemed faintly familiar . . .

But Graham was given no time to ponder this question, for they hustled him upstairs and into a bedroom. They pulled down the shade and turned on the lights.

"We gotta frisk you," said Lundquist.

They ran their hands over him, removing his knife, keys, watch-telephone—in fact all his petty possessions except his handkerchief and comb.

"Now," said Lundquist, "take it easy and get some sleep. The boss'll be here in the morning. But no tricks, my friend. We still got your girl, you know. And if you want anything, bang on the door."

"Okay," said Graham, and they went away.

When they had closed and locked the door to his room he at once began looking around. The bed was a small affair of steel tubing. Damn the people who built short beds! His feet would overhang the end, sure as shooting. There was a rickety chair, and a little old bureau bare of contents; that was all. Nothing to pick locks with, even if he had known how to pick locks.

He raised the shade and found that on the inside of the window a grille of stout iron bars ran up and down, about six or seven centimeters apart and bolted to the window-frame at top and bottom. A little examination showed that the nuts that held these bars in place were rusted fast to their bolts, and could not be unscrewed without a major operation.

He turned off the light so as to be able to see out. When his eyes became accustomed to the darkness, he observed that this one window overlooked the ocean: a calm ocean with mere one-meter combers. To the left a darker mass cut across the beach and extended on up northward, parallel to the shore-line. As it did not look quite like a boardwalk, Graham concluded that it must be the board fence surrounding a nudery.

The thought reminded him of where he had heard the name "Aurelio" before. A billboard on the Jersey Meadows, which he sometimes passed on the train, read:

ROYAL CHEST WIGS
Joseph Aurelio, Inc.
Newark, N. J.

The picture on the board showed three bathers at a resort like this one. Two of them were men to whom nature had not given abundant natural hair on the chest, and the third was an impossibly curvesome girl. Of the two men, one, resplendent in one of Mr. Aurelio's ROYAL CHEST WIGS, was getting all the attention from the girl, while the other lad, lacking both a natural and an artificial pelt, slunk off in disheartened dismay.

This was evidently Mr. Aurelio's summer beach-house. Judging by the permanent look of the bars in the window, the gang were probably using the house with the owner's knowledge and connivance. One more puzzle: what interest could a manufacturer of chest-wigs have in Gamanovia? Did he hope by some skullduggery to wangle an exclusive license for the sale of his product on the beaches of the new continent? If so he was doomed to disappointment; the shores of the new land would be deep-sea rock and ooze for many years to come, not at all nice for bathing.

And speaking of bars, this house did not impress him as much of a place. Old, and definitely crumbly. However successful Aurelio might be as a maker of chest-wigs, he had evidently not laid out a fortune here.

And if it was old and crumbly, perhaps something could be accomplished by main force. Graham grasped two of the iron bars and heaved on them. No, the house wasn't *that* far gone; the bars refused to give. He could, however, relieve the stuffiness of the indoor air by inserting his hands between the bars to open the window.

Looking out again, he saw a figure moving quietly around the front of the house. One of the gang on guard, he supposed.

He made another search of the room for some gadget or gimmick to get out of his prison with, when occasion required, but found nothing. The thought occurred to him that, like some old houses, this one might be equipped with glass window-panes. But when he rapped experimentally on the window, the dull sound indicated a methacrylate pane. So there was no hope of even getting a sharp sliver of glass to work with.

Not that he wanted to escape *yet*, before he had found out what the gang was after and whether they had Betty here . . .

At last, lacking anything better to do, he threw himself down on the over-short bed, his head in one corner and his feet dangling off the opposite one. And soon, soothed by the sound of the surf, he slept.

The next day, soon after he awoke, they brought him a sandwich and a glass of milk for breakfast and stood over him while he consumed them. To his questions Edwards shrugged his shoulders, saying:

"You got to wait till the boss gets here."

Afterwards they left him alone, except to look in on him every hour or so to make sure he was not up to mischief.

Lunch was the same. The beach filled up to some extent, though this house seemed to be south of the more densely settled section of Bay Head (towards Mantoloking, if he remembered the local geography) and comparatively few bathers resorted to this part. A few went into the nudery.

However, all were too far away for him to risk trying to call for help, now or later. Against the sound of the surf he'd have to scream his lungs out to attract attention, and the gang in the house would probably hear him before the people on the beach did.

Of course it was still pretty early in the season, and the water would still be cold even while the air was balmy. There was the usual man surf-fishing all day in hip-boots and not, so far as Graham could see, catching anything; and the youth who broke all the flying-regulations by buzzing his helicoupe a few meters over the heads of those on the beach.

Gordon Graham, suffering from galloping boredom, napped much of the afternoon. Dinner was a real meal, served, like the previous repasts, in his room. Not long after dinner, however, faint sounds of new arrivals filtered up through the floor-boards.

The door opened and Edwards said: "Come along."

He followed the small man downstairs to the living-room, whose previous occupants were ranged in a circle as though specially to receive him. He recognized the three men whom he had fallen afoul of two nights before: Lundquist, Edwards, and Warschauer, the last with his nose in a plaster cast. And two more men whom he did not know, and finally two extra-terrestrials: a dinosaurian reptile from Osiris, towering over the rest of the company, with its body painted in an elaborate blue-and-gold pattern; and a furry "monkey-rat" from Thoth (the other civilized planet of the Procyonic System) not much over a meter tall, with seven digits on each limb.

"Here he is, boss," said Lundquist, addressing the Osirian.

"So," said the reptile. "Come and look at me, Mr. Kraham!"

Graham, listening carefully, could just barely make sense out of the whistling accent that mangled half the sounds almost beyond recognition. Trusting to the helmet under his wig, he complied with the order. Presently he found the animal's two great green eyes glaring balefully into his own. His scalp prickled under the silver dome, and the room seemed to swim a little.

"Repeat after me," said the Osirian: "I, Kordon Kraham . . ."

"I, Gordon Graham."

"Take you, The'erhiya the Sha'akhfa."

"Take you, The'erhiya the Sha'akhfa." (To be my wedded wife? thought Graham. My God, what an idea!)

"To pe my absolute master."

"To be my absolute master."

"Until released py him."

"Until released by him."

"And will faithfully opey his orters."

"What?" said Graham.

"And will faithfully opey his orters! To you not unterstant, stupit one?"

"I didn't the first time—"

"Are you criticising my Enklish?" hissed the being shrilly, showing its crocodilian teeth. "I speak perfect Enklish! Not a trace of accent!"

Graham, thinking it better not to argue a point on which the Osirian was evidently touchy, simply said: "And will faithfully obey his orders."

"Efen unto teath."

"Even unto death."

So that was it! thought Graham. This Osirian must be

the one Betty had met at that extra-terrestrial clambake in Boonton, the one who had passed out surrounded by his oil-can-like drinking vessels. The famous speculator and his partner the Thothian—what was the name?—Adzik. Had The'erhiya not drunk himself silly, a lot of things might have been different. The Sha'akhfa would no doubt have been present at the meeting of the Churchillian Society, or at least in the background master-minding the procedure. Then the gang would probably not have committed those blunders that had led to the present situation.

Now what was he supposed to do? How did people act under the Osirian pseudo-hypnosis? All Graham knew was what he remembered of a scene in the movie *Perilous Planet*, where the heroine, played by Ingrid Demitriou, had been given the works by the villain, played by the eminent Osirian actor Faqhisen.

He therefore put his hands on his head and gave a theatrical groan, as if he had just found a misplaced minus-sign at the beginning of a week's calculations which he had just completed. He said:

"Mind if I sit down a minute? I seem to have a slight headache."

"That iss all right. You will feel petter in a short while," said the reptile.

At the end of his minute, Graham found them all standing around him expectantly. Then the Osirian squatted in front of him, extended its clawed hands, and caught him by the shoulders. The'erhiya said:

"You are Korton Kraham, the cheophysicist of the Kamanovia Prochect, are you not?"

Careful, now. "Yes, master. One of the geophysicists, that is."

"Ant you know where these maggots haff been planted in the ocean bet, to you not?"

That was public information, spread out before the populace in a hundred popular articles and news-releases. "Yes," said Graham.

"Well then, I want to know which maggots to fire, ant in what orter, to raise Kamanovia apuff the surface *pefore* Nofember twenty-ninth of this year!"

So this was it! But why, *why?* It still made no sense. November 29th was the date on which the World Federation's contract with Teófilo March became effective. So there was no doubt some connection. If the continent were raised before the contract date, that would no doubt cause some confusion, but nothing the W. F.'s lawyers couldn't straighten out.

Anyway, he couldn't answer this question off-hand. Therefore he said: "I don't know."

"O yes you to," insisted The'erhiya. "You must talk or we shall fint means to make you."

Still Graham shook his head. Lundquist remarked: "I guess he means that, boss. He couldn't hold out on you after you'd given him the treatment."

"I don't know about that," said Warschauer, the damage to his nose still de-nasalizing his speech. "Sometimes when an order contradicts the subject's compulsions and inhibitions too strongly, you'll get resistance to a post-treatment order."

Lundquist said: "I don't know as I follow Artie's fancy language, but we can soon enough find out. Just let me give his arm a good twist . . ."

The'erhiya waved a claw. "No, I haff a better methot. Ko ket our other guest."

"Oh, I get it," said Lundquist with what Graham took to be a grin of sadistic delight.

Lundquist and Edwards went out and in a few minutes returned, bringing with them a handcuffed Jeru-Bhetiru.

"Gorodon!" she cried. "What is this? What are they going to do to us?"

"I don't know, Betty," said Graham. "They want me to give 'em some—uh—dope I haven't got."

"You mean you say you ain't got it," said Lundquist. "Now, you two mursils hold her good and tight. You two, go get that old table out of the kitchen. And the hatchet."

When these articles had been brought, Lundquist said: "Okay, my friend, now see if you can't remember how to wuik those maggots. Because every minute you don't I'm gonna chop off one joint of this dame's pretty little fingers, until there ain't none left. Ready?"

They mashed her hand down flat on the old table. She screamed. The men paid no attention. Lundquist, a glint of amusement in his eyes, glanced upward. Following his glance, Graham saw that the ceiling was sound-proofed. One of the men had quietly brought a pistol out of his pocket in case of emergencies.

Lundquist raised the hatchet.

V.

"Wait," said Gordon Graham.

"Yes?" said The'erhiya.

Graham's mind had been working furiously. If there had been reason to believe that these gloops were out to blow up the Earth or conquer the Solar System or something fantastic like that, maybe he should be willing to sacrifice both himself and Jeru-Bhetiru. On the other hand there would be no point in letting her be mutilated to prevent some mere swindle or theft, which he suspected this of being. Of course if he were wrong ... He put that thought away with an internal shudder. He'd have to use what judgment he could bring to bear upon the situation.

Stall, that was the trick. His next statement would have the advantage of being almost true.

"I said I didn't know," he said, "but I didn't say I couldn't find out. You wouldn't expect me to carry around thirty pages of equations in my head, would you?"

"Ko on, tell us what you mean," said The'erhiya.

"I mean that if you'll g-get me my textbooks and log-tables and things, I could figure this out in a few days. After all you're asking me for data that took me and a dozen other men a year to work out in the first place."

The Osirian persisted: "Why can you not simply gif us the firing plan of the maggots? What tifference does it make whether the firing is started now or next Octoper?"

"A lot of difference," said Graham. "You have to take the lunar and solar tides into account, and the periodicity of the magmatic vortices, and a lot of other things. That is, if you don't want your continent to sink down again, or if you don't want to drown the coasts of Brazil and West Africa with earthquake waves."

"Fery well," said The'erhiya. "Gif him a paper and pencil, Warschauer, so he can make out a list of the things he will neet."

Graham made his list a good one, including not only all the reference-books he might need, and his slide-rule, but also his contour-map of the South Atlantic and his complete set of drawing-instruments.

"Get them out of my apartment," he told them. "Be sure you're there in the middle of a working-day when my brother won't be in. Here's my key."

"Goot," said The'erhiya. "Take our guests pack to their rooms, now."

Watching closely, Graham observed that Jeru-Bhetiru had a room two doors down the hall from his.

It was next noon when Warschauer and a man whom Graham had heard referred to only as "Hank" came in with the supplies he had ordered. Lundquist followed, saying:

"There you are, my friend. Now get to wuik like a good little boy and don't give us no more trouble, or we may have to liquidate you after all."

They stood around as he spread his papers and books out on the table they provided, and went through learned-looking manoeuvers. After an hour they got bored and went out, locking the door as usual.

Graham at once began examining his drawing-instruments. Stupid gloops; having once carefully searched him and taken away anything that might be used as a tool, they had willingly given him a whole other set at his own request . . .

Careful, he told himself; maybe they're not so stupid at that. Maybe they hope to pop in and surprise me. In any case they are assuming that The'erhiya's pseudo-hypnotic treatment and the fact of their holding Jeru-Bhetiru as a hostage would between them render me harmless.

He went to the window, reached through the bars, and began feeling around the outside. The house had been finished in stucco so old as to have become crumbly. Maybe if he could dig enough of it away he could remove the entire window-frame: window, bars, and all. At least it was worth trying.

He began pecking at the stucco with the sharp point of a drawing-compass. A thin little cascade of pale-gray dust sifted down from the scene of his operations to fan out on the roof below. Graham hoped the gang were not so fussy about the appearance of Aurelio's house as to notice it.

He had been hacking at the stucco for an indefinite time when it occurred to him that his guards might put their noses into his room any time to check up on him. Since they had taken his watch he couldn't be sure, but in any event he'd better quit for a while—which he was not sorry to do, as his arm ached from the strain and the awkward position. Next time he'd count his pecks to give himself a rough idea of the time that had elapsed.

He went back to his calculations until one of the men looked in on him again, then resumed his pecking. He now had a deep slot, a span long, in the stucco alongside the

window-frame. If he could get that much done each time
. . . He got to work again. Thank God for his long arms!

Two days later the slot ran all the way round the
window-frame. Graham grasped the bars and heaved. The
whole thing rocked towards him a couple of centimeters
with crunching sounds. As it came, plaster dribbled down
below the inside of the window-frame.

However, the frame refused to come any further. By
feeling around outside, Graham, who had never before
concerned himself with the construction of windows, discovered that the pieces of wood that ran around the
outside of the frame would prevent the window from
coming any further towards him. They would therefore
have to be removed.

Graham, going over his instruments again, decided that
his T-square offered the most promising possibilities. The
titanium cross-head had fairly sharp ends. Of course the
square wouldn't be worth much as a drawing-instrument
after being used as a pry-bar, but that couldn't be helped.
He got to work.

By the next day all four sections of the outer frame had
been pried loose, twisted off, and drawn back through the
bars to be hidden under Graham's mattress. He hoped
that the denuded condition of the window-frame would
not be too obvious from the outside.

Then he pulled on the bars again. This time the frame
came in as far as he wanted it to.

He'd better not go out now, though. He had been
thinking hard what to do when he got the window loose:
to make a dash for liberty, trying to find the nearest
public telephone to call Sklar; to reach Jeru-Bhetiru to
warn her of what he was doing, or to try to get her out
too; to make a clean getaway, or to 'phone Sklar and then
to sneak back into his room before they discovered his
absence . . .

He finally decided to make at least an effort to get
Jeru-Bhetiru out at the same time he escaped himself.
For, if he went alone and they discovered his escape
before he succeeded in bringing the forces of the law
down on the place, almost anything might happen. They
might kill the girl for the hell of it; or she might be killed
in the battle; or they might, on learning of his absence,
flee taking her with them as they had done from the house
in the Bronx.

Graham therefore cleaned up the plaster-dust on the

floor and waited until Edwards came for his dinner-tray. Edwards said:

"How you coming along with those figures, huh? The boss is getting a little impatient."

"I should have the answers in a couple of days," replied Graham.

Late that night, Graham waited until the man on watch had appeared and then disappeared from in front of the house. Then he heaved cautiously on the bars until the window came out completely. The combination of window, frame, and bars was heavier than he expected, so much so that his muscles stood out in knots from the strain of lowering the assembly gently to the floor. Fortunately the sound-proofing of the house helped him here; if it muffled sounds on their way to his room from elsewhere in the house, it also muffled sounds headed in the opposite direction.

Then he pocketed his drawing-compass and swung a leg over the window-sill. Luckily for him the slope of the lower roof was a mere 30°, so he felt he could crawl around on it without a life-line.

Next to his own window another gaped blackly. Was that room inhabited by one of the gang, and if so would the fellow be watching for him?

There was no way of telling short of putting his head into the room or calling out a challenge, neither of which acts struck Graham as the sort of thing a sensible young scientist would do. Therefore he crawled down towards the lower edge of the roof, sprawled like a spider on the shingles, and inched his way past the window.

Still no sound. His scalp itched from the several days' growth of hair under the helmet, but there was no possible way of scratching it through the silver.

He crept bank up the slope to Jeru-Bhetiru's window and rapped softly on the glass.

"Gorodon?" came a sharp whisper.

"Yes. T-take this." He passed her the compass. "D'you think you can reach out with it and dig at the plaster when they're not watching, enough to loosen the whole window?"

"I do not know," she said. "Let me try." And she reached out and began pecking as he had done.

It soon became obvious, however, that she had neither the strength nor the reach to do as quick a job as he had done. Moreover the point of the compass had been worn down from the previous operation. Graham said:

"At that rate it'll take six months to get the window loose, and I can't stall these bleeps that long."

"Could you not come out every night and dig a little?"

"That would be just as bad, and they'd probably catch me in the act sooner or later. In fact the man on watch now ought to be prowling around the front of the house again any minute."

"What, then?"

They were silent for many seconds. Finally Graham said: "If I could get you into my room, we could both go out my window. I wonder if you could get one of the gang to bring you around?"

"I do not know. That Edwards is not what you call very sympathetic."

"Well, maybe—tell him I'm your lover and you're going crazy because you haven't—uh—seen me for days, now. P-pour it on thick. Offer him your beautiful alabaster body if need be."

"Offer him my *what?* I thought alabaster was a mineral."

"Never mind; just use your feminine wiles to the utmost. You know what they are, don't you?"

"I think I do. When should I do all this?" she said.

"The best time would be the middle of the afternoon, when there's a crowd on the beach. If we get out my window, we'll jump off the roof and make a run for the nudery over there."

"What is a nudery?" she asked.

"An inclosure for folks who prefer to swim without suits. Every beach has one. I hope we can 'phone for help from there, and that there'll be enough people around so they won't dare try to chase us or shoot at us."

"Very well. I will try."

Now, Graham might have seized the opportunity to grasp Jeru-Bhetiru's hand, press it to his lips, and swear his undying love in the Romeo manner. But it occurred to him that neither his love nor anything else about him would be undying for long if the gang's watchman caught him at his tryst.

Therefore he contented himself with saying simply: "S-swell. Night."

He crawled back into his own room without incident. He was just heaving the window back into place when he heard his door being unlocked.

He gave the window a quick heave, driving it home with a resounding thump, and leaped into his chair just before the door opened. When Warschauer put his head into the room, Graham was poring over his calculations as studiously as could be.

"You all right?" asked Warschauer.

"Uh—yes, sure," said Graham.

"I thought I heard something . . ."

"Maybe you did, but it wasn't in here." Graham became uncomfortably aware of the plaster-dust that had fallen on the floor below the window as a result of his latest foray, and that he had not had time to clean up. Surely Warschauer must see it too; to Graham's overstimulated imagination it stood out like a ton of coal on a snowbank. He avoided looking in that direction.

"Well, okay, then," said Warschauer vaguely, and disappeared.

Graham's scalp itched worse than ever, but he did not dare take off the helmet to get at it. Not having any of the goo that Sklar had glued it on with, he was not sure he'd be able to replace it properly. At least, however, he could take out the splinters that his person had acquired from the roof-shingles.

The next day crawled along like all the others. After lunch, Gordon Graham began cocking his ear for signs that Jeru-Bhetiru had sold Edwards on the idea of letting her visit her supposed lover. (Supposed? Hell, in the older and purer sense of the word he *was* her lover.)

The day, as luck would have it, was overcast, drawing few people to the beach. Shortly after lunch a brief shower drove even these few away. But during the next hour the cessation of the rain and a few wan sunbeams lured some of them back. Graham would, have preferred to wait another day, but had no way of getting word to his fellow-prisoner during the daylight hours. He regretted that he had not made the escape attempt contingent on good weather. But then they might hit a rainy spell and delay too long . . .

The hours crawled past. Still no sign of Jeru-Bhetiru, daughter of Jeré-Lagilé of Katai-Jhogorai.

Then the lock clicked and in came the girl, with Edwards right behind her.

"D-darling!" cried Graham, holding out his arms. They went into a clinch, and Graham found that the reports to the effect that Krishnans had taken up the Earthly custom of kissing were not at all exaggerated. Graham found that he didn't have to pretend, and from the warmth of her reaction he hoped she didn't either. If it were not for more urgent matters he could go on like this all afternoon . . .

He finally forced himself to look up from the last lingering kiss and said to Edwards: "Why don't you—uh—just wait outside the door for a while?"

Edwards glanced at the bed with a slight smirk, then back at Graham. "Nope, gotta stay with you. The boss wouldn't like it. Anything you want to do, you can do it in front of me."

Oh yeah? thought Graham, remembering the ancient joke about the Frenchmen who were arguing over the definition of *sang-froid*. While wondering what to do next, he felt Jeru-Bhetiru stiffen in his arms. She was looking towards the window with an expression of terror.

"What is that?" she whispered, pushing Graham aside and running to the window. *"Surujo adhikol!* What is happening?"

"What's that?" snapped Edwards, crowding after her.

Graham took in the scene with one all-inclusive glance; then snatched up his drawing-board. Holding it edgewise to lessen its air-resistance, he brought the edge down with all his strength on Edward's red head. Edwards saw it coming out of the tail of his eye and started to whirl and reach for a shoulder-holster. But too late. The wood met the man's cranium with a sharp splintering sound. As Edwards folded up on the floor Graham saw that the tough board was split by the force of the blow.

He pulled the body out of the way, without bothering to see whether there was still life in it, and seized the window-bars. A straining heave, and the window came out.

"Come on," he said softly. "Move quickly but quietly." He slid over the sill of the opening and began crawling down the shingles. "D-don't jump off the edge. Take hold of the gutter with your hands like this, lower yourself to arm's length, and let go. You'll only have about a meter to drop."

From the sandy yard of the Aurelio house he caught her as she dropped. Then hand in hand they ran down the walk to the beach. On the beach they turned left and raced for the stockade of the nudery.

At the entrance to the nudery they paused to draw a breath and look back at the Aurelio house. There was no sign of pursuit.

"I'm sure somebody in here has a 'phone," Graham said. "Come on."

The entrance to the inclosure consisted of a passage between two parallel board fences. The passage made an L around the corner of the nudery so that nobody standing outside could see in. They made the turn and found that the inner fence ran on a couple of meters beyond the corner and ended in a counter and a row of lockers. Behind the counter they could see a few sunless sun-bathers sitting sadly on the sands.

"Hey," said the man behind the counter. "You can't go in there with clothes on! That's indecent non-exposure! Gotta leave 'em in these lockers."

"That's all right," said Graham. "I just wanted to fuff— to fuff—"

"You wanted to *what?*" said the man.

"To telephuff—"

He broke off and he and the man stared at one another in mutual recognition. The man was the member of The'erhiya's band whom he knew so far only as "Hank."

Before Graham could even tense his muscles for flight, Hank's hand swooped down below the counter and came up again with a pistol. He held this pointed at the runaways, in such a position that his back hid it from the nuders.

"Not a move," he said. "Just stay where you are." Then he dialled in his own wrist-'phone and spoke swiftly: " . . . well go look . . . yeah . . . got 'em . . . bring a trulp . . ."

Five minutes later Gordon Graham and Jeru-Bhetiru were being marched back to the Aurelio house by Lundquist and Warschauer, each pointing a scarcely-hidden weapon.

Back in the house they were conducted into the living-room, where The'erhiya and Adzik and the other man whose name Graham didn't know awaited them.

"Well?" said Lundquist. "What about Jim?"

"He iss det," said The'erhiya.

"Huh," said Lundquist. "Well, we'll take it out on these two." He put his pistol on safety, and took hold of it by the barrel.

"No," said The'erhiya, "we still neet him . . ."

But even as the reptile spoke, the pistol-butt whipped through the air and hit Graham's head with a muffled but distinctly metallic *bonk*. Graham saw stars and staggered, though the helmet and the thin layer of sponge-rubber inside it saved him from the worst of the blow.

"Stop it!" said The'erhiya sharply. "Later, perhaps, but not now!"

Lundquist paused, staring intently at Graham. Finally the man muttered: "Something funny about this wunk's head." He stepped closer and rapped Graham's skull with his knuckles. "Thought so." He began digging around the edge of the epidermoid with his fingernails until he had pried up enough to get a good grip. After much tugging the helmet came off with sucking sounds.

Graham put a hand to his head. Now at least he could scratch. His scalp bore a short growth of stiff bristly hair, perhaps half a centimeter long, and all gooey from the adhesive Sklar had glued the helmet on with.

"So," said The'erhiya. "Now we know why he has not giffen us any results. Now we have the information from One, he could only giff us a last-minute check. Not worth the risk. Kill them."

Lundquist said: "You mean right now? Why not save 'em and have some fun out of it?"

"I to not wish to risk more delay. This man iss dancherous. Stronger than he looks. Shut the wintows and shoot them right now. If it makes you unhappy, I will get you a rabbit to torture."

Graham exchanged an agonized glance with Jeru-Bhetiru. Before he let them simply execute him, he'd throw something or sock somebody, even if they killed him in the act. He taughtened himself for a spring.

As the men moved to obey, the taciturn Adzik piped up: "Wait." Then the Thothian engaged in a rapid conversation in a language unknown to Graham with its reptilian partner.

Finally The'erhiya said: "We haff a better itea. Now he does not have hiss helmet, we can use him." The Osirian thrust his scaly muzzle into Graham's face. "Kraham!"

"Yes?" said Graham. Those great green eyes really had hold of him now. It was as though everything else in the world had dissolved into gray mist, leaving only those eyes glaring through their slit pupils.

"Repeat after me: I, Korton Kraham . . ."

They went through the whole rigmarole again, but this time with a difference. As he repeated each phrase, Graham felt as though invisible but unbreakable handcuffs were being snapped shut on his spirit. He had committed himself morally to help these beings, and could no more disobey them than an ordinary man could shoot his mother.

"Now," said The'erhiya, "hit her. Hart."

Although Graham wanted nothing less, he could no

more help himself than one can help blinking at a strong light. He stepped over to Jeru-Bhetiru, drew back his fist, and, disregarding her horrified expression, let her have a strong right to the jaw. *Smack!* Down she went, cold.

"You see," said The'erhiya.

"He might still be pretending," said Lundquist sourly.

"No, I can tell." The'erhiya tapped a claw against the scales that covered his bulging cranium. "Now, Kraham, tell us who sent you to us with that thing on your het."

"Reinhold Sklar. World Federation Constable."

"Very well. You will ko with my men, who will put you out near the city. Then you will ko into the city, fint Sklar, and kill him. To you unterstant?"

"I understand." And the worst of it was, he did. Given the order, he knew he'd kill Sklar the first chance he got, that he'd use whatever stealth or deception needed, and that he'd be unable to warn his victim in any way.

"And when you haff killed Sklar," continued the Osirian, "you will immediately kill yourself. Iss that clear?"

"Yes," said Graham.

They led him out. He did not even look back at the crumpled heap on the floor that was the girl he loved.

VI.

Gordon Graham climbed out of the subway and walked like a remote-controlled robot towards Sklar's hotel in the west fifties. The dominant half of his mind thought of plans for killing Sklar. He must be careful, for instance, not to get excited and pump the entire magazine into the constable, because then he would have no shots left to kill himself with. And when he did kill himself, he must remember to shoot himself well back, over the ear. People sometimes shot themselves in the temple and blinded themselves without killing . . .

Meanwhile the rest of his mind, like a prisoner in a cage, raged futilely in vain efforts to regain control of his body, and was carried along, a helpless spectator, to witness whatever crimes the body had been ordered to commit. Whatever the Osirian pseudo-hypnosis was, it certainly seemed to work. Foolproof. Could it be that the other men of the gang were under The'erhiya's control in the same fashion? He knew from what Ivor Graham had told him that Osirians had to promise not to use this uncanny ability of theirs before they were allowed on

Earth. But if they broke their promise, there was no way of physically sealing up this faculty.

The hotel lay in the next block.

And why hadn't they done the same to Jeru-Bhetiru? Then he remembered reading somewhere that of all the civilized species, human beings were the most susceptible to this influence. Krishnans could be influenced for only a short time . . .

"No," said the clerk at the desk of the Baldwin, "Mr. Sklar isn't in."

"I'll wait," said Graham, and sat down in the shabby lobby.

Hours passed.

Still the autonomous part of Graham's mind lunged against the walls of its psychic prison, while the other half resigned itself with unwonted calm to waiting for his victim. Although darkness had fallen outside, and his stomach was protesting its lack of sustenance, he sat there in the moth-eaten old plushy armchair, waiting as quietly as a statue.

Then in came Reinhold Sklar. He saw Graham as quickly as the latter saw him, raised an eyebrow, and stepped forward with a hand out.

"Hello there!" he said. "I didn't expect you back so soon. Come on up to my room for a tuck, huh?"

Graham smiled, replied with a mechanical "Hello," and followed the constable to the elevator. This was going to be easy. As soon as the elevator started on its way he would simply take out his pistol and shoot Sklar—several times. As the magazine held nineteen shots, each with enough power to tear a limb off a man, a few shots should do a good job. Then the muzzle to his right ear, a pull on the trigger, and his brains would be spattered all over the inside of the elevator to finish a good job well done.

Stop! Wait! Watch out! shrieked the other part of his mind—but silently. This part of his consciousness could no more affect events than a spectator at a movie could, by wishing, alter the course of the plot.

The door of the elevator stood open. Graham remembered that he must do nothing to arouse the suspicions of Sklar.

Sklar stood aside and waved Graham in, then stepped in after him and punched the No. 9 button. The doors slid quietly closed, and the elevator started up.

Graham drew his right hand, clutching the pistol, out of his pants pocket.

And, just before it hit, he was aware of the blurred movement of a blackjack in Sklar's hand, swinging towards his own head with the speed of a striking snake ...

He woke up with a terrific headache, as if somebody had sent a miniature Gamanovian maggot boring into his head and then touched off its atomic pile. He also had a taste in his mouth something like the waste from an oil-refinery. He was lying on his back on a cot. When he tried to move his head he became aware of a gadget attached to it by means of wires that limited its motion.

"Now just you lie still," said a female voice, and a motherly nurse called: "Mr. Sklar!"

"Comink," said the brisk familiar voice.

The nurse continued: "Just hold still, Mr. Graham, so we can get the psychointegrator off you." There were metallic sounds, and the cap was pulled off his head.

He sat up, almost falling over onto the floor with dizziness. "Wh-what—" he mumbled.

One of Sklar's hairy, muscular hands was gripping his shoulders to steady him.

With great effort, Graham said: "How—How did you know—"

"That crew haircut of yours. I knew right away you didn't have your wig on no more, so I expected somethink like what happened."

"I n-never thought I'd be glad to have somebody bop me on the bean. Am I suss-safe now?"

"Sure; that's what for is the psychointegrator. Wonderful machin. You're in the hospital of the Division of Investigation Headquarters on Lunk Island. But quick, now, tell me what happened to you and where the gank is now hidink out?"

Graham furrowed his brow in an effort to think. It all seemed so long ago and far away.

"Let me see—Joseph Aurelio's house, something Atlantic Avenue, Bay Head, New Jersey ..." and he told his tale.

Before he had gotten out more than a few sentences, Sklar had dialled his 'phone and was rattling orders into it.

"G-going to raid the place?" said Graham.

"Yes, sure."

"Let me come too."

"Not you. You're still an invariable; you ain't up to it."

"O yes I am. You forget they've still got my girl."

"Oho. Okus-dokus, come alunk then."

The little squadron of W. F. D. I. automobiles purred slowly over Barnegat Bay, barely visible below as a paler strip against the blackness of the land. Graham could see the other cars only by their flying-lights.

He finished his account of his experiences, saying: "What did I do wrong this time?"

"You did pretty good, considering. For a man without special trainink you're a pretty keen absorber, which I would not suspect from that dopey absent-minded look of yours. That man in the nudery being a member of the gank was just a bad break. I don't think I'd have tried to rescue the girl too, but then you are yonk and romantic. One rizzon I sent Varnipaz to South America was that he is too damn romantic for this kind of work."

"Then you don't think he'll accomplish anything?"

Sklar made a rattling noise in his throat. "That gloop? Naw. He don't know his way around Earth good enough, for one think, even if he has been here a couple years. Didn't want an argument, so the easiest way to get rid of him was to send him off chasing wild geeses. But you now, maybe with a few years' trainink and experience we could make a constable out of you. Would you be interested?"

"I doubt it," said Graham. "After all I've put a good many years on getting to be a geophysicist."

"Sure, and you don't want to throw that away. I wish I knew who that 'One' that The'erhiya talked about was. If we knew that . . . You sure he said 'One?' "

"Yes; at least it sounded like 'One.' Of course with that accent it might have been almost anything to begin with."

"Sure," said Sklar. "You can't expect those lizards to spick good Enklish, like me for instance, because they ain't got human focal organs. 'One,' huh? Say, how many of the other Gamanovia brains do you know?"

Graham thought. "I know all the scientists on the job here at Columbia, and I've met a good many of those at Rio. It was down there last winter, and met Souza, the big chief, and Benson, and Nogami, and Abdelkader, and van Schaak . . . That's all the names I can remember just now."

"You keep trying," said Sklar. "Now, here we are. Remember, if we get close to quarters with this Osirian, don't let him look you in the eyes."

The cars manoeuvered with clockwork precision. While three of them hovered over the Aurelio house, the other four dropped into the streets nearby. As the swish of their rotors died away, uniformed men issued from them and filed silently around the intervening corners towards the house.

Sklar and Graham followed hard behind the uniformed men. Sklar whispered: "Now don't get excited and shoot one of your own pipple in the back. Very bad for morals. Don't shoot nobody unless to save your life or to kip them from gettink away."

"I won't," promised Graham.

"Now we got to wait," said Sklar. "You'll find the suspension of waitink is much worse than a fight."

Graham waited, heart pounding.

Nothing happened for at least a quarter-hour. Out of sight around the nearest house, the surf boomed lazily. Overhead the rotors of the hovering cars still burbled.

Then a whistle split the silence. At once lights came on everywhere: a searchlight in each of the hovering cars, a parachute-flare, several more lights that had been set up on the ground. Then came a crackle of shots and the sound of smashed methacrylate windows—like the tinkle of broken glass but duller.

Then silence again while the lights still played on the house. Here and there came the sound of windows opening in other houses and voices calling questions into the night.

"What is it?" said Graham.

"Gas," said Sklar, looking at his watch. "I'm afraid our pipple have flown the kite, gone, though. Okay, in we go. Here, stick these up your nose, and don't breathe through your mouth unless you want to be laid out cold like a turnkey."

There was a rending of wood as the men broke in the front door. By the time Graham arrived in Sklar's wake, the house resounded (despite its extensive sound-proofing) to the tramp of heavy feet, upstairs and down. The lights were already switched on. The gas made Graham's eyes sting.

"Nobody here," said a man in uniform.

For half an hour Graham had nothing to do but keep out of the way of the men, who took impressions of finger-prints, turned over furniture, and otherwise busied themselves in the search for clues.

He said to Sklar: "Say, it just occurred to me they might have—er—booby-trapped the house."

Sklar, puffing his usual cigarette, shrugged. "Sure, we

all knew that when we first came in. Got to teck chances in my business sometimes, you know."

Graham, increasingly bored and restless, wandered upstairs. The body of Edwards had been removed, though when, whither, and by whom Graham did not know. His broken drawing-board still lay where he had dropped it.

He strolled into the room that had been occupied by Jeru-Bhetiru. Perhaps he could find some trace of the girl that had been overlooked by the W. F. troopers.

But this room was as bare of tangible relics as all the others. The bed had been tipped up against the wall and the rug thrown back by the searchers, who had then gone on to other business.

Graham gave the room a good looking-over nevertheless. When he examined the floor, a slight streaky discoloration on the part that had been covered by the rug drew his attention.

By moving his head until he got a high-light from the room's one light-bulb to coincide with the discoloration, he saw that it consisted of a word written on the floor with some pigment almost but not quite the same as the color of the boards. The word was:

RIO

"Hey, Sklar!" yelled Graham. "Come here!"

Sklar saw it at once, and stooped closely over it, playing a pocket flashlight on the stains.

"Blood," he said. "Your girl-friend must have cut herself and written this for us to find. Good kid. Hey, who was in charge of searching this room?"

After a pause a very large trooper explained in a very small voice: "I was, sir."

"Your name?" said Sklar ominously.

"Schindelheim, Trooper, first class."

"That," said Sklar, "will go on your fitness report . . . What is it now?"

"Mr. Sklar," said somebody else, "one of these local cops has put tickets on all our cars for parking in the street with rotors attached."

Sklar made an impatient motion. "You take charge and take care of that, Roth. We're goink back to the city and then on to Rio. Come, Graham. How lunk will it take you to pack for a trip to South America, huh? Can you mit me at the airport at sixtin hunderd tomorrow? Good."

VII.

As the airliner banked with the ponderous aerial dignity of a condor, the great bay of Guanabara came into view through the window at which Gordon Graham sat. Although he had been to São Sebastião do Rio de Janeiro before, Graham never failed to get a thrill out of the approach to the world's most beautiful metropolis.

Below and in front of them the bay spread out like an immense fan, with clusters of islands in the foreground and behind them the scalloped line of sub-bays. Then the city, running along the edge of the scallop and trailing off into the valleys extending up into the mountains like the teeth of a comb. As the 'plane dropped lower the Corcovado and other peaks thrust themselves up against the skyline.

Even Reinhold Sklar, whom Graham would have thought to be about as aesthetically sensitive as one of Teófilo March's turtles, said: "Boy, ain't that something!"

Now the white line of the beach could be made out, and back of it the sharp diagonals of the avenidas with their rows of shining skyscrapers. Before them the vast airport thrust out into the bay like a welcoming hand. As they sank towards it, the map effect flattened out of sight. Graham found he was confronted by a solid wall of buildings, throwing back the pinkish-white light of the rising sun, and below them the green of the seashore parkways, along which he could see the movement of thousands of shiny dots: automobiles. In another traffic-lane, to their left, convertibles were buzzing in to the airport to leave their rotors, like queen-ants shedding their wings, while their owners drove them to work.

The landing 'chute blossomed behind them and they drew up to the ramp. As they walked down the companionway and into the reception building they met a tall, broad-shouldered, bushy-haired, smiling young man with a rather Oriental look. After a moment of uncertainty Graham recognized Varnipaz bad-Savarun, still in his Earthly disguise.

Shaking hands, Varnipaz asked: "Have you eaten yet?"

"No," said Sklar. They went into the restaurant and ordered.

"Well," said Sklar, "what have you found out, pal?"

Varnipaz said: "I reported to headquarters as you ordered me. Then I tried to follow the logical course. If the gang used a cult for a cover in North America, it seemed to me that it might use a similar organization in South America. Therefore I have been going around the city attending the meetings of all the queer little societies and cults—the Cosmotheists, the Brazilo-Israelites, the Hindu Center of Absolute Truth, the Society for the Abolition of Coffee, and so on." He shook his head. "You Earthmen may call us Krishnans backward, but you have some of the most irrational . . . Well, anyway, I have membership lists of several of them." He brought out a thick mass of papers. "I thought that if you could compare the membership of these with the list of engineers and technicians employed on the Gamanovia Project, you might find something."

"I apologize to you," said Sklar, leafing through the papers.

"For what?"

"For sayink you'd never make a W. F. constable. Your name ought to be Sherlock bad-Holmes. Any time you want to sign up for the candidate school . . . Here, Graham, you know who's who on the project."

"I don't know all of 'em," said Graham, "but I'll glance through these anyway." He too began running down the lists, and presently exclaimed: "Homer Benson! Why, old Homer's the second man to Souza; I know him w-well. That is, if this is the same Benson."

"It probably is," said Sklar. "There wouldn't be many men with a name like that in Rio. What list is that?"

Graham looked at the heading. "Soci—How do you pronounce it?"

Sklar looked. "*Sociedade Homagem ao Cortereal.* Society for Homage to Cortereal. Who's he?"

Varnipaz said: "João Vaz Corte-Real, an explorer who some people here think discovered the Americas before Columbus. They take it very seriously, though why anybody cares, when as I understand some Norwegian found the continents long before either, I fail to comprehend."

Sklar asked Graham: "Any more project pipple on that list?"

Graham sat in silence, running down the list. When almost at the end he said: "I think I recognize two here: Vieira and Wen."

"Who are they?"

"Gaspar Vieira is one of the local people, a chemist, and Wen Pan-djao is a Chinese mathematician. I met 'em both when I was down last year. I don't really know them, though."

Sklar drummed with his fingers on the table-top. "Come on, you two. I should go through the local poliss, but we ain't got the time."

They piled into a taxi. Sklar directed the driver to the Gamanovia Building, on the Praia do Flamengo out towards Botafogo Bay. As they rolled he told Graham: "Kip lookink through those lists. There might be others."

One of Rio's notorious traffic-jams held them up for half an hour, enabling Graham to complete his scrutiny. He said:

"I d-don't see any more, but that doesn't prove anything. We need the complete list of employees from Gamanovia's Personnel Department, to check against all of these."

"Hokus dokus," said Sklar. "Here we are."

They piled out, gave their names at the registration desk, and a few minutes later were in Souza's office. Meanwhile Souza's private secretary and six other girls were going over the lists in the adjoining room.

While waiting, Souza and his visitors engaged in small-talk. Graham had great difficulty in following this, for while Sklar's Portuguese was fast and fluent if badly pronounced, and that of Varnipaz was, like his English, painfully correct and formal, Graham could only read the language and speak it a little. When somebody rattled a string of nasal vowels at him he was helpless.

Presently Souza's secretary came back with the pile of papers. "Senhor Paulo," she said, "we found the name of Senhor Gjessing on the list for Mechanosophical Society."

"What?" said Sklar.

Varnipaz explained: "Those are the ones who worship the Machine. You should go to one of their services: An altar with a machine on it, all wheels and levers and colored lights. As far as I could see it does nothing but go round and round while they kneel and pray to it, but somehow it works them into a state of ecstacy. You Earthmen . . ."

"Is that all?" said Sklar.

"That is all," said the secretary.

"Good. That little metapolygraph in my suitcase has attachments for only four people. Senhor Paulo, will you get Senhores Benson, Gjessing, Vieira, and Wen?"

While these employees were being summoned, Sklar

employed himself with setting up his metapolygraph. He asked Souza: "You don't mind if I put the box on your desk?"

"So-no."

"*Obrigado.* I hope this will crack the case, because nothing short of deep hypnosis can beat this little machine."

One by one the experts appeared. Benign old Benson doddered in, and after him the hulking Wen with his perpetual grin. Then fat little Vieira, and lastly a bald man with a handlebar mustache whom Graham did not know.

Souza introduced each one as he arrived: "These are Mr. Sklar, Mr. Graham, and Mr. Muller" (for that was Varnipaz's alias). When the last man appeared he introduced him as "Dr. Gjessing," pronouncing it "zhessing" as if it had been Portuguese.

The owner of the name promptly corrected his boss by murmuring "yessing."

Wen's perpetual grin widened. "Roald always wants us to pronounce him as in Norwegian," he said. "Now me, I have given up trying to make people pronounce my name. It is really 'wun' but they all insist on saying 'wen.' "

"Then why do you spell it 'wen'?" asked Vieira.

"Because in Chinese, the 'eh' sound is always 'uh' except when it follows or precedes an 'ee' sound . . ."

Sklar cleared his throat in a marked manner and broke in: "Now, gentlemen, we'll discuss the science of fanatics later. With your permission I am going to attach this metapolygraph to you and ask you some questions about an urgent matter. You understand that you don't have to answer, or even put on the attachments. But as loyal employees of the World Federation I'm sure you want to coöperate, don't you?" The last words held the faintest hint of menace.

There being no objections, Sklar fastened the leads of the machine to the four men's head, wrists, and ankles. Then he sat behind Souza's desk and began asking questions:

"Do any of you know anything about a group, headed by extra-terrestrials, that wants to interfere with the Project?"

Graham, craning his neck a little, could see that the needles on the four dials remained steady as the men answered "*Não*" in turn.

"Have you ever been in contact with such a group?"

"*Não*."

"Do you know of *any* secret group opposed to the Gamanovia Project?"

"*Não*."

"Have you heard of any plan for firing the maggots ahead of time?"

"*Não* . . ."

Still no telltale movement of the needles. After half an hour Sklar gave up and removed the attachments.

"Wrong track," he said. "Looks as if the next person we'd have to interview would be Teófilo March, the turtle man. Would he be on Ascension Island now?"

"Oh," said Souza, "you will not be dealing with Senhor March."

"Why not? Is he dead?"

"No, he has sold out. An *Americano do Norte* named Aurelio bought the Rock, and March's contract along with it. I believe March keeps his turtle-farm, as the cable-employees keep their farms on Green Mountain, but . . ."

Sklar's sharp glance crossed that of Graham, in whose mind a sudden light shone. "Hey!" said Graham. "This is the man they t-t-t- . . ."

"Try again," said Sklar.

"T-t-t- . . ."

"Whistle it."

"The man the gang was talking about. You remember they said they'd heard from 'One'? They meant Dr. W-wen, of course, since that's how he pronounces . . ."

"Stop him!" yelled Sklar, reaching for his holster.

They might as well have tried to stop a rhinoceros. The big Chinese straight-armed Gjessing out of the way and plunged through the door, slamming it behind him. As they rushed for it they heard his feet pounding along the corridor, and they got it open just in time to see him disappearing around a corner.

"He seems to be headed for the control-room," said Souza.

Graham, the youngest man present, outran the others. He knew where the control-room was from his previous visits. They tore along the corridor, around a couple of bends, and up a single flight of stairs.

The control-door was both closed and locked when they got to it.

"Who's got a key?" snapped Sklar.

Souza arrived late, puffing like an asthmatic porpoise, and produced a key. It worked the lock, but the door, when they tried to open it, moved only a centimeter or two. Inside they could hear furniture being dragged across the room and placed against the door.

Then came a loud clank. Souza cried: *"Mãe do Deus,* he's throwing the maggot switches!"

Sklar said: "Gordon, you and Gjessing are the biggest. You push."

Graham and Gjessing threw their shoulders against the door, which moved a few centimeters more. Inside, another switch went *clank*.

"Again," grunted Gjessing, and under the impact the door opened a little wider.

"Duck," said Sklar, thrusting his pistol through the crack. Graham, rubbing his battered shoulder, got out of the way.

There was an earsplitting report and the sound of a falling body.

When they finally got the door open, Wen lay in a pool of blood in front of the panel on which were mounted the two hundred-odd firing-switches. Three of these had been thrown, their handles projecting down instead of up.

Sklar said: "Will it do any good to push those handles up again?"

"No," said Souza. "The reaction is irreversible, and once it is started the heat of the pile destroys the control equipment. It will keep firing until after a few days the heat finally destroys the automatic feed-mechanism too."

Sklar, not listening to the latter part, was bending over Wen, who seemed to be trying to say something. Graham, listening carefully, heard: "It was not my fault—I was to throw all the switches ahead of time . . ."

"That's why your metapolygraph didn't work," said Graham to Sklar. "You said a deep hypnosis would beat it. Well, the Osirian pseudo-hypnosis has a similar—"

"Sh!" said Sklar, still listening. "Where are they now?"

Wen murmured: "On Ascension. March's buildings. Stop them . . . *Duei bu chi, ching . . . Wo bu yau shĭ . . . Wei-shien . . ."* The voice trailed off to nothing.

"Dead," said Sklar; then to Souza: "What effect will those switches have?"

Souza and the other engineers had been comparing the numbers on the switches with those on the huge chart on the opposite wall, which showed the locations of all the Gamanovian maggots buried deep in the substratum below the South Atlantic Ocean. Other people, attracted by the shot and the commotion, were crowding in the corridor outside. Vieira kept them out.

Benson said: "Off-hand I'd say it would cause the bottom to drop east of Ascension."

"How much?" asked Sklar.

Graham shrugged. "As Doc Benson says, we'll have to c-calculate. Fifteen meters, maybe."

"And what will that do?"

"Cause a tsunami, I should think."

"What's a tsunami?"

"Earthquake wave." Graham and Varnipaz suddenly looked at one another in mutual understanding. "Betty—"

"Well," said Souza with a shrug, "if these people are on Ascension, let us warn the people of the neighboring coasts and then wait until the wave has passed. If it drowns them, so much the better, though after all Green Mountain rises to 900 meters and no tsunami could submerge that. What is that English saying about being blown up with one's own bomb?"

"Hoist with his own petard," said Graham.

Sklar shook his head. "In the first place we'd have to warn the cable-employees of Georgetown, who are not to blame for this. Second, the gang has a hostage with them, a friend of my two deputies here. And for what they've done for me, I've got to help save her. When will this wave come along?" He looked from face to face.

A Rio city policeman appeared, pushing his way through the crowd outside.

"Can't tell accurately," said Benson. "Not sooner than six hours and not later than forty-eight from now. If the maggots had been fired in their normal order instead of three at once, there wouldn't have been any sudden drop."

Sklar and the city cop were waving credentials at each other and arguing. Presently another uniformed gendarme appeared to join in with gestures.

Sklar silenced his colleagues long enough to say to Graham in English: "These blips will kip me tied up for hours while they untangle the red tapes. You and Varny are deputy constables; go find Colonel Coelho and make arrangements to fly us to Ascension with a platoon of polissmen."

"Who's he?" asked Graham.

"Chief of the city poliss. I know him."

"But look, w-wouldn't it be better to get—uh—some of your own World Federation people?"

"No. In the first place the nearest W. F. base is at

Bahia. In the second the Constabulary hasn't got the equipment for an attack like that. The Armed Force has, but it comes under the World Ministry of Defense, while we're part of the Division of Investigation of the Ministry of Justice. And Defense is always trying to take us away from Justice and swallow us up themselves. So we don't like itch other, and it would be almost as much trouble as to get help from the Brazzies. Now go on, hurry, if you want to save your little blue-haired girlfriend."

Although the city police seemed disinclined at first to let these two witnesses go, Sklar overbore their objections by sheer lung-power.

Graham and Varnipaz pushed their way out through the crowd and hurried down to the ground floor. They flagged a taxi, and on their way back downtown to the City Office Building they agreed that Graham should captain the party because he was wiser in the ways of Earthly bureaucracy, while the Krishnan should do the talking because of his superior command of the language.

Their W. F. identification cards got them into Colonel Coelho's outer office, where they sat for half an hour before being admitted.

Colonel Coelho, a stout balding man in horn-rimmed glasses, seemed first unable to understand what they were getting at. When they had gone over the whole story—how the gang had infiltrated the Gamanovia Project, and caused one of the scientists to fire the maggots prematurely, and so on—he seemed shocked by the idea they had come to him at all.

"Why," he said, looking something like an affronted owl, "my dear young men! I have no jurisdiction on Ascension! And moreover my airplanes are little putt-putts without the range required. While I have great esteem for the Senhor Reinhold, he must be mad to think I could undertake such an assignment."

Graham and Varnipaz looked at one another.

"The man you want," continued the colonel, "is my respected colleague Commander Schmitz, of the Federal District Police. I will give you a note to him. You will find him in the Federal District Building—"

"Perdon," said Graham, "but is that the same as the Federal Police?"

"Ah, no not at all. This is the Federal District, like your District of Columbia. In it lies the city of Rio de Janeiro, but the city does not occupy the entire district, which therefore has its own police. Make I myself clear?"

They thanked Coelho and went to find the Federal District Building. After getting lost a few times in the many little alleys that wandered off from the magnificent boulevards they found the building in question and settled down to wait in Commander Schmitz's office.

This time it took forty minutes. They had time to read clear through a newspaper that Graham went out and bought before they were admitted to the presence.

Commander Affonso Schmitz, a little terrier of a man with grizzling red hair, listened to their story and barked: "Coelho must be out of his head to send you to *me!* Not only have I no authority for any such enterprise, but also my budget for the year has been cut to where I can barely perform my assigned duties. Young men, you have no idea how hard it is to police the mountainous country around Rio with my little force. If you could persuade these pinch-milréis in the legislature . . . But I suppose there is no time for that. I am vexed with Coelho for dumping such a fantastic problem in my lap. I know! Go see Commodore de Andrada of the Rio de Janeiro State Police. If anybody can help you it should be he. I will write a note . . ."

"Excuse me," said Graham, "but is this something different from both the Rio city police and the Federal District Police?"

"So—yes! We have a city of Rio and a state of Rio, just as you have a city of Washington and a state of Washington, and the one is not inside the other—though in our case the State of Rio de Janeiro lies all around the Federal District that contains the City of Rio. Here . . ."

As it was now past noon, they were getting hungry. Graham and Varnipaz stopped at a coffee shop for a roll and a cup of coffee before proceeding on to the Rio de Janeiro State Office Building. Graham remarked:

"If we don't get somewhere soon the tsunami will be all over with."

Varnipaz nodded gloomily as they plodded towards their next destination. This time they waited in the outer office for nearly two hours while the Commodore took his afternoon nap.

When they were finally admitted, they found Commodore de Andrada to be a slim, elegant-looking oldster with a carefully tended white mustache. He listened with his head cocked and a sympathetic expression on his face. When they finished he replied:

"Ah, it breaks my heart and wrings my soul not to be able to help you. And such a romantic situation, too! Two brave young men flying to rescue the princess from the far planet! Were I but younger I should throw in my lot with yours. As it is, however, to my infinite regret, I must refuse you. You see I should have to get the approval of the State Legislature. In the first place they are not now in session; in the second, even if they were, it would take weeks to push through such an authorization; in the third, the Liberal Party is now in control whereas I am known to be of the Socialists, and they would like nothing better than an excuse to . . . But I think you follow me.

"However, do not look so downcast. If you will come back next month, when they are in session, I, Luiz de Andrada, will risk his future and sponsor a special appropriation . . ."

"I'm afraid that would be too late," said Graham.

"Ah, you *Americanos do Norte*, always in a hurry! You do not know how to live. You should stay here a while and learn from us . . . But do not despair; no true Brazilian ever turned the stranger from his gates, or proffered him a stone when he needed bread. I will write you a letter to General Vasconcellos of the Federal Police . . ."

"Beg pardon," said Graham, "but is that different from the Federal District Police? We've already been there, you know."

"Oh, but surely it is different. The Federal Police are the national organization. They are what would be the Armed Forces if individual nations were allowed to keep armed forces any more . . ."

General Vasconcellos kept them waiting a mere twenty-five minutes, and turned out to be a stocky Negro with a serious expression. A handsome young aide, Lieutenant Manoel Gil according to the sign on his desk, sat across the room from the general.

When Varnipaz had told their story for the fourth time, General Vasconcellos said: "Since you have already been to Coelho, Schmitz, and de Andrada, I suppose this is your last stop in Brazil. Now I should like to assist you, but . . ."

Here we go again, thought Graham.

"But," said General Vasconcellos, "I don't like the idea

of landing my men on the Rock just as this earthquake wave is due. If it drowned them . . ."

"That's unlikely, sir," said Graham. "Tsunamis rarely run over thirty meters high, and the island's much higher than that."

"But one cannot be sure, as this is the first man-made earthquake wave. And remember this hostage is not a Brazilian citizen; in fact not even a Terrestrial. While I sympathize with the young lady and my men are brave, imagine the political capital my enemies would make of my causing a score of Brazilians to be killed for the sake of one extra-terrestrial!"

"But—" said Graham.

Vasconcellos held up a hand. "I know what you are going to say, but I fear I can do nothing. Ascension Island is not under Brazilian jurisdiction—"

"Brazil handles the mail for it."

"But that is not sovereignty. When the March contract is fulfilled the sovereignty of the island will revert to the World Federation until the land is reclaimed and settled, but in the meantime Ascension is an independent nation. Nobody could stop Senhor March from selling it to the Martians if he wished, except that he has already contracted to sell it to you gentlemen."

Graham and Varnipaz sat in gloomy silence until Varnipaz said: "Since the island was originally British, I should think Great Britain would have a certain responsibility for it whether they want to or not. Could we, therefore, fly to Britain for help? Which way is it from here?"

Graham shook his head. "It's a third of the way around the Earth, and they'd give us the same sort of runaround."

"I must say," said Varnipaz, "I am getting a poor opinion of this so-called civilized planet. Brazil will not help us for this reason; Great Britain for that; the World Federation for another. If this were Krishna I should organize my own expedition. In fact I should do it here except that there is no time."

At this point the handsome young Lieutenant Gil spoke up, addressing his chief in such fast Portuguese that Graham could not understand a word of it.

After Gil finished, Vasconcellos said: "Perhaps all is not lost, senhores. My aide here has reminded me that we have to make training flights anyway, and that we were about to send one of our large rescue-'planes on a long flight over the ocean for navigational practice. Now if you and Senhor Reinhold would care to risk an attack on the island by yourselves, we could drop you by rotochute—"

"That will suit me," said Varnipaz.

Graham found the prospect of attacking a group of— he didn't know how many men—perhaps a score—an alarming one, but since he could not let his rival outdo him in gallantry, he nodded.

"And me too!" exclaimed Gil. "I want to volunteer for this expedition! I am tired of papers; I am tired of reports; I am tired of this filthy routine. I want to see some action before I die. *Por favor,* General . . ."

"*Paciencia,* my little one," said Vasconcellos. "If this plan goes through you shall have your chance. Could you be ready to leave by tomorrow noon?"

"Too late," said Graham. "Why not tonight?"

The general looked at his watch. "That would take some doing, but perhaps we can manage it. I know; we can drop you tonight and then return tomorrow morning to pick you up, if you are still alive and the island has not been all washed away. I have it! If an earthquake wave hits the Rock, we can land some of our men there as a humanitarian act to relieve the victims of a natural catastrophe. Our authorization extends to such emergencies."

Graham asked: "Then why couldn't you land men there before the catastrophe, to forestall it?"

Vasconcellos shook his head. "Not legal, I grieve to say. My predecessor got in trouble with the legislature for doing just that. But we will do what we can. Let me see: You will need some equipment, but I cannot just hand you a few thousand contos' worth of life-rafts, guns, and the like. What I can do is to give you a contract with the Office of Research, under which they lend you the equipment, and you promise not only to return it if possible, but also to write technical reports on how it worked. Is that agreeable?"

Graham and Varnipaz nodded.

"Good," said Vasconcellos. "Gil, take these visitors to the office of the Quartermaster General and see that some competent officer is assigned to help them choose equipment. Then draw up an engineering test contract and walk it through the Office of Research. It is an order that nobody in this building goes home tonight until the last paper is signed. That ought to get results. And call Captain Dantas about that navigation flight. I want these people delivered on the Rock before tomorrow morning ..."

VIII.

Lieutenant Manoel Gil squinted through the infra-red viewer of the machine-gun and said: "Have you gentlemen ever done rotochute jumps before?"

"N-no," said Graham, thinking he need not add that he hoped never to again. Although he considered himself, and justly, as quite an accomplished athlete, jumping out of airplanes had never attracted him.

So far everything had gone according to schedule. At times, though, he had to confess to a secret wish that the 'plane would break down or the red tape get fouled up to prevent the expedition from setting out at all. At the same time he burned to rescue Jeru-Bhetiru, and the conflict of emotions made him most unhappy. And here he was, in borrowed Brazilian Federal Police boots, shirt, and pants, crouching in the dimly-lit fuselage of the 'plane, watching Gil check over the other borrowed equipment, and listening to the monotonous whine of the engines.

"Then," said Gil ominously, "you had better precede me, so I can make sure you jump."

Sklar looked at his watch. Graham wondered if Sklar's face, which he could see only dimly, was as pale as his own felt.

"When are we due?" asked Sklar.

"Any time now," said Gil. "Remember, we must all go out in a hurry, or we'll be scattered all over that filthy island and never find each other. Do you all know your maps?"

Graham took another look at his. Georgetown lay on the northwest coast south of that northern peninsula. On the east side of the peninsula a pencil-mark showed where Teófilo March had his turtle-farm. They would try to drop on the east coast about a kilometer south of this point.

Graham said: "As I understand it, you're going to cache the raft on the east coast. That's the windward side, since it's in the p-path of the southeast trades. Wouldn't it be better for us to try to take off from the lee side?"

Gil shook his head. "No. There is something about the bottom formation on the west side of Ascension that gives the worst rollers you ever saw. Three, four meters high. It would take a trained coastguard crew to get through them."

"Then why did the British put Georgetown on that side?"

Gil shrugged. "I suppose because it was the only place they could find near enough to fresh water and at the same time to a good landing-place. The Rock is a lousy island to land on from the sea: but jagged pieces of lava under the water and little rocky beaches from which you have to scramble up cliffs to get to the interior. I think it would have been better to give it back to the terns and the turtles."

The squawk-box chattered in Portuguese, and Gil said: "The Rock is in sight; let us get ready."

They stood up and assumed their equipment. Every one of the four buckled on a pistol and a rotochute. In addition Gil took the machine-gun with the sniperscope attached, Sklar a paralyzer, Graham an extra infra-red viewer and some extra ammunition for Gil, and Varnipaz a bag full of explosives and pyrotechnics. Moving awkwardly under their loads, they wrestled the large bag containing their life-raft back to the door.

"We have a couple of minutes," said Gil. "Arraez is going to circle once before the drop."

Graham leaned against the nearest window and put his hands around his face to cut out reflections from inside the airplane. Up ahead, to the northeast, a dark shape on the water was cutting into the path of moonlight reflected on the sea from the recently-risen half-moon. As his eyes got used to the dark, Graham saw that Ascension Island was much bigger than he had thought from the nickname of "the Rock"—though it was impossible to judge sizes accurately from an airplane at night without some familiar object to give a scale of reference. He remembered from his work on the Gamanovia Project that the island was somewhere between ten and fifteen kilometers in its maximum dimension.

The whine of the engines had dropped to a whisper as they glided toward the northern peninsula. To starboard Graham thought he saw a twinkle of lights against the blackness. That would be Georgetown. There had been some question about how to warn the handful of cable-operators who lived there; a general broadcast about the approaching tsunami might be picked up by the gang and alert them. Then he, Graham, had thought of letting them know by cable, with a warning not to tell the folk at the turtle-farm. The Georgetownians should by now have fled with their household goods to higher ground.

Then, about there, thought Graham, should be March's turtle-farm. Far away to starboard Green Mountain reared itself against the stars as they dropped lower, then swung forward as the 'plane turned south.

"Get ready," said Gil. "Remember, even if I'm boss now, as we reach ground you, Constable Sklar, are in command."

One of the crew-members stood with a hand on the door. Gil stared at his wrist-watch. A sharp whistle came out of the squawk-box and the crewman yanked the door open. At once the 'plane was filled with draft and with the swish and whistle of the airstream outside.

Gil motioned Graham to give him a hand with the raft. They braced themselves, hands against the bundle, and waited.

The squawk-box whistled twice. "Out with it!" said Gil, and they pushed. Overboard went the bundle. Graham almost fell out the door, and instinctively caught the door-jamb to stop himself—and was catapulted out by a violent push in the small of the back. As he fell into the dark and the gale, he caught Gil's voice faintly above the air-sounds: "You next . . ."

For a heart-stopping second he was too frightened to do anything but tense all his muscles as if with a violent cramp, while the universe spun around him. Then he remembered to pull the ring. The blades of the rotochute opened like the petals of a flower, and the universe stopped whirling as he came right side up. The great wind ceased blowing up from underneath him, and its roar in his ears was replaced by the gentle whirr of the blades over his head. To one side and below him the moonlight caught the larger blades of the chute that was lowering the raft.

He looked towards the airplane, now invisible except for its fast-receding running-lights. He could however hear its engines starting up again. Somebody blinked a flash-light in the air on a level higher than his. Somebody else called:

"Hey, you there, Varnipaz? You there, Graham? Every-think all right?"

They called back and forth until all were identified. Graham, looking down, got another shock. They seemed to be dropping into the Atlantic Ocean.

"Hey!" called Graham. "Gil! We're going into the

drink!" And he began wondering how he could swim ashore laden as he was. He was a good swimmer but after all not a porpoise.

"The wind will carry us ashore," said Gil. "I only hope Arraez allowed enough for windage, or we shall have to drag that filthy raft a long way to the beach. Remember what I told you about alighting; the Rock is the best place for breaking the legs you ever saw."

The beach, marked by the phosphorescence of the breakers, slid up slantwise towards them as the wind bore them shorewards. Graham saw that it was, in fact, going to carry them inland. He got his flashlight ready for the landing. The sound of the surf below grew louder.

The beach slid under him, and from the dark below came the crunch of the raft-bundle striking the shingle. Graham flashed on his light, directing the beam downwards. The rough surface rose steadily towards him, hummocks of lava enlarging until individual stones and pebbles could be seen in the beam. He flexed his legs to take the shock, jarred home, and fell on his back. The rotochute crashed against the rock.

"Ouch!" he muttered. A sharp piece of rock had bitten into his left forearm, though otherwise he did not seem hurt. He freed himself from the chute and scrambled up.

As he did so the other three came down with a similar racket, one by one. Graham could hear them moving about in the dark and uttering a powerful symphony of curses: Gil in Portuguese, Varnipaz in Sotaspeou, and Sklar in what Graham guessed to be Slovakian or something of the sort.

Sklar said: "I came down on a goddam cactus! Here, all of you follow me to the bitch. Kip the talk down."

Graham found the warm wet wind, unnoticeable while he was borne along with it, now strong enough to ruffle his hair and his clothes. At least the sound of wind and wave would cover their approach. The place smelled of terns' nests.

By the light of their torches they finally got together and picked their way down a little ravine that opened on the beach. It was hard going, requiring a hand as well as a pair of legs as they slipped and crunched over the rough stuff and around the boulders.

At the foot of the clifflet they found the raft bundle. Sklar and Gil broke it out, and after a muttered consultation the latter turned the valve that inflated the raft. The carbon dioxide hissed gently from its cylinder, and the raft humped up like a live thing, its folds popping open audibly as the gas filled them.

"I don't like doink this in advance," said Sklar, "but when we get back maybe there won't be no time to blow it up. Let's tie it fast so it don't float away on the tide."

When the painter had been secured to the nearest rock of convenient size, they unzipped the outboard motor from its compartment.

"Better set it up too," said Sklar. "We'll want all the spid we can get."

Gil accordingly installed the motor, its propellor-shaft sticking out behind the raft like a tail. Meanwhile Sklar said:

"You two, how about pulling some of those spines out of my pants, huh? I don't feel like rescuink no dame with my tail full of niddles."

Graham and Varnipaz obliged by the light of their flashlights. Varnipaz said thoughtfully:

"I should like to know more about our legal status. I can see how you and Graham and I are authorized to make arrests by Earthly law, though I do not understand why we do not have to have warrants. And as for Gil . . ."

"Ouch," said Sklar. "We'll kip the lecture till later."

Gil said: "The motor's ready."

"Come alunk," said Sklar, leading the way north along the beach. The going was easier here until the beach ended in a rocky point, over which they had to scramble as best they could. The cliff to their left rose far above their heads, then came down to eye-level again, then rose once more and strode out into the water.

"Hey," said Sklar, "no more bitch! Can we wade?"

"I don't know," said Gil. "Hold my gun." And the Brazilian began feeling his way forward past the end of the beach, leaning against the cliff-face. A few steps, however, brought him up to his hips in the water, which rose and fell with the swells. A big wave splashed water all over him. He turned his face back in to the beams of the flashlights.

"No good this way," he said. "We'll have to go back and find a route inland."

Graham could not help remembering that any minute the water might start to rise, up—up—up, scores of meters above its usual level. The only safe places in such a case would be either on high ground inland or well out to sea where the tsunami's slopes were gentle. Since the water usually receded in advance of a tsunami before it started to rise, they should have at least some minutes' warning, perhaps even a half-hour. If they started seaward the minute this recession began, they might get a safe distance out before the wave arrived.

With this consideration in mind, Graham said: "Why don't we take the raft? We could land right in front of the turtle-farm . . ."

"No," said Sklar. "No cover to approach. Might work, but if anybody was watching the bitch we'd be sittink ducks."

They straggled back until they found another ravine cutting up into the cliff, and picked their way up it. A few sparse plants grew among the rocks, but otherwise the land seemed practically lifeless.

As they rounded a big boulder in the ravine, something whitish snorted and scrambled out of range of their flash-lights. Graham's heart leaped into his mouth until Gil, with a nervous little laugh, said: "Goat. They run wild here."

They scrambled up the ravine, sweating with exertion, until they could climb out on level land. After a short rest they set out again, checking their direction by the map and the stars. Graham walked behind Sklar, the wind pushing at him gently but continuously.

The half-moon was high in the sky, and Graham was sure they had covered many kilometers, when Sklar said: "Lights out; we're getting close."

Graham stumbled on the rough lava. The land at this point sloped all the way down to the beach on their right, instead of dropping off in the form of a cliff as it did elsewhere. As they came over a rise Graham could make out, in the moonlight, a group of structures ahead running up from the shore like steps. Behind him he heard Gil fall down with a crash and a string of whispered oaths.

"Quiet," murmured Sklar. "Spread out."

He led them down the slope towards the beach. As they got closer Graham could begin to make out the form of the turtle-farm: the buildings proper well back from the water, and between them and the beach dozens of tanks in which March raised his stock. He sent a glance out to sea. Still no sign of the tsunami, the terrible mountain-ridge of water . . .

"Let's see that viewer," said Sklar. Graham passed it to him. While Sklar looked through the viewer, Gil did likewise through that attached to the machine-gun. After a while Sklar passed the viewer back to Graham, who looked through it. Gil offered his gun to Varnipaz, who whispered: "No thank you. My retinas are sensitive farther down in the infra-red than yours, so I can see well enough."

"They seem to all have gone to bed," said Sklar, "but unless I miss my guess they'll have Miss Jeru locked up somewhere and a man watching outside her door. They don't know about Wen yet, so maybe they ain't expecting company. Varny, you come with me around the left side of the tanks, while you other two go around the right side and try to find this guard. Go slow and kip your heads down."

He set off in a crouching position, and the others did likewise. Graham followed Gil, who every few steps raised his head above the level of the tanks to peer through his scope. From the tanks came faint bumpings as the turtles moved about.

They had reached the upper end of the tanks and had just turned left towards the other side of the layout when they heard a sharp "Pst!" They hurried ahead to where Sklar and Varnipaz crouched. The former whispered:

"We found him! In front of a little buildink at the south end."

"A concrete building with only small weendows, high up?" inquired Gil.

"That's it."

"That would be the sea-water distilling-plant."

Sklar said: "We can't blow up these buildinks until we know for sure which one she's in. But we can make a diversion. Varny, take your stuff around to the north end and get it ready to make a nice big explosion and fire. But don't set it off unless you hear shootink from us. Then come back and join us quick."

"Gil had better do it," said Varnipaz. "I do not know much about explosives."

Gil accordingly took the bag and faded off into the night. The others began stalking the guard outside the distilling-plant.

"He's around the next corner," breathed Sklar, passing his viewer back to Graham. The constable took out his paralyzer, raised it, and peered around the corner of the building they were hiding behind.

The gadget went *brrrp!*

There was an exclamation from the unseen guard, cut off in the middle, and then the clatter of a dropped gun.

They rushed around the building that sheltered them, to

find the man lying in the moonlight, his gun beside him. His eyes were open and he twitched in a way that showed he was still much alive. It was Hank, the attendant at the Bay Head nudery.

Graham examined the building the man had been guarding. It was, as Gil had said, a small concrete structure with no outside openings save one small square one high up on each wall, which looked more like ventilator-openings with bars across them than windows and did not seem promising as means of egress.

The door was of wood, but stout and strong. It was also locked.

Sklar fumbled through the guard's pockets. "No key. That The'erhiya is smart. See if you can make her hear."

Graham put his mouth to the door and murmured: "Betty! Betty!"

After he had done this for half a minute he heard a faint: "Is that you, Gorodon?"

"Yes. Hold tight; we're going to get you out."

"Out of the way, sonny boy," said Sklar, and attacked the lock with his lock-picker. After several tries he said disgustedly: "Don't fit. We'll have to blast the lock. Graham, take the viewer and find Gil. Tell him to light a lonk fuze and then come back to us."

Graham took the viewer and stole off towards the north end of the settlement. He found Gil laying out an elaborate series of noise and firemaking preparations against the northernmost building.

When Graham had given his message, the Brazilian said thoughtfully: "I theenk I will keep the gelatin. It'll be useful on our way back; in that loose rock it will be as good as a fragmentation bomb."

He finished pegging out his fuzes, snapped his cigarette-lighter into flame, and applied it to the ends. When the fuzes were all fizzing, they headed back towards the other end of the hamlet.

Back at the distillery, Graham asked: "The fuzes are lit; what are you going to do?"

Sklar replied: "When they go off I'm going to blast the lock with this." He patted the machine-gun.

"Won't the shots go through the door and hit Betty?"

"I told her to get behind the cooling-coils, so she'll be pretty safe . . ."

Wham! A sudden glare lit up the night sky and the shock-wave buffeted them. The main explosion was followed by a series of lesser reports, and the pinkish flare of the incendiary mixture cast long lurid beams among the buildings.

Voices called into the night, to be drowned by further explosions. Somewhere doors opened and running feet pounded.

"Get back," said Sklar. "Around the corner. Don't want to hit you with a ricochet."

The constable lay down on his back with his feet against the door of the distillery and began firing bursts at the wood around the lock. The hammering of the gun drowned out the other noises.

"Okus dokus," said Sklar, and the three others ran around the corner of the building behind which they had taken refuge. Where the lock had been the door showed a gaping jagged black hole. With a little shaking the door came open.

"Betty!" called Graham.

"I come," she said, and stepped out from behind the coils.

"Hurry," said Sklar.

As Jeru-Bhetiru stepped out of the building, Graham saw that all she had on was a pair of men's pants much too big for her and a pair of rope-soled Spanish shoes.

"Hey!" cried a voice, and a man started towards them between the rows of buildings.

Sklar, still holding the machine-gun, whipped it to his shoulder and fired a burst. The man dropped. As he did so, the gun gave a final click and stopped firing, its bolt open.

"Take it," said Sklar, and tossed it to Gil, who fumbled at his belt for another clip as he ran. They all trotted south back over the route by which they had come. The light of the fire allowed them to run without their flashlights—for a while at any rate. As if in answer to the fire, the eastern horizon had now begun to show the first faint pallor of dawn.

Somewhere behind them a gun cracked. And again. And again. A bullet hit a rock and screamed off.

Then they were out of the firelight and had to slow down to avoid stumbling. Gil said: "You go on; I cover you." He knelt behind a rock and sighted on the little black figures boiling out of the buildings, silhouetted against the glow of the fire.

Graham, his earlier fears forgotten, lusted to feel the kick of a gun. He rested his pistol on another rock. As the machine-gun clattered beside him the little figures ducked this way and that. Graham squeezed his trigger. The pistol bucked in his hand, but it was too far for pistol-shooting and he could not tell if he had hit anybody. They were all out of sight, now, but from among the hummocks came little twinkling flashes and the sound of shots.

"Go on," said Gil. "We have to take turns at this."

Graham reluctantly went on, soon catching up with the others by virtue of his long legs. They picked their way, unable to use their lights for fear of drawing fire. Presently Gil panted up after them, saying: "If you want a turn, Meester Gordon, here it is," and handed him the gun. "Don't stay too long; just enough to make them stop and take cover."

Graham found a place between a couple of boulders that gave him a loophole of convenient size. He waited while the footsteps of the others died away behind him. Too bad, he thought, that Sklar's paralyzer had such a short range . . .

After a long time a light appeared. Somebody was coming ahead slowly, sweeping the surface of the lava with a powerful flash. Graham sighted on the light and fired a burst.

The light went out. There were cries and the sound of men running and stumbling. Graham, calculating that they would shoot at the flash of his machine-gun, ducked back behind the larger of the two boulders. Sure enough, a rattle of shots came, mingled with the shrill *ptweeoo!* of the ricochets. Then there was a sharper crack and a straight line of blue arc flashed into being. It ended among the rocks on the seaward side of Graham. That would be an Osirian shock-gun. *Crack!* The blue arc winked again, close enough to make Graham's muscles jerk with the electrical surge.

Graham edged around the other side of the large boulder and held his fire until he was sure he was lined up on the flashes of one of the guns of the pursuers, and fired a burst. Then, without waiting to see the result, he slid back behind the boulder and began crawling away. It would take them some time to find he had gone.

He could move a little faster now, for the light in the east was just beginning to show up the form of the rocks over which he was walking, though not yet their color. He caught up with his party just before they reached the ravine up which they had come from the beach, and which could now be seen as a darker gash in the dark tumbled surface.

"Here," said Gil, leaning on his elbows, half in and half out of the ravine. Graham handed him the gun.

There was a sudden rattle of rock and a groan from the darkness below.

"What is it?" said Graham, lowering himself into the gash.

"I have turned my ankle," said Varnipaz. Then: "It is all right; I can still walk on it."

Graham followed his companions down the ravine to the beach, using hands like a monkey. Whatever the differences between the internal structure of human beings and Krishnans, it was interesting to know that the latter had ankles subject to sprains like those of people.

Behind Graham the machine-gun clattered once. Then over the sound of the surf he heard the overturning of rocks, and Gil stumbled and scrambled his way after them.

"Just a meenute!" called the Brazilian. "Before you run, give me a couple of those gelatin sticks!"

Varnipaz paused and fished the explosives out of the bag he carried. Gil and Graham fitted a couple of lengths of slow fuze into them, lit them, and tossed them as far as they could up the ravine.

Then they ran. Sklar and Jeru-Bhetiru were already far ahead of them. Graham passed Varnipaz, who limped painfully from his mishap. Graham knew they would have to hurry from now on. Hitherto conditions had been with them. The rough terrain favored the defense, and the light had been just strong enough to see one's way without being bright enough for accurate shooting. Now however they would be out in the open with the light waxing every minute.

When they reached the place where the raft had been left, Graham found that Sklar had already untied the painter and tossed his paralyzer into the vessel, saying:

"Graham, you and Varny take the rear end, on account of that's heaviest. I'll take the front. Don't hit the propellor on the rocks."

They picked up the raft while Gil flattened himself against the base of the cliff and aimed his machine-gun back towards where the ravine debouched onto the beach.

As they neared the place where the sea should be, Graham saw with a thrill of horror that the water was not where it had been. It had begun to recede, and even as they ran towards it it fled before them, faster and faster.

"The tsunami!" Graham yelled. "Catch that water and

get out to sea, quick!" He shouted back: "Come on, Gil! The wave's coming!"

The gun clattered briefly, and then Gil was running after them. A muffled *boom* came from the direction of the ravine, and out of the corner of his eye Graham saw the puff of dust and rock fly into the air. He could not tell if they had harmed the enemy by the explosion. Gil panted after them. They stumbled over loose shingle, sank ankle-deep in mud, and meandered around outcrops of jagged lava. On the exposed sea-bottom seaweeds lay sprawled, and stranded sea-creatures flopped and scuttled.

The sharp crack and bright flash of the electrostatic projector made Graham cast a glance back. In the dim pre-dawn light he could make out forms moving on top of the cliff and others sliding down it to the beach. He thought he saw the tall tailed reptilian figure of The'erhiya among them. Gunshots sounded, and the nasty crack of h-v bullets whipped about their ears.

Gil turned, threw himself down behind a rock, and aimed his machine-gun—and suddenly collapsed, dropping the gun.

"Hold it!" said Graham, letting go his corner of the raft. He ran back a few steps. One glance at Gil, the top of whose head had been taken off by a bullet, was enough to tell him the young man was dead.

Graham picked up the machine-gun and fired at the moving figures. The gun barked once and then stopped. Mud in the works, thought Graham, and worked the bolt a couple of times until it seemed to slide easily. Then it fired several bursts without difficulty. The pursuers sought cover or threw themselves down flat.

Bullets and high-voltage arcs whipped past Graham. He felt a sudden blow on his right arm that almost knocked him over, then a sharp pain. He looked down: A bullet had gone through the sleeve of his shirt and grazed his arm. Luckily it was a flesh-wound only; a square hit might have taken his arm clear off as a result of the terrific m-v of modern firearms. He fired another burst—why does a target always look so much smaller over a gunsight than when looked at in the normal fashion? The bolt clicked and the gun, now uncomfortably hot, was empty again.

Graham got up and ran to catch up with the others. At least it was light enough now so you could really see where you were going. He zigzagged around the larger rocks and leaped over the smaller.

Varnipaz was still limping, and Jeru-Bhetiru was manfully carrying the corner of the raft that Graham had dropped. "Gil?" asked Varnipaz.

"Dead," replied Graham. They had almost caught up with the receding water.

Sklar splashed into the surf and dropped the front end of the raft. The others pushed it off and piled aboard. Graham threw the machine-gun into the body of the little vessel, pushed the raft ahead of him until he was knee-deep, and leaped in himself. Then he hunted around the outboard motor until he found the starting button. The motor buzzed into life, sending the water foaming back from the spinning screw. The raft gathered speed, which, added to the rapidly increasing velocity at which the receding water was bearing them away from Ascension, made them seem to be leaving at airplane velocity.

Shots still came after them. Graham put one of his reserve clips into the machine-gun and fired back at the shore, though the pursuers were now so distant that from this unsteady platform he could do little more than spray the landscape in the hope of keeping down the return fire. Sklar and Varnipaz added to his barrage with a few shots from their pistols.

"Oh-oh!" said Sklar in the bow. "Here comes that wave of yours. Does anybody know how to pray?"

Graham put the gun on safety and looked around. He had always been in the habit of saying that, having studied tsunamis, he had no desire ever to see one in person. Now, it seemed, he was going to meet one whether he liked or not.

The earthquake-wave did not take the steep cliff-like form of a breaker. Instead the horizon—close at hand from their low position amongst the swells—seemed to hump itself up against the paling eastern sky little by little. The raft slowed as it headed up a steeper and steeper slope. Behind them the exposed sea-bottom and the beach spread themselves out below their level. Ahead the slope of the tsunami extended away like that of a great rounded hill.

"Look!" cried Jeru-Bhetiru, pointing shoreward.

They were now on a level with the top of the small cliff, and rising higher. The water had stopped receding and was now rushing back shoreward. Far ahead and below them the edge of the water foamed over the exposed bottom towards the beach. They were still rising, so that now they were above the highest point on the northern peninsula, and could see clear across to the ocean beyond. To their right Graham glimpsed the March turtle-farm before the waters overwhelmed it, liberating all the thousands of March's turtles. Now their great hill of water was carrying them swiftly back towards the peninsula.

Along the beach, little figures, mere specks in the distance, could be seen frantically scrambling back up the cliff. The water roared up the beach, spurted high as it lapped against the cliff, and then submerged the cliff itself. Then the curve of the watery hill hid the land ahead from those in the raft. The raft went faster and faster, drifting north and shoreward, and began to spin round and round like a top. A great current was rushing around the northern tip of Ascension Island, rising higher and higher until most of the peninsula was one vast cascade over which sped a sheet of water. Graham gripped a couple of the rope hand-holds and hoped they would stay right side up. The roar of the water drowned everything else.

The raft pitched and heaved madly. Gouts of foam burst all around it, spraying its passengers with salt spray. Ascension Island slid past them as deep water poured over the northern peninsula. Ahead of the raft the water sped over the land to meet the other water that had poured around the northern end of the island in a millrace of leaping waves splashing tens of meters high.

Graham screamed: "Hold on!" at the top of his lungs, but could not even hear himself.

Now the whole peninsula was submerged, all but a few of the highest rocks, past which they spun. Then they were sliding down the long slope towards the maelstrom on the lee side which, though it had subsided somewhat, was still boiling.

Then they were in it. Graham snatched a quick breath and held it. They seemed to run head-on into a wall of water, and for a few seconds there was nothing but green-and-white smother all around them. Then, when it seemed as though his bursting lungs could stand it no longer, Graham realized that his head was clear. The raft righted itself and there they were, drenched and coughing, and gripping their loops of rope with the grip of desperation. The raft still tossed, and water sloshed back and forth around their legs, but at least they could breathe. The machine-gun and the other loose gear had disappeared, and the engine had stopped.

When he had coughed the water out of his lungs and squeezed the water out of his eyes, Graham looked towards the island. The air was filled with the screams of tens of thousands of terns flooded off their nests. In the dawn light he could now make out the rugged reddish-brown form of Ascension and see many of its forty volcanic cones, culminating in Green Mountain with its cloud-cap.

As they watched, the land of the peninsula began to appear above the water—first a rock here and there, then continuous stretches, and finally the cliffs around the edges.

Meanwhile the backwash from the first wave sucked them northward around the tip of the peninsula. As the minutes passed the whole of the peninsula emerged, the water running off its top in sheets and cascades. The water slowly sank to its normal level; then another rise sent them spinning back westward around the tip of the peninsula again. However, this and subsequent waves came nowhere near submerging the peninsula; they merely rose and fell like speeded-up tides.

The four people in the raft, two human and two Krishnan, stared at the rusty, barren land. Graham picked up the bucket that was attached by a line to the raft and methodically began bailing.

"What was that?" said Varnipaz, coughing.

"What?" asked Sklar.

"It sounded like a voice crying for help. In—that direction, I think." Varnipaz pointed.

"I don't think nobody could have come through that alive," said Sklar. "Probably one of these sea-gulls."

Graham was fussing with the engine, which stubbornly refused to start. At last he got out the oars.

"If you'll move a bit," he said, "I'll try to row. Mr. Sklar, you take the paddle in the stern."

"You know about boats and thinks?" said Sklar with raised eyebrows.

"I've—uh—had a little experience."

"Okus dokus, then you be captain."

The sun was now half above the horizon. Graham looked at Jeru-Bhetiru, who in her unembarrassed semi-nudity looked like the most desirable thing on earth. He asked:

"Betty, why are you wearing that rig?"

She eplained: "In Rio I tried to get away when they were putting me into their airplane to fly out here. They caught me and my dress got so torn they gave me these instead. What is wrong with your arm? Were you wounded?"

"Just a graze," he said, but submitted gladly to letting her bind up his wound.

The cry came again so that all could hear it. Sklar steered the raft in that direction. Presently as the swells lifted them they began to see a couple of black dots bobbing about between them and the shore. Graham pulled hard, and soon they drew alongside the swimmers. One was the fat bald Warschauer, the other a lemur-like extra-terrestrial: Adzik of Thoth.

"Well," said Gordon Graham, "fancy meeting you here! Don't b-be afraid; you're among fiends."

He reached for his pistol, but Sklar said: "Hey! (*cough*) Don't shoot with your gun all wet. You'll blow it up."

Graham therefore hunted among the compartments of the raft until he found a fish-spear in three sections. As the raft came closer to Warschauer, who struck out strongly and caught one of the ropes, Graham assembled the spear. He said to Warschauer:

"All right, now t-tell us what this whole plot was about."

"I'm not talking until I see my lawyer," said Warschauer.

"Yeah?" said Graham, thrusting the spear into the man's face. "Want me to stick this into your guts and turn it around a few times?"

"You wouldn't do that!"

"Try and see. The s-same for you," he told Adzik, who had paddled up alongside Warschauer and had hold of another rope.

Warschauer coughed up some sea-water and said: "Okay, you win. Especially since it looks as though Adzik's gang has double-crossed us. Adzik (*cough*) was the head of the syndicate on Earth; The'erhiya was just the hypnotist who kept us in line. He had control of me too, so I couldn't tell you this except I've been half drowned and that seems to break the hold."

"What was the objective?" asked Graham.

"To colonize Gamanovia with Thothians, stupid."

"How?"

"Adzik's a member of a private syndicate, most of them government people as well. That's how they do things on Thoth. They wanted Gamanovia raised ahead of time to break the contract so March would own the whole continent. Or rather Joe Aurelio, who bought the Rock from March."

"What then?"

"Joe signed an agreement to sell the continent to the syndicate, who would in turn sell it (at a colossal profit) to the Thothian planetary government. Before Earth knew what was happening, the continent would be full of surplus Thothians dumped there from space-ships."

"They couldn't get away with that!"

"Think so? Remember the case of Thor versus Earth? When the Terrestrials grabbed a continent on a similar deal, and then argued that since ancient wrongs could never be righted they should be left in possession?"

"It's not the same—"

"Legally it is. At that time the court set up the precedent that legal immigrants to a planet might not be expelled except for individual crimes."

"But the W. F. wouldn't allow this immigration in the first place!"

"How could they stop it? Under their constitution the right to limit immigration is reserved to the nations—and the World Court says that means immigration from other planets too."

"But this immigration would be based on fraud! Kidnapping people, hypnotizing the project scientists . . ."

"Sure, but you'd have had a hell of a time proving that if the plans had gone through as scheduled."

"So the W. F. spends billions to make a home for monkey-rats! Is that so, Adzik?" said Graham, pointing the spear at the Thothian.

"Yes," squeaked Adzik, "though I must protest your use of the insulting term 'monkey-rat.' May we come aboard now? I am tired of swimming."

"Okay, but one false move and back you go. Where are the rest?"

Warschauer snorted. "What d'you think? Drowned. Lundquist stopped a bullet before the tidal wave came. The'erhiya couldn't swim, and the only reason we're alive is I'm too fat to sink and Adzik swims like a seal. What the hell happened? Earthquake?"

"You'll find out in the clink," said Sklar. "Say, ain't we driftink?"

The trade-wind had indeed blown them several kilometers to the northwest. Graham made one more fruitless effort to start the motor, then got out the sail and the waterproof instruction-book for setting it.

Half an hour later they had the sail rigged: a simple triangular lateen sail swung from the top of the stubby mast. Graham, who knew at least the theory of sailing if not the practice, thought he could tack back to Ascension. However, he soon found that despite its stiff-rubber keel the shallow craft drifted to leeward faster than he could beat to windward. Ascension continued to recede.

"We'll have to row," he said. "Mr. Sklar, keep the spear on these two. Warschauer, take one oar and I'll take the other. Betty, you take the paddle. Mr. Sklar, poke him every time he catches a crab."

"How should I catch a crab out here?" asked Warschauer innocently.

Sklar, who had given up trying to light a soaked cigarette, asked: "How lunk are we going to last in this boat?"

"We've g-got food and water for some days in the compartments. And if we run out, there's always our friends." Graham nodded towards Warschauer and Adzik.

"I have been looking into the Earthly law on cannibalism," said Varnipaz. "To kill a man for the main purpose of eating him is illegal, but if he dies for any other reason it is all right. So if Mr. Warschauer forces us to kill him by acting obstreperous . . ."

Warschauer's expression showed that he considered this a joke in very poor taste.

With the oars they made time back towards the island. They were still a kilometer from shore when a noise overhead caused them to look up: a *swoosh* like that of a gasoline blow-torch amplified. Graham recognized the blast of a space-ship's rocket motor.

"There she is!" said Sklar, pointing.

Down came the ship, growing from a speck to a spot to a rocket standing on its tail. It dropped towards the northern peninsula of Ascension. To Graham it somehow looked neither like a standard Viagens Interplanetarias ship nor an Osirian ship . . .

"They have come!" squeaked Adzik. "We are saved! Warschauer, we can still put it over! The contract is in March's safe, which is still in his house even if wet!"

"Hey!" said Sklar, gripping his spear.

The space-ship hovered over the peninsula, drifting this way and that as the pilot sought a patch of level ground. Then down it came on its tail in a burst of steam and dust from the earth beneath. The jet sputtered and died.

The Thothian shrieked: "If we can get my people to

destroy these, there will be no more evidence! They are the only ones who know the whole story! Follow me!"

As Adzik dived overboard, Sklar sent a futile jab after it. The raft rocked as Warschauer, too, went over the side.

"Throw the spear!" said Varnipaz.

As Sklar hesitated with the unfamiliar weapon the fugitives drew out of range, Warschauer holding the tail of the powerfully-swimming Thothian.

"Grab that oar!" said Graham to Varnipaz.

They started rowing vigorously, but it soon transpired that with the wind against them they were outclassed.

Jeru-Bhetiru said: "Little people like Adzik are getting out of the space-ship."

"They're Thothians, all right," said Sklar. "Look up!"

Overhead appeared six more dots, circling slowly and balancing on their jets.

"The rest of the Thothian colonists," said Sklar.

Graham said between strokes: "They won't—land until the—first ones mark—out level spaces—for them. And—that'll take some time—on Ascension."

Jeru-Bhetiru said: "Adzik and Warschauer have reached the shore. They are standing up. A big wave knocks Warschauer down, but he is getting up ... The Thothians from the ship are running down to shore ... They are talking ..."

Sklar said: "You guys better head out to sea again. They're settink up some kind of gun."

The raft spun and headed back northwest, faster because the sail now helped. Again Ascension shrank until the Thothians became mere moving specks. Now that he was facing shoreward, Graham could see that they were indeed setting up some kind of weapon, though it was too far for details. He hoped that, being crowded with colonists, the ship could not have carried anything heavy.

Something went *wheep*, and there was a loud crack. A column of water rose in the air near the raft.

Wheep-*crash*! Another, nearer.

"They've got us—ranged now," panted Graham. "The next one'll get us ..."

Wheep-*crash*! But this was farther instead of nearer.

"My God!" said Sklar. "Look!"

A long gray shape had emerged from the waters of the South Atlantic, water running off its decks in sheets, and was now accelerating to full surface speed. As its atomic engines forced it up to sixty knots or more towards

Ascension, spray leaped in huge splashes as its pointed nose butted through the waves. The column of water from the last explosion towered in this ship's wake.

A cupola on the forward deck opened out and a girder structure appeared. With a *whoosht* a rocket leaped towards Ascension. The missile accelerated to a streak, its path curving as its guiding mechanism led it towards the space-ship.

"Cover your eyes!" cried Graham.

A blinding flash visible even through closed lids came from the island, followed by a tremendous roar and a puff of air-blast that carried away the sail and almost upset the raft. When they opened their eyes a huge cloud of smoke and dust was boiling up from the peninsula. The space-ship had vanished.

They sat half-stunned while the six space-ships overhead filed off to westward out of sight. The warship circled towards them.

Jeru-Bhetiru said: "Will that mean war between your planets?"

Sklar shook his head. "You can't have real interplanetary war for logistic risens, yonk lady. Besides, the Thothian government will say these were private pipple and they are not responsible. Maybe there will soon be a new government on Thoth."

The warship drew alongside to windward, the checkered flag of the World Federation flying from its staff. The name *Nigeria* became visible on the conning-tower, and a crew with shiny-black faces appeared on deck. A squirt of oil flattened the waves, and the sailors hoisted them aboard.

An African officer with a major's stripes said: "I'm skipper and my name's Nwafor. Are you Reinhold Sklar?"

Sklar introduced himself and his companions. Major Nwafor said:

"We were out on a routine cruise from Freetown when we got a wireless from General Vasconcellos of the Brazilian Federal Police. He seemed to think there might be trouble at Ascension and asked us to stop by. We ordered that fellow to stop shooting, and when he fired at us we had to defend ourselves."

Sklar looked up. "Where are the other Thothian ships goink?"

"I ordered them to Bahia, for arrest and internment. Now go below, please. When you get yourselves dried off I should like to hear your stories."

The whine of turbojets made them look around. Against the western sky a seaplane with the markings of the United States of Brazil was bearing down on them.

"Late as usual," grumbled Sklar, and led the others below.

IX.

On the airliner for New York, Jeru-Bhetiru sat facing Graham and Varnipaz in an Earthly dress bought in Rio; an enchanting sight even if the costume made less of her mammalian attractions than her native garb. The others' hair was beginning to grow out again after they had discarded their helmets and wigs for good. She said:

"I am so sorry about that poor Mr. Gil. It was not worth while rescuing me if he had to get killed in the doing."

Varnipaz nodded somberly. "He said he wanted to see some action before he died, and he did." The Krishnan turned to Gordon Graham. "I owe you more than I can pay, Gordon. As in my own world I am a person of some importance, you shall have anything you wish if I can manage it. Name your reward."

Graham looked up from the engineering report he was writing for the Brazilian Federal Police and exchanged glances with Jeru-Bhetiru. The Krishnan had turned out to be quite as fine a fellow as he had seemed, and you couldn't very well respond to his offer by telling him you wanted his girl.

"Go ahead," said Varnipaz. "Anything you desire."

"Well—uh—" said Graham.

"Be frank."

Graham took a deep breath and said: "If you r-really w-w-want to know, I'm in love with your fiancée."

Varnipaz raised his antennae slightly. "Interesting. That however is something for her to decide. What about it, Jera-Bhetira?"

"I love Gorodon too," she said. "Madly. But of course I shall still marry you as planned."

"What?" said Graham. "How d'you figure that?"

She explained gently: "In my country this state you call being in love has nothing to do with marriage. We think that people who mate on a basis of interest and advantage are happier in the long run than those who do so on a basis of a temporary sexual attraction. While the latter does sometimes happen, we consider the victims to be pitied. This romantic idea of the Earthly Western culture makes no sense to us.

"Now, the engagement of Varnipaz and myself is a stroke of statesmanship, to set up a tie between Katai-Jhogorai, the most cultured state on Krishna, and Sotaspé, the most scientific. We like each other and shall get along well, and we certainly should not spoil such an excellent plan because of a temporary infatuation, especially with an Earthman. You and I, Gorodon, could not even have young."

"W-we could adopt . . ." began Graham, but she stopped him.

"Adopt what, an Osirian with scales or a Vishnuvan with six legs? No, Gorodon darling, you know as well as I that it would not be the same . . ."

And then they were at the New York Airport. Varnipaz shook hands with Graham and Jeru-Bhetiru kissed him soundly, and off they went, the Krishnan girl on the arm of her betrothed.

Graham turned to Sklar. "How about a drink before we go into town?"

"Sure think," said the constable, and they walked towards the bar. "Don't look so sad, pal. After all you're a hero."

"I do feel sort of let down," said Graham. "Of course it's nice to have the President of Brazil shake your hand, and Souza offer you a permanent job on the Project, and that sort of thing. But I was hoping . . ."

"That the little squid would—uh—make some arrangement, huh? You'll be glad some day. When you been married as lunk as I have, you take a relaxed view of such thinks. After all you saved the continent for the W. F., didn't you? What do you want, an egg in your beer?"

"I'm afraid I do."

"Okus dokus." Reinhold Sklar turned to the bartender. "A Martian special for me, and for my friend here one stein of lager. Put an egg in it."

SIGNET Science Fiction You Will Enjoy

☐ **CLARION An Anthology of Speculative Fiction and Criticism from the Clarion Writer's Workshop edited by Robin Scott Wilson.** The Clarion Workshop is the only writers' program dealing with speculative fiction. The alumni represent twenty states and from this workshop many fresh and important voices will emerge to set the tone and influence the direction of science fiction in the seventies. Included are **Fritz Leiber** and **Samuel Delaney.** (#Q4664—95¢)

☐ **TOMORROW I A Science Fiction Anthology edited by Robert Hoskins.** Five fascinating speculations on tomorrow featuring **Poul Anderson, John D. MacDonald, James H. Schmitz, Clifford D. Simak** and **William Tenn.** (#T4663—75¢)

☐ **NO TIME LIKE TOMORROW by Brian Aldiss.** Fantastic stories of the future—adventures that soar beyond the barriers of time and space, yet remain perilously close to the boundaries of reality. (#T4605—75¢)

☐ **THE SHORES OF ANOTHER SEA by Chad Oliver.** Royce Crawford's African baboonery becomes a laboratory for a terrifying extraterrestrial experiment. From the author of the prize-winning novel **The Wolf Is My Brother.** "A prime contender for the Heinlein-Clarke front rank of genuine science-fiction."—**The New York Times.** (#T4526—75¢)

THE NEW AMERICAN LIBRARY, INC.,
P.O. Box 999, Bergenfield, New Jersey 07621

Please send me the SIGNET BOOKS I have checked above. I am enclosing $_____(check or money order—no currency or C.O.D.'s). Please include the list price plus 15¢ a copy to cover mailing costs.

Name_____

Address_____

City_____State_____Zip Code_____
Allow at least 3 weeks for delivery